The Ghosts of Blood and Innocence

Author's Note to the Second Edition

While there have been no major changes to '*The Ghosts of Blood and Innocence*' in this edition, typographical errors have been corrected, as well as grammatical and stylistic mistakes. I have also inserted minor adjustments to the text to ensure this story is consistent with current Wraeththu terminology and canon, which has developed over the past fifteen years, through my own writing and that of other authors who have contributed to the Wraeththu Mythos

A glossary of terms, places and characters has also been added for the convenience of readers who might not have read the original trilogy.

The Ghosts of Blood and Innocence

Book Three of the Wraeththu Histories

Storm Constantine

IMMANION PRESS
Stafford, England

The Ghosts of Blood and Innocence: Book Three of the Wraeththu Histories
By Storm Constantine

This is a work of fiction. All the characters and events portrayed in this book are fictitious, and any resemblance to real people, or events, is purely coincidental.

http://www.stormconstantine.co.uk

Cover by Ruby
Interior Layout by Storm Constantine

ISBN: 978-1-907737-94-7

Catalogue Number: IP0145

An Immanion Press Publication
www.immanion-press.com
info@immanion-press.com

Chapter One

Darquiel's pearl hatched on the eve of midsummer when, outside Phade's Tower, clouds of mosquitoes hung above the pools in the courtyard, so thirsty they would drink water rather than blood. It hatched in that strange hour when neither light nor dark holds sway, and hara walk home through the balmy air, drunk on the perfume of wild roses, thinking of love. But high in the tower room, where it had long been twilight, there were no thoughts of love. The walls to the room were white, and they glowed in the dusk. The narrow window-frames were painted black, devoid of drapes or blinds, and the floorboards were bare and unvarnished. It was a room that was never used, not until now.

The pearl rested in a nest of woollen blankets, surrounded by lamps, on an old wooden table. In the soft glow the pearl gleamed, semi-translucent. Limbs writhed slowly within it, pressing against the decomposing membrane. Eventually, the pearl ripped and a meaty, sweet smell came from it.

For some moments after the leathery sac fell apart, the lone har who observed the event feared the harling within the pearl was dead, for there was no further movement for over a minute. Then Darquiel's head emerged, his brow creased in a frown. He pulled aside the scraps of leather that had once enfolded him and wriggled forth from his bower of nutrient slime. His head waved this way and that, like the head of a cobra. His black eyes surveyed all that he saw before him with what appeared to be a critical view. He expressed a sigh of ennui. Life had come. He did not, nor ever would, resemble a normal child.

While nighthawks hovered outside the window, and dogs in the courtyard pulled upon their chains and wept at the night, Phade har Olopade, sole witness, lifted the newly-hatched harling in his hands and held him at arm's length. Its body was covered with viscous fluid, and the smell of the nutrients that had nurtured it within the pearl stung Phade's nostrils. He half expected the harling to spray him with black venom or utter a curse. Surely his tongue would be forked? 'I name you Darquiel har Aralis,' Phade said, and the child went limp in his hands.

The second heir to the throne of Immanion had gone to sleep, exhausted by the thought of what was to come.

Nohar had come to witness the hatching, except for Phade, and he had had no choice, because the pearl had been transferred into his care. There was an air of desolation in that stark chamber, high in the main tower of Phade's domain. He had not asked for this responsibility and did not welcome it. If a harling of high birth had to be hidden away in this forgotten corner of the world, it could not bode well. The harling must be reared ignorant of his parentage. Phade must attempt to raise him as an ordinary child, but it was clear, from the very first breath that he took, that Darquiel har Aralis was far from ordinary.

Ten days before, a *sedu* had emerged from the Otherlanes, bearing a tall, aquiline-featured har, whose hair was the colour of bright platinum and who was swathed in black.

The visitor had been presented to Phade in his office, on the second floor of the tower, which overlooked the yard. It had been a blustery day. Phade had been called from the stables and knew he smelled of horse. He tied back his thick black hair to appear more businesslike, then sat behind his desk.

Somehar knocked on the door and Phade called, 'Come in.' He folded his hands before him.

One of his househara came into the room and bowed. Behind him, the white-haired visitor loomed in an imposing manner. Phade cleared his throat. He wondered what kind of business such an exotic creature could have with him.

'Your visitor, Tiahaar,' the househar said, and fled.

The har was not known to Phade and did not offer his name. At first, he said nothing, but appraised Phade overtly and perhaps came to private conclusions.

'Good day, Tiahaar,' Phade said. 'Forgive my househar, he did not tell me who you are.' He raised his eyebrows expectantly.

The visitor said only: 'I come from Tiahaar Thiede. He has a task for you.'

Phade went cold from head to foot at once. In the past, he'd been used to dealing with Thiede's often bizarre requests, but since Thiede had left the realm of earth, Phade had been left unmolested. He could now run his domain independently, free from the nagging fear of what tomorrow might bring. He could walk the fields with an easy stride. He was free. Hardly anyhar outside of Samway knew he existed.

'What task is this?' he asked, noting that the har before him was concealing something within the voluminous folds of his robes.

His visitor brought forth the pearl and unwrapped it. Phade stared at it for some moments, unaware of what it was. 'In perhaps as little as ten days' time, this pearl will hatch,' said the visitor. 'Thiede requires you to care for this harling and raise it, here at Samway.'

'Whose pearl is it?' Phade asked, knowing that this was the most important question.

His visitor barely paused. 'It is a child of the Aralisian dynasty,' he said. 'Its father is Pellaz, Tigron of the Gelaming.'

Phade was silent for a moment. 'He is known to me.'

The visitor inclined his head. 'Indeed. I understand the Tigron came to Samway before Thiede presented him in Immanion.'

'Yes. He stayed here for a while.' Phade cast his mind back to that time and remembered the shrivelled husk who had been brought to his domain, and the golden har who had later risen from that husk, reborn. Pellaz har Aralis. Phade had not forgotten him. 'Is my tenuous connection with Pellaz the reason why a child of Immanion is brought to my tower?' he asked.

'No,' said the visitor. 'It must simply be concealed.'

'Like a changeling child in a fairy tale,' Phade observed.

The visitor pulled a mordant face. 'Perhaps. Thiede creates stories. The child must never know who created it.' He swept back his platinum hair with both hands. Phade saw there were black pearls plaited into the hair, and the har's jewellery was also set with pearls. He must be high-ranking. 'The Olopade are hidden,' said the visitor. 'Samway is virtually unknown.'

'And why must the harling be concealed?'

The visitor pulled a wry face. 'Let's simply say it is a child of Grissecon, born before its time. Many powers of the realms would desire to own it, should they know of its existence. What you see before you is, or could be, the seed of our kind's destruction. Or it could be a saviour. It's difficult to say. Far better that it lives a normal life, ignorant of its heritage. It must not know its origins.'

Phade stared at the pearl and tried to match the image with the words. It wouldn't work. The pearl looked like a gourd or a wizened black melon. It did not look like destruction or salvation.

'I have no experience of raising harlings,' Phade said. 'I've no idea what to do. None of my hara here have... *bred*. It's not our territory.'

'You will learn,' said the visitor, in a tone that reminded Phade eerily of Thiede. 'Harlings are simply miniature hara. Feed it as you would a young hound. Discipline it well, for I expect it will be wilful. Put it to work in your domain. Train it as you would one of your own hara. You will name it Darquiel har Aralis, but will tell it only the first part of its name.' The har placed the pearl carefully on Phade's desk. 'Keep it warm,' he said, and turned around in a dramatic swirl of cloth to leave the room.

Keep it warm.

Phade continued to stare at the unwelcome object on his desk for some moments, the fingers of one hand tapping his lips. It was hard to credit it contained new life within it, that it had been expelled from the body of a har, as a fish or a bird might lay eggs. But as Phade stared at its dark knobbly surface, he thought perhaps he could see something moving inside it. It was not an altogether pleasant image.

Phade called for one of his household staff, a sixteen-year-old har named Zira, an attractive creature with strawberry-blond hair to his shoulders and a heart-shaped face. Phade got up when Zira entered the room and walked around to the front of his desk. He felt more comfortable examining the pearl with another har beside him. Altogether, he felt somewhat light-headed. He explained the situation, omitting to mention who the harling's father was. 'I'd like you to care for this... *pearl* until it's ready to hatch,' Phade said.

Zira looked dubious. 'And how long will that be, Tiahaar?'

'I don't know exactly... days, a couple of weeks.' Phade walked back behind his desk. 'In the meantime, I relieve you of all other duties. Instruct Malech to take over your daily tasks.'

'But I've never...' Zira began, bewildered.

'None of us have,' Phade interrupted. 'Do as you're told. Take this thing away.'

Phade had forbidden Zira to attend the hatching, unsure himself of why he felt the need to be alone. Perhaps it was because, on those occasions when he'd inspected the pearl, he had felt strange emanations wafting from it, like a steam of dark thoughts. He believed that the harling within the pearl suffered from nightmares. It turned uncomfortably in its protective cell. While he'd been caring for it, Zira had complained of feeling depressed, assailed by a terrible melancholia, which was unusual, for he was a har of sunny nature, incepted quite recently from one of the pairs of breeding humans that Phade kept in the village next to his tower.

Phade knew that the visitor who had brought the pearl to him had neglected to tell him the most important aspect of this pearl's history. Pellaz har Aralis would not have given up a son willingly, Phade was sure of that. No har would: unless there was something unusual about it, something warped or something bad. Who was its hostling? The Tigrina? Perhaps it was an undesirable conception, some bastard offspring from an unsuitable har.

Although Phade kept away from harish society, he also kept himself informed. He knew that the infamous har, Calanthe, had recently gone to Immanion and that he had been responsible for removing the self-styled leader of Wraeththu, Thiede, from power and banishing him to another realm. Calanthe had become joint Tigron with Pellaz, and had therefore acquired for himself a Tigrina, in the form of Caeru. Now, a triumvirate ruled the Gelaming, or rather acted as figureheads for the all-powerful Hegemony.

Phade had little more information than that. He kept himself apart from the world. Phade had been, and perhaps still was, one of Thiede's most loyal servants, but he was also somewhat grateful to Cal for what he'd done. Phade had felt that with Thiede's removal from the earthly realm, he'd been released from a subtle kind of slavery. But no. Even beyond this world, Thiede could still call upon him.

Phade, still holding the harling at arm's length, left the room at the top of his tower and went down to one of the lower floors, where the décor was homelier. He went into one of the empty bedrooms that he'd allocated for the harling. It was a small, cosy room and seemed right for a child. Phade had already ordered a crib to be placed in the room, and he now lowered the sleeping harling into it, drawing the covers over the small, perfect body. Phade had never seen a harling before. Just hatched, Darquiel appeared like a tiny version of a human child who was perhaps two years old. It was uncanny. He had a thick growth of black hair upon his head, and his dark eyelashes lay long against his smooth cheek. A beautiful thing, a homunculus created by magical means. A changeling. An elf. *A demon.*

Phade went to the door and found Zira waiting outside in the hall. The young har had wrapped his arms around his body protectively. He looked haunted. 'I felt it,' Zira said. 'I felt it... *come out*. It feels so tired already.'

'We must call it "he",' Phade said. 'It's - *he's* - hatched now. He's a har, like you are.'

'*Not* like me,' Zira said, rather too quickly. 'Must I still care for it?'

'I would like you to,' Phade said. He reached out briefly and touched Zira's hand. 'See how you get on. Keep me informed. He's asleep now. When he wakes, feed him. Give him something soft to eat, like soup.'

'Is that what harlings eat? Won't he need milk?'

'No,' Phade said. He paused. 'Go to the village. Bring your mother here. A harling is not like a human child, but she is undoubtedly more qualified to deal with this situation than we are.'

Zira did not bother to conceal the relief he felt at this instruction. He left at once.

The human community had been collected by Phade over the years he'd lived in Samway. They had been imported from Megalithica and Alba Sulh, and some even from Almagabra. Phade was a conservationist at heart, and felt that humanity should not become extinct. He had the same feeling towards rare animals, and felt sorry for the bewildered human souls who had lost all that they knew. He settled his collection in the beautiful country of Anakhai, where Thiede had installed him a long time ago to create the relatively small, and certainly private, tribe of Olopade. Samway, and Phade himself, had been used by Thiede for various purposes over the years. He was happy to indulge Phade's hobby, as he saw it, and had gathered some prime human specimens himself, from all corners of the world. This was easy for Thiede, because at the same time he'd been scooping up the cream of harish specimens to create the tribe of Gelaming.

It was not Phade's practice to incept automatically every young human male; he allowed them to make their own choices. In the beginning, hardly anyhar had had a choice about what they became, since inception had been forced on every available body, in order to enlarge the harish population. But, as time went on, and humanity waned, there were fewer people to incept anyway. In Phade's community, few suitable young males resisted the idea of becoming har. Why remain human and die at an early age, when you could become something else, with an expanded lifespan, and dozens of other physical benefits? These boys had grown up with hara; they didn't fear the transformation to androgyny. Phade knew that eventually this would cause problems with his breeding program. It would ultimately become more difficult to find fertile humans to bring to Samway.

But for now, the human community functioned like an old-fashioned settlement from hundreds of years before. Olivia, Zira's mother, had borne three children. She was thirty-four years old, a strong-boned creature, who had survived against all odds in a world that no longer nurtured her kind. Whether she was grateful to Phade, who had rescued her from certain slaughter at the age of five and brought her to his domain, was difficult to say. Certainly, she had later submitted without complaint to being paired with Raymer, and even called him her husband. She worked with the other humans, alongside hara, who treated her well, much in the same way that they were kind to their horses and dogs. She had surrendered her first-born son to inception without a word, even though she had been forbidden to attend the ceremony or care for Zira during his althaia, the time when the transition from human to har took place. He had gone to visit her two weeks later; no longer her son, yet wearing his face. Now, she came to Phade's tower in the middle of the night, a shawl cast over her dark green homespun dress, her thick auburn hair coming loose from a bun at her neck. Her wide handsome face was expressionless.

Phade took her to inspect the harling. Olivia peered into the crib, betraying nothing. 'I've appointed Zira as the harling's guardian,' Phade said. 'It would help if you could advise him and so on.'

Olivia had noted at sundown that the blackbirds in her garden had not sung their welcome to the night. She had noted that the smell of wormwood was very strong on the air. 'The child needs a bath,' she said. 'In lavender and thyme. In hawthorn. At once.'

'Hmm,' murmured Phade, then: 'Why?'

'It will clean him good,' said Olivia. 'Then you will all feel better.'

'Will you do this?'

'Yes.'

Phade nodded thoughtfully. 'Olivia,' he said, 'I want this harling to be absorbed without trouble into my household. He will be raised here, no different from any other har. Your skills will help in this matter. If things go well, your family will be rewarded.'

Olivia rolled up her sleeves and picked Darquiel up. She did not appear as discomforted by the harling as Zira and Phade had been. 'I'll bathe him,' she said. 'Show me where.'

Chapter Two

When Darq was exactly one-year old, he decided he was a twin, even though it took him a day longer to discover the actual term. The idea came to him as he walked beneath the shedding oaks and beeches, in the woods that skirted the town of Samway. Gold and scarlet leaves filled the air like promises, or messages, or dreams. As he looked up through the branches, towards the pale sky, he felt a tugging in his heart. It was as if he could very easily jump out of his body and fly up as a white spirit towards the aching space above. The feeling made him both happy and sad at the same time. Something was missing. Something as big as the sky.

He walked back along the path, his gaze upon the ground. Beechnut cases crunched beneath his boots. He was very young, but because he was har he looked far older than a human child of his age would look: not an infant but an independent creature who could walk and talk and think for himself. If you'd seen him, and imagined him to be human, you'd have found it difficult to guess his age. He could have been anything between four and seven years old. Physically, he was still small, but he was more like a miniature teenager than a child.

Darq's thick black hair hung just past his chin. In certain lights, it had threads of gold in it. His skin was a honey, olive shade, his eyebrows straight and dark. He was beautiful, as all harlings are beautiful, but he was also different.

At such a tender age, Darq felt like an outsider, unable to connect with the hara and humans around him. But this did not particularly bother him. He did not crave affection or reassurance. He was quite happy in his own company, and already loved passionately the landscape he inhabited.

He knew that Phade didn't approve of him wandering about in it on his own, but it was easy for Darq to slip away from Olivia's supervision. Often, she was too busy to notice when he'd crept away from her garden, crouched down like a robber, out of the picket gate and onto the road that led to the forest. It was more of a problem to escape Zira's attention, but he was only in charge for three days a week, when he gave Darq lessons. The rest of the time Darq considered his own. He always returned to Olivia's garden before he had to go back to the tower for dinner, and although she stared at him through narrowed eyes, her lips pursed disapprovingly, she would rarely upbraid him. 'You be careful among the trees, now,' was all she'd say.

'Yes,' he'd answer. 'I know how to take care.'

Darq had met other children, albeit human ones, because Phade encouraged it. There were no other harlings in Samway, so Phade decided Darq should mix with the humans. It would be the nearest he could get to friends his own age, and Phade was anxious for Darq to be normal: Darq could feel that desire steaming off his guardian like hot sweat. Unfortunately, Darq didn't understand the other children at all. They seemed to him like leaves on the wind, blowing this way and that, one moment laughing out loud, the next screaming in distress like maniacs for what he considered to be very little reason. They were curious about him and sometimes wanted to include him in their games. They ran around him in circles, the bigger boys repressing with the greatest difficulty the urge to poke fun or bully. They were afraid of him, attracted and sometimes bewitched, but always wary.

On this day of revelation, Darq returned to Olivia's garden to find her taking down her washing, great billowing sails of white that made his eyes ache. Her daughter, Amelza, eight years old, stood holding the laundry basket, from which the swathes of fabric lolled like sleeping ghosts. Amelza stuck to her mother's side like a witch's familiar.

Olivia eyed Darq shrewdly. She had wrapped up her hair in a head scarf, which had tassels. Darq liked the way it made her seem somehow mysterious. He knew a lot of the villagers called her a witch, and for that reason they came to her for aid very often. 'You could help,' she said. 'Help Ammie fold the sheets.' She placed the last one in the basket.

'OK,' Darq said. He didn't mind helping. Amelza was considered to be an odd girl by her peers, but not by Darq, who had no opinion. She often talked to herself and, when other children came by, put her apron over her face.

She laid down the basket and lifted out the first sheet. Darq took up one end of it. 'Olivia,' he said, folding carefully, 'why don't you try to stop me going into the forest?'

'Why waste my breath?' Olivia replied, dropping washing pegs into a bag.

'Because Phade would be angry with you if he knew.'

'He doesn't know,' Olivia said. 'Be quick. There might be time for hazelnut cake before you go home.'

'Why is he afraid for me and you're not?'

Olivia smiled, an expression that rarely crossed her face. 'Because you can ask a question like that at one-year old, that's why! You're safer than I am. If something tried to get you, you'd sense it from a mile off and run away.'

'No, I wouldn't,' Darq said.

'You would. You're special.'

'I mean, I wouldn't run away. I'd just kill whatever was after me. That's safer. Then they wouldn't try it again.'

Olivia shook her head. 'Who have you been talking to?'

'Nohar. I watch Phade's guards. It's what their minds are like.'

'You might be bright, Darq,' Olivia said, 'but you're still a harling, and you're not strong. Don't ever consider trying to kill something, especially something hostile. You don't know everything.'

'You don't need strength to kill something,' Darq said, taking up the end of another sheet that Amelza offered him. 'I could use a bow or throw a knife. I could dig a hole and make them run into it.'

'Now you sound like one of the bully boys,' Olivia said.

Darq could see the thought forming in her mind that she would suggest to Phade that his ward be kept away from the boys. 'What's so bad about it?' Darq asked.

'It's just not the way you're supposed to be,' she said. 'At least, I don't think so.' She sighed. 'Why should I care?'

'I don't know. Why do you?'

'Just finish folding those sheets,' Olivia said. She went into her kitchen.

Darq felt confused. He wished Olivia could answer his questions.

Amelza pulled on the sheet to get his attention. 'I'd kill them too,' she whispered.

From this simple remark, Amelza became Darq's friend. When he heard those words, it was as if he'd seen her for the first time: a thin girl with a curtain of reddish brown hair and a long serious face. He realised that in some ways she was like him. Therefore, it was to Amelza that he confided his belief that somehow part of him was missing. The very next day, in Olivia's garden, as Amelza weeded round the raspberry canes, Darq told her his heart.

Amelza patted down the soil, digging her fingers into the rich earth. Darq could hear her breathing and smell the scent of her skin and hair, which was sweet like honey. 'Maybe you were a twin,' she said.

'What's that?'

'There should be two of you, a brother. Rufus and Simeon are twins. They look the same.'

'Then where is my twin?'

Amelza shrugged. 'Maybe he died.'

Darq frowned as he thought about it. 'It doesn't feel that way,' he said.

That evening, Darq was compelled to confront Phade over dinner. Phade treated Darq like an unpredictable animal. He was fair and often generous, but rarely initiated conversation. Darq knew that Phade would rather he took his dinner with Zira and the other staff, but something wouldn't let him order it. They always ate in a room on the first floor; its long windows welcomed the morning sun, but in the evenings it could be rather gloomy.

As unobtrusive hara glided around the table to clear away the soup bowls, Darq asked: 'Was I a twin?'

'What? No,' Phade said. He was reading some reports on his equine breeding stock, occasionally making notes on the papers. Now he glanced up, apparently irritated at being interrupted. In a lot of ways, he reminded Darq of a bird of prey. Although his hair was very dark, his eyes were almost amber and his features were hawklike. His hands were strong. He could control the wildest of his horses. But in the evening, in lamplight, he appeared softer, beautiful rather than handsome. Darq knew the difference, because he had discussed Phade earlier in the day with Amelza, who was fascinated by all hara.

'How do you know I'm not a twin?' Darq persisted.

Phade put down his pencil. 'Because you came from a pearl and I watched you hatch. If you'd been a twin, there would've been two of you.'

'Maybe there were two pearls and you only got one.'

'It doesn't work that way,' Phade said, although he didn't sound that confident about it. 'Ask Zira to tell you things. He can teach you some biology.'

'OK.'

Unfortunately, approaching Zira about the subject inadvertently led Darq to spill the secret of his lone excursions into the forest. He didn't say anything about his strange feelings until Zira had been teaching him basic biology for a couple of weeks. Darq hadn't meant to confide in Zira; he'd just mentioned how he'd felt when he'd looked up at the sky through the trees, and how the idea of being part of something had come to him then. He intended to broach the subject of twins and so on, but was unprepared for Zira's reaction.

Zira's eyes had widened. He raised a hand to silence Darq. 'Shut up. You mean you were out on your own?'

'Well... yes.' Darq realised he'd revealed too much. The expression on Zira's face – a mixture of anger and smug satisfaction – stemmed the fountain of questions that had been ready to break from Darq's mouth.

'You stupid harling,' Zira said. 'Phade will be furious.'

Darq knew it was pointless to suggest the information be kept from his guardian. Zira took Darq to Phade at once. Phade was out in the fields with his animals, as usual. As Darq and Zira approached him, Darq became aware of an unfamiliar feeling within him. It was apprehension. He didn't like it at all.

Once Zira had related what Darq had told him, Phade felt obliged to administer discipline. 'You will stay here in the tower for a week,' he said. 'Don't take advantage of Olivia's good nature, Darq. No more wandering around on your own. If you want to go into the woods, wait until Zira can take you.'

It was torture for Darq to be kept indoors, which is of course what Phade intended. It was even more irksome that Phade locked him in his room at night, to bring home how serious the punishment was. Darq felt that even being confined for a week meant he would miss so much of what was happening outside. He also missed Amelza's company. They'd only known each other for a couple of weeks, but had quickly become firm friends. Perhaps by the time Darq was let out, the trees would be bare, the gold all gone, and a cold wind would come slicing down through the high pine forests that surrounded Samway's valley. The older deciduous woods were Darq's domain. He loved them, and resented bitterly being kept away from them, which he considered unreasonable. Olivia knew he was safe, so what was Phade's problem? Darq had tried to explain, but Phade wouldn't listen.

Three days into his incarceration, and exasperated by rules and punishments he didn't understand, Darq absconded into the night. The tower was surrounded on either side by outbuildings and stables, and at the back by a walled garden. In front was the wide yard, with a well in the centre, and the great gates that were kept closed at night and guarded. Darq scrambled out of his window, intending to exit the tower via the gardens, since he knew a place where he could climb a tree next to the wall and thereby get over it. He experienced some perilous moments as he teetered on the sill, some thirty feet above the ground, and then inched towards the thick, ancient ivy that covered part of the tower walls. He climbed down, stems coming away from the wall in his hands. Dust and insects got into his eyes and hair and mouth. Eventually, he jumped down the last few feet.

Oh, how big the world was at night. Excitement coursed through Darq's veins in an intoxicating flood. He saw a great white owl swoop down from the sky, heard the squeak of the creature it killed. He ran across the lawn, past the sundial and the sleeping fountain, into a stand of ancient yew trees that hugged one part of the wall. Within moments, he was on the other side, free. He paused a moment and breathed deeply, taking in the scent of the night. The wind had a voice, full of secrets. The last leaves of the trees trembled to hear them. A fat moon sailed majestically above the reaching branches of the oaks around him, and Darq could feel the presence of hunters in the nearby forest: not animals, hara or men, but spirits who rode on spectral black horses, hounds baying at their sides.

He laughed aloud, drunk on his forbidden freedom, and ran towards the trees. Then, inspired by a spontaneous idea, he veered off along the lane to Olivia's cottage.

Olivia and Raymer held high positions within the human community, and therefore had one of the larger dwellings in the town. It had a spreading lower story, and a smaller one on top, which was a big attic room where Olivia and Raymer slept. Amelza and her older sister, Silbeth, slept on the ground floor, in a room at the back of the cottage, next to the charcoal house.

Because Olivia believed it was beneficial to breathe fresh air while you were sleeping, the window was open and Darq was able to slither into the room quietly. He saw Silbeth lying on her back, mouth open, snoring. Amelza was curled beneath her blankets, silent and still. Darq crept to her side and put his hand upon her. Instinctively, he did not speak or even shake her, but thought the shape of her name in a loud way, as if he were shouting. Amelza woke at once and uttered a soft gasp. Darq felt her body go rigid beneath the blankets.

It's me, he told her. *Don't be afraid. Let's go out.*

Amelza peered out of her nest, her face creased into a frown. She glanced at her sleeping sister, paused for only a second or so, then got out of bed. She pulled on a pair of work trousers and stuffed her nightdress into the waistband. Together, she and Darq left the cottage, and neither had said a word out loud. Samway was sleeping. A few dim lights burned high in cottage windows, but mostly it was dark and silent.

Once they were on the track that led to the forest, Amelza said, 'I hope you don't get caught. Ma told me what happened.'

Darq shrugged. He didn't care about getting caught. The only important thing was his ability to escape the tower.

'If they find out, they'll put locks on your door,' Amelza said.

'There's already a lock on the door,' Darq said.

'Then how did you get out?'

'The window.'

Amelza laughed. 'You're mad. You could have fallen.' She took Darq's arm and they left the main path to walk into the trees.

'But I didn't,' Darq said. 'You're right about the locks though. I hadn't thought of that. I won't be able to get back in the way I came out or through the door either, so I'll have to wait 'til morning when the guards open the courtyard gates.'

'Maybe Phade will beat you,' Amelza said.

'Maybe,' Darq said, brushing aside a branch that blocked their path. 'But he *will* lock the window.' He grinned. 'I must enjoy the night. It might be the last until I think of another way.'

'Don't you care about being beaten?'

'I don't know. I've never had it done to me.'

'You won't like it,' Amelza said.

They went to a secret place, deep in the forest, they'd claimed as their own. There was a pool there, which sometimes caught the moon in its depths, and wonderful burrows and warrens of ancient rhododendron. There had once been a monastery in Samway, and the ruins of a very old church lay deep among the trees. At one time, the human lord of the area would have worshipped there with his family. Now, it hid close to the pool, where sometimes the moon came to swim.

'You know,' Amelza said, clambering over the mossy stones of the fallen masonry to find a good seat, 'I can't work out whether you're a girl friend of mine or a boy. Not that you're either, of course. But sometimes, I feel like you're one or the other.'

'Hmph,' grunted Darq, uninterested. 'You're just you. So am I. Isn't that all there is?'

In the moonlight, Amelza frowned, clearly unsure what Darq meant. 'And you look so old too! You could be the same age as me, yet Phade looks much younger than Ma, even though he's much older. It's so weird.'

'We're different,' Darq said. 'Different species.'

'I know...' Amelza paused for the space of three heartbeats. 'Maybe we should do something while we're here,' she said. 'It's a forbidden night so we should do something forbidden.'

'Like what?' Darq came to sit beside her.

'Like... call up your dead twin.'

Darq could tell that was not the only thing on Amelza's mind and that, in fact, she was eaten up with curiosity to discover how he was different from her and the other children. However, she lacked the courage to ask him to show her. 'I don't have a dead twin,' he said. 'Phade said so.'

'And you believe him?'

'Yes, he wasn't lying. I know when hara are lying… and humans too.'

Amelza looked away. 'Don't you have that feeling anymore… about missing some part of yourself?'

'Yes,' Darq said. 'But it's not a twin, not in the normal way, anyway. I don't know what it is. Perhaps we *could* try to find out.'

'You should ask the moon,' Amelza said. She took hold of Darq's arm, and when she spoke again, her voice was a whisper. 'Look…'

At that moment, the moon had slid above the trees and now its reflection was cast in the pool. It was as if it had come to them at their request. While Darq was extremely practical and logical in many senses, he also appreciated the power of the world of the unseen. When an omen walks past your window, or comes down from the heavens to wallow in a pool, you should not ignore it. He jumped from the jumble of old stones and approached the water. He knelt down beside it. How clear it was, fed by a secret spring, and yet so still, because the current ran deep beneath the surface.

'Drink it,' Amelza said, creeping up behind him.

Darq shivered. He realised that Amelza was far more like her mother Olivia than her brother and sister were. Amelza had a bit of witch in her; it was obvious. She could hear Darq's unspoken messages, and as far as he knew humans weren't supposed to be able to do that.

'Go on,' Amelza urged.

If Darq stretched out, as far as he could reach, his fingers could touch the cold image of the moon. If you drink of the lunar fire, you are given the power to see beyond the veil of mundane reality. Darq didn't know whether he'd read, been told or had overheard this, but he knew it to be true. So, he leaned out and scooped up a handful of water. The image of the moon shattered like crystal, and ripples bloomed over the surface of the pool. Darq drank quickly before all the water ran from his fingers. It was cold in his mouth, so cold, and tasted of earth and sky. *Show me,* he said in his mind.

For some moments, all was quiet, but for Amelza's breathing, which for some reason was quite heavy. Darq was just about to stand up and say something, when a sibilant voice hissed in his mind: *there are four of you.*

It had been so loud, and so definite, that Darq jumped up, uttering a small, shocked sound.

'What is it?' Amelza asked. Her eyes looked completely black, open wide.

'A voice,' Darq said. 'It told me there are four of me.'

Amelza began to laugh, then smothered it. 'A voice…'

Darq was conscious now of the forest spreading away from them in all directions, so ancient. He was aware of every small natural sound in the undergrowth, and the other sounds beyond normal hearing. The hunters of the forest had heard the voice too. They had pulled their horses to a halt and signalled their hounds to be quiet. Darq did not want to attract their attention. He did not fear them exactly, but neither did he want to confront them. He told himself it was because the sight of them might drive Amelza mad for, if they should approach, the girl *would* see them. She was different from other humans in that way. 'We should go,' Darq said.

'Yes,' Amelza agreed.

Darq knew the two of them shared the same fear, but also knew that if either of them spoke of that fear aloud it would become far worse. He held out a hand and Amelza took it.

Just as they left the glade, Darq looked back. It seemed to him that, for a moment, a spectral figure floated above the pool. It was like a dancer, arms held out straight, hovering on one foot, the other leg bent up. It had smoky holes for eyes and its long waving hair was white.

'Come *on*,' Amelza said, her eyes fixed on the path ahead of them. She pulled on his arm. He followed her.

Darq returned to Olivia's cottage and, because he knew he could not get back into the tower, slept with Amelza in her bed for the rest of the night. Shortly after dawn, Olivia came in to wake her daughters and uttered an outraged cry when she caught sight of Darq snuggled against Amelza's back. 'Darquiel!' she cried. 'You are a bane, I swear, by all the gods and their swift messengers! Get out of that bed!'

Darq woke up from a rather unpleasant dream, and was instantly alert. 'I had to come here,' he said. 'I couldn't get back in at home.'

Olivia sat down heavily on a chair. Silbeth and Amelza were also awake now, both eyeing their mother anxiously. 'Do you wish me such ill?' Olivia asked Darq. 'Will you bring the wrath of Olopade down on my head? Why do you do this to me? You're an ungrateful wretch, young har.'

'I won't tell anyhar,' Darq said, getting out of bed. 'I'll go back home at once. I won't tell them where I've been.'

Olivia sighed. 'What do you take me for? Come on.' She grabbed Darq by the wrist and dragged him from the cottage. Despite his protests, she would not talk to him until they reached the tower gates. Here, she demanded to see Phade, and the guards, seeing who she had with her, did nothing to obstruct her.

Phade was not yet out of bed, but came to his office on the second floor at once, still wearing his dressing robe. As the office overlooked the yard, Darq could see the guards talking together down there, occasionally glancing up towards the window. They knew he was in trouble.

Phade's eyes widened when he caught sight of Darq, but he remained outwardly calm. 'What is it, Olivia?' he asked.

Olivia thrust Darq at him. 'I found this in my daughter's bed this morning.'

Phade's lips twitched a little, and Darq could tell he wanted to smile, but he restrained himself. 'Indeed! That's quite a feat for a harling who was locked in his room last night. Darq, are you such a magician? Can you turn into smoke and pour through a keyhole?'

'No,' Darq answered. 'I climbed out of the window.'

Phade flared his nostrils. 'Thank you, Olivia,' he said. 'You may go.'

Olivia hesitated. 'I know it's not my place to say so, Tiahaar, but... the harling is not unsafe in the forest. He knows his way, in this world and the ones you cannot see.'

'I'm sure,' Phade said. 'Thank you, Olivia. You were right to bring him to me personally. Ag knows where he might have strayed if you'd sent him home alone.'

Olivia ducked her head and left the room.

After she'd gone, Phade stared at Darq for a whole excruciating minute. Darq did his best to return the stare.

'It's not advisable to disobey the orders of your elders,' Phade said.

'The order was unreasonable,' Darq said, sounding braver than he felt, for he could see in Phade's calm manner just how angry he was. 'Olivia is right. I *am* safe. There's no reason I can't go around by myself.'

'My order was unreasonable?' Phade sat down on the edge of his desk. His hair was still messy from sleeping and the front of his robe hung open at the chest. 'Do you presume to think you know better than I do?'

'I just don't know why you want to lock me up. Olivia isn't scared for me, and she's human, so why are you scared?'

'Sit down!' Phade ordered, pointing to a row of chairs near the door.

Darq hesitated for a moment before he obeyed. There was a wide space between him and Phade now. It made him feel uncomfortable.

Phade folded his arms. 'I'm not scared, Darquiel. Let's just say I'm concerned for your welfare. It's not the forest you should fear, harling, nor the night creatures, nor ghosts, nor beasts of the air. It's hara you should fear.'

'Why?'

'I can't tell you.'

Darq sensed that Phade had erected barriers in his mind to shield his thoughts. He did that often when Darq asked difficult questions. Did that mean he lied?

'All you need to know is that I'm entrusted with your safety,' Phade said. He pulled his robe closed and belted it more tightly. 'It's my prime concern.'

'Where did I come from?' Darq asked.

'The ethers,' Phade replied.

'Who was the one who bore me, my hostling?'

'I've no idea.' Phade ran his fingers through his hair. 'A friend asked me to care for you. I imagine your parents are either dead or disgraced. Your life is here now. And as we're both condemned to live with this incontrovertible circumstance, you will obey me, as if I were your hostling.' His dark eyes appeared to have gone completely black. 'You will *not* go out alone again. You'll stay in your room for another week. And you can be sure the window will be locked.'

'That's not fair,' Darq said. 'Why can't I go out with Zira?'

'It's called punishment,' Phade said. 'When you do something bad, you have to see the error of your ways. You lose privileges. If you're good, you get to do things you like. I'm sure you can understand the concept.'

Darq felt so full of rage, he was shocked at himself. He didn't like being told what to do, or having his movements restricted. This har wasn't even his parent. What right did he have to issue orders and give punishments? *I'll run away*, Darq thought, but because he was so angry, his thought was too loud and Phade heard it.

'If you attempt any such thing, I'll do more than lock you up,' he said. 'I have no wish to hurt you, Darq, but if you continue in this way, I'll have no choice but to administer a more physical form of punishment. Perhaps that's something you will understand.'

'Amelza said you'd beat me,' Darq said sarcastically, hoping to imply insult that a human child could know such a thing.

'You'd be wise to listen to your friend in the future, then,' Phade said, perhaps deliberately misinterpreting the message. 'If you're good for a week, then Amelza can come to the tower and play here in the garden with you.'

Phade sent out a mind-call to Zira, who presently came to the office.

'Take Darq back to his room,' Phade said. 'Have his breakfast taken there. There will be no lessons today because Darq needs time to think about things on his own. Don't you, Darq?'

Without a word, Darq followed Zira out of the room.

The guards had lost no time in gossiping with the household staff, so Zira already knew most of what had happened. Once they were in the whitewashed corridor outside Phade's office, Zira pinched Darq hard on the arm. 'If my family ends up in trouble because of you, I'll kill you,' he said in a low, hard voice.

'You're not allowed to have human family any more,' Darq said, repeating something he'd picked up from Zira's thoughts, which were occasionally troubled.

Zira uttered a cry and smacked Darq across the head. 'You're a little beast! I hope to Ag all harlings are not like you. You're unnatural and vile!'

Darq rubbed his head for a moment, strangely unmoved. He was surprised and awed by the fact he no longer felt angry, even though Zira had hurt him. 'You're just afraid of me,' he said. 'And if you hit me again, I'll blind you.'

'Nohar likes you,' Zira said. 'You're not a child, you're a malevolent adult hiding in a harling's body. Everyhar thinks you're a freak. The only person who'll speak to you is my sister, and the whole world knows she's "touched".'

'Your mother likes me too,' Darq said primly. 'You don't want to ask how I know, because if you do, you'll also realise how much I know about what goes on in *your* head!' Darq laughed. 'I wonder, does Phade know how much you dream of him?'

'Beast!' Zira hissed. 'I do no such thing.'

'Yes, you do. You do more than dream. You touch yourself and imagine it's him.'

Zira growled and Darq considered the har both looked and sounded like an angry dog. 'You're too young to be able to mind touch,' Zira said. 'You're just a spiteful liar.' He took hold of one of Darq's arms and hauled him up the passageway.

Left alone in his room to await his breakfast, Darq stared at himself in the mirror. He remembered what he'd heard and seen at the pool the previous night. *There are four of me.* 'Where are you?' he asked aloud. '*Who* are you?'

But there was no message in the mirror. Only his reflection stared back at him: an adult hiding in a harling's body.

Chapter Three

Phade came to Darq's bedroom early the next morning. Darq had hardly slept because his mind had been in a spin all night. For the first time, he had begun to think about himself. Where had he come from? Who were his parents? Why had he been given to Phade? Did he have brothers somewhere? It seemed the only way to get the answers to these perplexing questions would be to win Phade's favour. And Darq knew he'd overstepped the line the day before. Zira would have told Phade everything. Well, nearly everything.

As soon as Phade unlocked the door and came into the room, Darq could tell the har felt a little contrite. Memories of Phade's own childhood, which had often been unhappy, had plagued his dreams. Echoes of them wafted round Darq's room, lamenting. Now Phade smiled, obviously in an attempt to put Darq at ease. Darq reflected that Phade looked better when he was smiling, or when his heart was soft. When Phade was in a good mood, Darq appreciated more what Zira saw in him.

'What are we going to do with you?' Phade asked, shaking his head.

'I didn't ask to come here,' Darq replied. 'I didn't ask to be made. Who were my parents? I know you know.'

'Zira's not wrong about you,' Phade said. 'I know harlings are different to human children, but surely not *this* different. You're too adult.' He sat down on the bed. 'Tell me what you remember about hatching. Do you remember anything before that?'

Darq considered, and a hot wave coursed through his flesh. It was as if Phade's question had been a magical key to unlock a door Darq had known nothing about. For just an instant, he saw utter blackness, but within it there was movement, something violent, and the sound of screaming. 'I remember something bad,' he said. Should he tell Phade? He decided to bargain. 'I'll tell you, but only if you tell me something in return. Who are my parents?'

'I don't know,' Phade said, and perhaps he was lying, because his thoughts were again impenetrable to Darq. 'You came to me as a pearl. Perhaps your hostling died.'

'But who brought me here? You said yesterday it was a friend.'

'An old friend. He didn't explain much. He just asked me to raise you here, because Samway is safe and hidden and…' Phade narrowed his eyes. 'Enough. Tell me what you remember.'

'Screaming,' Darq said, briefly closing his eyes. 'And... something like fighting, but it was in darkness. I couldn't see anything.'

'Perhaps that's because you were in the pearl,' Phade said, 'though it's interesting you recall so much.'

'I think I was stolen,' Darq said. 'That's the only possible explanation.'

'That conclusion is not unreasonable,' Phade agreed.

Darq hugged his knees through his bed covers. 'My parents must have been important.'

Phade folded his arms. 'You don't know that. Perhaps we'll never know the circumstances of your conception. The fact is, Darq, you are with me now, and I don't want there to be hostility between us. You'll carry your childhood with you for the rest of your life. Let's make sure your memories of it are mostly happy ones. Respect my wishes and I'll respect yours.'

'You think I'm in danger,' Darq said. 'You must do, otherwise you'd let me out alone.'

Phade stared at him thoughtfully. 'Perhaps I *am* over-protective,' he admitted. 'You don't really get along with Zira, do you? You need a harish companion, so that you can go out together. Amelza is a good friend, I know, but she wouldn't be able to protect you, if you ever needed her to.'

'Make her har like Zira is, then,' Darq suggested. The idea seemed logical.

Phade smiled. 'I can't do that. She can't be made har like you.'

This was news to Darq. 'Why not?'

'Hara can't incept human females. Also, she is too young. She could become Kamagrian one day, perhaps, but not har. Kamagrian are similar to us, but not exactly the same.'

Darq was delighted with this information. 'Make her that, then!' he said. 'I don't want her to shrivel up and die like humans do. I like her.'

Phade smiled and reached out to ruffle Darq's hair. 'I know. I'll bear it in mind, I promise.'

Emboldened by this strange new intimacy, which made him feel slightly drunk, Darq laughed and said, 'Zira is in love with you.'

Phade didn't laugh as had Darq expected. 'Did he tell you that?'

'No. It's what he thinks about. He's sad you didn't go to him after althaia, that it was somehar else.'

Phade exhaled through his nose and folded his arms. 'Hasn't Zira told you it's very rude to pry in other hara's thoughts?'

Darq glanced away. 'I don't know. He might've done.'

'You mustn't do it.'

'It wasn't prying," Darq insisted. To him, this seemed true. 'He thinks so loud about you it's like he's singing.'

'Well, whatever – curb yourself,' Phade said. 'If you hear something like that, tune out and turn off. You *do* know how to do that, don't you?'

Darq shrugged.

'Darq, *don't* listen in. It's bad. Also, you're far too young to know about what happens after althaia.'

Again, Darq received a brief impression of Phade's bittersweet childhood memories.

'Enjoy being a child,' Phade said, more gently. 'Enjoy being innocent. It won't last forever, and one day you'll wake up feeling sad because it's gone. Understand?'

Darq shook his head. 'Zira says I'm not a child, so what's the point of trying to cling on to something I'm not?'

Phade sighed again. 'Physically, you *are* a child. That's the way it is and the way we will look at things. You upset Zira yesterday. You should apologise.'

'He pinched and hit me.'

'You should *both* apologise. Believe me, Darq, life is far easier if hara can get along.'

Darq could see that Phade was right. If you displeased somehar, things often got awkward. But how to cope with the dilemma that something you wanted to do was in opposition to what others wanted? Presumably, you just had to find a way to do it so that nohar would know about it.

'So, if I apologise to Zira you'll let me out of my room?' Darq asked.

'If I went back on punishments, that'd be wrong,' Phade answered. 'I must stand by what I said, otherwise the punishment is worthless.'

'I don't understand,' Darq said. 'You made me see what happens when I'm bad, and all day yesterday and all night I was in the punishment. I felt what it would be like not to be let out for a week, and I suffered. You came and explained to me why you did it, and now we're friends, so what's the point of there still being this horrible thing between us? I won't climb out of my window again at night. I understand everything you've said. I agree with you. Why must I still be punished?'

Phade stared at Darq for several seconds. It was clearly difficult for him to believe he was talking to a one-year-old harling. 'All right,' he said at last. 'But be nice to Zira. Threatening to blind him indeed! A harling your age should have no such ideas. Come on, get up. We'll go and have breakfast.'

After breakfast, Darq went to the room on the first floor that Phade had appointed as his classroom. It was a light and airy place, its walls lined with book shelves. The shelves were far from full, but Darq put other things on them that interested him, such as animal skulls he found in the forest and brightly coloured fungi that eventually shrivelled up and smelled bad. Zira was already in the room, still looking furious.

'I'm sorry,' Darq said.

Zira raised his eyebrows. 'What for?'

'Saying those things to you. I won't blind you.'

Zira smiled. 'If you tried, there might be rather a scuffle. All right, apology accepted. I'm sorry I whacked your head.'

Darq was astounded at the power of the simple words 'I'm sorry'. It was like a magic spell. 'Will you take me to see Olivia?' he asked. 'I think I should apologise to her too. I didn't want to get any of your family into trouble. I just like being outside and... well... can we go to the cottage?'

'Of course,' Zira said.

'I could pick her some flowers,' Darq offered, 'or find some branches with red berries on.' He realised a bit of coy simpering might also be useful and batted his eyelashes a few times.

Zira responded exactly as Darq wished. 'That's a thoughtful idea. She'll be pleased. Afterwards, we can go into the woods, if you like. We can do today's lessons there. Perhaps Ma will let Amelza come with us.'

This is amazing, Darq thought. *It's so easy.* He giggled as he'd heard human children do when they sought the favour of adults.

Zira ruffled his hair. 'Perhaps you're not as freakish as I thought,' he said. 'Maybe it's just that nohar round here really knows how to be with harlings. We'll just have to learn.'

So will I, Darq thought. He felt he'd made a major breakthrough already.

Chapter Four

Loki har Aralis' first name would have rested far more comfortably on Darquiel's shoulders. It was the name of a trickster god, and Loki the harling was anything but a trickster.

He was the half-brother of Darquiel, but did not know it. He lived in the Gelaming city of Immanion with his parents, in the country of Almagabra. As far as Loki was concerned, he had only one other sibling, who nohar talked about. From gossip around the palace Phaonica, Loki had determined that his much older brother, Abrimel, was in prison somewhere, a criminal. His parents wouldn't speak about it, nor his hura, Caeru, nor his tutors and servants. They would say things like 'when you're older', which was no use at all. Loki was inquisitive and bright, but knew his place. When adults said 'no', he complied with their wishes.

He was as unlike Darq as it's possible to get. Where Darq was literally dark, Loki was fair. He enjoyed the company of others. He was popular among his peers, not least because he was a son of the Tigrons and therefore royal. His father, Calanthe, took him everywhere with him, whenever it was possible. His hostling - well - that was another matter, but then Pellaz was always busy. 'Don't worry,' Cal said once. 'I was just like that when I hosted Tyson. Maybe some of us are just cut out to be better fathers than hostlings. He'll be fine when you grow up.'

Adults, of course, did not normally say such enlightening things to harlings, but Cal was different to all other adults Loki knew. He loved Cal so passionately, it sometimes made him hurt inside. He had nightmares about Cal disappearing, or flying away on a great bird, or being smothered by strange shadowy monsters. Loki would wake weeping from these dreams and run to his father's rooms. He could always climb into bed beside Cal and whisper his fears, and Cal would sling an arm around him say, 'No chance. I've had my lot of disappearing.'

It was Cal who had given Loki his name, and also who told him what it meant.

'Isn't that a… *bad* name?' Loki asked; polite but slightly alarmed.

'No,' Cal replied. 'It's a very strong name. I chose it on purpose. It comes from a country where the gods of the north live.'

'Can we go there?'

Cal grinned. 'I think one day we might, yes.'

Loki grew up surrounded by love, and given every privilege a young har could want: his own *sedu* to ride, his own rooms and attendants, noble-born harlings imported from several realms to be his companions. He never brushed his own hair or cut his own fingernails. He had no idea how food was prepared; it was simply delivered to his table, perfect, whenever he was hungry. The Tigrina, Caeru, doted upon him as if Loki were his own son. Loki had many relations. There was his hura, Terez, in Immanion, and Mima in Jaddayoth, who was Terez and Pell's sister back from when they'd been human. She wasn't har, but Kamagrian, which was apparently similar. Loki called her his huri, rather than hura, to make the distinction. The Parasilian family in Galhea, on the other side of the great ocean, were also his kinshara, not least because his half-brother, Tyson, was a Parasilian, and also his hura, Snake, another of Pellaz's brothers. Loki was comfortable within this organism. He was praised and pampered by every har who was a part of it. He was the heir to the throne in Immanion.

You can be sure that Loki would never, under any circumstances, have climbed out of his bedroom window at night and teetered perilously thirty feet above the ground. He liked approval, and did all that he could to get it. A cynical har might say that there was an underlying selfishness in Loki's manner. Perhaps he learned the game long before it even occurred to Darq there was one to play.

He was always extremely courteous, and the only thing he didn't like was disrespect – not that many other harlings would dare to show it to him. This rather prim attribute might have originated from Cal's influence, who often told him he should never 'take shit' off anyhar (a delicious secret Loki never told a living soul, because the language was bad), or it might simply have been because it was in his blood, the particular corpuscles that had come from Pellaz, his hostling. Pellaz could wither hara with a glance, and on several occasions Loki had slunk from his hostling's presence feeling utterly wilted. He noticed very early in life that Pellaz rarely apologised, even when he was wrong about something, and Loki took this to be the way a son of the Tigron should also behave. However, in his view, one should never do anything that requires an apology. Really, it was very simple. Thus, it followed that by the age of nearly seven, Loki had never said the words 'I'm sorry' and had had no cause to.

The early years of Loki's life had been full of adventures, of only the safest kind, but devoid of more significant events. He had travelled the Otherlanes at only two years of age, held by his father on the front of his saddle. He had visited his relatives in Megalithica, and in Roselane, in Jaddayoth. In fact, one summer, he and Cal had spent three weeks in Jaddayoth. Cal had taken him to wonderful places, like the underground city of Sahen, and the cliff city of Shappa, where the narrow streets were nearly vertical. Like all privileged individuals, Loki grew up thinking life was grand, or perhaps he didn't even consider that. He simply took it all for granted.

Once a week, the Aralis family met together to share a meal. This was on the evening of Aghamasday. When the weather was fine, which it usually was in Immanion, the fairest of Wraeththu cities, the six of them would sit round a table on Caeru's terrace, which faced the ocean. Sometimes, there were visitors, such as Parasilian hara from Galhea: Tyson and his chesnari Moon, or Snake and his chesnari, Cobweb. Occasionally, members of the Hegemony would join them for special occasions like birthdays and festivals.

One Aghamasday evening, in the height of summer, the Aralisians met as usual to share a meal. Loki, arriving with his father, could tell at once that Pellaz was not in a good mood. He sprawled in his seat, with his feet up on the table, his beautiful features set into a scowl. Loki knew better than to seek approval from his hostling when his face wore that expression. Terez was also already present, and he and his chesnari Raven were usually late arrivals at these gatherings, much to Caeru's annoyance. Tonight, Raven was not there, however. Loki got the impression Terez had been summoned very quickly. Something must be wrong, he realised.

Loki went at once to the Tigrina and hugged him; gentle Caeru, who was so willowy and fair. That day, Loki had been into the city with his father, who had taken him to a hair stylist, where only the very rich stepped over the threshold. He'd had his hair cut very similar to Cal's and now felt extremely grown up and handsome. Pellaz cast him a glance and raised an eyebrow. 'Well,' he said, 'you could be brothers.'

'He looks very like his father,' Caeru said, a hand hovering just above Loki's head, so as not to ruffle the artful messiness.

'Doesn't he just,' said Pellaz, in a voice that sounded to Loki as if it was full of wasps.

Loki wanted to look exactly like his father, of course, and was warmed by Caeru's comment. The fact was he had his hostling's eyes, which were very dark, and also his lips, which were fuller than Cal's. His skin tone was somewhere between the two of them, darker than Cal but fairer than Pellaz. But his hair was the same shocking white gold as his father's and he was of a similar build, long and lithe. At nearly seven, Loki looked like a young teenage human. Within a year or so, he would be adult, when feybraiha, the Wraeththu equivalent of puberty, would steal over him. In harlings, the process occurred very quickly, taking weeks rather than years. Like all harlings his age, desperate to be adult and gain some freedom, Loki awaited this magical time impatiently.

'You look like you're sitting on a nail,' Cal said to Pellaz. 'What's up?'

Pellaz sighed deeply. 'Communication from the north,' he said.

Cal sat down at the table, and Loki sat beside him. '*The* north?' Cal enquired.

'Yes.'

'In what respect?' Cal helped himself to an apple from a bowl on the table and began to munch it. Loki could tell that his father was now also somewhat tense. He sat very still, hoping that if he became invisible, the adults would talk more frankly in front of him.

'There have been anomalies in the ethers around Freyhella,' Pellaz said. 'The Council in Freygard considered we should be informed.'

'What kind of anomalies?' Cal asked.

'I don't know. They suggest we send a delegation to see for ourselves.'

Cal raised his eyebrows and stopped chewing. '*Really!*' he said, after a few moments. 'Who made contact?'

'I've no idea. The Listeners received a message, that's all.'

'Who will you send?'

'I expect Eyra will see to it. The Listeners and the ethers are his province.'

Cal gestured at Terez. 'I think our deadly assassin should go.'

'I am *not* an assassin,' Terez said, clearly pleased at being called that. 'But I'll go if you want me to, Pell.'

'Yes, maybe,' Pellaz said irritably. 'Be part of the delegation.'

Cal took another bite of his apple and shook his head slowly. 'Well, after all this time, all this silence... I thought Freygard had dropped off the map.'

'They must be really concerned to contact Immanion,' Terez said. 'I hope to all dehara this doesn't mean something's happening again.'

'We'd have felt it,' Pellaz said sharply. 'Snake and Cobweb are always alert. They never rest and never will. If there's the faintest glimmer of abnormal activity, they'll sense it, probably long before it happens.'

At that moment, Raven arrived, which meant the conversation ceased for some minutes. Raven was another favourite of Loki's, mainly because his skin was so black, when you stroked his arm it made the taste of dark chocolate appear in your mouth. He smelled good, like purple berries, aromatic coffee and thick syrup. All in all, he was a delight to the senses. Raven sat down, and Caeru's servants began to bring out the first course of the meal.

'Freygard's been in touch,' Terez said to Raven. He outlined what Pellaz had told them.

'And you of course will be heading north now,' Raven said. He glanced at Pellaz. 'Shall I go with him?'

'As you wish,' Pellaz said. 'Freygard asked for a delegation. That could be a dozen hara. We'll meet at Eyra's office in the morning.'

'I think I'll go to Freygard too,' Cal said.

There was a moment's silence around the table, then Pellaz said, 'Why?'

Cal pushed Loki's shoulder playfully. 'I think our son should see it.'

'You can't be serious,' Pellaz said.

'Why not?'

Pellaz blinked at him meaningfully, and Loki sensed a secret.

'Come on, Pell,' Cal said in a cajoling tone. 'Let him see it. Let him smell the air, the sea. He should visit. You know he should. It's…' He smiled at Loki. 'It's a very magical place. All hara should go at least once in their lives.'

'I'd really like to go,' Loki said hopefully.

'I don't know,' Pellaz said, clearly uncomfortable. 'It might not be a good idea.'

'Trust me,' Cal said. 'It'll be fine.'

Pellaz nearly choked.

'Why shouldn't he go?' Caeru asked. 'Think about it, Pell. What happened is ancient history. It's nothing to do with Loki, and relations should be patched up politically. Cal should go and build bridges.' Caeru fixed Cal with the hardest stare he could manage. 'That *is* what you'll do, isn't it?'

Cal displayed the palms of his hands, pulled a rueful face.

Unexpectedly, Pellaz laughed. 'Yes, you're right. You should all go.' He smiled at Loki. 'You'll like it. Well, I expect you will. I've never been there.'

'Perhaps you…' Cal began.

'Shut up,' Pellaz said mildly. 'My presence will do nothing to facilitate any bridge-building, I assure you.' He narrowed his eyes. 'I do hope you don't have knives concealed beneath your good intentions, my beloved. Please assure me that is not the case.'

'My good intentions are laden with flowers,' Cal said. 'I've never seen Freygard either.'

Later, in Loki's own rooms, Cal told his son to look upon the trip as work. 'It won't be long before you're sitting in the Hegalion yourself,' he said. 'You should develop the diplomat's forked tongue as soon as you can.'

'Forked tongue?' Loki asked dubiously.

Cal laughed. 'A figure of speech. I think you'll be an exemplary diplomat.' He took Loki's face in both hands and kissed his brow. 'You're so grown up. Time has flown by. I can't believe it.'

Cal's words made Loki feel insecure somehow. It implied a growing distance, an approaching horizon when the sun would set on gilded days. He hugged Cal fiercely, suddenly having to swallow a lump in his throat.

'Hey,' Cal said. 'What did I say?'

Loki pulled away. 'I don't know. It felt like winter coming.'

'There's no need to worry. Life will be full of wonders, Loki.'

Loki smiled bravely. 'Why are we going to Freyhella?'

Cal grimaced. 'Some time ago, the ethers and the Otherlanes went strange. It was part of some trouble we had to deal with. Now, something odd has happened in Freygard, and the hara there want our opinion.'

'What was the trouble?'

Cal glanced at the ceiling for a moment, skewed his mouth to the side. 'It's a long story. Basically, before you were born, the Gelaming were involved in a conflict with some hara who… let's just say didn't really have the well-being of Wraeththu at heart. We formed an alliance of tribes, and Freyhella was one of the tribes that showed up. They're fiercely independent, and really didn't want to ally with us, but…' Cal shrugged. 'Anyway, as soon as the conflict was over, they sailed back to Freygard and closed communication. They must be worried now to contact us.'

'Will we sail to Freygard?' Loki had never been a long distance on a boat.

'No. We'll use *sedim* as usual. It'd take too long on a boat.'

Loki was disappointed by that. He liked the thought of travelling over the sea.

Two days later, the *sedim* leapt out of the Otherlanes in the hills beyond Freygard's walls, bearing a delegation of Gelaming. Loki was impressed at once by the majesty of the landscape, even though the cold hit him sharply. Freyhella was shrouded in mist and seemed watchful. There were forested mountains and deep fjords, fanged with sharp rocks. This land might be the haunt of dragons and wolves with burning eyes. The air smelled strongly of brine and fish.

Immanion had sent a party of twelve hara, which as well as including members of the Aralisian family, also included the Hegemon Eyra Fiumara, Hegemony Clerk Velaxis Shiraz, and a few guards. Velaxis always unnerved Loki. He was a watchful har, like a sly cat and his abundant hair was the colour of untouched snow. He favoured winding it with black pearls and usually dressed in clothes of white or black. He was the sort of har who knew everything and everyhar. Loki knew this, because Pellaz often said snide things about him. Velaxis was very friendly with Rue, and Loki knew Pellaz thought that was a strategic friendship. It didn't surprise Loki that Velaxis was part of the group.

The Freyhellans had sent no welcoming party, which even Loki knew was a little odd, if not rude, and the Gelaming rode into town along the main road, which followed the river. The call of seabirds drifted mournfully through the mist and, as the party approached the walls of Freygard, the sound of water on wood could be heard, and the gristly clunk of hulls rubbing together. As they drew nearer to the gates, the peaked roofs of Freygard could be glimpsed through the swirling vapor; still and dark and immense. Wooden hex-beasts snarled from the highest eaves, moisture dripping from their bearded chins. Loki could hear voices, the sound of wheels on cobbles, the tock of blacksmiths' hammers. The warm scent of horse dung mingled with the aroma of the sea. He had a strange feeling inside, as if he'd walked into one of his own dreams. He felt he'd been to this place before. He felt excited, wistful, fearful and ecstatic, all at once.

'Do they have strong magic here?' he asked Cal.

Cal glanced over at him. 'Why do you say that?'

'I feel strange.'

Cal had no opportunity to respond to that, because the gates of the town opened ahead of them and a delegation of Freyhellans rode forth. Like Cal and Loki, they had pale hair. They rode stocky chestnut horses, whose manes and tails were the same pale colour as their riders' hair. Their leader urged his mount ahead of the others, and touched his brow in a gesture of respectful greeting. 'You are welcome, Tiahaara. Allow us to accompany you to the Hall of Assembly.'

Eyra, a rather stern-faced har, who wore his shining black hair in multiple braids, had assumed leadership of the Gelaming group. 'We are happy to oblige,' he said, and the company rode beneath the arch of the gate.

Cal appeared content to blend into the background, as if he were there simply to observe events. Loki perceived a slight tension in his father. There was history between Freygard and the Aralisians, Loki already knew that, even if he was unaware of the details. Cal had told him about the war, when the tribes of Wraeththu had had to ally against a common threat, but Loki had sensed something else beneath his father's casual words, a feeling that had smelled like burned meat.

The Hall of Assembly stood upon an immense dais in the centre of the town, so that it was approached by a flight of steps on all sides. Banners on poles surrounded it, hanging limp like seaweed in the damp, motionless air. The building was surrounded by a wide square, and smaller administrative buildings and stables lay behind it. It was in this hall that the archon of the Freyhellans held court.

The great chamber was stuffy, filled as it was with hara clad in musty furs. A huge fire grumbled in a hearth the height of two horses. Smoke-blackened beams arched high overhead, and massive pillars, with twisty carvings, supported the roof. As Loki followed his father inside, he found he was short of breath. He felt light-headed and wondered why. After all, it wasn't as if he was unused to large gatherings or strange places.

There were so many hara in the room, Loki could see little of what transpired. Cal had asked Raven to take care of Loki while business was undertaken. Now, Loki stood by Raven near the back of the crowd, while the Gelaming went to the dais at the end of the room to confer with the Freyhellan councillors. Voices were low; it was a private conversation, not for all present in the room.

Raven sighed, perhaps in boredom. 'I wish somehar had been polite enough to show us to guest quarters before this,' he said. 'Then you and I could leave here, do some sight-seeing.'

Loki was straining to catch a glimpse of the Freyhellan archon, but the dais wasn't that high, and there were too many tall bodies in the way.

'Maybe we should go anyway,' Raven said. 'What do you think?'

Loki smiled up at Raven. He'd always do what adults wanted of him.

They walked down to the beach, past the docks, where the long boats of the Freyhellan warriors were moored, along with fishing boats of more squat proportions. Pale-haired hara worked on their nets, sitting on upturned lobster pots, with their dogs nearby, which were nosing through seaweed and flotsam. The Freyhellans paid scant attention to the strangers among them, or else delivered the occasional expressionless glance. Loki felt uncomfortable. He sensed they weren't welcome in this place, in which case, why had they been invited?

Raven ignored the less than companionable emanations from the locals and took Loki down to the shoreline. 'In this place,' he said, 'your huri Mima was thrown from a ship. She and her friends washed up here.'

Loki shivered. 'It's such a cold damp place. It doesn't seem very magical now. Were the hara rude to Mima too?'

Raven laughed softly. 'I don't believe so. It was long ago. This is all about politics, Loki. The convoluted web of relations between tribes. The Freyhellans are suspicious of us, because we are powerful. In situations like these, we must remain courteous and reserved. We observe local customs. We are patient.'

'I understand,' Loki said. He wanted more than anything to be a good ambassador for his tribe.

'I wasn't always Gelaming,' Raven said, 'so I appreciate how others feel sometimes. It's up to us to allay their fears, to be respectful. Project that intention, and you'll find that eventually hara warm to you.'

'I will.'

They walked towards the headland, where the black cliffs were pocked with caves. A few harlings were sitting on the sand outside one of the caves, having built a fire. They were frying shrimp in butter, a battered old skillet placed right on the flames. Raven went up to them, and Loki followed, trying to project respect.

'Smells good,' Raven said.

The harlings all stared at Raven, in a manner so outrageously without manners that Loki squirmed in embarrassment for them.

'We're visitors,' Raven said, 'from the south.' He hunkered down among them.

One of the harlings reached out and briefly touched one of Raven's hands.

'You're Gelaming,' said another in a strongly-accented voice.

'Yes,' Raven said. 'We are.'

'Why is your skin painted that way?'

Raven laughed. 'It isn't. It's made that way. It helps me be attuned to strange things. Have you seen any strange things around here?'

One of the harlings poked at the shrimp in the skillet with a charred wooden spoon. The others exchanged glances. Then the one who had first spoken said, 'They can't understand you. They don't speak your language.'

'How come you do?'

'My father was from the south. I speak both tongues.'

'Useful,' Raven said. 'So, is there anything you can tell me about what's going on here?'

'You mean, like the spirit window?'

'Yes,' Raven said, 'like that. I'd like to see it.'

'We're not supposed to go there now. It's unstable, they said.'

'Can you tell me where it is?'

Loki could tell, from Raven's tone and posture, that he had slipped into Hegemony officer mode. He was determined to get some information.

'You shouldn't go,' said the Freyhellan harling. 'Things can come out of it.'

'But I have my magical skin to protect me.'

The harling regarded Raven with some scorn. It seemed he believed Raven was mocking him.

'That was a joke,' Raven said. 'But even so, I'm more than capable of protecting myself.' He reached into a pocket and pulled out a glittering Almagabran coin. 'You can have this if you show me the spirit window.'

'All right,' said the harling, getting to his feet.

'Thanks.' Raven helped himself to a shrimp before standing up.

The harling led them along the cliffs to where a path snaked upwards between brittle, salt-bleached shrubs. Raven asked the harling his name and received the short reply: 'Taldri.'

The Freyhellan ran up the almost vertical path, Raven and Loki struggling to keep up. At the top, Taldri stood with hands on hips to wait for them. 'It's back here,' he said. 'Not far. It came where the water spout rises.'

The top of the cliffs was a series of slick black platforms, interspersed with puddles. Loki found the surface treacherous. His boots slipped alarmingly. He took Raven's hand, even though he wanted to appear adult and aloof in front of Taldri. Taking Raven's support, however, was preferable to losing his dignity in a fall.

The area around the spout hole was covered in tiny limpets; presumably they'd been thrown there by the spout. A grove of gnarled ancient hawthorns huddled nearby, leaning together like malevolent imps, stunted and deformed by salt and wind. Even from a distance, Loki perceived a strange sensation pulsing from that grove.

'There,' Taldri said, pointing to the trees. 'I won't go in there anymore. My friend Eshric found it, and he's been ill ever since. He went too close for too long, I heard.'

'Thanks.' Raven flipped the promised coin to Taldri, who caught it deftly.

Taldri hesitated a moment, then said, 'Be careful.' He ran off across the black rocks, pale hair flying.

Raven raised his eyebrows at Loki. 'They should have a guard here if it's so dangerous. I'll take a look. Wait here.'

'Don't!' Loki said, unable to contain himself.

'It's OK. I won't go too close.'

Loki edged a little nearer as Raven went into the grove. The small hairs on his skin had started to lift. There was a buzzing sound in his ears.

Presently, Raven called. 'Come closer, Loki. It's quite safe.'

Nervously, Loki approached the dark of the trees. He could see Raven limned in a strange violet light. 'What is it?' Loki asked.

Raven wheeled round. 'Loki, get back! Don't come in here!'

'But you said…'

Raven came out of the trees. 'It's a real phenomenon. I've never seen anything like it. I've no idea what it is.'

'You called me,' Loki said.

Raven frowned. 'I didn't.'

'I heard you.'

'Strange,' Raven said, 'but perhaps a warning. We should leave.' He took Loki's hand again.

'What does it look like?' Loki asked, as Raven dragged him swiftly across the slick rocks.

'A sphere of violet light,' Raven said, 'then nothing at all but a feeling, then a sound. It doesn't belong here.'

They returned to the Hall of Assembly to find that the Freyhellans had become slightly more hospitable. A table had been laid with food and now hara milled about, talking. Loki saw Eyra Fiumara conversing with a tall har whose flag of pale hair cascaded down his back. Loki had a strong desire to see his face. It was almost a compulsion. Cal was sitting on the table with his feet on the back of a chair, staring at Eyra's companion, his face set into a faintly sour expression he was attempting to present as cynical amusement.

'Who's that with Eyra?' Loki asked Raven, as they made their way through the crowd towards Cal. 'Do you know?'

'That's Galdra har Freyhella,' Raven replied. 'Archon of this tribe.'

Cal noticed his son's approach and smiled more genuinely.

'How did it go?' Raven asked.

'Well, we've endured the airs and graces,' Cal replied. 'Later, we're being given a guided tour.'

'I took a look at the phenomenon already,' Raven said. 'They were right to inform us.'

'What is it? His Mightiness, Emperor Galdra, told us it's some kind of gateway, like an Otherlanes portal.'

Raven shrugged. 'I've no idea if it's that or not. The harlings around here call it a spirit window. They say things can come out of it.'

Cal nodded. 'We were told that. Shadows. Shadows that stand outside houses, looking in.'

Raven grimaced. 'Nice.'

'Definitely spooky. Nothing bad has happened, except to the harling who discovered the thing. He's been weakened by it. Healing does no good. There's no evidence the phenomenon is hostile, though. It could be that a sort of alien energy from it affected the harling. It might not have been a deliberate attack.'

'In your opinion,' said Raven, 'is this anything to do with… well, what happened before?'

'It's too early to guess,' Cal said. 'As others have said before, Wraeththu travelling through the Otherlanes might have had effects we were unaware of, that affect this reality. We have no way of knowing.'

'And as you're the only har of our acquaintance who can travel the Otherlanes without a *sedu,* I guess it's down to you to investigate this,' Raven said.

'I'll take a look, naturally,' Cal replied, 'but even with my experience, I'll not risk anything stupid. I'll report this to Thiede.'

'Maybe we should contact Galhea. It might be worth Snake and Cobweb taking a look too.'

'That could be a good idea, yes.' Cal got down from the table. 'It's difficult to negotiate here. The Freyhellans hate having to involve us. But this is beyond them.' Cal sounded irritated by that.

Loki had been stealing covert glances at the Freyhellan leader, but now when he looked over at Eyra, he saw that Galdra was staring back at him. Astonishingly, he was facially very similar to Cal: a chiselled face with wide high cheekbones and a finely drawn mouth. A severe jolt shook Loki's body. He felt strangely ashamed.

Cal had noticed that Galdra was staring. 'Keep your eyes to yourself,' he muttered.

'Cal,' Raven said in a warning tone. 'Was this really a good idea?'

Cal uttered a wordless sound in response.

Galdra turned away, but Loki felt the Freyhellan's attention was still focused upon him. He felt very uncomfortable. 'Cal, why did he look at me like that?'

'You are my son,' Cal replied lightly, 'and I am not his favourite har.' He grinned. 'Come on, let's try the local cuisine. I'm starving.' He guided Loki further down the table.

The Freyhellan leader kept his distance, and eventually a har of the tribe approached the Gelaming, who had gravitated towards one another, in order to conduct them to their accommodation. They were taken to a house reserved for official guests to the town, which was comfortable and spacious. Loki liked the peaked eaves that were covered in carvings of strange mythical beasts from the sea: serpents and merhorses and giant octopi, some of them a meld of several different creatures. Cal said they were put there as protective spirits. Loki could believe there was some kind of life in them; they appeared to stare down disapprovingly at the hara who had been placed beneath their protection.

Galdra was due to arrive within the hour to conduct them to the site of the phenomenon. The Gelaming sat in the main salon, along with their scant luggage, while Eyra and Velaxis questioned Raven about what he'd seen.

'What did you think of it?' Cal asked Loki.

'I didn't see it really,' Loki replied, 'but I heard Raven call me to go to him while he was looking at it. Only he didn't. The thing must have done that.'

'Called you,' Eyra said, pondering. 'Hmm.'

'Perhaps it calls to harlings,' Terez said. 'It was discovered by one, who has suffered ill effects. To me, that seems sinister.'

'I agree,' Eyra said. 'Well, soon we shall see for ourselves.'

'The Freyhellans should close off the area,' Raven said. 'I think they're lucky they haven't had disastrous consequences, leaving it open to all like that.'

'You got a bad feeling from it, then?' Velaxis asked.

Raven shrugged. 'Not bad particularly, but I didn't understand it or recognise it. Fire is dangerous, in the hands of a har who doesn't know about burning. I think it's the same.'

A sharp knock came upon the door, and without waiting for a response a Freyhellan walked in to announce he was Fyala, their housekeeper. 'I prepare breakfast, and keep the place in order,' he said, in thickly-accented Almagabran. 'I don't do lunch or evening meals. Tonight, I believe you are the guests of our archon for dinner, in any case. If you stay longer than tomorrow, the inn *Fair Winds* does good meals.'

'Thank you,' Eyra said icily.

Fyala ducked his head and withdrew.

'Wait!' Eyra called.

After a moment's hesitation, the Freyhellan reappeared.

'Do your duties extend to coffee or tea?' Eyra asked icily. 'If so, please bring some here.'

Fyala grimaced. 'I'll have to go and buy milk.'

'Then do.'

Fyala closed the door.

Eyra shook his head. 'Our friends are going to great effort to make us feel welcome.'

Cal laughed. 'Yeah.'

They were sitting down and had only just begun to drink mugs of coffee, which Fyala had taken over half an hour to prepare, when the door opened again, this time without the forewarning knock. Galdra har Freyhella marched into the room, accompanied by a pair of armed hara. For a moment, Loki was frightened, wondering if the Freyhellans were going to turn on them now, lock them up or attack them. They were tall and dressed in tailored animal skins and leathers. Their necks were hung with protective fetishes of horsehair and shells. Their appearance contrasted strongly with the well-groomed Gelaming, whose flowing garments were of jewel-coloured velvet and soft linen. There was a wild dangerous edge to the Freyhellans that the Gelaming did not have.

Galdra's expression was far from warm. 'Are you ready?' he asked abruptly.

'Indeed,' said Eyra fastidiously. 'Remember we are here at your request, Tiahaar. A little more courtesy would not go amiss.'

'I am courteous to you, Tiahaar Fiumara,' Galdra said. For a moment, his eyes rested on Loki, who wanted to squirm back into his seat. 'My feelings for Gelaming have never changed. However, I appreciate you have at your disposal resources that we do not. That is why I asked you here.'

'Then let's get on with our business,' Velaxis said, rising fluidly to his feet.

Loki had noticed that Galdra's gaze never wavered from Eyra or himself. It was as if he couldn't bear having to look at the other hara in the room. What was the hidden history between Freyhella and Gelaming? Loki knew in his gut it was more than tribal politics.

'It seems you look upon this visit as a holiday,' Galdra said, as the Gelaming put their coats back on. 'Bringing harlings here.'

'This is the son of the Tigrons,' Eyra said, indicating Loki. 'It's part of his education to visit other tribes, hardly a holiday.'

'What is your name?' Galdra asked Loki.

Loki told him, in a small voice he was powerless to make louder.

Galdra raised his eyebrows and almost smiled, but his eyes were dark and furious. 'That name comes from this land,' he said.

'I know,' Loki said. 'It's the name of a god.'

'Then it's fitting your family brought you here, to see where you came from.'

Cal came up behind Loki's chair and put a hand on his son's shoulder. 'Stay here,' he said. 'We don't know how dangerous this phenomenon is.' He glanced at Raven. 'Would you…?'

Raven raised his hands. 'Harling-minder again? No problem. We'll explore the house.'

Loki didn't think he needed a minder, but he was glad Raven was staying behind with him. He was confused and upset, feelings he rarely encountered. In just a few exchanges, Galdra had unsettled him greatly. He felt responsible for something, almost guilty. He couldn't understand it. Was Galdra angry because the Gelaming had used a Freyhellan name?

After the party had left the house, in a cloud of emotional energy that felt positively infected, Loki started talking before Raven could say anything. 'That Galdra hates me,' he said. 'He makes me feel bad. I don't like these hara. They're so… so *angry* all the time! It's because of my name, isn't it?'

Raven stared at Loki for a few moments. 'Partly,' he said. He shook his head.

'Tell me,' Loki said. 'Please. What happened between the Gelaming and the Freyhellans?'

Raven appeared troubled.

'I'm nearly adult,' Loki said. 'I'm supposed to be Aralisian, a politician. Aren't I? I should know the truth.'

Raven smiled, and it seemed directed inwards on a memory. 'Sometimes we forget,' he said. 'We forget how quickly our harlings grow.' He sighed. 'All right, I'll speak to you as an adult, but only if you react like an adult and keep it to yourself. It's best you hear from me anyway I suppose, rather than from some har who just wants to gossip.'

Loki swallowed. He felt apprehensive, wondering if he'd asked for more than he could cope with.

'Your hostling was once close to Galdra har Freyhella,' Raven said. 'Pell and your father were parted for a while, and in that time, we went to war. Galdra worked with Pell intensively during that time, very... *intimately*. Everyhar knew he fell in love with Pell. Some say he acted opportunistically, taking advantage of Pell when he was vulnerable. Some say he had designs to take Cal's place as Tigron. Personally, I don't think he had any real agenda; he was just besotted.

'But whatever plans he might or might not have had, he was cast aside when Cal returned. Cal made sure of it. I hope you can understand now why Galdra seems a bit prickly around you. You were conceived almost immediately after Cal came back to us. And then, for whatever reason, Cal named you for an ancient Freyhellan deity. Galdra must see that as a mordant joke. Knowing Cal, it was meant that way. I'm sorry. It's best you should know. In the future, you'll have to deal with this tribe.'

Loki actually felt relieved. He had thought it would be worse than that. 'It makes sense to me,' he said. 'Cal wasn't pleased about what Galdra did. He stole a name, because Galdra tried to steal something important from him.'

Raven put his head to one side. 'Astute,' he said. 'He took the name because he could. Galdra could never take what he wanted.'

'Pell became close to Galdra because he looks like Cal, and Cal wasn't there.'

Raven laughed. 'Already you're learning about more than one form of politics. Relationships can sometimes be more complex than any inter-tribal dealings.'

Loki felt very pleased with himself, proud of his conclusions. It all made perfect sense. Perhaps, in his dealings with the Freyhellans, he should be more accommodating. Galdra had been hurt. Now he had to endure Cal's presence here. It must burn his skin like acid. *And I am living proof of a love he couldn't have,* Loki thought. The cells of his body had reacted to Galdra, because once Pellaz had been close to him. Pell's memories were inside him in some way. 'Did my hostling ever love Galdra?' Loki asked.

Raven frowned. 'I can't answer that. How can I?'

Dinner was held in the Hall of Assembly, where long tables had been laid out to accommodate around sixty guests. Galdra, perhaps grudgingly, invited the Gelaming to share his table. Eyra sat on one side of him, Cal on the other. Loki sat next to his father, one side of his body freezing cold, owing to the invisible pane of ice that separated Cal from Galdra, the effects of which crackled far. Amazingly, they were able to converse in stilted fashion. Cal was on his best behaviour and didn't mention Pellaz once, Loki noticed. Eyra kept up a professional stream of conversation – a hardened diplomat. Terez and Raven, sitting on Loki's other side, appeared to befriend the hara near to them. The flowing mead and wine might have had something to do with that.

'I'll send some of my Listeners to Freygard,' Eyra was saying. 'The phenomenon should be monitored constantly. It might be best if you cordoned off the area.'

Galdra nodded shortly. 'I'll see to that now.' He glanced at Cal. 'Previously, a word from the Assembly was enough to keep our hara away.'

'It might be nothing to worry about,' Cal said. 'I'll take another look tomorrow, open a portal next to it.'

'Is that wise?' Galdra asked.

Loki could almost hear Cal's unspoken response: *As if you care!*

'Probably not,' Cal replied, 'but it might produce results.'

'I don't want to put my hara in danger.'

Cal smiled politely. 'Trust me, Tiahaar. I *do* know what I'm doing.' He stood up. 'Please excuse me for a moment.'

As he left the table, Eyra turned to speak with Velaxis. Loki became excruciatingly aware that he and Galdra were sitting next to one another, with nohar else to talk to. He felt he wanted to say something, but had no idea what. Eventually, inspiration struck. He cleared his throat. 'Tiahaar…?'

Galdra turned to him and Loki's confidence nearly fled. He grabbed it by the scruff of the neck and plunged on.

'It is my wish…. I'll be part of the Hegemony in a few years. It is my wish for there to be no bad feeling between us.'

Galdra raised his brows, smiled. 'Tiahaar, there is no bad feeling between us. Of that, be assured.'

'I understand the history,' Loki said gravely.

Galdra laughed. 'Do you?'

Loki glanced at the Freyhellan, and realised that perhaps he didn't understand at all. Raven didn't know everything, clearly. 'I wish only to build bridges between our tribes.'

Galdra reached out and briefly touched Loki's cheek. When he spoke, his speech was formal. 'My dear harling, you already are a bridge.' He stood up. 'I think perhaps you were brought here as a spear, but it does not wound me. Far from it. Your hara speak of courtesy, yet they do me the greatest discourtesy. Perhaps it is done in ignorance. I have no way of knowing.'

'Tiahaar…' Loki felt strangely helpless; the situation was spiralling beyond his control.

Galdra raised a hand. 'Please. Enough. With those words, I should perhaps excuse myself also.' He bowed his head respectfully and left the table.

Loki watched him go. There was a quiet dignity in Galdra's posture that spoke of great pain. Loki's face was flaming. He was a symbol of all Galdra had lost, brought here to pour bitter salt into a wound. That must be why he'd felt ashamed in Galdra's presence. He wasn't sure what feeling gripped his body, and for a brief moment wondered whether it was some kind of adult thing. But no, it didn't feel like that. It was something else.

Chapter Five

Shortly after their founder, Tyr, wrested power from what was left of humanity in the area, the Freyhellans devised their own alphabet, a new set of runes, imbued with symbolism that embraced their androgynous condition. These runes were called the Harrark, and they were used to write down the history of the tribe. On the day the Gelaming came to Freygard, the historian of Freyhella began to record recent events. He wrote it in a beautiful hand, on the thick creamy pages of a book crafted by local hara. Within the words, as subtle as a faint scent borne on a soft breeze, twined the story of Pellaz har Aralis and Galdra, archon of Freygard. Its spectre still haunted the soul of the tribe.

The Gelaming Hegemony had never paid an official visit to Freygard. Before the second war with Fulminir, this was because Tyr, who was then still archon of Freyhella, had had a great mistrust of any tribe setting themselves up to be superior to all others. Then Tyr was murdered in a mysterious fashion and Galdra became archon. Tyr's death had been the catalyst that forced Galdra to contact Immanion, albeit with the greatest of misgivings. And during the following conclave of tribes in Immanion, as Wraeththu attempted to consolidate to ensure a safe future, Galdra had fallen in love. It had been a love doomed to tragedy.

After the war, the distance between the Gelaming and Freyhella increased. Hara might have spoken about it together, safe in their dwellings, but no official statement came from the Hall of Assembly. Everyhar was aware of some of what had transpired, and felt that Galdra had been used. Tigron Pellaz was a hard and ruthless creature. Although Galdra did not show it, many believed his spirit was, if not broken, then cracked and bleeding. He had wrapped part of himself in the banner of his pride. He had put it into a secret chest and locked it away. The light of Freyhella had dimmed, if only slightly, and the hara of the tribe could not forgive the Gelaming for that. Many waited for the day of retribution, for they felt that it would come.

Their historian recorded the events of the first official visit. He wrote of how Calanthe har Aralis went to the site of the spirit window and had there used his ability to open an Otherlanes portal. Cal quickly discovered that the phenomenon, whatever it was, was not a gateway to the Otherlanes. It was something else entirely, a different kind of portal. It would not allow him to enter it, even though he was brave and foolish enough to try. He learned only one thing. It was an exit, not an entrance. But whatever might squeeze from it, he could not say. It was beyond his experience.

The Freyhellans dreamed strange dreams. They saw shadows from their windows. They heard whispers in the rustling of leaves, in the song of the wind through the fishing nets strung out to dry. They were haunted.

The historian did not record everything, because some things were kept from him. He did not know that Galdra spoke privately to the Hegemony officer, Terez har Aralis, or that he gave Terez something to carry back for him to Immanion. Why he should have trusted Terez at all is perhaps a puzzle, but he did. He gave the Gelaming a letter.

Pellaz har Aralis too was haunted, and had been from the moment that Loki had hatched from his pearl. While the greater part of his family was in Freygard, Pellaz dreamed of Galdra every night. Several times, he almost told Caeru the truth, because he thought he might burst if he didn't. But he also knew it would be folly to do so. Some secrets had to remain secret, and the greatest secret kept in Immanion at that time was that Cal was not Loki's father.

To overthrow the forces of Ponclast, erstwhile leader of the Varrs, and his otherworldly aides, who were ranked against the allied tribes, Pellaz and Galdra had performed Grissecon, ritual aruna, on many occasions. They had learned strange and amazing new things about the magic of Wraeththu sexuality, but ultimately they'd had to use it to fight. The climax of that conflict had had a debilitating effect on them.

There is a special kind of aruna, which hara had always believed was used only to create new life. Pellaz and Galdra had learned otherwise. They learned that hara could enter the etheric realms through the cauldron of creation: that strange phenomenon, which could not be called an organ exactly, since it existed both within and without the harish body. Now, it was known the cauldron could enable contact with distant points and otherworldly entities. It was not just for reproduction after all. Pellaz had been able to prevent conception during the work, but on that final occasion, when the outcome of the conflict hung upon Pell's expertise and strength, his defences had been down. He hadn't guarded himself sufficiently, and Loki had been the result.

A son of the noble houses of Freyhella and Gelaming could have been disastrous. It would have given Galdra more power than some hara in Immanion wanted him to have. Although Galdra did not know it, he had allies too: those who would gladly have seen him take Cal's place at Pell's side. Cal had to protect his position, and part of doing that had been to claim paternity of Loki. Politically, both Tigrons had considered it the right thing to do. The Tigrina had never been told the truth.

Pellaz, who was far from stupid, realised what a dangerous game he was playing, allowing Loki to go to Freygard. He wondered whether Galdra would recognise the harling as kin, and part of him secretly hoped he would. It was not that Pellaz intended to wound or taunt. Part of him pined for Galdra continually, and he knew that should he dare to lay eyes on the Freyhellan again, old feelings could be resuscitated very quickly.

This would be awkward in many senses. For a start, Cal was not sympathetic to Galdra, so therefore any relationship between the Freyhellan and Pellaz was out of the question. Then there was the possibility that factions within the Hegemony, who were still suspicious of Cal, might attempt to use Galdra to oust Cal from power. Through Loki, Galdra could rightly try to claim power in Immanion: the conception of harlings was regarded as sacred by Gelaming. Pellaz had been trapped into a bloodbond with the Tigrina through a similar event many years earlier, and this could be taken as a precedent. Pellaz did not want to risk that happening. Any political scuffle, apart from being humiliating and potentially dangerous, would effectively kill any fondness he had for Galdra.

And fondness remained. It was the ghost in his bedchamber on the nights he slept there alone. It haunted his dreams. Over the years, he'd learned to live with it, slightly puzzled why another har could have such an effect on him, seeing as Cal was his soul mate, part of his being. It troubled him he could feel that way.

While the Hegemony delegation was in Freygard, Pellaz felt on edge. He wished he'd put his foot down and stopped Cal taking Loki with him. He knew there were going to be difficult repercussions, but he'd been stupid. However, when most of the party returned, after only two days, it seemed his fears were groundless. Eyra had remained in Freygard and two of his Listeners had travelled to join him. Everyhar else had come back to Immanion.

Pellaz questioned Cal at the first opportunity, which was when Cal came to the Tigron's office to make a report away from the ears of others. 'Galdra doesn't drop a grudge,' Cal said, 'but he knows he needs us. The atmosphere was strained, but not exactly hostile.'

'And Loki?' Pellaz asked. He was turning a fragile paper knife in his fingers, trying to resist the urge to snap it in two.

Cal pulled a wry face. 'The Freyhellan wasn't impressed by his name, but other than that, I think it was fine.'

Pellaz sighed. 'I hope you're right.'

'What can he do, anyway?' Cal said, sitting down in a chair opposite Pellaz. He put his feet up on the desk top. 'There's no proof of what happened with you two.'

'Don't be ridiculous,' Pellaz retorted. 'If he chose to make an issue of it, Eyra's hara would sniff out the connection in seconds. Nohar has seen it, because nohar has looked for it. You and Galdra look alike. But if the Listeners put their minds to it, Loki's heritage would scream out at them. You should know that.'

'I don't think the Freyhellan would do anything,' Cal assured. 'He's still too angry. He wants no connection with Immanion.'

'Does he have a son in Freygard?' Pellaz asked.

'Not that I saw.'

Pellaz grimaced. 'Then don't say he'd do nothing. Loki is half his. Nohar can be so angry as to deny a harling.'

Cal raised one eyebrow. 'Excuse *me*, father of Abrimel?'

'Shut up,' Pellaz said darkly. 'That was very different.'

Cal got up from his seat and went to Pell's side. He gripped Pell's shoulder. 'Loki enjoyed himself. He was in his element. He'll make a fine hegemon one day.'

Pellaz reached up to touch Cal's arm, then turned his head to kiss it. 'You are very good to him. It's like he really is your son. That means a lot.'

'He *is* my son,' Cal said. He sat down again, this time on Pell's side of the desk. 'I raised him.'

'Doesn't his parentage ever bother you?' Pellaz asked.

'Why ask me this, after all these years? Isn't it obvious the answer is no?'

Pellaz nodded. 'I know. I don't know why I asked that.'

Cal leaned over to kiss Pell's forehead. '*I* do. Don't worry.'

'And the phenomenon you studied? What of that?'

'I'm not sure. We'll talk later. I need to rest.'

Terez came to Pell's apartment in Phaonica after Cal had left. Pellaz had the distinct impression that his brother had been waiting for Cal to leave, which was strange. It also made his heart beat faster. He took Terez to his office and closed the door. 'The meeting went well?' he asked, sitting down behind his desk once more.

'As well as it could,' Terez said. 'The phenomenon does need to be observed. Nohar knows what it is. I expect Cal told you about it.'

'Not really,' Pellaz said. 'He's tired. We hardly discussed it.'

'It's definitely some kind of portal, but doesn't seem to be associated with the Otherlanes. The Freyhellans have witnessed strange things, something like shadows. So far, nohar has been directly threatened, but until we're sure what the phenomenon is, we should all be on alert.'

'That makes sense. Get our esteemed general, Ashmael, to send hara to Freygard too, as protection.'

Terez drew in his breath. 'Galdra might not look kindly upon that. Technically, Freygard doesn't come under our jurisdiction. The Freyhellans are still independent.'

'I know that,' Pellaz said. 'But Galdra is stupid if he refuses our aid. If anything should happen, and he loses hara because of it, he'd be furious with himself. Get Ashmael to send some of his hara. If there are any repercussions, direct Galdra to... direct him to Tharmifex.'

Terez raised his brows. 'To the Chancellor, not to you?'

'It wouldn't be the best action to direct him to me.'

Terez sighed. 'You know, I've been in two minds whether to do this or not.'

'Do what?' Pellaz asked.

Terez reached into one of his jacket pockets and pulled out an envelope, which was crumpled, as if he'd crushed it in his fingers many times. He held it out. 'Galdra asked me to deliver this to you.'

For some seconds, Pellaz stared at the envelope as if it were drizzled with poison.

'Will you not take it?'

Pellaz stood up and came from behind the desk. He took the envelope from Terez and with his back to his brother, opened it. Inside was a single sheet.

Pellaz, we must meet. I could come to Immanion or you could visit Freygard. The choice is yours, but I expect you would prefer discretion.

It was a pleasure to meet Loki. You must be very proud of your achievement.

G

'Damn,' Pellaz said.

'What does he want?'

Pellaz turned back to his brother. 'He wishes to speak to me.'

Terez gestured with one hand. 'Understandable. Perhaps he wonders why you did not come to Freygard with us. You haven't spoken since before the final Grissecon at Fulminir. That leaves a lot unsaid, my brother.'

Pellaz stared at the paper in his hands, acutely aware that Galdra had touched it. 'He made no attempt to contact me. He knew that was the way it had to be.'

'Well, now his tribe is perhaps in trouble. You were the only Gelaming he ever seemed to trust. It might help if you replied to him.'

Pellaz nodded slowly. 'I must think about it. Come here tomorrow after breakfast, before we meet at the Hegalion. Speak of this to nohar, and I mean *nohar*. Not even Raven.'

Terez inclined his head. 'I already understood that.'

Once Terez left, Pellaz read the note dozens of times. He knew in his heart what it meant. He could not ignore it. Before dinner that night, he sent a message to Terez. They would secretly visit Freygard the following morning. The Listeners would be asked to relay a message to Galdra har Freyhella to say that Terez har Aralis wished to speak with him in response to the request he'd made. They would ask for a liaison point to be determined.

Pellaz and Terez emerged from the Otherlanes at the preordained location, some miles north of Freygard. In this place, a long age ago, humans had built a chambered barrow as a tomb for the kings of their people. In later years, it had been excavated and preserved, roofed with tough glass. There were no remains left within. Here, Galdra har Freyhella had asked to meet with the Tigron of Immanion.

Pellaz left Terez outside with the *sedim* and ducked into the low passageway that led to the main chamber. It was dark only for a few moments. Vegetation had grown over the roof, making the light inside the main chamber green, but it was still well lit. Galdra sat in one of the niches where once a body would have lain. He hadn't changed at all. His bright hair seemed to glow with sunlight.

'Thank you for coming,' he said.

Pellaz said nothing. He didn't trust himself to speak. Galdra was entirely luminous in the gloom of the chamber. A dozen images flickered across Pell's mind's eye: Imbrilim, rain, Galdra's damp hair, warm flesh. And later, at Fulminir, when he and Galdra had transcended everything that Wraeththu understood about aruna. Pellaz closed a fist of iron over his heart. He had to remain focused, betray nothing.

'I'm sure you know why I asked to speak with you,' Galdra said. 'I don't know what motive you had in sending Loki here, and I hope that now you will tell me.'

'Say what you have to say,' Pellaz said.

'I'm not stupid, Pell, and I was more aware than you were when our work ended at Fulminir. I did wonder whether there had been... unexpected results, but I thought – clearly foolishly – if that were the case, you'd have sent word to me. The suspicion has nagged at me for years, until the moment I saw Loki in the Hall of Assembly. Then I knew for sure.'

Pellaz did not let himself react.

Galdra sliced the air before him with both hands. 'When I first saw the harling, and recognised him, I was angry. But I've considered the matter and now I understand why you kept him to yourself. I wonder whether even Cal knows he's not Loki's father'

'*Say* what you have to say,' Pellaz said again, in a low voice.

'I want no claim over Immanion; you've always known that. I appreciate the difficulty of this situation. But you have no right to deny me my son.'

Pellaz felt his skin prickle. 'What do you want?'

'The chance to know him, that's all. He recognised me too, but he doesn't understand what it is he sees in me. He wants to make peace between our tribes. His mere existence facilitates that, but only if you let me be part of his life.'

Pellaz folded his arms. 'Cal raised him. Cal cares for him. I don't think he'd allow it.'

'Does he know you're here now?'

'That is not your concern. If I don't agree to this demand, what do you intend to do?'

'I *will* take it further, Pell. I gave up a lot for you, not least my dignity and my heart. I vowed to leave you be, and would have kept to that, but Loki makes a difference. I have no other sons, and I doubt I ever will. Since you...'

'You can't blame me for that,' Pellaz said quickly, anticipating what Galdra might say next. 'It's your choice.'

Galdra shrugged. 'I know, but the facts remain the same. I *will* go to the Hegemony about this, if need be, and I know you won't want that.'

'Blackmail, then. I see.'

'Perhaps it is as low as that, yes,' Galdra said. 'What other choice do I have?' He jumped down from the niche and Pellaz took a few steps back. 'All I ask is that you allow Loki to spend some time here. I won't tell him about my relationship to him. That I promise you, although you ill deserve it. I'll keep quiet for his sake, not for yours or Cal's. He was stolen from me, Pell.'

'Even if I consent to this, I can't see Cal agreeing,' Pellaz said.

'Then you must convince him. How would he feel if he knew the truth?'

Pellaz expelled a short bark of laughter. 'It appears you learned a lot from me.'

'I did. Well?'

'I will speak to Cal about it.'

'I want Loki to celebrate his feybraiha here, because I can see it will be soon. His first aruna should be with one of my hara. That seems only right. It would go down well with the Hegemony. It would seem like a gesture of alliance and friendship.'

'True,' Pellaz said. 'There is sense in the idea.'

Galdra narrowed his eyes. 'Cal wouldn't want Loki to leave Immanion at that time, and yet I get the impression you don't care either way. All you care about is the political ramifications of his heritage being revealed. That's sad. Do you resent him so much?'

What Galdra hadn't guessed was that the reason Pellaz wanted Loki to visit Freygard was so that his son could be close to Galdra, as he himself could not. Instead of revealing this, he found himself saying something harsh, which he didn't mean at all. 'If you really want to know,' he said, 'I would've preferred not to have had him, but he has turned out to be a good har. I admire and respect him.'

Galdra shook his head. 'Why do I love you? You're made of stone. You lost one son, under terrible circumstances, and he is most likely dead. Another is your enemy. However Loki came to be, he should be a balm to that hurt. Your indifference only convinces me more I should take a part in my son's life.'

Pellaz tried to calm his heart, which had begun to beat faster. 'You hardly know me, Galdra. You love a fiction. I'm not allowed to be anything but what I am. I'm like stone, a statue, a figurehead. I belong to Wraeththu, not to myself.'

Galdra appeared unimpressed by this speech. 'I find myself grateful to Cal, for loving Loki, and that's a strange and unexpected feeling. But if he knew the truth...'

'He *does* know the truth,' Pellaz said.

Galdra was clearly surprised. 'Then he's more than I believed him to be.'

'He is that,' Pellaz said. 'He's very protective of Loki, but I will speak to him. He doesn't want this matter to be made public either, for obvious reasons.'

Galdra hesitated for a moment, then said, 'Why did he bring Loki here, Pell?'

'I don't know,' Pellaz replied. 'I advised against it – rightly so, as it turns out. Maybe he's never felt that Loki was truly his son. Maybe he sought to put a ghost to rest.' He paused. 'You don't want to make an enemy of Cal, Galdra. Trust me on that.'

'I don't wish to make any enemies,' Galdra said. 'It appears we might be facing a common threat again. Loki is a side issue, but an important one.'

Pellaz nodded. 'It was foolish of me to allow Cal to bring Loki here. This is only the inevitable result and he's brought it on himself. But if you promise to keep silent, then I see no reason why Loki shouldn't spend some time in Freygard and celebrate his feybraiha here. It won't do his education any harm.'

Galdra smiled coldly. 'I'm glad you're being rational.'

Pellaz grimaced. 'Hardly that. However, whatever you might think of my feelings for Loki, I don't want him to come while there's any risk or threat. I'm talking, of course, of the phenomenon that's appeared here. Surely, you wouldn't put your own son in danger?'

'I don't think it poses any danger. We're unclear what it is, but it appears that if hara stay away from it, there are no ill effects.'

'What of the harling who discovered it?'

'He's still ill.'

Pellaz nodded once. 'I see. Then let me take him back to Immanion with me. As you know, our healers are second to none.'

'So are ours,' Galdra said dryly, 'but I'll do anything to give the harling a chance. It seems a reasonable idea.'

'I still think the phenomenon should be regarded as potentially dangerous,' Pellaz said. 'I'd like to examine it.'

Galdra inclined his head. 'Of course. I'll take you there myself.'

'As you wish.'

Terez was still waiting outside with the *sedim*. Pellaz swung into his *sedu* Peridot's saddle and communicated with the creature to examine the portal also. The *sedim* might have insight into it, Pell guessed. Few hara communed easily with the *sedim*, but Pellaz enjoyed a closer relationship with his than most.

The day had turned dank and a thick fog was rolling across the waters to the west. Galdra mounted his own horse, a stocky Freyhellan beast with plaits in its mane and tail. 'Follow me. It's on the cliff top.' He urged his horse into a canter and, after exchanging a glance, Terez and Pellaz followed.

At the hawthorn grove, the party dismounted. Fog was tumbling in thickly now: it muffled sound, warped shapes and crept across the slick cliff tops in curls. Two of Eyra's Listeners were at the site, along with three Freyhellan guards. Pellaz told them he had come to investigate the phenomenon himself and asked them to draw back, to give him some privacy. He and Galdra went alone into the trees.

'Where is it?' Pellaz asked. The atmosphere felt electric in the close interior of the grove, where the hawthorns huddled together so closely, but he could perceive nothing with his physical eyes.

'This is how it is,' Galdra said. 'Sometimes, it appears as a violet glow, like a globe. Sometimes, it's just a sound, like the distant tolling of a bell. On some days, it makes your hair stand on end merely to be in here. Today is one of those days.'

'And what exactly have you seen come out of it?'

'Nothing. Hara have seen strange things in the town. Animals behave oddly, jumping at things we cannot see. There are noises, the feeling of being watched, but other than that...' Galdra shrugged. 'It's difficult to perceive this as hostile. It just seems... well... *unknown*.'

'Cal and I both wonder what effect hara have had on the Otherlanes, intruding into them,' Pellaz said.

'Well, it's only the Gelaming who have the privilege of Otherlanes transport,' Galdra said in a terse tone. Pellaz could tell that the mention of Cal had wounded him. He hadn't meant to do it.

'It's not only us,' Pellaz said. 'We know that Ponclast's hara had the ability, or some of them did, and they had darker motives than Gelaming could ever have.'

'You think Ponclast could be responsible?'

'I doubt it. Lileem is perfectly capable of keeping him in confinement.'

Galdra spoke carefully. 'Have you contacted her since...?'

'No,' Pellaz interrupted and swiftly changed the subject. 'Perhaps this is just some kind of side effect, a random portal. I don't know. The *sedim* are not very familiar with this area.'

'No. The last time I know of them visiting was long ago, when your sister Mima passed through.'

Pellaz called softly to Peridot and the *sedu* came into the grove, head lowered. Pellaz stroked his neck. 'Peridot, if there is something hostile here, send me an image.'

The *sedu* raised his head and sniffed the air, ears flicking back and forth.

'It's incredible,' Galdra said. 'He really seems to understand you.'

'He's rather more than a horse; you know that.'

'Even so...'

'We have limited communication,' Pellaz said, which was far from the truth. 'Hush. I need to concentrate.' Pellaz closed his eyes, attuned himself to Peridot's essence. *What do you sense?*

Nothing emerges from it but shadows and memory. It amplifies memories.

So, the Freyhellans are just seeing things from their own minds?

Yes, and feeling them.

What of the harling who fell ill?

I can perceive no reason for that. The energy here is not toxic to harish forms, or to mine.

That is strange. Can you tell me anything else?

No, there is nothing else to tell. It is not an Otherlanes portal. It is a tear in reality to an indistinct realm, perhaps a realm of nothing. It should be healed.

Can you do this?

For some moments, Peridot ended communication. Pellaz opened his eyes. The *sedu's* legs were splayed, his head lowered. His whole body shook.

'Pell…' Galdra said, 'is he…?'

'It's all right,' Pellaz replied, his hand firm against Peridot's trembling flank. 'He's just investigating.'

After some moments, the *sedu* relaxed and shook his mane, like any normal horse.

Well? Pellaz asked him.

Peridot did not answer immediately, and when he did, Pellaz was conscious of a strange kind of distance between him and the *sedu.*

The phenomenon may well heal of its own accord over time, Peridot said.

Then do you know what caused it?

Peridot was silent for some moments. *I will communicate with my brethren later and attempt to find out.*

Thank you.

Pellaz opened his eyes once more. 'You'll be pleased to know Peridot also assumes it's safe.'

'That's good…'

'But it concerns me he doesn't know why the harling who found this thing was so affected. Perhaps it was coincidence and his malady stems from another source.'

Galdra sucked his lower lip, ducked his head. 'That would be a great coincidence – too great.'

'Perhaps.' Pellaz ran his hand down Peridot's neck and the *sedu* nudged him affectionately. 'Well, it seems feasible to allow Loki to come to Freygard for the time being, but I think the Listeners and their guards should stay in attendance also. They can be Loki's household.'

'I'll be pleased to make arrangements for that. Looking at him, I'd say his feybraiha is near.'

'I expect so.' Pellaz paused. 'Cal and I must have some say in who you choose for him.'

'Naturally. I want the best for him, as you do.'

Pellaz smiled grimly. 'Good. Then we are in accord.'

He made to leave the grove, but Galdra caught hold of one of his arms. 'Pell...'

Pellaz stiffened. 'What?'

'It doesn't have to be this way between us... surely.'

Pellaz fixed him with a stare. 'It does, Galdra. You think ill of me. I believed you were bright enough to understand the way I have to be.'

'I don't know what you mean. I accept that you and Cal...' He broke off. 'I can't say it aloud. You know my heart. But if there's to be healing between our tribes, we should at least be friends.'

'We're not enemies,' Pellaz said. 'Don't for one moment think that what happened was any easier for me than for you.' Let the Freyhellan make of that what he willed. Pellaz pulled his arm from Galdra's hold and left the cover of the trees.

Chapter Six

When Darquiel was seven years old, rapidly approaching his own feybraiha, he had to watch his best friend change into a completely different creature. He and Amelza had always been close. She was his ally and his conspirator. They believed themselves to be superior to all other beings; partners in a world containing only two creatures. But then, seemingly overnight, Amelza became possessed. That was the only way Darq could describe it to himself. She developed a self-consciousness that was completely alien. She became secretive. He'd come across her in the woods, weeping alone. When he called to her, she'd run off. Some days, she'd be sharp with him, to the point of real aggressiveness, while on other days she'd want him to hold her, as if she were a kitten or a puppy, and then her eyes would fill with tears and she'd cry all over his shirt. She even looked different.

Finally, and it almost hurt him to consider it, Darq realised that Amelza was no longer a girl. She had lost something fragile and precious. Time had claimed her, put an iron collar on her. It was hideous. Becoming a woman seemed to mean she could no longer be his soul mate. His attempts to discuss it with her came to nothing. The friend he knew would have confided in him utterly, but this awkward stranger went mute or angry in his presence.

'You're different,' he said. 'What's wrong with you? Go back to how you were.'

'I want to!' she yelled at him. 'By all the gods, you have no idea how much I want to.'

'Then, just do…'

'You don't know anything, Darquiel.' She shook her head, looking as if she was about to cry, then sneered. 'You're just a child. You have no right to look the way you do.'

'What do you mean?' Darq asked, puzzled. 'What's wrong with how I look?'

Amelza uttered a strangled sound. 'Nothing! Absolutely nothing! That's the trouble.'

Then she'd stormed off, leaving Darq utterly bewildered. He knew he'd have to get some information about this distressing circumstance from somewhere, but shrank from questioning Phade or Zira. He knew what they'd say: it was none of his concern. Amelza was human. What was happening to her was inevitable.

As the years had passed, Darq had also come to spend more time in Olivia's company, not least because he usually felt like an outsider among hara. Among humans, he knew he was supposed to feel that way, which was strangely comforting. He also liked Olivia's personality; her dry words that were always right, and her ability to make sense of nonsense. As Amelza wrestled with the demons of puberty, sometimes hiding from him for days at a time, Darq would sit with Olivia in her kitchen or garden. Often, they didn't talk at all, but he knew Olivia liked him. He sensed she was full of words she thought inappropriate to say.

One day, he said to her, 'When Amelza is through with this… changing thing… will we be friends again?'

Olivia glanced as him askance.

'It's all very confusing to me,' Darq said. 'She won't speak to me in the way we used to speak. Why's that? I'm still the same.'

Olivia pursed her lips. She was kneading dough at the old kitchen table. Flour particles drifted in sunlight. 'Darq,' she said. 'It's hard for her.'

'I can see that,' Darq said. 'But it's as if I burn her. I don't care what hara or people think of me, but I do care about what she thinks. It's like she's part of me.'

'Yes,' said Olivia, in a dark sort of tone. She sighed, stopped working. 'It's not my place to say certain things, but I can say this: she's been cursed with the open eyes that will never shut.'

'What do you mean?'

'You'll understand, one day. It'll happen to you, I'm sure.' She glanced at him. 'Well, it should do.'

'What?'

'Amelza grew up with you. She looked on you as a female friend, I think. Now, she sees you differently, because she's a woman and you're not. Hara can confuse humans like that. Your kind can be desirable to us, and then we don't know what it is that we desire. It feels either too wrong or too right. But then again, it's beyond us.'

'Oh.' Darq frowned. 'You mean Ammie feels for me like Zira does for Phade?' It was no secret, in either the human or harish community, that Zira still entertained his pointless longing.

'You must never speak to her of it,' Olivia said. 'But I decided you should know. It's why you can't be close any longer. Humans and hara can never come together in that way, and it's sad that the heart doesn't care about that.'

Darq was silent for a moment. 'I must speak to Phade.'

'Why?'

'He told me about Kamagrian. That's something we could do for Amelza. She can be made quite like a har.'

'I've not heard of that,' Olivia said. 'We've always known that women can't be har, ridiculous though that seems.'

'They can,' Darq insisted.

Olivia looked dubious concerning that suggestion, so Darq decided it was time to leave. 'Thank you for telling me, Olivia. I'll not say anything about what you told me.'

The gods of Wraeththu, known as dehara, had not yet penetrated the farthest corners of the world. The Olopade knew of them, vaguely, but favoured their own gods, which were flavoured by ancient archetypes, fashioned from the old beliefs of humans. In the late springtime, a great festival was held, which coincided with the first of the summer horse fairs. The Olopade did not interact greatly with other tribes, but their own was far flung, sometimes as few as four hara occupying a hidden farmstead in the mountains. They emerged from their hideaways for the fairs, bringing with them the wind-spirited colts and fillies they had bred in the rarefied air. Other events took place at the fairs, such as magical caste ascensions for those who pursued a spiritual path and who required a Samway hienama for the task. The mountain hara, unlike their tribe-mates in the town, had also begun to breed. Perhaps it was because they had more time, were closer to the land, or simply free from the influence of Phade, who clearly regarded the whole process with distaste. However, as the years had passed, harlings began to appear at the horse fairs with their families. Most recently, it was considered particularly auspicious if feybraihas were celebrated at the first fair, when wild, young harlings at the brink of adulthood would be joined with members of Phade's elite guard, a circumstance that parents looked upon as a privilege and Phade's hara as a treat, there being no second-generation hara in Samway, apart from Darq. Also, during these gatherings, Phade would oversee and judge small matters that required his decision. It was altogether a busy time, and certainly not the best for Darq to approach his guardian over the issue of Amelza.

Over the years, despite his good intentions, Darq had had many run-ins with Phade over differences of opinion. Quite often, Phade made what seemed to Darq to be unnecessary rules and restrictions. He forbade Darq to travel to other settlements, or even to explore the mountains. He didn't like Darq going out at night, even if he stayed close to home. Although he'd spoken of Darq having harish friends, he discouraged his ward from establishing relationships with outsiders, even if those outsiders were only Olopardic hara from the mountains. Sometimes, the arguments Darq had had with Phade had lasted for days; both were stubborn creatures. On several occasions, Darq had considered running away, but he sensed it would be better to wait until he was adult before attempting this. He could wait. But some things couldn't wait.

Darq cornered Phade in the yard of his domain, where a few yearlings were being trotted round for his inspection. It was important to Phade that his stock was the best on show at the first fair, so his attention was hardly on what Darq was saying, as he reminded his guardian of their conversation concerning the Kamagrian.

'How do we call these hara?' Darq wanted to know.

'I'm not sure,' Phade replied vaguely. He gestured at one of the grooms. 'Bring that colt forward, Agante.'

'How can I find out?' Darq asked.

Phade went over to inspect the colt's legs. 'This one is fine. He must lead the procession.'

'Phade?' Darq said.

'Not now, Darq. It can wait.'

'Actually, I don't think it can. Given what I know, I'd say that now is the best time for Amelza to undergo this change, before she's fully a woman.'

Phade turned to Darq and appraised him with a critical stare. 'Is your own feybraiha approaching, do you think?'

Darq considered. 'I don't think so. But then, how would I know?'

'I'm sure you'd know,' Phade said. He shook his head. 'You look no different to me. I'll speak to one of the hara from the mountains at the fair, somehar who has a son of his own. He'll be able to advise us in this matter.'

'And the matter of Amelza?'

'I suppose I could communicate with… hara who are more experienced in this regard than I.'

'Like who?'

'The Gelaming, I suppose. It must wait, Darq. I'll send a message as soon as I can.'

This response was not the one that Darq had hoped for. He could tell that Phade wasn't really interested in Amelza, and no doubt regretted his rash words to Darq on the Kamagrian.

'Is there anything I can do?' Darq asked, refusing to give in. 'Could I contact the Gelaming?'

'No, you could not.'

'But I'm very good at communicating telepathically, you know that. If you haven't the time, you could teach me how to do it over long distance and...'

'Darq, no! I expressly forbid it. The Gelaming are unpredictable and dangerous. They require careful handling. I don't want them meddling in our affairs.'

'But...'

'There's nothing else to say. Make yourself useful. Help with the horse-breaking. It'll take your mind off Amelza.'

Darq liked to help with the animals. There was nothing more exhilarating than winning the confidence of a horse, so that it allowed you to ride it. The Olopade did not regard the breaking to saddle as breaking an animal's spirit. The trick was to convince the horse it wanted to be ridden and that there were advantages to having a harish companion. However, horses were powerful, strong-minded and often disposed to cause injury, so it was rare that Phade had allowed Darq to take part in the riskier early stages of breaking. Darq sensed that Phade had only relented now to shut him up. This was slightly annoying, if not insulting. 'Thank you,' Darq said, somewhat stiffly. 'I'll do that. But just one more question. Amelza will need to go through what Zira went through, only with one of these Kamagrian hara?'

'I suppose so,' Phade said.

'You can't do it? You're sure of that?'

'No woman has survived inception to Wraeththu, as far as I know.'

'I see.'

Darq went next to Zira, who was in fact waiting for Darq to appear in the schoolroom. 'You're late,' he said.

'I had to speak to Phade,' Darq replied. He sat down at his desk and folded his hands on top of it. 'Zira, tell me about your inception. How did it happen?'

'Phade gave me his blood,' Zira said, then hesitated. 'Why do you want to know?'

'I think I *should* know. It's an important part of our history and perhaps one day it will no longer happen, since Wraeththu can have harlings now.'

'That's true,' Zira said. He had a faraway look in his eye, and Darq could tell that Zira had been thinking about what it might be like to have a harling of his own. He was also thinking about Phade again, and had probably never stopped since his inception. The feelings inside

Zira were quite alien to Darq. He could not imagine ever having such a hunger or need for one particular har. It seemed like a waste of energy. He could appreciate the pleasures of aruna, but couldn't say he was impatient to discover them for himself. It would happen when it was meant to happen.

'So, tell me, Zira,' Darq said insistently. 'How did Phade give you his blood?'

'The hienama cut me.' Zira displayed the long faint scar on his inner right arm. 'Phade was cut too. The wounds were pressed together for a long time. It made me swoon. It wasn't pain, but I felt him go into me, his essence. His blood tasted mine and then changed it.'

'Just that?' Darq said, surprised.

Zira nodded. 'Usually, the hienama gives the blood, but Phade wanted to give me his. I thought…' He pursed his lips.

'You know why Phade has no chesnari, don't you?' Darq said.

Zira glanced at him askance. 'What do you mean?'

'The thoughts you have are the thoughts he fears; that's why. To be chesna with somehar, you have to be totally open with them, give yourself to them, I think.'

'How do *you* know? You're not even adult, Darq.'

Darq shrugged. 'I've talked about it with Amelza and I pick things up. For some reason, Phade is scared of being too close to one har. He's scared of having harlings. Perhaps he's still too human, and that's why he devotes himself to the human community. He feels guilty for being har maybe, or…'

Zira bristled. 'Darq, shut up! You've been told a thousand times.'

'Don't listen in, I know,' said Darq, rolling his eyes. 'But even a human could read *your* mind, Zira. I'm only trying to help. Phade likes what he is, the way things are. If he didn't, he wouldn't be living here. He's had many opportunities for advancement, which he's never taken.'

'You know too much. If Phade found out, he'd be livid.'

Darq shrugged. 'Sometimes, I'm invisible to him, especially when he's thinking. In my opinion, you should put aside your desire for him.'

'Thank you,' Zira said coldly. 'I think we should return to your lessons.'

'There is little left you can teach me.'

'Hmph,' said Zira.

Darq did a lot of thinking over the next few days. He wandered around the fields just outside town, where the fair would be held, mulling things over in his mind. Pavilions of flowers had been erected in the fields and effigies of the gods placed on pedestals between them. Hara began to arrive, at first in a trickle, then in a greater stream from the high meadows and valleys. Darq watched them riding into town in wagons and on horseback. He saw a few bare-footed, brown-skinned harlings among them; like him, but not. Darq missed Amelza. He had nothing in common with anyhar, and now his only companion had vanished. They were inextricably linked in some way, like twins.

It became clear to him what he should do, but he still had to think about it. He tried to divine the outcome of his idea, by casting sticks and stones and reading the formations they made. He watched for omens in the sky. All were inconclusive, riddled with hidden variables. Then, on the afternoon before the opening of the fair, a vixen ran across Darq's path as he walked in the forest. She stopped and stared at him, and he stared back. The fox reminded him of Amelza as she'd been before; wild and beautiful, a creature of nature. In that moment, he made up his mind.

He found her at the edge of the camp, in the field next to where the horses would next day be shown off by proud breeders. Evening was stealing in, bringing with it the special magic of summer. Amelza was wandering around the periphery of the fires, perhaps watching the hara who ate there, the younger ones tumbling around like cubs at play. Darq appraised her from a distance for some moments. She was taller, shapelier, in the way that a human female is shapely. She seemed a creature of enchantment, removed from all that was familiar.

'Amelza.' He called to her from the shadows of a grove of oaks.

She paused in her wanderings, but did not turn to him. Grief streamed off her, pooling at her feet in a misty cloud.

'Come to me,' he said.

Now, she raised her head and spoke across the distance between them. 'I can't, Darq. Not anymore.'

'Don't you trust me?' he asked her. 'Please, come here. I've got something to tell you. It's important.'

She walked across the grass towards him. 'What is there for me to trust you about?' She folded her arms, appearing defensive.

'I don't want to lose you, Ammie. You're my only true friend. You have to be made to be like me.'

She shook her head. 'That can't happen. You know it. What is it you're trying to say?'

Darq took a deep breath. 'I can give you the gift of my kind.'

'What?' Now she sounded harsh, impatient, somewhat more back to normal. 'You're mad!'

'No, I'm not. I can't make you har, but I can make you something similar, something more like me. Then we'll be the same again.'

Amelza shook her head. 'No, you can't do that. It would kill me.'

'I don't think it would,' Darq said. 'I'm different to other hara. I've thought long and hard about it. I've cast the stones and read the flight of birds. A fox came to me, and I saw in her a you that might come to be. Also, I just *feel* it will work. Trust me, Ammie, and come to me.'

Amelza narrowed her eyes. He could see himself through her gaze, how she perceived him. She saw him as beautiful, an unattainable creature, unbearable to be near. It confused her, because she didn't know whether she desired the male or the female in him. But then again, why should she care about that? If he'd been female, she could have loved him. But he was har and beyond her. He could tell she wanted desperately to believe he could change her, and wondered whether she was dreaming, or whether he was mad. She wondered about the scent of the evening, the essence of pine wafting down from the high passes, the perfume of the night-blooming flowers, and how it made the whole of life seem unreal, yet filled with unguessed potential. She was young, and would no doubt one day forget about him, if she'd only give herself the time, but she believed, in her blossoming, that she would die if she could not be with him. If there was the slightest possibility that this could happen, she should take it. If she should die, well… there would be no more pain.

All these impressions washed over Darq from the simple contact of her gaze. He was aghast at the depth of her feelings; it was worse than what Zira felt for Phade, which in Darq's opinion was a very bad way to be. He should do what he could to alleviate this pointless suffering. He had no desire to share her feeling, because it seemed utterly without value or purpose, but if it would make his friend happy to be able to touch him intimately, he would allow it. Perhaps it might be interesting.

'Come, Ammie,' he said.

They went into the deepwood, which at that time of year was growing so fast you could hear the rustle of it. They approached the moon pool, where once Darq had learned he was part of something. Here, they sat on the grass, holding hands.

'Before we do this,' Darq said, 'you should know the truth.' He stood up and took off his clothes. He showed her the thing she had always been so curious about; the ouana-lim and soume-lam, the refined genitalia of his kind. He explained he was not yet fully adult, of course, but at least Amelza could now have some idea of what hara were like.

Amelza's eyes were wide and dark, drinking him in. 'Yes,' she said. Simply that.

Darq put his clothes back on. He had with him a knife, which he'd stolen from the kitchen, after making sure its blade was as sharp as it could be. He'd used the whetstone on it. But even so, it isn't easy to make a cut in flesh, unless you mean to wound or kill.

'Are you ready?' he asked.

Amelza appeared dazed. 'Kiss me first,' she said. 'In case it doesn't work.'

'I don't really know how to.' He observed her expression. 'Well, all right.'

He put his lips to hers. She was hot, feverish. He couldn't give her the passion she wanted, even though he could tell she was afraid she was about to die. It just wasn't in him yet; maybe it never would be for a human. Amelza would die content if she could do so with his taste in her mouth. He believed she wouldn't die, but even so he kissed her until she broke away from him. Anything to make her happy again.

Amelza knelt beside the pool, with her hair hanging forward and her arms held out, wrists uppermost. She seemed barely in control of her senses. On the way to the glade, Darq had told her what he would do, but he wasn't sure she'd heard him properly. She trembled as he pressed the blade against her skin and he had to press really hard, and make several attempts, before he cut her. Then he thought he'd cut too deep, because the blood came out, black as ink in the moonlight. He was trembling too as he applied the knife to his own forearm. *Is this the right thing to do?* He was sure it was. Sure…

He slumped to his knees beside her and pressed their wounds together. It was the most intimate thing he had ever done, more so than the kiss. He could feel the pulse of their hearts, the linking of their essences. Amelza hung heavy and limp against him, her breathing laboured. Presently, she began to twitch.

The blood had congealed by the time Darq pulled away from her, and it crackled like shattering resin as he broke their bond. He laid Amelza down in the dew damp grass. Her eyes were closed and she looked deadly pale. He knelt beside her, staring down, his fists plunged between his thighs. His arm was throbbing. He sat with her all night. It seemed she was sleeping, and hopefully changing.

Just before dawn, Amelza uttered a cry and sat bolt upright. It was as shocking to Darq as if she'd been a corpse, springing back to life.

'Ammie?'

Amelza merely dropped open her jaw and emitted a continuous

low scream. She beat at her face, and the wound on her arm came open, so that blood flew from it. It smelled too strong, like carrion.

Darq tried to grab hold of her arms to restrain her, prevent her from harming herself, but she was stronger than him. She threw him away from her, as if he was only a kitten, and leapt to her feet. Then she was running away, between the trees, all the time uttering a terrible cry.

Darq ran after her. She was easy to follow, because she was making so much noise crashing through the shrubs and thickets. He called her name, all the while knowing it was useless to do so. She was transforming. He'd incepted her. Even now, he couldn't believe he'd done it. She wasn't dead, so it must have worked. As he ran, Darq became aware of other presences in the wood. At first, this did not bother him, but then he realised it was the spectral hunters. They had heard Amelza's screams and had smelled her blood. It had drawn them. He couldn't think about that now. He had to put them from his mind, for they were only spirits after all, and their only weapons were the inflictions of madness. They kept pace with him, and he could hear the panting of their hounds. Sometimes, they might bay in the night, but now they were silent.

He found Amelza among some ruins. Once a house had stood in this place, in landscaped gardens, but the forest had taken all of it years before. The upper stories of the house had long gone, and only a few walls, about four feet high, remained. Amelza had squeezed herself into a corner where the first rays of the sun had not yet penetrated. The hunters were nearby, and usually they vanished at daybreak. Darq sensed them beginning to break up, melting into mist, but still their curiosity chained them to this spot. Perhaps they would rematerialise here at dusk and wonder where they were and why they were there. They avoided the old habitations of men.

Amelza was now a dreadful sight. She had become a crone as she'd barged through the forest. Darq suspected the process hadn't gone quite as well as he'd thought it would. He went to her, cautiously, but she did not appear to see him. Her jaw hung slack, emitting black drool. Her skin was scabrous, and it was as if the flesh were melting from her bones.

'Ammie,' Darq breathed. She was dying. Darq pressed bunched fists against his eyes. He screamed: *Help me!* in his mind. He sent out a call to Phade, to anyhar, or anything else that could hear. Perhaps there was some sympathy in the cold breasts of the hunters, but the daylight was their enemy and they would soon be gone completely.

It was as if a thick fog filled the ethers. Darq's own inner cry was muffled, thrown back at him. He had never felt panic before, and was frightened of it, because he couldn't control it. He hadn't known fear before either. It was terrible, like being possessed. He knew he should focus, think rationally, but it was virtually impossible. *Think: what would Phade do?*

He would call to those who knew about this process. He would call to the Gelaming. They were reputed to be the most powerful of hara. Surely, they would hear a desperate plea?

Darq summoned every shred of strength he possessed and squashed it into an arrow of intention. This had to work, because if it didn't Amelza would die and he'd be her murderer.

I call upon you, Gelaming. Come to me! Come now! A life depends on it!

After some minutes' concentrated effort, Darq released his breath and lowered his hands from his eyes. A mist had crept in at ground level, covering the forest floor, seeping into the ruins. Amelza's breath wheezed in her chest. It seemed to be slowing down. She was mostly motionless, but occasionally a violent tremor would shake her body.

Had he been heard? He was sure he must have been. He had never invested such effort into a psychic call before. But nohar came, and Amelza's body made strange bubbling and popping sounds. The end was near.

Darq put his face in his hands and wept. He was overcome by such powerful feelings, it was almost divine. He realised, for the first time, how fragile life was. 'Forgive me,' he said aloud. 'Please forgive me.'

He heard the sound of horses' hooves behind him, not galloping, but walking slowly. He thought it was Phade and jumped to his feet, wheeling round. But it was not Phade. For a while, he saw nothing, and it seemed the approaching animal was invisible, but then through the mist a huge white horse appeared. It was a beautiful creature, lifting its knees high. Its mane flowed down on both sides of its neck, hanging to its chest. It bore a tall, cloaked har.

The horse came to a halt before Darq, and its rider stared down at him. All he saw was a penetrating, silvery grey gaze, a long straight nose, a well-shaped mouth and chin. Long drifts of dark red hair fell over his breast. He looked magnificent, even though his hood shadowed his face. Darq didn't care who it was. 'Help me,' he said, gesturing at Amelza. 'She's dying. Help her. I gave her blood...'

The har dismounted from his horse and without speaking approached Amelza, brushing past Darq as he did so. Darq could pick up nothing psychically from this har; he was like a blank stone. The har squatted down to examine the girl and spent some moments doing so. Then, he rose to his feet and turned to Darq. He threw back the hood of his cloak and Darq physically winced. He had never seen such a powerful and beautiful har: he must be Gelaming.

'You are a fool, Darquiel,' said the har.

'I know,' Darq said. 'I thought I could change her…'

'No! What I meant was that you are a fool for shouting like an imbecile into the ethers.'

Darq got the impression this har was not that concerned about Amelza. 'Can you help her?'

The har sniffed. 'It might be possible. The question is: why should I?'

'Because…' Darq faltered. 'Because you came when I called?'

'I am not here to deal with botched inceptions. You should know that harish blood is poison to femalekind.'

'Phade, my guardian, he said the Kamagrian…'

'And is this female in any condition to travel the Otherlanes to reach them? I think not.'

'Then bring them here.'

The har laughed. 'You are quite amusing. Why should I do that? Give me a good reason.'

'She shouldn't die because of me. Her family serves my tribe. It isn't right. I did wrong. I'll do whatever you ask if you'll help.'

'That is a rash promise,' said the har, 'but very well. I'll risk taking her. It might be too late, so pray to the dehara it isn't.'

'Who are you?' Darq asked.

'Somehar who should not be here. Somehar who came because you are very stupid and have possibly put yourself in grave danger. I am Thiede.'

'Are you Gelaming?'

'Go home, Darquiel.'

Thiede picked up Amelza in one arm and somehow managed to mount his horse again, which Darq now noticed wore no bridle or saddle. Thiede slung the girl before him, over the animal's withers. 'I will return. Phade is looking for you.'

Thiede turned the horse with some unspoken command and the animal trotted off towards the trees. Then the air fractured and it vanished.

Darq remained staring at the spot for some minutes. He was dazed. If it wasn't for the fact that Amelza no longer squatted behind him, he'd have believed he'd just dreamed the past five minutes. This har called Thiede had known him by name. He knew of Phade also. His horse had just vanished from this reality, and had no doubt appeared in a similarly bizarre manner. A shiver ran over Darq's skin. *Is this the har who brought me here, as a pearl?* What powers he possessed!

I am Gelaming, Darq thought. *I must be.*

As he retraced his steps to Samway, which was difficult because this was a part of the forest Darq did not know well, conflicting feelings brawled inside him. He was full of remorse for what he'd done to Amelza, extremely excited and intrigued by Thiede, and angry with Phade. It was an old resentment: the certainty that Phade knew much more about Darq's origins than he'd revealed. Darq was resigned to the fact that Phade would be furious with him too, if only for being out all night. He contemplated whether to reveal what had happened or not. Thiede had said he would return. If Thiede was one of his parents, or had known them, he would no doubt be angry with Phade for not keeping Darq under control. Whatever happened, Darq was sure life was just about to get very interesting indeed.

Two of Phade's guards came upon Darq before he'd even left the forest. Darq knew them well: Keroen and Farn. At first, they thought he'd been attacked because his shirt was covered in dried blood, but he told them he'd cut himself.

Keroen hauled Darq up before him on his horse. 'You're in trouble,' he said.

'No doubt,' Darq replied.

'We've been searching half the night. Where did you hide yourself?'

Darq shrugged, and Farn laughed. 'I wouldn't be in your place when we get back.' Neither of the guards mentioned anything about Amelza.

By the time they reached Phade's Tower, Darq felt quite ill. This was also an unusual circumstance. He wondered whether all those perplexing feelings he'd experienced had somehow affected him physically. The wound on his arm burned. He was light-headed, and his entire body felt like it was crawling with ants, within and without.

Phade came into the yard, even before Darq had got down off the horse. He was unusually white of face, which meant he was bubbling with fury of the most severe kind. His lips had virtually disappeared into a thin line of disgusted disapproval.

Darq almost collapsed as he dismounted. Pulling himself straight, he braced himself to confront his guardian. Phade's blow to his face took him totally by surprise. He didn't feel it, but one moment Darq was standing, the next on his back, with lights shooting out of his eyes.

'You little fuck!' Phade yelled. He lunged forward.

For the second time that day Darq experienced fear. He had never seen a har so incandescent with rage.

Farn pulled Phade back and said, in a low worried voice,

'Tiahaar…'

Phade shook the guard off. 'Get up!' he said to Darq. 'Come to my office.'

Darq sat in the dust and wept. He wasn't himself anymore. He had become like Amelza or Zira, full of these ridiculous swirling emotions. Keroen squatted beside him and put an arm round Darq's shoulders. Darq slumped against the har in relief. He wanted to be held. He didn't want to face Phade.

'He didn't mean what he did,' said Keroen. 'He's worried, that's all. You scared him, disappearing like that.'

Darq was too exhausted to argue. He didn't think that concern should be displayed by punching somehar in the face.

Keroen helped him to his feet, and Darq had to hold onto the har's arm all the way to Phade's office. He couldn't see properly. He wanted to be sick. 'Stay with me,' he said to Keroen. 'Don't leave me.'

Keroen uttered a soft sound. 'He'll dismiss me. You know he will.'

'I'm afraid. I think he wanted to kill me.'

'No, not that. Apologise. Keep weeping. He's not that hard a har.'

Once Darq reached Phade's office, the reason for Phade's excessive anger was revealed. Thiede was already there. Darq could tell that Phade was frightened of this har, and now that his initial burst of fury was over, he was very concerned about Darq's condition, not least, no doubt, because he would be blamed for it.

'I'm sorry,' Darq said. 'I'm sorry, Phade. I didn't…'

'I know,' Phade said. 'I've been told.'

'It is only the folly of youth,' Thiede said. 'He meant no wrong.'

'He never does,' Phade snapped. 'Keroen, get out!'

Darq heard the door close behind him; his ally had gone.

Phade turned to Thiede. 'He can't stay here any longer. He's your responsibility.'

Thiede gestured languidly with both hands. 'It would be unwise to leave him here, yes. In the ethers, he was shrieking "Here I am!" to all and sundry with half an ear to hear.'

Phade paced up and down the room, clearly in a state of extreme agitation. 'Then take him and go. I did what I could. Don't say that I didn't.'

'I can't take him, Phade,' Thiede said calmly. 'I'll arrange for somehar else to do it. You must be patient.'

Phade threw up his arms. 'And what might come pouring out of the Otherlanes in the meantime?'

'We have time. I have made sure of it; for my own protection, if not for Darquiel's.'

Darq listened numbly to this exchange. These hara were discussing his future, yet he could not care. He sat down on a chair, because otherwise he'd have fallen down. Phade didn't even look at him.

Thiede stood up. 'Have your hara care for Darq. He cannot yet travel, in any case.'

Now Phade glanced at Darq; it was clear that what he saw pained him. 'He brought it on himself. What did he do? Butcher the girl? What am I to tell her people?'

'Tell them she is undertaking training with the Kamagrian,' Thiede said.

'Will she live?'

Thiede shrugged. 'Time will tell.'

Phade shook his head. 'Darq, you are beyond me. If you didn't butcher *her*, you nearly butchered yourself. You look half-dead!'

'That isn't butchering,' Thiede said smoothly. 'It seems events have precipitated a natural phenomenon.'

'What do you mean?' Phade asked sharply.

'He has begun his feybraiha, that's all.'

Chapter Seven

Phade took Darquiel to his room. He did not call for Zira, for which Darq was relieved. He didn't feel capable of looking Zira in the eye, and he wondered whether Olivia and her family would believe the story about Amelza and the Kamagrian. They would certainly not be pleased.

'Why did you do that?' Phade asked. 'What possessed you?'

'I was just sure it would work,' Darq answered. 'You wouldn't listen to me.'

Phade shook his head in exasperation. 'You're too impatient. We only discussed the matter a short time ago.'

Darq pressed his fingers against his forehead, rubbed it. 'You wouldn't have done anything. You didn't care.'

Phade sighed. 'You've brought Thiede here. That's the last thing I wanted.'

Darq sat down on his bed. 'Who is he? Is he Gelaming?'

'In a way, yes,' Phade replied. He seemed back to his usual self. There was a light of contrition in his eyes, which Darq sensed meant that Phade was uncomfortable with the fact he'd struck a harling.

'He brought me here, didn't he?'

Phade nodded. 'He appointed me as your guardian, yes.'

'He's very powerful.'

'And dangerous.'

Darq grimaced. 'Must I go with some stranger he sends here? This feybraiha thing - must I take aruna with somehar? What's going to happen to me?' He began to weep again, unable to prevent it. Somehar else was living unlawfully in his body; he hoped this emotional interloper wouldn't squat there permanently.

Phade sat down beside him, and put an arm round Darq's shoulders. 'I really can't answer the first question yet, but all I can say is that Thiede brought you here for a reason: to keep you safe. When you called for the Gelaming, Thiede heard you, which means others could have heard you too. You are special, Darq. Your abilities, I think, are stronger than most hara's.'

Darq wiped his face with his hands. His mouth felt full of salt. 'I want to be normal again… I want to know who and what I am. I feel I can't be until you and that Thiede tell me the truth.'

Phade sighed through his nose. 'I can't tell you. That issue is between you and Thiede. But as for your second question, is there any har you'd like to be with you for your feybraiha? I can deal with that at least.'

'I don't care,' Darq said. 'I have no interest in it. Pick anyhar.' He pulled away from Phade and shook his head vigorously. 'I nearly killed Amelza. I'm glad you struck me. I deserved it. I should take aruna with a *troll* as punishment.'

Phade laughed, then checked himself. 'Darq, you are right. This isn't you.' He paused. 'You seem to get on well with Keroen. How about him?'

'If you want. I just want to get it over with.'

Phade squeezed one of Darq's shoulders. 'At this point, I should say that once you're in the moment, you won't feel like that, but somehow I don't think I *can* say that to you. I'll talk to Keroen. We'll see.' He stood up. 'I shouldn't have struck you. I'm sorry about that. I was just…'

Darq interrupted him. 'I know. I don't blame you.'

Phade smiled tentatively. 'Things will work out Darq, I'm sure they will. Get some rest. I'll be back later.'

After Phade left, Darq lay down on the bed and stared at the ceiling. He kept seeing Amelza's face, how she'd changed to become something hideous. He'd been so sure it would work. His whole world seemed shaken apart, because he could no longer trust his instincts.

Eventually, he drifted off to sleep and slept for most of the day. When he awoke, it was dusk and he saw that somehar had left a tray of cold food on the table by the door. The last thing he felt like doing was eating. He felt wretched. Physical discomfort conspired with anger and self-loathing within him. He knew he couldn't run away, because Phade's hara would find him. Nothing in the future seemed remotely attractive. Olivia and Zira would hate him now. Keroen would probably feel sick having to touch a har every living creature in Samway thought was a freak. Normally, Darq wouldn't care about such things. He hated what he was becoming. It was all too vile.

Darq groaned and turned onto his side. He put a pillow over his head. And in his mind was a small, silky voice that said, *Hello…*

Darq sat up at once and held his breath. He didn't recognise the voice. It was outside his experience, somehar he didn't know. He shouldn't reply. He should put up barriers right away… and yet… *Who are you?* he asked.

Who are you?

Darq lied at once. *Phade har Olopade.*

Laughter in the mind is a strange thing to experience. It was like prickles of electricity in Darq's head. *Look out of your window...*

Darq couldn't help himself. He had to see. He went to the window, drew aside the curtain, and looked. Around the outer walls of Phade's domain he saw several riders on motionless horses. They were not hara; they were spectres of the forest, clothed in dark apparel, the details of them indistinct. They seemed to be waiting for something.

If you go to them, they will bring you to me...

Darq could not respond, because at that moment the door to his room swung open and banged against the wall. A figure pushed past him and drew the curtains roughly over the window. Darq winced. He saw it was Thiede.

OUT! Thiede's psychic command was not to be disobeyed. Whatever had tried to communicate with Darq vanished at once from his head. Thiede's mental shout echoed round Darq's skull for some moments afterwards.

'Darquiel,' Thiede said. 'This is what I feared would happen.'

'Who was it?' Darq asked.

'Whoever it was, they weren't known to you, so you should *not* communicate with them. It could be anyhar.'

'You knew who it was. You knew what they said.' Darq jerked his head in the direction of the window. 'You closed the curtains. There were ghost riders out there.'

'An illusion,' Thiede said, 'plucked from your mind. Whatever you think you saw, it was something else. You must now guard your thoughts at all times. I will show you how.'

'I want to know about myself. Tell me.'

'Now is not the time,' Thiede said. 'You remain in ignorance for your own protection, believe me. If you knew, it could be picked up. You were heard in the ethers, Darquiel, and recognised as unique. Some no doubt think you could be useful to them. There are many factions of Wraeththu, and within them small cabals of powerful individuals who are not to be trusted. You called to the Gelaming, but I don't believe the Gelaming heard you. Others did. They must not know your heritage.'

'I'm Gelaming, aren't I?'

Thiede appeared to consider whether a truthful answer would be acceptable. Eventually he said, 'Yes. I can see little point in dissembling over that; you have already made up your mind about it.'

'Are my parents still alive?'

'You must not think about them, because if you do, you'll want to find them. That could be exploited. I will not answer your question.'

'You *have* answered it,' Darq said. 'What will you do with me? Where will you send me?'

'You must keep on the move for a while,' Thiede said. 'That would be best.'

Darq felt that all his life he had somehow been trying to escape Samway. Now that the reality was upon him, he was uncertain. Samway was home, Phade his virtual parent. 'I'll guard my thoughts,' he said. 'I'll feel safer here.'

'You can't stay here,' Thiede said. 'I'm sorry. You will soon be har, not a child. You must be trained to protect yourself. I can see to this.'

'And when will I find out about my history? After the training?'

Thiede considered again. 'I'll be honest with you; there might never be a time. Much as this irks you, you must accept it. Your pearl would have been destroyed, if it wasn't for me. There is still a potential threat. If not death, then abduction. I'll not risk either. You must disappear into the world, Darq. Become yourself, as you are, with your memories of Samway. Look upon Phade as your father or hostling. Trust nohar.'

'Perhaps then I should remain with you.'

Thiede laughed. 'Neither of us are safe, Darquiel. I can't risk taking you to my domain, and I must return there soon. I have been out of this world for a while.'

'Really? Where have you been?'

Thiede drew Darq back towards the bed and gently pushed him down to sit upon it. 'There are many layers to what you see as reality, Darq, but then I suspect you already know that.'

'I've felt it… sometimes.'

Thiede nodded. 'Naturally. I am able to travel between these layers, as can many others. Because of certain conflicts in this realm, I have had to hide far beyond where I can be traced.'

Darq frowned. 'How?'

'You saw the animal I rode today? It is not a horse. It's a *sedu*, a creature that can travel the Otherlanes, the spaces between the realms.'

'Would I be safe in another realm?'

Thiede pulled a sour face. 'Unfortunately, those who might have an interest in you are as mobile as I am in the Otherlanes. Earthly reality is best for you, because you can blend in and hide yourself. This realm tends to hide "otherness". Mundane reality holds sway here. It is not so in other places. In my domain, for example, your essence would shine like a beacon to anyhar trained to see it.'

'Who is interested in me? And why?' Darq felt overwhelmed by all this new information, but relieved too.

'It's a long story, and I hope one day you will hear it.' Thiede drew in his breath and folded his hands together. 'For now, we must concentrate on more physical matters: your feybraiha. This is a rite of passage, Darq, and although you are impatient with it, you should pay it the attention it deserves.'

Darq's shoulders slumped. 'Given what's happened recently, I find that difficult. It's just an inconvenience. I don't think I have the urges other hara have.'

'That is a possibility,' Thiede said. 'We shall have to see.' He put his hands together and tapped his lips with steepled fingers, clearly deep in thought. Then he said aloud, 'Hmm, there is no reason why not.'

It was nearly dark now, and Thiede's looming presence was a strangely glowing flame in the room. Darquiel felt unnerved. It was the same feeling he had when the spectral hunters were near.

'Very soon, a har will arrive in Samway who will take over your education,' Thiede said. 'I had thought he should be with you for your feybraiha, but now another idea occurs to me.'

'Phade is going to ask Keroen,' Darq said.

Thiede wrinkled his nose a little. 'Whoever that is, he is unworthy of you. Phade is too parochial at times. No, it's clear to me that I should be the one to guide you at this time.'

'Yes!' Darq said at once. He could see that Thiede was devoid of all the hot turbulent emotions that other hara seemed governed by. With him, aruna would be academic, like taking exercise for the body. To Darq, this was preferable to any situation where he might be expected to react with pleasure or gratitude.

Thiede, however, appeared surprised by this immediate acceptance. He raised his eyebrows and did not smile. Darq presumed his response had not been that flattering. But he could not lie about himself. He could not pretend to yearn and desire, because it wasn't in him.

'Not yet,' Thiede said. 'We must give your body more time.'

'It won't make any difference,' Darq said.

'Perhaps not, but even so.' Thiede stooped down and took Darquiel's face between his hands. 'I will share breath with you. Even if it doesn't kindle desire, I think you will find it interesting. Also, I must construct some temporary wards to stop spies snooping around in your head.' With no further preamble, he put his mouth to Darq's.

This was very different to the kiss Darq had shared with Amelza. For a start, it involved the mingling of breath, and with that came strong psychic impressions. Humans couldn't achieve this. Darq's first impression was of hot stone, wet after recent rain, and the smell that came from it; crumbled brick mixed with damp moss. It was a feeling of something incredibly ancient, yet forever new. He was on the battlements of a high castle, his hands on the stone, gazing out over a landscape that went on forever. Then he was walking through a room where everything was blue. It was lined by columns of turquoise. At the far end, the room was open to the elements. Darq walked out onto a balcony. Again, he was high up, and below, at the bottom of cliffs covered in dark-leaved trees, was the ocean. It too was incredibly blue. He could smell brine, but also a tart lemony scent. These were some of Thiede's memories, perhaps, or his dreams. Darq saw a herd of white horses galloping across the sea. Then they had fishes' tails and were diving beneath the surface. A tall figure walked past him, visible on the edge of his vision. He turned to see and saw a har with wings whose hands dripped red. Reality shifted, and Darq was running down the room, and there was a hole in the ceiling with steps leading up to it. At the top, was a sandy courtyard where severed limbs lay scattered about. The winged har was with him. He said, 'This is a killing ground.'

Darq gasped. He blinked and the reality of his room in Phade's tower swung back into focus. Thiede had drawn away from him. 'There are no sunny vistas in my breath,' he said, and laughed.

'Did you see anything in me?' Darq asked him.

Thiede nodded. 'Yes. You are very alone.'

'I like it that way.'

Thiede went towards the door. 'Until tomorrow, Darquiel. Sleep well.'

Darq slept most of the following day, waking only to discomfort and strange feelings of uncertainty, as if something hideous were about to happen. He felt too lethargic to get up and dress himself, and the thought of food was sickening. What had occurred the previous evening had faded like a dream. Had there really been a voice in his head? He wondered whether, in fact, feybraiha had made him hallucinate. It seemed so long ago that he had walked with Amelza in the night-time forest and had drunk from the moon in her pool. The feelings he'd had back then must be connected with the few things he'd learned since Thiede's arrival, but it was beyond him to care. It was as if his entire life had run into a stone wall. He was still reeling from the impact.

Phade came to Darq's bedroom in the afternoon, accompanied by a har named Ganaril, who lived in a mountain settlement. Ganaril was dressed in clothes the colour of pine needles, and his hair had a weirdly mossy sheen. Clearly, Darq thought, the har spent too much time among the trees. Ganaril had hosted a son, who had gone through feybraiha the previous year. Darq submitted to a cursory examination from this har. He wanted somehar to tell him this feybraiha inconvenience would all go away.

Ganaril merely frowned and spoke to Phade, who was standing with folded arms on the other side of the room. 'You say he started this yesterday?' Ganaril asked.

Phade nodded.

'It's very strange – I'd say accelerated. It took our son Faril a few weeks to reach this stage.'

'What stage?' Darq asked quickly.

'Heat and swelling in the soume-lam suggest you're ready for aruna,' Ganaril said shortly. 'But that is unusual. I'm not sure.'

'But otherwise, he is normal?' Phade asked.

Ganaril nodded. 'All looks in order to me, but I'm no real expert.'

'And after this aruna I'll be back to how I was?' Darq asked.

'You'll feel better,' Ganaril replied. 'I can send Faril to talk to you, if you like.'

'No.' Darq pulled the bedclothes over himself. 'I know what I need to know.'

Ganaril gave him a narrow-eyed glance. 'Well, if you change your mind…'

'Thank you,' Darq said, and heard in his own voice the tone of dismissal.

Ganaril inclined his head politely, and Phade ushered him out of the room.

Sooner rather than later: that suited Darq fine. He wanted to be free of the carping, whining interloper in his head.

Phade made a swift reappearance. 'I know that Thiede has spoken to you,' he began.

'Yes,' Darq said. 'I'm happy with the arrangement.'

'OK, well in that case, he'll no doubt come to see you later.'

'No,' Darq said. 'I'll find him. Tell him that. Outside. Not in here. I want this to happen in the landscape; it's what's meant for me.'

Phade adopted a darker tone. 'You know you shouldn't wander around on your own, especially now.'

The last thing Darq wanted to deal with was Phade's over-protectiveness. He tried to keep his voice level. 'Nothing bad can happen to me at the moment. I'm sure of it. Tell Thiede I'll find him tonight.'

Phade shook his head. 'You are quite possibly mad, but if Thiede is content with your suggestion, it's between you and him. If I ever wanted any real proof you were no ordinary har, now I have it: I can't imagine anyhar wanting to take aruna with Thiede. I imagine it would be like jumping into molten metal.'

'And when I come out of the metal, it'll go hard, and I'll have really safe armour,' Darq said.

Phade smiled. 'Let's hope that's the case!'

Thiede did not come to Darq's room as Phade predicted. Instead, one of the househara came to deliver a message, to say that Thiede was agreeable to Darq's plan. That was all; no other details. Darq, in a kind of delirium, had no idea what had inspired him to make that request, or how he'd go about finding Thiede later. At one time, it would always have been Zira who delivered messages of that type. Not anymore. He wondered what Phade had told Amelza's family. Did Zira know that Darq had hurt her? Or was Phade keeping him away so that Darq didn't have to answer any awkward questions? And what of Olivia? Wistfully, Darq wished he could see her now. She would, he was sure, understand more about the horrors of feybraiha than Phade. If only Amelza were here too, to lighten things with abrasive comments and laughter. Darq wondered where she was and how she was doing. He'd done wrong to her, and had tipped his world upside-down with his arrogant pride.

At sundown, Darq drank three glasses of water one after the other, from a jug that had been left for him. He sat on the edge of his bed, fully clothed, but with bare feet. The automatic movement of raising his arm and swallowing the liquid was calming. He felt he could do it for eternity. When the jug was empty, he stood up and stretched. There were no voices in his head, just a high-pitched humming. His face felt very hot.

The tower seemed empty as he walked along its dusk-dark corridors, heading for the outside. Perhaps hara withdrew at the sound of his feet and hid themselves behind closed doors. Even the dogs were silent in the yard. Darq walked beneath the shadow of the great gate and onto the road that led down to the town and beyond. He could see orange and yellow lights in the fields where the horse breeders were camped, and now the thin strains of music reached him: the sound of a fiddle, the cardiac beat of a hand-drum. Every sense was especially alert. He realised he felt greedy for something Thiede could give him that was beyond mere knowledge. After tonight, his life would make sense. He would *know*.

His feet led him to the path that led to the moon pool; it seemed the most appropriate place. If Thiede was not there, Darq planned to lie down on the cold grass and wait for what might happen next. If the hunters came for him, so be it. He was utterly without fear.

He walked into the glade and it was full of the cold crystal light of the stars. It fell down upon a ghostly form sitting cross-legged next to the pool: a luminous figure with a veil of hair that shone red even in the colourless starlight. Thiede looked young, like a har not much above Darq's own age. Darq was not surprised. He supposed Thiede to possess several other unusual abilities.

'Come to me,' Thiede said, and his voice too was different; more wistful, less commanding.

Darq went to stand over him and didn't say anything. Thiede was naked but for his hair. His skin had a matte satiny sheen, and glowed slightly, as if starlight was attracted to him and could not escape.

'I was not incepted and have never experienced feybraiha,' Thiede said. 'I had no rituals, no formal recognition. I just *was*. Because of what I am, I am alone. There are few who can tolerate intimacy with me.'

'What are you?' Darq asked. He suspected the question was desired.

'I was the first of all Wraeththu,' Thiede said simply. 'There were others, but they... *failed*.'

Darq squatted down. 'The first... but he is a god, he is the Aghama.'

'Aghama is an idea. It is me and yet it is not. It's a part of me that exists in the minds of hara as a god, as a dehar. It's separate from me in most respects. Wraeththu created Aghama as I created them.'

'Are you my father or my hostling?' Darq asked.

'No, but we are in some way related,' Thiede replied. He took a deep breath. 'Darquiel, I've been thinking since our last meeting. There's something I wish for you to know.'

Darq nodded and settled himself more comfortably on the grass. This was more than he'd dared hope for.

'For many years, Wraeththu pondered how and perhaps why they had come to be. At first, I believed my existence was accidental; a freak birth that somehow kick-started a new evolutionary step for humanity. Other hara felt otherwise, including some who are very wise. I ignored their thoughts as wishful thinking. But so many things have happened since, I've come to the conclusion I was wrong. We *were* created by something, or someone.'

Darq nodded in encouragement for Thiede to continue.

'Humans lived for the main part in the prison of their senses; they believed that what they perceived was all that is. Those who felt differently were often regarded as heretics or lunatics, mad fringe-folk who had more imagination than sense. A few sensed the truth, I think.

'I have a friend, who is named Malakess har Sulh. He is High

Codexia of the Library of Kyme, on the island of Alba Sulh, to the west of this continent. He and his colleagues collect as much information as they can from the ruins of human civilisation, concerning the more controversial theories that certain human scholars devised. The Sulh are looking for seeds of truth. I, on the other hand, experience them.'

'Who created us and why?' Darq asked, fearing Thiede's pause signalled the end of the revelations.

Thiede shrugged. 'I have yet to find out. Whoever did it has hidden themselves completely. And as to why they did it, who can say? But that's not what I want to talk to you about.'

Darq frowned. 'Then what?'

'Worlds are power sources,' Thiede said. 'Some beings can tap into and drink the life essence of a living, breathing world. No doubt there are beings beyond *their* perception that drink of them too. But as Wraeththu, all we need to concern ourselves with is those who stand above us in the hierarchy of creation. In return for sustenance, our world is fed with a different kind of energy that is creative and inspirational. It's responsible for all the greatest breakthroughs in understanding and awareness. Under normal circumstances, the inhabitants of a world would remain unaware of this transaction. But something is happening that has changed that situation.'

Thiede reached out and put a long-fingered hand on one of Darq's thighs. 'When you were created, it was at the start of what amounted to a fairly small skirmish in a war for power. Those who have stood over us for millennia are being challenged for dominance, mainly because of us – Wraeththu. We are greater than humanity. We have the potential to perceive far more of reality than creatures of our level of existence would generally possess.'

Darq was aware of the painful beat of his heart. He hardly dared breathe, in case the slightest sound reminded Thiede he should keep silent.

Thiede smiled, probably having interpreted Darq's feelings. 'I said I wouldn't speak of your parents, and I still won't, in any great detail, but I've decided you should know that you were conceived deliberately. Your parents acted in haste and ignorance, obeying a drive without any comprehension of its source or reason. You were created as a magical creature, the sum of the essence of three hara, not two. Your body is a vessel that attracted a potent soul. You can't remember any of this, because the rules of incarnation decree that all previous states of being are not recalled. But you can look upon yourself as an embodiment, or avatar, of the world itself; a concentration of its energies. Most of this potential is yet locked inside you, and should remain there. You are a beacon to those we should look upon as our allies - fearsome though they may be - and also those who are opposed to them. You should understand there is no compassion in our allies; we are a precious resource to them, that's all, but they will defend us as long as it's viable to do so. '

Darq stared at Thiede, wide-eyed. 'And this is why you sent me here?'

Thiede nodded. 'Yes. I've kept you here with Phade to protect you, to keep you from this bigger picture until you are mature and able to hold your own ground. I'm still unsure as to whether you should ever step forward to take part in any confrontation; you could be used against us by either side. But I have listened to my heart and it has spoken. This is why I'm telling you these things.'

'Thank you,' Darq said. 'I will think about them.'

Thiede smiled gently. 'You're such a grave soul Darq; you should enjoy a little light.'

Darq grimaced, then shook his head. He did not want to discuss his state of being; it hardly interested him. 'I want to tell you something too,' he said. 'Something that happened to me when I was very young.'

'Of course.'

Darquiel told Thiede the story of his visit to this very spot where they were sitting. 'I was told there were four of me,' he said. 'In your opinion, would that refer to the fact I had three parents? Me being the fourth component?'

Thiede narrowed his eyes in thought for a moment. 'Perhaps, although...' He paused and stared at Darq thoughtfully. 'No... we must not focus on your family. Remember that powers beyond your perception are interested in you. You should mistrust any information that comes to you via psychic means. The way these powers manifest in this reality can be tricky; they speak in riddles and conundrums. It has always been so. You need to stand far back from them to see any sense. In my opinion, since you asked, I think that you were instilled with the idea at that time that you were part of something greater - which was no lie. It was designed to whet your interest, to keep you alert and hungry for similar messages.'

'But I received no more after that time.'

Thiede shrugged. 'It could be that others were waiting, as I was, for you to reach maturity. Once you have access to aruna, your abilities become sharper and more potent. I think that whatever tried to contact you last night had the intention of sitting where I am sitting now, although the information you'd have received would have been somewhat different, I'm sure!'

'That makes sense,' Darq said. 'I appreciate you speaking to me in this way. My whole life has been a fog of riddles, and Phade would never be honest with me. I know why now, of course, but it was still annoying.'

'Phade knows little about you,' Thiede said. 'It was safer that way.'

Darq nodded. He paused, then said, 'How did you know where I'd come tonight? Was it my thoughts or the place itself that drew you?'

'I just followed my nose,' Thiede said. He reached out and took hold of a strand of Darq's hair. 'Darq, we are here for a reason.'

'I know,' Darq said. 'I'm ready for whatever must happen.'

'I hope so.' Thiede smoothed his own hair, as if to bring Darq's attention to his physical attractions. 'I said to you that few can tolerate my essence, and that's because it's stronger, or perhaps just different, from that of most hara. I know it won't damage you in any way, and for this reason tonight is special for me. For this one night, I am like any other har, alive in the spring, with the scent of the season all around, and a beautiful young har before me, who has come to the sacred altar of our kind. I ask you now to step out of your mind for a short while, to simply "be" in this moment with me. Put aside judgment and observation. Celebrate life for its own sake. Neither of us knows what the future will bring.'

'Tell me what I must do,' Darq said.

'Let your body off its leash,' Thiede said. 'You keep it tightly controlled. Let it be free.'

'I don't want to be a slave to my body as others are,' Darq said.

'Thought, vehicle and essence are all one thing, Darq. You're unbalanced if you neglect one in favour of the other aspects.'

'Oh, all right,' Darq conceded. 'I'll try. Shall I undress?'

Thiede laughed. 'No, not yet. We'll share breath again, but I want you to concentrate on the physical aspects. Just let go.' He grinned widely. 'You might even like it.'

'That's possible, I suppose,' Darq said, unable to imagine it could be so.

Thiede drew Darq towards him. 'Put your arms around me. Touch my skin. Inhale its scent.'

Darq did as he was told. He smelled Thiede's hair and neck. It was a warm living scent, vanilla and musk. He ran his hands over Thiede's back and couldn't help thinking about how the skin was just an organ holding all the other ones inside the body. He knew he shouldn't be thinking that. The skin was sensitive, designed to respond to the slightest stimulus. It liked to be stroked. Thiede ran one of his hands over Darq's shoulder blades, beneath his shirt. It wasn't unpleasant,

Darq supposed. Then they were sharing breath, at first in shallow lapping waves, then deeper, with great breakers of sensation and images crashing over them.

Darq noticed his body was eager to respond in various ways and eventually he relented and allowed it to happen. There was some confusion, as if his flesh was separate from the rest of him, and almost hysterical at the notion it might do what it liked. It had a desire both to plunder and be plundered, which felt very strange. But it was also like an unbearable itch Darq could not reach to scratch. He pulled away from Thiede's lips. 'Now,' he said. 'It doesn't feel good. We have to...'

'Hush,' Thiede said, and put a finger against Darq's mouth. Slowly, he pulled off Darq's shirt and then covered his chest with soft kisses.

'Stop it,' Darq said, hardly able to speak. 'It hurts.'

'That's not pain,' Thiede said. 'Remember, let go.' He pushed Darq back onto the grass. There were some frantic moments of fumbling as Darq refused to let Thiede take things slowly. He didn't care what role was required of him, as long as it was *something*. It was amazing how all thoughts of control had simply disappeared. His entire being was one throbbing need. If he didn't get what he wanted, he'd explode. Thiede paused for a moment and said, 'Darq, in feybraiha, the younger har first takes a passive role, but...'

'Whatever!' Darq said. 'Don't talk to me, just do something.'

Thiede laughed. 'All right, you asked for it.' He rolled Darq onto his back.

It wasn't so much pain as a kind of stretching discomfort that went on for too long. Then Darq relaxed and uttered a long sighing groan.

'Are you all right?' Thiede whispered in his ear, his body motionless.

'Dislocated,' Darq murmured.

'What?'

'Dislocated limb. It's gone back in now. That's what it's like. I'm put back together. Now I can move it.' He experimented with this concept for some moments. 'Yes,' Darq said. 'It's good. You can move too now. Let's not talk.'

'That is the usual way,' Thiede said.

Chapter Eight

Freyhella in the summer was very different from the dour forbidding land Loki had first seen. The great mountains, swathed in clouds like ephemeral silks, dominated the landscape, filling it with sentience and power. Freygard nestled in the creases of these mountains as they stretched their toes to the ocean, creating the long steep-sided rivers for which the land was famous.

It was late in the afternoon as Loki arrived, feverish with feybraiha, still reeling from the surprise of being sent to this place. Half of him was afraid, yearning for the familiar comforts of his childhood home at this delicate time, while another part of him, already beyond feybraiha and hale again, welcomed the adventure. He would be staying in a house, in the hills not far from town. This was where Eyra's Listeners had lived for some while. It was similar to the one where Loki had stayed before, but with smaller rooms, even if there did appear to be more of them. The wooden panelling on the walls was unvarnished, as were the floorboards. Curtains at the windows were heavy and the floors covered in animal skins and thick rugs. Houses in Freygard required furnishings to combat the winter cold.

The strange portal still existed in the hawthorn grove, about a mile away, but had remained dormant. The Freyhellans now simply accepted its existence. Nohar had been harmed by it, and even the harling who'd found it had eventually become well again, cared for by hara in Immanion.

Cal and Pellaz both accompanied Loki to Freygard, in order to inspect the har that Galdra had chosen to consummate the feybraiha. His name was Seydir. None of it felt real to Loki. He could not imagine life beyond this rite of passage. Galdra escorted the Aralisians to Seydir's house in the evening. The har was fairly young, only three years past feybraiha himself, and lived alone. Galdra said he was a trusted member of the Assembly staff, and that he would regard it as a great honour to be Loki's guide.

Loki sat with his parents and Galdra, before a great fire, feeling as if the flames licked at his bones. He was surrounded by a strange bristling fog of emotions, and before him, in a carved wooden chair, sat the har with whom he would share the most intimate things. It seemed unimaginable. Cal nibbled the skin around his fingernails, and said hardly anything. Pellaz talked as if he was in the Hegalion, in clipped formal speech. Seydir too said little, so it was up to Pellaz and Galdra to keep the conversation going.

All the while, Galdra's gaze kept wandering to Loki, who was sensitively aware of the intense scrutiny. He wondered what interest this har had in him. Why, after all the hostility, had this invitation been extended? Loki wasn't sure he was comfortable with being a political tool. Yet hadn't he talked of building bridges when he'd been here before? He hadn't thought Galdra had really been listening, but obviously he had.

In the morning, after staying overnight in the Listeners' house, which was now reserved for high-ranking Gelaming when they visited Freygard, Cal and Loki went for a walk along the beach. Seydir came with them. Cal appeared to warm to the Freyhellan somewhat, because he talked at Seydir quite freely about inconsequential things. The Freyhellan said hardly a word and was clearly uneasy, perhaps in as much of a daze as Loki was. They strolled to the docks, where a refreshment shack for fisherhara stood. They sat outside at a sea-bleached table, sipping a strong, sweet brew of tea, serenaded by the greedy gulls, which strutted up and down, hoping for gifts of food.

Cal sighed. He'd spent the best part of an hour trying to put Seydir at ease and had obviously failed. Loki was utterly tongue-tied and wanted to go home.

'Have you seen anyhar through feybraiha before?' Cal asked, clearly having decided to face things head on.

Seydir shook his head and raised his hands in a gesture of helplessness.

'It's nothing to worry about,' Cal said.

'No.' Seydir put down his mug of tea, squinted out to sea.

'If you don't want to do this, you should say,' Cal said, his patience sounding thin.

'I don't speak your language good,' Seydir said abruptly. This had not been obvious, because he'd said so little.

'Have you understood half of what I've said to you?' Cal asked, grinning.

Seydir smiled, rather sheepishly. 'I don't speak well.'

'Fortunately, language is not an essential,' Cal said. He took a sip of the scalding tea, winked at Loki. 'What do you think of him, loveling? He can't understand us, so say what you like.'

Loki was unconvinced that was true. He already knew from his own language studies that it was easier to understand a tongue than to speak it. 'I like him.' He risked a smile at Seydir, and realised they had both thought the same thing about language. It was a brief mind touch, and it proved that language was clearly irrelevant in psychic communication. Loki hadn't considered that before.

'He looks good,' Cal said. 'Of course, they all do here.'

'You could be Freyhellan,' Loki said. 'You and Galdra look very alike.'

'So I've been told,' Cal said, and from his tone Loki wished he'd kept his mouth shut. 'Well, you two walk back down the beach. I'm just in the way. I'm supposed to chaperone, but I'll keep a beady eye on you from here. Off you go!'

Seydir looked momentarily confused as Cal flapped his hands in the air, but Loki sent the message, *Let's walk,* and Seydir got to his feet.

They went down the worn sandy steps to the shore. The tide was far out and harlings carrying wicker buckets picked for shellfish among the rocks. Seydir took Loki's hand rather shyly and they walked in silence, not even communicating by mind touch. They reached the caves where Loki and Raven had met Taldri. Today, nohar was around. Loki glanced back up the beach. He couldn't see Cal sitting outside the shack; it was too far away.

You are beauty, but also darkness.

Loki was surprised by the words that slid into his mind. *Dark? Me?* He'd never considered himself to be that.

Tigron blood, Seydir told him, but he was smiling. *Your mind talks strongly for one so young.*

I was taught to do it.

Seydir took Loki's hands in his own. Loki had never been touched by another har in this way, with this different intention. It was odd, another world. He felt strangely detached from it, when surely the spirit of feybraiha should have him painfully in its clutches. He could tell that Seydir thought they should share breath, because that was the usual way of things. He could also tell that the Freyhellan was still uneasy. His usual desire to please took control. *You are my teacher now. I know nothing.*

Seydir nodded and took Loki's face gently in his hands. For some moments, he gazed into Loki's eyes as if searching for something. Then they were sharing breath and the crash of the distant waves became thunder. Loki no longer felt detached. The union was euphoric, an utter sharing of being. It was like living Seydir's own life, seeing all those pictures, sensing his feelings. Suddenly, Seydir was the most desirable har in the world. It was remarkable how physical sensation took over. Loki became a single nerve of craving. And then Cal's voice was in his head. *Loki, come back now. Enough.*

He broke away, breathless. Seydir's eyes looked glazed. *I have to go back. My father called me.*

Seydir nodded. *He was right to do so. The feybraiha hunger is becoming very strong in you. Now is not the time.*

I look forward to the time, Loki told him, and Seydir laughed.

Among the Freyhellans, a feybraiha is celebrated among the whole community. If a har of status is involved, hara will come from outlying settlements, sailing down the coast in their long wolf-prowed ships. Offerings are made to the dehara of the sea, and the young har undergoing the rite of passage is required to spend a night in one of the sea caves, communing with the spirits gentle to his kind.

Galdra wanted his own son to experience a Freyhellan feybraiha to the full, although he did allow Loki to forgo the night in the cave. So, while physical symptoms of a minor yet annoying nature plagued Loki's body, he dutifully complied with Galdra's wishes, all the time wondering why Pellaz and Cal allowed the Freyhellan to take charge so much. Not that they stayed in Freygard for long. It seemed that once they were satisfied that Seydir wasn't a troll who might rip Loki's throat out, they were content to go back to Immanion, although they would return for the feybraiha party, when Seydir would initiate Loki into the rites of aruna.

Galdra spent a lot of time with Loki, instructing him in Freyhellan lore: that of the sea, the sky, and the beasts who rode them. He taught Loki about the winds and the sons of the winds, those capricious elementals who held the fate of ships in their cloudy hands. The attention Galdra showered on him made Loki feel breathless, and somewhat confused. It wasn't that he didn't enjoy or appreciate it: it just felt as if Galdra was running out of time, he had so much to say. Perhaps he was taking the idea of education to heart too earnestly. All the awkwardness and tension Loki had experienced on his first visit had melted away. He wondered what his parents had said to Galdra to change this. Was it just that Galdra was so flattered by being asked to instruct the Tigrons' son that he'd forgotten how bad he'd felt? Loki couldn't convince himself that was the reason.

But still, it would be churlish not to be grateful for all he'd been given. He loved the house where he lived; it had quickly started to feel like home. He enjoyed exploring its rambling garden. The Listeners, Samarchis and Lantovar, were young, second-generation hara. Away from Eyra's watchful eye, they were more disposed to light-heartedness and made easy living companions. They teased Loki constantly about his forthcoming feybraiha rite, but it was good-natured and he didn't mind it.

He made friends among the Freyhellans and every day met with Seydir, who was teaching him the language. Seydir would speak to Loki in mind touch, so he understood the meaning, and would then speak the words aloud in Freyhellan. It was easy to learn that way. Loki would look at this har, with whom very soon he would be sharing the most intimate experiences, and somehow it didn't feel real. Seydir had become a friend very quickly, and on those occasions when they shared breath, Loki could appreciate what delights were in store. Still, it seemed some part of him was distant from it, observing from afar. He wondered whether it was because once Seydir had called him darkness. Those words had been like a magical spell. He had not forgotten them.

There is darkness of the sky, darkness of the earth, and then the darkness of the soul, which is the greatest darkness of all. Loki had been conceived in a time of great turmoil; his was an accidental conception among a race where the creation of new life was always planned and preordained. He was an anomaly, and the dark flux of Fulminir's end, when Ponclast's unworldly allies had clashed with the *sedim,* when otherness had spilled through like oil from alien realms, and had touched his being. Like Darquiel, Loki was no ordinary harling, but he did not know it. He believed he'd been created in the golden light of peace, at war's end. He did not know that his creation had occurred at the very moment that Pellaz had wished himself dead.

Leaders from all the local phyles of Freyhella converged on Freygard for Loki's feybraiha. The Aralisians came from Immanion, with several members of the Hegemony, and Parasilians from Galhea in Megalithica. A ritual was held on the beach to mark Loki's ascension to Ara, first level Kaimana in the magical caste system. There was a feast, and the food and drink seemed supernaturally replenished, for it never diminished, no matter how many hara gorged themselves. There were recitals of songs, tales of hara from the north and their mythical meetings with gods. There were races and competitions, in which the Freyhellans demonstrated the agility and intelligence of their horses. Overseeing it all, crowned in flowers and throned like a monarch, Loki sat beside Seydir, his body newly calm, as if it knew the long wait was over.

Once the sun set, Galdra came to Loki to escort him back to his house. In the night sky that was filled almost obscenely with the starry riches of the heavens, strange lights danced in the north. As Galdra and Loki walked through the streets, which were quiet, because everyhar was at the party, Galdra asked, 'You're not afraid, are you?'

Loki shook his head. 'No, I'm not afraid.'

'You seem detached somehow. Do you feel numb?'

'A bit, yes. So much has happened today.'

Galdra laughed softly. 'I know, and this is the crowning moment. Come back into it, Loki. You shouldn't be numb.'

Loki smiled at Galdra and realised then how much he must have grown in the past couple of weeks. He was nearly as tall as Galdra now. At the door to the house, Galdra said, 'Would you like me to come in with you for a while?'

'I think I'd prefer to be alone, if that's all right,' Loki said.

Galdra stroked his hair. 'Of course.' He gripped Loki's shoulders. 'I have grown to love you, as I would... my own son. May the spirits shine upon you.'

Inside the house, Loki walked from room to room in the dark. He tried to imagine the immediate future: Seydir's footsteps on the porch, the sound of the front door opening. He tried to imagine the heat of another body alongside his own, and it didn't feel real. *It wasn't real.* Loki mounted the stairs to his bedroom, walking towards the dark feathery shadows at the top landing, where ghosts might huddle and whisper. He realised he didn't feel excited, frightened or anxious, simply because it wasn't going to happen. How he knew this, he could not tell, but it was a certainty. He went into the bedroom.

The night sky looked purple through the window. Loki didn't draw the curtains across it. He undressed and got into bed, then lay on his back staring at the ceiling. The shadows of tree branches outside writhed above him. He could hear the song of the wind, and it seemed that within it were voices from far away, calling. If he got out of bed now, he could open the window and walk a path of starlight into a new world. When Seydir came, nothing would be left of Loki but an impression in the sheets and a faint lingering warmth.

He must have dozed, because he became aware of waking, and that the quality of the light had changed. The wind had dropped and the shadows of tree branches were now a lattice of stillness across the ceiling. How late was it? Seydir was not there. Loki was alarmed. Even though he'd felt that peculiar certainty as he'd ascended the stairs, it now seemed unthinkable that Seydir had not come.

As he thought this, he realised that somehar was sitting in the old wing chair that stood in the far corner of the room. Or perhaps he was mistaken. Loki always threw his clothes there and sometimes didn't move them for days, so that a pile built up that in darkness resembled harish or monstrous shapes. He stared at the chair, not quite certain if somehar was staring back at him or not. Then a figure stood up, and he saw for sure that he was not alone.

For a moment, Loki knew pure crystalline terror. It was not the appearance of his as yet unknown visitor, for he could see very little; it was the feeling that came with it, a feeling he could not describe, but it too was a certainty. The figure approached him, and although its progress was not slow, Loki still had time to consider a thousand rushing thoughts. He remembered the feeling that had engulfed him when he'd dreamed of Cal dying and had woken up still thinking the dream had been real. He felt like that now: a terrible inevitability, a crushing reality that turned the world black. He said the name 'Seydir' without much hope.

A har he did not know was standing next to his bed. This har had long hair, blacker than the shadows around them. He was dressed in leather: trousers and a jerkin that left his arms bare. His skin shone dully, but not with light. It was like oil shifting over the surface of water. 'Seydir cannot come,' he said.

'And *you* have?' Loki propped himself up on his elbows. He didn't know how he was feeling now. A certain normality had re-established itself. There was an explanation.

'Yes. Don't be afraid.'

'Who are you?' Loki hesitated. 'I don't know you. Has Galdra sent you?'

The har sat down on the bed, brushed back his hair with one hand, which made him seem more ordinary. His face was bony, the eyes slightly slanted. He had a look of Pellaz, in a way. Perhaps Loki's parents had sent this har, at the last moment deciding they did not want a Freyhellan in their son's bed. 'I am Skripi,' he said. It sounded like a Freyhellan name.

'What happened to Seydir?'

'I've come in his place.' Skripi smiled then, and in that smile was the promise of the arcane and wondrous. Loki was aware of a connection between them, and even though he felt as if he was in a dream, and there was something most definitely not right about what was happening now, he threw aside his bed quilt in invitation.

Seydir's body was discovered at first light, when the hara he worked with went out to see to the cattle. Seydir lay in the byre, between the great living sides of beef, who appeared to be guarding him. His throat had been cut. His eyes stared sightlessly in surprise, and perhaps the image of the one who had killed him was captured in that lifeless stare.

Galdra was informed at once, and took it upon himself to run without his coat straight to Loki's house, before the Aralisians got wind of what had happened. He didn't understand it. Seydir had left the feybraiha celebrations some moments after Galdra had returned from escorting Loki home. Seydir had been in high spirits, but not drunk. There were no enemies in Freygard, and not even the most sensitive har had picked up any discomforting ripples in the ethers.

Galdra burst into Loki's house without knocking, dreading what he might find, but there were only the Listeners in the kitchen, sleepily drinking coffee. 'Where's Loki?' Galdra demanded.

Samarchis said, 'What's wrong?'

And Lantovar said, 'He hasn't got up yet. We didn't disturb them.'

Without further words, Galdra ran for the stairs, leaping up them three at a time. Part of his mind dithered at the threshold like a frightened harling, but his body had no such hesitation and threw the door wide. He took in the rumpled bed, the figure lying on its stomach within it. He strode straight over and hauled back the quilt. Loki raised his head and Galdra's feeling of relief was so immense, he dropped to his knees and let out a choked cry.

'Galdra,' Loki said. His eyes were wide and appeared strangely unfocused.

Galdra drew Loki into his arms and held him close. He kissed the top of Loki's head. Loki struggled feebly within his grasp. His breath was sour and his skin felt hot.

'You're hurting me.'

Galdra drew away. Loki rolled onto his back and lay there panting. His chest and stomach were covered in small v-shaped cuts. He lay on a crusty film of dried blood.

Samarchis and Lantovar had followed Galdra upstairs. 'Samarchis, go to the healers' guild and fetch somehar at once,' Galdra snapped. 'Lantovar, summon the Tigrons.'

'What's happened?' Samarchis asked.

'Go!' Galdra's command was a growl.

Left alone with Loki, he knelt beside the bed and took the young har's hands in his own. 'Loki, can you remember what happened?' His voice was steady but behind his words was a scream.

'Seydir didn't come,' Loki said in a slurred voice.

'Somehar did…'

'Yes… Skripi…'

'Can you describe him?'

Loki shook his head. He frowned. 'I can't really remember. I feel very strange. Am I supposed to feel like this? I'm so thirsty.'

'Just lie still. I'll fetch you some water.'

Galdra went down to the kitchen and for some moments leaned against the sink, his mind awhirl. At any moment, Pellaz and Calanthe would arrive. There would be a scene, recriminations, blame. What had happened? There was no har named Skripi in Freygard. The injuries on Loki's body were bizarre. They were like the bites of a hundred reptile jaws, tiny reptiles. Galdra filled a glass with water and took it back upstairs. Loki had struggled into a sitting position and now leaned against the headboard of the bed staring at his stomach. He touched one of the wounds tentatively then withdrew his hand quickly.

'Here,' Galdra handed Loki the glass. 'Can you hold it?'

'Yes.' Loki drank greedily and handed the glass back to Galdra, who put it on the bedside table.

'Something went wrong,' Loki said. 'I don't think that har was supposed to be here. Did you send him?'

Galdra shook his head. 'No. Did you take aruna together?'

'Yes. He took me to some very strange places, but I liked them, in a way. It was very good, but all the time I felt I shouldn't really be doing it. I couldn't stop myself.'

'Did he make those cuts on you?'

Loki frowned in a dazed manner. 'I don't know. I don't remember. Maybe he took me someplace where it happened.'

'Your parents will be here soon,' Galdra said. 'Try to remember as much as you can.'

Fortunately, the healer arrived before the Aralisians. Galdra left him to examine Loki and went quickly to organise a search of the town for any interlopers, even though he did not believe for a moment that whoever had visited Loki would still be around. What was the motive? Who would kill a har to take his place at a feybraiha? Loki seemed fairly undamaged, despite the cuts, but perhaps he'd been poisoned. Galdra shuddered inside. He heard himself issuing orders in a clipped manner, while his mind asked itself a hundred unanswerable questions. He was not looking forward to a confrontation with the Aralisians.

Pellaz and Cal were already at Loki's bedside when Galdra returned to the house. He awaited a torrent of accusation, but the Tigrons appeared so concerned for Loki, they were bewildered rather than angry. The healer could not tell what had made the injuries; they were in many ways like bites. There did not appear to be any poison in the wounds.

'This is deliberate,' Pellaz said. 'We must take Loki back to Immanion as soon as possible.'

Galdra could not disagree. What protection could he ensure if an assailant could walk into this house without obstruction?

Loki had been given a potion that had made him fall asleep. His cuts had been dressed, his bedding changed. Galdra indicated that he and the Tigrons should go downstairs to talk.

They went to a small sitting room that overlooked the garden. Here a fire had been built, but to Galdra the air was stuffy rather than simply warm.

Cal sat down next to the fire, in an old padded chair, over which a sheepskin had been draped, while Pellaz leaned against the window sill. He was not comfortable enough to sit down, Galdra thought.

'I'm inclined to think we now know the purpose of your spirit window,' Cal said.

Of the two Tigrons, Galdra had expected a tongue-lashing from Cal, but Cal was surprisingly cordial, given what had occurred.

'Do you have any evidence for that?' Galdra asked. It was not an arch question; he hoped Cal had intuited or sensed something.

Cal shook his head slowly. 'Not hard evidence, just a feeling. The etheric residue in that room was faint - almost too faint - but it was unfamiliar. I think that somehar or something has orchestrated this whole scenario.'

'Who could orchestrate you bringing Loki to Freygard in the first place?' Galdra said, and now his voice was bitter. 'What enemy would know you that well?'

Cal smiled grimly. 'Perhaps I'm too predictable, after all.'

'We shouldn't jump to conclusions,' Pellaz said. 'As yet, we don't know the purpose of what happened. I find it hard to believe that somehar - whether enemy or opportunist - would go to such lengths as creating that portal and so on, simply to be the first to take aruna with Loki. What purpose would that serve?'

Cal gave Pellaz a cold glance. 'We both know that the boundaries of aruna have yet to be fully explored. Who knows what might have been accomplished? For all we know, Loki might well now be a ticking time bomb.'

'A what?' Galdra said.

'A device that's made to explode after a certain time,' Cal said dryly. 'Read your history books, Galdra. Some things it's best not to forget.'

'Surely you're not implying that Loki...'

'I'm implying he could have been affected in some way without knowing it. He could have been given instructions he can't remember. He could murder us all in our beds. If I were an enemy of ours I'd consider that quite an elegant way to dispose of us.'

'Then perhaps he should stay in Freygard after all,' Galdra said, 'for your protection as much as his own.'

'I'll work with Loki,' Cal said, 'mind to mind. I've been trained well. If anything has been planted in his head, I'll find it. As for where he should go, I'm thinking the safest place for him would be with Thiede.'

'What do we have to brace ourselves for?' Pellaz said bitterly. 'What does all this presage? I must speak to my brother Snake as soon as possible.'

Galdra rubbed his hands over his face. 'I'm sorry this has happened.'

'It could have happened in Immanion too,' Pellaz said. 'We have no way of knowing. It could be unconnected with that portal.'

'I doubt that,' Cal said. 'But there's nohar to blame but me. I take full responsibility. Don't look so shocked, Galdra.'

'We are all responsible,' Galdra said. 'In one way or another.'

Loki woke up in the evening and lay in his bed, listening to his own breath. When he turned his head to the side, he could hear the wet pulse of his heart in his ears. What had happened? He didn't know. It seemed like a dream now. Somehar had come to him, somehar made of oil and smoke, who had touched him and woken him up, who had left him wounded and befuddled. Loki still did not know Seydir was dead, because Galdra had decided he shouldn't yet be told. All Loki knew was that a stranger had taken Seydir's place and that stranger was now part of him, inextricably woven into his bones and blood.

Dusk came softly on the wings of owls. The tree branches wove their shadow dance across the ceiling of Loki's bedroom. He felt strangely at peace, languorous and detached. The future, in terms of days following days, had no meaning. Soon, Lantovar or Samarchis would bring him something easily digestible for his evening meal. He could hear them in the lower parts of the house, and if he concentrated very hard, he could hear their hearts beating too. They were talking in low voices, even though they thought there was nohar else around to hear. They spoke of death, of pelki, though both concepts were far removed from Loki's feelings on the matter. Gradually, as he listened, so still upon his bed that if anyhar had come into the room they'd have thought him dead, Loki realised that somehar had indeed died last night. Disoriented, he had to question whether that was in fact himself. He ran his fingers over his chest and stomach, felt the faint ridges of the scars that had already nearly healed. He could not remember receiving those wounds. Surely, they were not fatal?

'You are very much alive, Loki.'

Galdra had put guards around the house. Two of them were on the front porch, while others hid in the garden at the back and on the road that led to the town centre. Nohar could get into this house without detection. Yet here he was again.

'Skripi,' Loki said. 'They're looking for you.'

Skripi came out of the shadows, perhaps his portal to this place. 'That's of no consequence,' he said. 'Get out of bed and dress yourself.'

'I can't, there's something wrong with me. I'm too tired to move.'

'You're fine,' Skripi said. 'Get up.'

Loki was about to protest again, but realised he did in fact feel very alert and full of energy. The languor had dropped from him, presumably at Skripi's words. He must be working magic. Downstairs, Samarchis had put a ceramic bowl on the kitchen table, and Lantovar was about to ladle soup into it. In a few short moments, one of them would begin to climb the stairs. Loki knew that was dangerous for them. 'What do you want with me?' he asked Skripi.

'We're going on a journey,' Skripi answered. 'It's one you want to take. We must go at once.'

The kitchen door opened and closed, and floorboards creaked as Samarchis walked across the hall.

'If you care for that har, you will come with me now,' Skripi said, and although the words were threatening, Loki knew that he was not in danger. Samarchis, however, was. Loki got out of bed and pulled on his clothes. He was finding it difficult to think properly, but his body moved swiftly and precisely.

Just as the door opened and Samarchis came into the room, Skripi pulled Loki backwards into a shadowed corner. The shadows wrapped around them both like a concealing cloak. Loki saw Samarchis stare at the bed for some seconds, before he yelled, 'Lantovar!' and fled the room.

Skripi's arms tightened around Loki. 'Are you ready?' he whispered.

Loki did not answer. They were leaving whether he was ready or not. For a brief moment, he considered breaking free and following Samarchis in a hectic flight down the stairs, but before the idea could take shape properly, the air folded and fractured around him.

He was being taken into the Otherlanes. Very few hara can travel the etheric highways without the use of a *sedu*. The only har Loki knew who could do it was Cal. Now he was plummeting through a void, gripped by a creature he could no longer see. He was confused and numb, but just before he was taken to another world, Loki sent out a pulse of his own essence: a symbol and a sign. He hoped that Cal would be able to find it.

Chapter Nine

In the realm of Thanatep, the sky is black, even though a solar disk burns high above the twisted landscape. There are no stars. The land itself is red and black; sepia in the shadows. The first words Loki heard in this place were, 'You must protect yourself from the Thanax.' The words meant nothing, and seemed to come from nowhere, because Loki's senses were addled. The air he breathed had a bitter tang to it, and his eyes were running. He felt hands upon his arms, and a living presence behind him, while he blinked to clear his vision, struggling for breath. He wanted to say things like 'What is this place?' or 'Take me home,' but the act of speaking was too difficult. He was in an alien realm, powerless and a captive.

Skripi, who held him, released his grip and turned Loki to face him. 'You'll get used to this place. Soon, the air will have no taste. But we must make haste. You're too vulnerable, and the Thanax will sense your warmth.'

By this time, Loki was able to take in more details of his surroundings. He and Skripi were standing on the brow of a stark cliff, where black, straggling herbs snaked across the ground. They looked undernourished and poisonous. Below, was a wide flat plain that looked as if it had been created by some kind of massive impact, as it was surrounded on all sides by cliffs. Upon the plain was a forest of towers, some with bulbous cupolas at their peaks, others with stone crowns of spikes. Some had fallen completely, others were half standing. About a third remained intact.

As for Skripi himself, he was an attractive har, even if his aura felt rather strange and dark. His hair was not quite black, almost purple, as were his eyes. But despite these aesthetic qualities, he was still an abductor.

'That is the city of Thannaril,' Skripi said, 'though nothing lives there now… except for us.'

Loki still could not speak. He wanted to weep, but felt that if he did so, the tears would turn into some caustic substance and burn his skin.

'Come,' Skripi said, and took hold of one of Loki's hands. If he was aware of Loki's distress, he ignored it.

There was a narrow, treacherous path that led down to the plain. Several times, Loki stumbled as loose shale gave way beneath his feet.

Skripi hauled him on relentlessly. He appeared to be in a hurry.

When they eventually reached the bottom, Skripi paused. 'You must be wondering why I didn't bring us out of the Otherlanes directly into Thannaril, but this has proved difficult. Ancient wards about the towers still contain a residue of power.'

Loki had been thinking no such thing. He could barely think at all.

'But we're nearly there. Hurry.'

Skripi dragged Loki onwards. The shadows of the towers fell over them, and Loki heard a threatening sibilant hiss. Skripi tensed, whilst also increasing their pace. 'Don't look at them,' he advised.

Loki had not been aware there was anything to look at, and the simple injunction not to look made him glance to the side. The image would stay with him forever. He saw three skeletal shapes, whose skins were as dark as the world around them, yet it seemed as if it were not *colour* exactly. Their eyes were black holes, and their long, tangled hair a dirty white. Hunger poured from their beings and they were edging out from the shadows.

'Thanax,' Skripi said. He broke into a run.

Guided by survival instinct, Loki ran just as fleetly. He thought he heard the words 'Flesh fire!' hissed behind him.

Skripi and Loki ran towards a nearby tower. There was a gaping entrance just above ground level, reached by a short flight of steps, but there was no door. Skripi leapt up the steps and plunged into the unsavoury darkness beyond the threshold, dragging Loki with him. Loki could not see how an open doorway provided any measure of security, but then Skripi was hauling him up wide spiralling stairs on the inside wall of the tower. If there had been floors to the building, the lower ones were long gone, but around thirty feet up, a ceiling appeared from the darkness, in which there was an opening. The stairs led through it into a circular room, with a high-beamed ceiling.

Here, Skripi let go of Loki's hands and braced his hands upon his knees, breathing deeply. He groaned and straightened up. 'I took the drain. You didn't feel it, did you?'

Loki stared at Skripi mutely. He had no idea what the har meant.

'Well, you seem unscathed,' Skripi said. He ran his hands through his hair. 'Don't worry. The Thanax won't follow us into a tower. This is Mutandis, once the lair of a powerful creature, we believe. We visit it rarely, but it was the closest to hand.'

The room was empty, but for a few shadowy chests arranged around the walls. Loki was puzzled as to how he could see so well, seeing as this realm had little light. Now that he was more himself, he could take in more details: Skripi looked little older than he did, but it was clear the other har was more experienced, in many ways. He had a confidence and inner strength that Loki thought he lacked himself.

'Why?' Loki managed to ask. 'Why have you brought me here?'

Skripi flashed him a crooked smile, and did not answer, but walked across the room to a strange metallic structure that sprouted from the wall. It looked like a flower of metal struts. 'This is a water tap,' Skripi said. 'You must drink now, because the Otherlanes can dehydrate you. The water here is drawn from deep beneath the ground. There's little that is drinkable to be found on the surface around here.'

He turned one of the spiky metal petals, and a gush of fluid burst from the tap's centre. The whole room filled with a damp smell of earth.

Skripi picked up a battered metal cup from the floor and filled it. 'You'll get used to the taste,' he said, and offered Loki the cup.

Loki drank, and although in some ways it felt as if he were eating soil, he also felt refreshed. He wiped his mouth. 'You must tell me. Why have you brought me here?'

'To be with us,' Skripi said, 'your kin.'

'My *kin*?'

'We are surakin, Loki.'

'What's that?'

'I'm the son of your brother, Abrimel, who the Tigron has imprisoned in Immanion. Abrimel is my father. You're my hura, believe it or not. But I prefer the term surakin, don't you? It makes us sound like equals.'

'Whatever. It means nothing to me.' Loki sat down on the floor. He'd had no idea he possessed this relative, if indeed Skripi was telling the truth. It was a shock, not least because if it was true, a very close blood relative had recently taken him through feybraiha. Was that forbidden? Loki pressed his hands against his eyes briefly. 'What do you want with me? Am I a hostage to barter for your hostling?'

'No,' Skripi said. 'You're here to learn a part of our family's history. Nohar's ever told you about it.' He hunkered down in front of Loki. 'My true name is Geburael. Call me that from now on. You won't have heard of it. You were conceived at the time when my hostling, Ponclast, was vanquished by the Tigrons and my brother Diablo fled with me to sanctuary. I was a tiny harling then, but even so, I felt your soul flower in the earthly realm. I've waited to make contact with you. There are many things you don't know, not least that your father's former consort was not slain by the Teraghasts, as hara believe. He was slain by those who wished your father to make contact with the Aralisian, Pellaz.'

Loki almost laughed. 'Skripi... Geburael... my father's former consort was killed virtually by his own hand. It was his choice to die.'

Geburael got to his feet. 'We're not speaking of Terzian har Varr, Loki. Calanthe har Aralis is not your father. That's just one of the lies.'

Loki felt as if Geburael had punched his stomach. For a moment, it was difficult to draw breath, then he managed to say, with dignity: 'I don't believe you.'

Geburael shook his head at these words. 'Loki, you must believe. I have no reason to lie. Your father is Galdra har Freyhella. We've been given information about this. You were conceived on a field of battle, while the Aralisian performed Grissecon with the Freyhellan to defeat my hostling. That is a fact, and not even Pellaz would dare deny it if you asked him outright.'

Much as this news was distressing, Loki felt the information settle within him and knew instinctively that it was true. It explained a lot. Galdra was aware of this truth, which was why he'd said the Gelaming had done him a discourtesy in bringing Loki to Freygard. But some arrangement had been made, some understanding arrived at, in order for Loki to be educated with the Freyhellans. Everything made sense, except for one thing. 'You still haven't said why I'm here,' Loki said. 'If we are kin, why didn't you just tell me?'

Geburael laughed harshly. 'Because of who my parents are. If I'd made myself known to you, and you'd revealed that knowledge, the Tigrons would have tried to imprison me, as they did my parents. Not that they'd have succeeded, but I don't want them to be aware of me just yet. Pellaz is mad, drunk on power. He's a threat to Wraeththukind. It's important you know the truth, because you're his heir.'

'*You* are his enemy,' Loki said. 'That's why you're saying these things. Don't think me so stupid. I know who Ponclast is, what he tried to do. *He* was deranged. How do you plan to use me?'

'I don't plan to *use* you,' Geburael said. 'I want to make you aware of the facts, that's all, and then you can make up your own mind. Naturally, you're prejudiced against me at the moment. I expect that. But I'll show you things that will enlighten you.'

Loki had already resolved to appear to co-operate, since this could buy him time. He realised he must concentrate on drawing Cal to him, for he had no doubt Cal would be looking for him. Did Cal know the truth about Galdra? Somehow, Loki felt that he must, which made his sincere love all the more precious. 'What things?' Loki asked. His mind went back to the creatures from which they'd fled. 'What are the Thanax?'

'Leeches,' Geburael replied. 'They feed on living essence. I'll show you how to protect yourself from them. They're drawn by warmth; you must learn to project cold, and then they'll ignore you.'

'What is this place exactly?'

'Another realm, another exit point of the Otherlanes, like the earthly realm is. Diablo found it years ago. He brought me here for safety after Fulminir fell. We have... assistance here.'

'Did the Thanax once live in these towers?'

Geburael shook his head. 'No. Diablo gave them that name. He learned the name of this city, and this realm. The Thanax are a fairly recent phenomenon, he thinks. We've tried to kill them, but it's impossible. They never get that close and can move quicker than a thought flies through the psyche. But we've been drained by them and it's not pleasant. They're not deadly, but they'll send you into a stupor, take all your strength and energy.'

'If they feed on life force, who else do they draw nourishment from, apart from you? This place seems almost barren.'

'They don't,' Geburael said, 'well, not here. That is why they're constantly hungry, although Diablo thinks they can access other realms, feed from those who frequent the Otherlanes, for example. The majority of hara travelling the ethers are most likely unaware of it. We look on the Thanax as Otherlanes parasites. Why there's a colony of them here, we don't know. Once you can protect yourself, they're no bother.' He smiled. 'If you've refreshed yourself, I'll take you to Diablo. Remember to project cold. You've had some caste training, I take it?'

'Scant,' Loki said. 'I've just passed feybraiha, remember.'

'I remember,' Geburael said.

Loki could recall little of the night when Geburael had first visited him, other than that he'd felt strangely drawn to him. Still, it was difficult to imagine they had taken aruna together. Loki could remember the strange wounds he'd woken up with. What had Geburael done to him? He did not seem to be entirely har. 'Why didn't Seydir come to me?' he asked. 'What did you do to him?'

Geburael frowned. 'I don't know that har.'

'He was the one who had been chosen for me for feybraiha, the one whose place you stole.'

'Diablo dealt with certain aspects of the operation,' Geburael said. 'I had no part in that.'

'But what did...?'

Geburael held up his hands. 'You have many questions, I know. I'll answer as many of them as I can, but now we should leave this place.'

Loki nodded. 'Take me to your brother.' In his voice, he heard the ringing tone of Aralis, his bloodline. He must not let these strange and possibly dangerous exiled hara forget who he was.

Once outside Mutandis, Loki expected the Thanax who'd spotted them earlier to be lurking around, waiting for him and Geburael to re-emerge, but apparently the creatures did not have that much of an attention span and had wandered off. Still, Loki was nervous as he and Geburael jogged between the shadows of the silent, looming towers. He kept expecting a hideous shape to leap out at them.

Years before, Diablo had escaped from Fulminir, or rather had been expelled by Cal, during the battle between the *sedim* and the *teraphim*. On his flight, Diablo had had the wits to scoop up the harling Geburael from Abrimel's arms. At the time, Abrimel had been rendered senseless and didn't notice the abduction. Ponclast had already been delivered into Lileem's custody and the battle outside had been nearly over. Diablo had been injured by Cal, but even so his determination had kept him going, and he had slipped into the Otherlanes, to relative safety.

Although Ponclast had not known it, Diablo had been making his own investigations of the Otherlanes for some time. Wraeththu, perhaps subtly influenced by the *sedim*, steadfastly refused to explore other realms, believing them to be hostile to harish life and therefore deadly. Diablo had no such concerns. If he emerged into a realm where the air was unbreathable, he'd be out again in the blink of an eye. If he emerged into solid rock and died, then he died. He didn't really hold his own life in much esteem, but he was a creature full of curiosity.

After many abortive attempts to emerge into realms other than earth, Diablo eventually tumbled out into Thanatep. Something about the place appealed to him: the silent, sentinel towers of the city; the crumbling hints of a civilisation long dead. Little was left as evidence, but once Diablo composed himself in trance, the name Thannaril came to him, which he supposed was accurate. The Thanadrim, who'd built the city, and had once occupied the entire world, were gone, but their ghosts, their memories and their feelings remained. Diablo did not discover the Thanax until the time he brought Geburael to Thannaril. He supposed this was because his own life force was not particularly palatable to parasites.

When Loki laid eyes on Diablo for the first time, he was shocked. It wasn't that Diablo was deformed particularly, or even horrific to behold, but he was so different, he barely looked harish. His eyes were abnormally large, his cheekbones like blades, his chin narrow and pointed. His hair was blacker than the eerie sky and so thick it resembled lush jungle vegetation rather than hair. His dark gaze was compelling, like that of a hypnotic predator. Loki felt Diablo could see right into him. It was also clear, from first acquaintance, that he felt no kinship to Loki. Whatever motives Geburael might have for bringing Loki here, Diablo's were different. Loki wondered what kind of monster Ponclast must be to spawn such progeny.

Diablo did not smile or utter a greeting when Loki stepped into what was clearly his personal space. He merely inclined his head, and indicated that Loki should sit down. There were some ragged cushions on the floor that had seemingly once been quite plush. Loki settled himself, and Diablo went to prepare food.

Apanage Tower was perhaps the least dilapidated in Thannaril. All its floors were still intact and these had been equipped with a few bits of furniture that Geburael and Diablo had filched from the earthly realm: as well as the cushions for seating, there were small tables, even bed rolls for sleeping. The realm was not as barren as it first appeared. Geburael explained there were small mammals and reptiles to hunt for food, as well as a few species of reptilian birds. The plants, though tough and stringy, were plentiful and nourishing. There were no hearths or chimneys in the tower, so fires for cooking and warmth had to be built directly on the floor. Fortunately, the wood from the local hardy shrubs was virtually smokeless, if carefully dried beforehand.

When Diablo served the meal, it looked unappetizing at best. There was no meat, but a stew of dark weeds that tasted bitter. Salt or spices would have made it more palatable, but Diablo had no such condiments to cook with and clearly considered the matter too trivial to amend by fetching some from the earthly realm. Loki forced down the stew, knowing he should keep up his strength.

Geburael had been brought up in this place, Loki realised, suddenly sensing what a lonely harlinghood his surakin must have had. Diablo was hardly lively company, being dour and mostly silent, although it was obvious he had a fierce protective streak concerning his half-brother. Even so, Loki thought that Geburael should really have been brought up in Immanion, among kin more savoury and sane. He could not imagine that Pellaz would have been cruel to the harling; after all, Geburael was his high-son. Diablo loathed the Gelaming, with a passion beyond imagining, and Geburael had been indoctrinated into his brother's beliefs. Now, he sought to indoctrinate Loki in a similar manner, but Loki was aware that could work both ways.

While they ate, Geburael explained how Loki should protect himself from the Thanax. 'Imagine a shield of cold, and put all your intention into it,' he said. 'It's a kind of camouflage, like the ones that some animals use. There are creatures here that can look like stones and their skins are so tough it's hardly worth the effort of hunting them. Be like that. Make yourself a tasteless morsel.'

Loki did not look forward to the time he must test this defence. While Geburael talked, as if they had known each other for years, and this was a social visit, Diablo studied Loki with a hard gaze. At first, Loki was intimidated by this, but gradually the feeling mutated into annoyance. He was the heir of Aralis. He would not be regarded this way by such a freak. 'What do you want of me?' he asked Diablo, in a haughty tone. He was curious as to what the har's answer might be.

Diablo gave him a grisly smile. 'You will decide your own fate,' he said.

Loki shuddered, and hoped it didn't show. 'I find that hard to believe. I was brought here mostly against my will. Did you kill to bring me here?' He managed to hold Diablo's gaze after this question, wishing strongly he'd never voiced it.

'We did what had to be done,' Diablo said coldly.

'How much do you know of the Rout of Fulminir?' Geburael asked, clearly to change the subject.

Loki stirred the mess on his plate with a spoon. 'I know that following the First Fall of Fulminir, Ponclast har Varr was imprisoned by Thiede in the Forest of Gebaddon for his crimes against harakind. I know that he later broke free with otherworldly assistance, and attempted to reform his tribe and apply himself to regaining control. He tried to rebuild Fulminir, but was vanquished by my hostling... and Galdra har Freyhella. Now he is imprisoned somewhere and his hara have scattered.'

'That is the surface of the story,' Diablo said. He put down his plate very carefully and composed himself in a cross-legged position, his long limbs curling up like those of a large spider. 'The fact is that the Gelaming are the tools of a faction whose representatives in the earthly realm are the *sedim*. The Gelaming are ignorant, proud and arrogant. They believe these unearthly creatures are simply willing vessels of transportation. They are wrong. All the realms are constantly in flux, for they are resources for higher beings. The earthly realm is under dispute. Its lowly denizens have no awareness of this. They have no need for it. But those of us who do have it, are aware of something else too: it makes no difference to us who has control, because we have no evidence for it in daily life. When a stronger force wishes to take what is theirs, they should not be opposed, because that could cause the destruction of the world. It is in the interest of all living beings on earth that the stronger forces should have their way. The *sedim* care nothing for Wraeththu; they are simply pawns. The *sedim* should be removed. Our masters know that Wraeththu have tasted the Otherlanes and that the privilege should not be taken from them. Other means will be provided, once the *sedim* are no more.'

Loki had ridden *sedim* many times, and anyhar who travels with them forges a strong bond with the creatures. He could not believe that any *sedu* was this heartless thing that Diablo intimated. 'Have you ever travelled with a *sedu*?' Loki asked.

Diablo pulled a sour face. 'No. I have no need. Neither would they carry me. I am their enemy.'

Loki said nothing about this, and hoped his pointed silence was noted. He took another mouthful of food, chewed it, conscious of Geburael's attention upon him. It was clear to Loki that Geburael wanted Diablo to warm to him. The two hara had different agendas, and perhaps Geburael wasn't as mature and worldly as he liked to project.

'Are you responsible for the strange portal in Freygard?' Loki asked Diablo. 'Is that how Skripi… Geburael… reached me?'

'That is not ours,' Diablo replied. 'It could belong to our allies or to their enemies. Be assured it has some purpose.'

Loki nodded. 'That's obvious. Well, now that I'm here, and you have *enlightened* me with your version of history, what next?'

Diablo flared his nostrils, an expression implying utmost contempt. 'You wait,' he snapped. 'Our masters the Hashmallim will come, for I've told them I have you. But when that will be, I don't know. They can't be summoned. They simply arrive when it suits them.'

'Hashmallim,' Loki said. 'What are they?'

Diablo smiled. 'You'll find out.' He jerked his head at Geburael. 'The Aralisian will sleep with you. Don't let him wander.' He put down his empty plate. 'Now go. I don't want to look at you.'

Loki got to his feet, his food mostly untouched. 'With pleasure, Tiahaar. There is just one thing I would like to say. You don't *have* me. I might be here against my will, and I might be your prisoner, but there is more to imprisonment than physical confinement.'

He knew these words were perhaps unwise, given his predicament, but the whole situation made him angry. He sent another silent scream into the ethers. *Find me, Cal! Find me!*

Diablo did not react as Loki expected. 'Believe what you will,' he said. 'It makes no difference to me.'

Geburael took hold of one of Loki's arms. 'Come,' he said.

Loki pulled away from him. 'I can follow.'

Geburael led him to a room higher in the tower, which was his own space. Loki felt a twinge of pity as he regarded the wretched attempts that Geburael had made to make the place feel like a home. There were half-hearted efforts at decoration, coloured scarves tacked to the walls, rows of candles in a multitude of different holders, small ornaments, some of which appeared to have come from a Nayati. Did Geburael, in his lonely moments, commune with dehara? Loki thought that unlikely. He dreaded to think what Geburael might commune with.

'I can't believe you've lived here for so long,' he said. 'You should have left. You should have come to your family.'

'I'm with my family,' Geburael said coldly. 'What's left of them. You're here now. That's enough.'

'I think it's driven you mad, being here.' Loki sat down on Geburael's rumpled bedding. 'You sleep on a floor and eat weeds. You live with a gargoyle and there's no light here. It's like the realm of the dead.'

Geburael's eyes widened. 'You can mock me, if it gives you satisfaction. I didn't have your privileges and neither did Diablo. He was raised on poisoned ground. He's the way he is because of the mercy of the Aralisians. Did you ever think about that, Loki har Aralis? All those hara exiled in Thiede's hell? Hara whose only crime was to follow the orders of their leader, as all hara are supposed to do. Was that justice?'

'They committed crimes,' Loki said. 'Their punishment was fitting, because of what they did. They were perverted.'

'Some of your family's dearest friends were once Varrs,' Geburael said. 'Are the Parasilians perverted? Are the hara who work their fields debauched? The Varrs in Gebaddon were once no different.'

'Parasiel made its choice,' Loki said. 'The Varrs in Gebaddon were Ponclast's elite. They paid the price.'

Geburael sliced the air with one hand. 'They had no choice! Ponclast was no better or no worse than the Gelaming. It was simply a struggle for power. You're blind if you can't see this.'

Loki laughed harshly. 'No, *you* are blind. Don't you know what happened in Fulminir? Acts of unbelievable vileness. Even erstwhile Varrs will tell you that. You can't conveniently believe it was all Gelaming propaganda. Take me home, and I'll arrange it so you can meet some of the survivors. Look into their eyes and then try to believe what Diablo has told you.'

Geburael turned away and shifted some of his candlesticks around.

Loki could tell he'd touched the har in some way, perhaps made the first crack in Geburael's wall of belief. 'It doesn't matter,' Geburael said. 'The struggle for power is no longer between Wraeththu factions. Diablo is right about that. And when you meet the Hashmallim, you'll look into their eyes and know a different kind of truth.'

'We'll see.' Loki sighed. 'What do you do to pass the time here?'

Geburael paused. 'I write stories. I study the books the Hashmallim have given to me. I draw maps of the towers.'

This revelation also conjured a pang of pity in Loki's breast. He saw an image of Geburael as a very young harling, wandering around the bleak forest of stone, making up stories. This was followed by another, altogether less pleasant image. 'Who took you through feybraiha?' Loki asked.

Geburael again paused before replying. 'I think you know,' he said.

'No, I don't. That time with me could have been your first also.'

'Well, it wasn't.'

'Oh.' Loki felt nauseous and didn't know what to say next.

'It was important to me, what we did,' Geburael said. 'It was very important.'

I am really going to throw up, Loki thought. He swallowed. 'You injured me. What was that all about?'

'When Diablo... I...' Geburael closed his eyes briefly. 'After feybraiha, I was changed. It's something to do with the taint of Gebaddon. It's as well you're told this. During aruna, there are thorns.'

'What?' Loki laughed nervously.

Geburael laid a hand on his stomach. 'Thorns,' he said. 'The wounds aren't bad. They bring pleasure.'

Loki narrowed his eyes. 'Sounds like something that would have gone down well in Fulminir.'

'You didn't complain at the time.'

'Happily, I have no recollection of the event.'

Geburael smiled grimly. 'Loki, I've watched you for a long time. I know our purpose is to be together. As you noticed, there's little to do here, but we have each other.'

'Not in that way we don't,' Loki said. 'It's not going to happen, I promise you. I can't take aruna with a har who's imprisoned me against my will, thorns or no thorns. The matter is non-negotiable. Naturally, I can probably do little to prevent you taking what you want by force, seeing as you have your gargoyle accomplice, but that's the only way you'll have me.'

Geburael did not react angrily, as Loki expected. 'You're annoyed now,' he said. 'I understand that. But you'll come to me eventually,

Loki. You won't be able to help yourself.'

Loki pulled a face to indicate his revulsion. 'You overestimate your charms.'

Geburael smiled. 'How like your hostling you are: Pellaz the Imperious. I know all about him. You should learn to be humble. One day, those words will make a fool of you.'

Loki decided it was pointless to argue. He thought he knew Geburael's heart: this lonely har, who was desperate for company and physical closeness. He had no sense of right or wrong, because he hadn't been taught it. In his simple, warped world, he had simply taken what he wanted and would now be confused because Loki wouldn't play the game. Pathetic really.

'I want my own tower,' Loki said.

Chapter Ten

Diablo could hardly refuse Loki's request, since it was clear that Loki wasn't going anywhere. Geburael complied because, as Loki had rightly deduced, he was now confused as how to win Loki's favour. He'd fondly believed that once Loki knew 'the truth,' as he saw it, he would share Geburael's viewpoint. Diablo had not warned him about the most likely consequences of Loki's abduction, and probably did not care. All Diablo cared about was having Loki in his power.

Loki chose a tower about a hundred yards away from Apanage. It was a narrow, elegant structure, missing only its summit, so that the top storey was open to the sky. Loki liked to sleep up there, in the slumber periods he designated as "night". Before sleep, he would gaze at the immense blackness, with its baleful, lightless sun. Somewhere out there, in a different reality, Cal was looking for him. Loki felt closer to Cal when he stared at the sky.

The name of the tower was Ninzini. Loki was surprised how easy it was to discover this title, almost as if the very stones were soaked in that single piece of information. On his first night there, he closed his eyes and wondered *What is the name of this place?* And almost immediately, the tower sang to him in his mind. It was all that was left of its former majesty. Loki often wondered about the race that had once lived here. Would there come a time when the earthly realm was like this, and all of human and harish history but a dim memory in the shattered stones of forgotten temples?

He had to admit that Thanatep did have its attractions. On the second "night" there, it occurred to him: *I am in another realm. This is a totally alien place. Few hara have experienced anything like this.* From then on, he viewed his new, hopefully temporary, home with greater respect. He felt sorry for Thannaril; he sensed it brooded mournfully for past ages. *Here I am,* he told it, *as much a victim of Fate as you are. I want you to know I care for you.*

Whether Ninzini, or any of the other towers, could understand this, he could not tell, but it made him feel better thinking it.

The entrance to Ninzini was about a third of the way up the tower; steps led to an arched entrance outside. Loki investigated all the levels of the tower, but every circular room was empty. Those who had once occupied them had left nothing behind, or perhaps time had dissolved all evidence of the vanished race.

Geburael and Diablo left Loki alone; Geburael no doubt in the hope that Loki only needed time to come around, and Diablo because he knew Loki could not escape. The only time Loki saw them was when they ate together, since Loki lacked the knowledge of how to procure and prepare food. During these times, they ate mostly in silence.

Loki did consider leaving Thannaril and wandering the world, but he felt that if he did that, it might be more difficult for Cal to find him. He thought it was safer and more sensible to stay put. The Thanax were also a hazard, although he rarely caught sight of them. They tended to avoid the city, although sometimes Loki heard them in the hills, singing strange, sad songs. They would make cries like birds or wolves. It seemed as if sometimes something spooked them, because a racket would start up that might last for what felt like nearly an hour, then all would be silent for a long time.

Thanatep was a bizarre yet serene realm. There was little weather to speak of; no rain, no storms. Light breezes lifted the dusty sand from the empty thoroughfares between the buildings and sometimes made music high in the air among the broken tower crowns, but the winds were rarely strong enough to make Loki feel cold. The mountains around the city were gaunt, jagged and dark. There were no tall trees in the landscape, but many stringy hardy shrubs. Lichens abounded, and occasionally delicate ferns sprouted between bricks. There were no rivers: the only natural water came from a few warm pools that sprang from beneath the ground. These were sulphurous, or tainted with a mineral that smelled similar to sulphur, but were not poisonous. Geburael told Loki to use these pools for bathing, since the water from the taps in the towers was precious, and sometimes it dried virtually to a trickle. Neither Geburael nor Diablo knew how the plumbing worked, or where the water came from, but presumed there were underground reservoirs that serviced the towers. Loki wondered what other parts of the world were like; at home, different countries had different climates and geography. Thanatep must be the same, and perhaps there were verdant fields somewhere, far away. But then, he told himself, how could any land be verdant beneath the cold, mean eye of that virtually lightless sun?

Loki had no clock other than his inner sense. He slept when he was tired and turned up at Apanage when he smelled the faint aromas of cooking. He measured days in meals and periods of rest. After being in Thannaril for what he assumed was a week, he said in private to Geburael, 'If I'm to tolerate this hell, at least make it more bearable.

You can travel the Otherlanes. Get food from home.'

Geburael was surprised by this request, but also clearly pleased, as he saw it as a concession. 'What do you want?'

'Salt,' Loki said. 'Salt would be good. Can't you bring other things, like fruit and vegetables?'

'I've never thought about it,' Geburael said.

'You should have done. Why make this exile worse than it is?'

'I'm not in exile; this is my home. The food here is nourishing. You're too spoiled.'

'Whatever. Will you get the stuff or not?'

'Maybe.'

But Geburael did comply with Loki's request. Diablo refused to use salt or any other condiment in cooking, but Loki simply added it to his own meals. It made the food more bearable. Geburael also brought fruit, which Loki devoured as if it was the sustenance of the dehara. He suggested Geburael should try it, but when he did Geburael found the taste too strong. Even an apple made his eyes water. He and Diablo were used to the bitter or bland flavours of Thanatep's flora and fauna. Sweet and salty tastes made Geburael feel nauseous.

Once, Loki visited Apanage when he was not expected. He knew that Geburael had gone into the Otherlanes, since Loki had asked him to bring back some cheese. Thoughts of the mouth-watering flavour of cheese drove Loki into an insane desire to taste it, so when he sensed the shiver in the air that indicated an Otherlanes portal opening, he went directly to Apanage to satisfy his craving. Such simple pleasures had become the focus of his existence.

The sight of what he found within the tower shocked him more than he would have believed. He saw Geburael and Diablo taking aruna in the middle of the floor of their living space. Loki's first thought was that it was like watching a clockwork toy that had gone mad. Their union was passionless, mechanical. As soume, Geburael's eyes were closed, his brow furrowed. He did not look as if he was in the throes of bliss. Loki's heart contracted. He felt that what he saw was a violation of an act that should be sacred. It was made all the more difficult for him, because it reminded him that he hadn't taken aruna since that first time with Geburael. His body craved it, but he'd managed to suppress his desires, relying upon satisfying his body's need himself. It wasn't enough, however, and Loki found it deeply disturbing to be slightly aroused by what he considered to be a grotesque sight.

Diablo sensed him standing at the threshold and raised his head.

'Wait,' he said. That was all.

Loki backed out, his heart beating too quickly.

Later, he hadn't the heart to go to Apanage for a meal, and eventually Geburael turned up with the cheese. Loki was loath to take it. He felt it was contaminated, having been in the same room as Diablo possessing Geburael, but then perhaps most of the food he'd eaten had been. 'Next time,' he said, avoiding Geburael's eyes, 'bring it straight to me. Don't leave it with him.'

Geburael considered. 'If you will give me what he does.'

'I can't,' Loki said. 'Even more so now. I can't. Not after him.'

Geburael sighed. 'You wouldn't anyway, but it was worth a try.'

When he left, Loki finally gave in to the grief that had condensed inside him. Would he never escape? Could Cal not hear his calls? He wept until he fell asleep exhausted.

After that, Loki resolved he'd have to find his own food and learn how to cook it. He would just have to take his chances with the Thanax, although he'd come to the conclusion they weren't as threatening as Geburael had implied. He'd had to argue with Diablo, who was extremely reluctant to give Loki any kind of weapon. Loki only got his own way when he swore he'd starve himself to death, and how would the Hashmallim feel about that? Diablo must have known Loki didn't really mean that, but eventually gave him a hunting knife, which he could use to cut plants also. 'Try to use this on me or Geb and I'll scar you for life,' Diablo said. 'You could lose an ear or a hand and the Hashmallim won't care.'

Loki said nothing, but took the knife. He had watched Diablo cook often enough to know the rudiments of how to prepare a meal, even down to gutting a small creature. He now went on foraging missions just beyond the towers, to hunt animals and to seek other means of sustenance. The first time he killed a small armoured reptile, he was physically sick, but steeled himself to cut it into pieces with the knife. He had to survive.

Loki had received little caste training, but found he was able to handle a plant or fungus and discern intuitively whether it was poisonous to his body or not. He had applied himself to flexing his skills, because there was little else to do in this world.

On one occasion, Loki ventured farther than he ever had before, beyond the shadows of the towers. He walked towards the hill where he and Geburael had first arrived in Thannaril. There seemed nothing to fear.

Once he'd scrambled to the top of the cliffs, there were several pathways that snaked off between the rocks. The landscape was quite beautiful. Mineral pools were surrounded by blooms of crystals and salts of different reddish hues. Insects with huge gauzy wings hovered over the waters. Loki squatted down to examine one of the pools, in case there were aquatic creatures within. One of the insects alighted on his shoulder and began to clean its triangular face with threadlike limbs. It weighed nothing at all. The surface of the pool was glassy, almost too perfect to be water. It looked hard. Loki reached out to touch it, but at that moment he saw in reflection that he was not alone. Quickly, he jumped to his feet and turned. The insect flew away from his shoulder, uttering a thin humming squeak. Behind him were three Thanax, perhaps the three he had seen on arriving in Thannaril. They had crept upon him in utter silence. Up close, they looked terrifying; like hara, but not – emaciated and feverish. They were so dark, and yet not black. It was as if they were hara-shaped holes in reality. At once, Loki surrounded himself with a protective aura of cold. He began to back away.

'Don't fear,' one of the Thanax said. He held out a skeletal hand.

Another glided forward. 'We are so cold, just that. So cold. Share your warmth with us.' He blinked his dead black eyes.

'Get back,' Loki said, without much conviction. He was astonished they could speak his language.

'The cold is hurtful,' said the first. 'You are good. I see that in you. Share your warmth with us.'

'No,' Loki said. 'I can't do that. It'll hurt me.'

The first Thanax sighed and his companions went to his side and pressed against him. They looked so forlorn, Loki experienced a pang of pity. 'What are you?' he asked. 'Where do you come from? You speak a language of Earth. You look sort of… harish. Are you har?'

The first Thanax disengaged himself from his companions. 'The others have never asked us that,' he said. 'They want to kill us, even though we are not strictly alive. But that is because they guard their warmth jealously. We are not thieves. We want only to be warm. Would you deny us that? We are the half-born, the unrealmed.'

'What do you mean?' Loki asked. 'Are you har or not?'

'We are history,' said the Thanax. 'When Wraeththu incept a human, a harish spirit is born. If the body dies, as it often does, the spirit has no home but here. We are the failed inceptions, and more. We are the murdered, the suicides and the great leaders who fell.'

'We are forever cold,' said another. 'We go into the paths to find warmth. We listen for the calls of magicians, and ride on the tails of invocations. We are those who hide amongst the cloaks of gods and elementals. But always we return here, for this is the warmest of all realms to us. In others, the cold is beyond bearing, and we freeze into pillars of stone.'

Loki's first thought at this information was: *Trust Diablo to find this place.* But his second was that of compassion. 'Can't you find other bodies, new souls to inhabit?'

'Inceptions are few now,' said the first Thanax.

'But hara are born, as harlings,' Loki said. 'Couldn't you find flesh through them?'

The Thanax regarded one another thoughtfully, then their apparent leader said, 'We don't know how. You have been courteous to us, so I'll tell you this: Some of us are very angry, and envious of those with warmth. You should avoid the envious.'

'This is the first time I've seen any of you since I first arrived,' Loki said. He paused. 'I wish I could help you, but I'm a prisoner here. I'm sure my hara could do something for you, but I don't think any of them know you exist. If I ever get home, I'll make sure they know.'

The Thanax inclined their heads to him, and it was in Loki's mind to offer them some warmth, then he thought better of it. Perhaps their apparent meekness merely hid their voracious need, and once he lowered his defences, they'd fall on him like locusts. 'Could you help me leave here?' he asked.

'No,' said the Thanax in unison.

Loki wasn't sure if that word implied "won't" or "can't". 'Then I can't help you,' he said. 'If you think of anything to help me, you know where I am.' He steeled himself to turn his back on the Thanax and walked away from them.

When Loki returned to Ninzini, he found Geburael waiting for him, in a curiously agitated state. 'I've heard something,' Geburael said, 'something very important.'

'What?' Loki asked, fearful that Geburael had spied on his encounter with the Thanax, which he had intended to keep secret.

'A cry,' Geburael said. 'It was a cry of our blood.'

Loki went cold, a dozen unwelcome images of death and injury flooding his mind. 'What do you mean? Who?'

'I thought it was you,' Geburael said.

Loki had never seen the har so discomposed. 'It wasn't,' he said. 'Was it Cal or Pellaz?'

Geburael shook his head. 'No, I could tell it wasn't. It was a har in distress. A young har. He called for help, and it felt like you. Loki...'

'What?'

'Do you have another brother?'

'Only Abrimel. Was it him?'

Again, Geburael shook his head. 'I'd know my father.' He rubbed his hands over his face. 'It has made me feel... very strange. I have *not* told Diablo.'

This disclosure changed things in Loki's mind. 'Sit down,' he said, indicating some of the cushions Geburael had brought for him. 'I'll heat water.' Loki had also been experimenting with hot drinks. He'd found a dry wizened fruit that when crushed in hot water, and mixed with sugar and nutmeg, tasted rather like spiced coffee. It smelled rancid, but the familiar ritual of drinking it made Loki feel more at home.

Geburael sat down. He sighed, and his whole body shuddered. 'The cry hit me like a flying fist,' he said. 'It shook me.'

Loki took some of his coffee figs, as he called them, and began crushing them with a pestle and mortar, another request that Geburael had fulfilled for him. He thought about what Geburael had said. 'Why didn't you tell Diablo?' he asked at last.

'I didn't want to.'

'Yet you've told me.'

'Yes. It had to be you. Loki... do you know about the stolen pearl?'

Loki knew very little, since his family and tutors had kept the information from him. From friends less sheltered than he, Loki had heard whispers about how his hura Rue had been attacked while he was with pearl. It was not exactly something a young har would read about in history books. 'Yes,' Loki said. 'Sort of.'

Geburael took a breath. 'Diablo took the pearl.'

Loki's first instinct was to hit Geburael, which quickly subsided before he could act on it. 'Diablo,' he said, deadpan.

Geburael nodded. 'He was meant to kill it, but didn't succeed. It was taken from him. It wasn't dead. I think... I think the cry I heard was *him*, your brother. I can't tell Diablo because it's his purpose to kill that harling. I can't let that happen; he is part of you. He's not Aralisian, because he doesn't know who he is. When I heard him, I felt empathy, as I did with you.'

'Where is he?'

'In the earthly realm, I could tell that much, but not precisely where. It was a place unknown to me. Loki, I couldn't do anything to harm him. It would be like harming you. I couldn't do that.' He put his hands over his face.

Loki bowed his head. He wasn't sure what to think, but one thing was radiantly clear: Geburael was in love with him. If it wasn't for that love, perhaps Diablo would have been told of the cry. 'You were right in telling me,' Loki said. 'We need to know who took the pearl from Diablo, and why, since they never returned it to Immanion. The har it held will be right around about the same age as us. Can you contact him?'

'The cry was brief,' Geburael said, lowering his hands, 'then it was silenced, like a blanket was thrown over it. Still, it entered my body through the heart. I can't go back to Apanage yet. Diablo will sense it in me.'

'Stay here,' Loki said. 'Let him think we're together in the way you desire. He'd believe that story.'

'He'll come looking for me.'

'Stay here,' Loki said. 'I meant it. Sleep beside me if you need that long away from him. If he turns up, we can act. He won't disturb us, will he? Is he jealous?'

'No. He thinks I should've forced you. He's not jealous.'

'Good.' Loki ran the bitter smelling fragments of the coffee figs through his fingers. 'Geb… thank you for not forcing me.'

Geburael shrugged.

'Anyway…' Loki tried to adopt a carefree tone. 'Try my Thannaril coffee. You might like it.'

Geburael wrinkled his nose a little. 'OK,' he said.

As Loki continued his preparations, it occurred to him that Geburael could simply disappear into the Otherlanes for a while. Diablo wouldn't question that either, and it would be easy to make up some story about how he'd gone to get Loki something from the earthly realm. Yet neither Loki nor Geburael had suggested it, and even now, something held Loki's tongue. He wasn't sure what exactly. The thought of lying beside Geburael made him feel angry and pleased at the same time, as if he wanted to torment Geburael. Did he desire power over another so much? Was it a cruel kind of revenge? He hoped Diablo's rotten presence hadn't corrupted him somehow.

When Geburael tasted Loki's drink, he said, 'It's not too bad.'

'I left out the sugar and the spice,' Loki said.

'Considerate of you.'

Loki rolled his eyes. 'Yeah.'

At that moment, Geburael tensed. He put down his cup. 'He's coming. He's sniffing me out. He knows something's happened. He's climbing the stairs.'

Loki said nothing, but pulled Geburael towards him, wrapping him in his arms.

There is no way to pretend sharing breath, it just happens. In the inky swirls of Geburael's soul, Loki received impressions of their time together in Freygard. He remembered, and was grateful for the fact he hadn't known about Diablo at that time. Had feybraiha changed him also?

Diablo came into the room, and Loki tried to immerse himself in Geburael's breath. *Think only of me, Geb. Remember us. Keep him out.*

Diablo laughed, in a sly humourless way, but at least he left the tower. In the heightened perception of breath-sharing, Loki heard Diablo's creepy footsteps padding away.

Loki drew away from Geburael, wiped his mouth. 'He's gone. We convinced him. He fell for it.'

Geburael smiled wistfully. 'So did I,' he said.

Chapter Eleven

As soon as the Aralisians returned from Freygard, the Chancellor of the Hegemony, Tharmifex Calvel, requested Pellaz to meet with him in the private offices of the Hegalion. When Pellaz arrived there, he found that the ubiquitous Velaxis Shiraz was also present, as well as Eyra Fiumara, who looked harried, as if Tharmifex had recently upbraided him. Eyra was dressed in his official Arch Listener robes, which suggested he'd recently come from a meeting with his staff. Pellaz had barely slept for the past few days. He was full of self-recrimination, confusion and a certain amount of numbness, which was the worst thing of all. Perhaps he was destined never to have heirs: they would all be taken from him. Perhaps he should have acknowledged Galdra as Loki's father all along, and accepted the consequences; now he was being punished for it. Perhaps Loki was dead. Innocent, wide-eyed Loki; a charmed harling. They'd kept him in ignorance, when knowledge might have given him some protection.

'Pellaz,' Tharmifex said shortly, as the Tigron closed the door behind him. Cal had wanted to come too, but Tharmifex's request had been very clear. This did not bode well.

'Matters become serious,' announced Tharmifex, an imposing figure behind his wide dark-wood desk. His deep brown hair was plaited severely and lay in a gleaming rope over his shoulder. His angular face was expressionless. He wore splendid robes of dark purple velvet embroidered with scarlet metallic thread.

Pellaz caught Eyra's eye, sensed an ally, and sat down opposite the Chancellor in the empty seat that had been waiting for him. 'Before you say what it is you wish to say, there's something you should know,' Pellaz said.

Tharmifex gestured abruptly with both hands. 'Speak.'

'Loki was not conceived here in Immanion. It happened at Fulminir.'

Tharmifex was silent for a moment, while Eyra shifted uncomfortably on his seat and paid more attention than was necessary to arranging the folds of his robe. Velaxis stared at his hands, his face expressionless.

'Galdra har Freyhella is Loki's father,' Pellaz said. 'For obvious reasons, I didn't want this fact known. Now, I think the Hegemony should be aware of it. Naturally, I expect this revelation to be treated in the strictest confidence.'

Pellaz could feel Eyra's embarrassment; the Listener wished he was anywhere but in that office. Velaxis, as usual, was unreadable, though Pellaz couldn't help thinking the Hegemony Clerk felt smug. Tharmifex, however, smouldered with suppressed annoyance.

'You created a pearl with the Freyhellan,' Tharmifex said, deadpan. 'Clearly, you were considering the suggestions that had been put to you concerning Galdra. You didn't expect Cal to return to you.'

'That is not the case,' Pellaz said. 'The pearl was an accident.'

'Hara don't have accidental conceptions,' Tharmifex continued. His eyes looked completely black.

'Well, clearly they do. When involved in the kind of work that Galdra and I undertook, it's a risk. I was exhausted. I lost control. That's all there is to it.'

'And now Loki has disappeared.' Tharmifex tapped some papers before him with one hand. 'I read the report and find it perplexing. Why was no guard placed in Loki's chamber?'

'There were guards all around the house,' Pellaz said.

'And yet everyhar was aware of the phenomenon in Freygard which they referred to as…' Tharmifex flicked through the papers, '…the "spirit window". Did it not occur to any of you that entities might emerge from that portal who could enter premises undetected? We were all at Fulminir, Pell. We all saw the strangest things. We know Cal can traverse the Otherlanes without a *sedu,* and that hara under Ponclast's command possessed a similar ability. Frankly, I'm aghast security was so lax. Have we learned nothing from what happened to Rue seven years ago when his pearl was taken?'

'The *sedim* pronounced the portal as safe,' Pellaz said.

Tharmifex shook his head, expressed a sigh. 'And yet there was a young har from Freygard in our infirmary who patently discovered that was not the case. The Freyhellan took a long time to heal, Pell. Our healers could find no cause for his malady.'

'I accept security was lax,' Pellaz said, 'and that we should now apply ourselves, through every means possible, to discovering what happened. I have lost a son, Tharmifex. Another son. You can be sure I intend to put every resource behind this investigation.' Pellaz was far from pleased Tharmifex was speaking to him in this manner in front of Velaxis. It was inappropriate. Perhaps Tharmifex deliberately wanted to discomfort the Tigron. Pellaz managed to catch Eyra's eye again, briefly. The Listener blinked and shook his head, almost imperceptibly. He wasn't happy about being present at this meeting either.

'You will, of course, attempt to contact the Kamagrian, Lileem Sarestes,' Tharmifex said.

'I...' Pellaz frowned. 'Why would I do that? Cal will communicate with Thiede. That should be enough.'

'Lileem took Ponclast into her custody,' Tharmifex said. 'I think at the very least he should be interrogated about this matter. Many of his hara escaped Fulminir, including two of his sons: Diablo, and the harling of Abrimel. We still have enemies out there somewhere. Part of me wonders whether, in fact, Ponclast should be brought back to this realm, kept in captivity here.'

'That's impossible,' Pellaz said. 'You can't just go in and out of the realm Lileem discovered. She's different to hara. She possesses abilities none of us have. Ponclast is like us. He's quite safe there.'

Tharmifex was clearly in no mood to be deterred. 'But perhaps we're dealing with creatures who are more like Lileem than like us. I personally don't relish the prospect of somehar, or something, freeing Ponclast from his prison. And that is something we should consider deeply.'

Velaxis cleared his throat and turned to Pellaz. 'I think perhaps you should try to speak to Lileem, Tiahaar,' he said.

'Do you? And of what use is your advice to me?' Pellaz glared at Tharmifex. 'I'll be honest, Tiahaar. I object to the fact that your *clerk* is present at this meeting, when my consort is forbidden to attend.'

'Object all you wish,' Tharmifex said mildly. 'Tiahaar Shiraz is of more use to you than you know. I trust his judgment and so should you. I will speak to Calanthe separately. You must appreciate that my prime concern is Gelaming security. And I am *very* concerned. If an enemy has taken Loki, we can only conjecture about what they want from him. Hostage, ransom, or perhaps a source of information. Of all the Aralisians, he is the most vulnerable, because of his age.'

'I know that.'

'Eyra, your Listeners need better training,' Tharmifex said.

Eyra raised his hands. 'We'll do whatever we can to improve our service.'

Tharmifex nodded. 'Good. Pellaz, I would like you to speak to Lileem about this matter. I'll ask Cal to do the same with Thiede. If we have these *powers* floating about in etheric realms, it's about time we made proper use of them, otherwise they're pointless. The Kamagrian claims that all knowledge resides in this library she discovered. Well, you should encourage her to do rather more research. I will, of course, also contact the Kamagrian leader, Opalexian.'

'Tharmifex,' Pellaz said, his patience fraying, 'that would not be helpful. If Opalexian knew anything about this, she would have contacted me. None of our psychics have picked up anything, not even Snake and Cobweb, who I consider to be more in tune with our needs than Opalexian. We should deal with this ourselves, but if you want me to communicate with Lileem, I'll try. However, I can't guarantee success. The conditions required for that communication are... difficult.'

'You have Cal, your soul mate,' Tharmifex said. 'Take that superior kind of aruna with him. I'd have thought it would be very easy for you.'

'For some reason, you are angry with me,' Pellaz said, 'which I don't think helps this situation. I'll do what I can. Please remember that when I was in contact with Lileem before, it was under certain circumstances. I've had no contact since.'

'Then try,' Tharmifex said. 'If you fail, we must communicate with Opalexian. We know that when hara and parazha come together, they can create portals. Perhaps the time approaches for that to be explored.'

'Opalexian would never agree to that.'

'We all share this world,' Tharmifex said. 'It's about time Opalexian woke up to that fact, and Thiede and Lileem accepted that they've chosen, in whatever obscure way, to remain part of our reality. Yes, I *am* angry. I'm angry with all the whimsical nonsense I see around me. I see fog, clouds, puzzles, half-answered questions and mysteries. I want facts, action and sense. You should want them too. Contact Lileem, and find out what she thinks is happening. I believe it's time for her to return to us. If she's learned anything, both Kamagrian and Wraeththu need her knowledge. She can't hide away in her studies any longer.'

'I think perhaps you place too much importance on...' Pellaz began.

Tharmifex raised an impatient hand. 'I know what's important and what isn't. We can't simply accept the things we experienced seven years ago. We have to question, seek answers, and arm ourselves with information. If we merely dither along the way we've been doing, we could regret it. There's nothing else to say. You know what you have to do.'

Pellaz stood up and bowed. 'I'll take that as dismissal, then, Tiahaar.'

'Do!' Tharmifex turned to Eyra. 'And you can go too. Have all of your Listeners working constantly. I don't want anything occurring in the realms, to which we do have access, without knowing about it.'

Once they had escaped Tharmifex's presence, Eyra rubbed his hands over his face. 'I've never seen Thar that angry. He's like a different har.'

'He's worried,' Pellaz said, 'and most of what he said is right. I'll do as he suggests. It'd help me if you could contact Galhea, bring the Freyhellans into the picture. I'd do it myself but...' Pellaz sighed. 'I need to devote myself fully to the Lileem issue.'

Eyra clasped Pell's right shoulder. 'No, don't worry. I'll do that for you, of course.'

Pellaz had travelled to his own inner space many times with Galdra, but now he wondered if he could remember how he'd done it. He had memories of the experience, but the concentrated feeling had gone. Also, at the time, Lileem had been trying to make contact with him too. The intense energy surrounding the whole Fulminir episode had meant that even inexperienced hara, like Tyson and Moon Parasiel, had been able to emulate what Pellaz and Galdra had done. But the energy had dissipated, and circumstances were now very different.

That evening, Pellaz asked Cal to come to his private apartments and there told him what they had to do. Cal had undergone his own interview with Tharmifex, which surprisingly had not been as caustic as the one Pellaz had endured. 'Tharmifex is right,' Cal said. 'We have to do everything we can to find Loki, and discover the reasons behind his abduction.'

'Have you communicated with Thiede?'

Cal frowned. 'No. The channels to his realm are closed. I can only presume he feels under threat himself. It's rare I can't reach him.'

'I think Tharmifex feels something similar to Fulminir is about to happen,' Pellaz said, 'but I can't feel that way. The fact is, I don't know *what* is happening. We have one strange phenomenon and the abduction of a young har.'

'Hmm,' Cal murmured. 'Another abduction. It might be that the delightful creature who took Rue's pearl is responsible for Loki's disappearance too. Pell...'

'What?'

'There is another Aralisian heir, you know that.'

'Abrimel is safely in confinement. I'm sure we'd have heard if he'd disappeared too.'

'I didn't mean him. I meant... the harling he had with Ponclast.'

'Yes, Tharmifex mentioned him too.'

'Ponclast's son Diablo fled with the harling. Abrimel told us that under interrogation. Diablo took Rue's pearl. It seems pretty clear to me he's involved in Loki's disappearance.'

Pellaz raised his arms in exasperation. 'And what does Diablo want? His hostling reinstated? The downfall of the Gelaming? He has no army, Cal. He's an addled freak. If he's responsible, then you and Thiede should be able to track him down.'

'I think the guard should be doubled on Abrimel,' Cal said. 'I think Eyra should put a Listener near him.'

'That makes sense. I'll see to it at once.'

Cal sighed. 'Diablo might be an addled freak, but he might also still be in contact with Ponclast's erstwhile allies. They could simply be waiting for another chance.'

Pellaz felt a cold wave course through his body. 'Cal, Rue's pearl… where is the harling? Thiede hid him away, but where? He needs protection too.'

'I can't tell you because I don't know. Thiede didn't tell me. It was best that way.'

'And now you can't contact Thiede.'

'That harling was… well, I know Thiede was right to tell us to forget about him. That's his greatest protection.'

'I wish I could be as sure about that as you are.'

Cal took Pellaz in his arms. 'I know. Go and send a message to Eyra, then come back to me. Let's go to the realm of dreams together. We'll solve this thing, I know we will.'

But intentions and certainty are sometimes not enough. A har can conjure up the most intense feelings; he can soar through the ethers on silver wings in the arms of aruna's sweet waves. He can take it to its furthest point, when the cauldron of creation opens and potential for life comes flooding through. What he finds beyond that portal can barely be described in words. Pellaz achieved those things. He went into himself, to the dark pulsing core of his own being. He could prevent conception as easily as he ever could, but there was no way he could project himself beyond that space, as he'd once been able to do. There was no Lileem, and no way to call her.

Pellaz wanted to keep trying, at least for several days, but a message came from Tharmifex's office the very next day, demanding a report. It arrived while the Tigrons were still taking breakfast together in Pell's apartment. Outside, the day was somewhat overcast and drizzly; an uncommon phenomenon in Immanion.

'He'll want to contact Opalexian,' Pellaz said glumly to Cal. 'She'll be furious. You know what she's like.'

'Mmm,' Cal murmured, 'don't I just.'

'She won't do anything to help.'

'No.'

'We'll just have to continue ourselves and let Thar do what he wants.'

'Perhaps.'

'What does that mean?'

Cal leaned back in his chair. 'It might not be your fault... I mean, maybe I'm just the wrong har for the job.'

'Whatever you're thinking, don't voice it,' Pellaz said darkly.

Cal ducked his head, stuck out his lower lip. 'Why not? What's your problem if I don't have one? Loki is Galdra's son too. Perhaps you and he should be the ones to penetrate Lileem's realm, or rather you might be the combination that would work. I've no great love for the Freyhellan, you know that, but I have wondered recently - since spending some time with him - whether my absence during the Fulminir crisis was somehow preordained. You two did wondrous things together, even *I* can see that. Perhaps it wouldn't have happened if...'

Pellaz didn't want to hear this, not least because part of him agreed with it. His feelings for Galdra were too complicated. 'Cal, shut up. I can't do that. It's too prickly an area. Galdra is in love with me. He'll read all sorts of things into it if I offered that kind of invitation. I couldn't bear it.'

Cal laughed. 'Now, taking aruna with a har who hates you: I can understand the "no" factor in that, but...'

'*No,* it is. Leave it.'

'You shouldn't feel guilty, Pell. Remember my relationship with Terzian. We're all grown up now. You don't owe me anything.'

Pellaz was silent, only too aware how accurate Cal's aim had been with those remarks.

'I want Loki back,' Cal said. 'I'd do anything to achieve that. Anything. He's not my biological son, but he's the child of my heart. I think I care more for him than anyhar. Call Galdra to Immanion, Pell. Do it.' He paused. 'Please.'

Cal was not the only har in Immanion who'd had that idea. Pellaz went again to Tharmifex's office, once more finding Velaxis in attendance. He reported the bare facts: no success. He waited for Tharmifex to start talking about Opalexian, and was therefore unprepared for the Hegemony Chancellor's next remark. 'You could, of course, attempt to repeat the procedure with Galdra har Freyhella.'

'Politically, that might be unwise,' Pellaz said.

'Perhaps, but I think the ends would justify the means in this case, don't you?'

'Cal thinks Diablo, Ponclast's son, is responsible for the abduction.'

Tharmifex nodded abruptly. 'I know. Eyra told me of your

communication last night. Security has been increased around Abrimel's accommodation.' He paused. 'Well, shall I send a message to Freygard or will you?'

Pellaz glanced at Velaxis, furious he was present. The Hegemony clerk was staring at his hands, which were folded in his lap; a picture of polite decorum. The sight made Pellaz grit his teeth. 'Cal has expressed a similar suggestion,' Pellaz said. 'He believes we should do whatever we can to help Loki. I'm not happy with this, but very well. If it requires Grissecon with the Freyhellan, then I'll do it. I've done it before, so it's not beyond me to do it again.'

'Grissecon?' Velaxis looked up and spoke for the first time. He was frowning. 'You don't need to do that.'

'Your puppy is barking,' Pellaz said to Tharmifex.

'Do you have something to say, Velaxis?' Tharmifex asked.

'Just that this is not a matter of Grissecon. The Tigron and the Freyhellan should simply do what they did before, and that was not part of a public ritual.'

'I agree,' Tharmifex said.

Pellaz felt sick. He thought he could just about cope with a formal, unemotional form of aruna with Galdra, but anything private would be excruciating. He dreaded what Galdra might say, and also how his own body might react in the heat of the moment. Then he'd have to dread what he himself might say. Perhaps Cal could be part of it. 'This must be discussed,' he managed to say. 'You send Galdra the message and ask him to come here. Don't explain the purpose of the meeting. I'd prefer that to be revealed once he's here. Simply say we require his help in a procedure to locate Loki.'

Tharmifex nodded. 'Of course.' He paused. 'Lileem might be our only strong ally in any unpleasantness to come. I heard Thiede is not communicating at the moment, either.'

'Yes. Cal fears that Thiede is under threat.' Pellaz looked Tharmifex in the eye. 'Will you still send word to Opalexian?'

'No. For now, I'll keep her out of it. I'll send a message to one of our Listeners in Freygard at once. If the response is favourable, and I know it will be, Velaxis will go there directly with *sedu* transport for Galdra. He will be here by later today.'

'No time to catch my breath, then,' Pellaz said lightly.

Tharmifex smiled, a little grimly. 'Time to put away old weapons, perhaps,' he said. 'Lay down your arms, Pell. Galdra didn't take Cal's place, despite the wishes of some who'd have liked to see him at your side. Don't blame him for the aspirations of others. We both know he had no desire for the throne of Immanion. There was only one desire he had.'

'Thank you for that insight,' Pellaz said dryly. 'If you need me presently, I'll be out with Peridot. I won't go beyond easy communication distance.'

Peridot carried Pellaz out into the hills behind the city. Here, the soft rain hissed down like mist. Pellaz asked Peridot to halt at a high vantage point and from there he watched the sea. He remembered the glorious day when he'd ridden down to the docks to see the Freyhellan fleet arrive for the first time in Immanion. Today, the sea was sullen and heaving. The sound of waves crashing against the rocks was audible even from here.

Peridot, must I do this thing? Speak to me. Where is Loki? Help me now.

Peridot tossed his head. *Calanthe is right. The har Diablo is involved, but all is not clear to us, not clear at all. Loki is alive, but he walks towards a very strange light. Its radiance is alluring to him. Sweet child, you must do as your heart dictates, even though you bar the door firmly upon its insistent demands. Didn't I once tell you that you had much to learn from the brother to the wolf and the hare? Don't be afraid of your heart, Pellaz. There are many fires at which you can warm your cold flesh.*

Some fires burn too hot, Peridot. I'm afraid of what I feel in the presence of Galdra har Freyhella. He is not my Cal. I don't want Galdra to become too alluring a light. I don't trust myself. How can that be?

Pellaz could feel the *sedu's* warm laughter rather than hear it. *You ask me, a creature beyond all hara and humans, that? What makes you think a* sedu *knows how to love?*

Angels know how to love, Peridot. I have felt it. I felt it at Fulminir when your brothers fell around you.

I know you intimately, beloved, as you apparently know me! All I can tell you is to follow your heart. Ultimately, such truth cannot lead to pain. What you and Cal enjoy was forged in fire and blood; it cannot be broken by any living thing. But perhaps you must be more generous of yourself.

That's it. Perhaps I can't be that generous. I resent the fact that Galdra will be overjoyed if he knew the way I felt. I don't understand myself. His adoration irritates me, even as I sometimes yearn for those days we spent together.

That is your dilemma to solve. Galdra will help you connect with the Kamagrian, Lileem. Tharmifex Calvel is right about her too. She cannot hide away forever.

And what is the position of the sedim *in all this? Are we to face another war? What do you know?*

Our kings are alert; that is all I can say. If enemies move, they do so covertly. I stand by my words in Freygard: the portal there is harmless.

The Hegemony doesn't agree about that.

Their opinion is irrelevant. I'm telling you, *and that's all that's important.*

Pellaz reached down and ran his hand down the *sedu's* broad neck. 'We talk well together now, don't we? One day, perhaps, I'll be able to endure your true form. That would please me.'

It would please me too, but I fear you'll have to travel beyond this life for us to experience such intimacy.

As Tharmifex had predicted, Galdra appeared to leap at the chance of coming to Immanion. Pellaz was not cheered by this: for years, there had been utter silence between the Gelaming and the Freyhellans. Pellaz had had the impression that Galdra would rather have eaten his own tongue than set foot in Almagabra again.

It was arranged that Pellaz and Cal would meet with Tharmifex and Galdra at Tharmifex's home in the Thandrello area of Immanion. Pellaz requested specifically that Velaxis should not be there. Even though he had no liking for Velaxis, he didn't distrust him particularly. What annoyed Pellaz was that Velaxis seemed to be everywhere at once. He had a finger in every Gelaming pie, and probably others besides. He was the archetypal civil servant, perhaps representative of the true power behind thrones. But the matter of Galdra was a personal one; Velaxis had no place in it. Tharmifex was only tolerated as an arbitrator.

Cal and Pellaz arrived half an hour or so before Galdra. They sat in the garden with Tharmifex and Ryander, his unobtrusive and gracious chesnari. The sky had cleared and the air was fresh and crisp, smelling of salt. Seagulls called raucously, and bullied the songbirds who had come to taste the scraps left out for them by Tharmifex's househara.

A har came out of the house and murmured something to his employer. Tharmifex nodded and stood up. 'The party from Freygard has arrived.'

'Party?' Pellaz said frostily.

'Three hara; Galdra and an escort.' Tharmifex turned to Ryander. 'Perhaps you could take Galdra's hara to the kitchen area for refreshments.'

Ryander inclined his head and also got to his feet.

Tharmifex gestured at Pellaz and Cal. 'Please go to the meeting room. I'll bring Galdra there.'

The Chancellor's meeting room was of modest size, space enough for up to ten hara to sit comfortable around a large table. It was constructed of glass, attached to a side of the house that overlooked Tharmifex's tiered water gardens. Vines grew over the roof so that the light was green. Sitting there, Pellaz was reminded of the roofed tomb in Freygard. He remembered Galdra jumping down from the niche, his bright hair swinging.

Cal took one of Pell's hands in his own. 'Breathe,' he advised, grinning.

Tharmifex ushered Galdra into the room. 'Please, take a seat, Tiahaar.'

Galdra bowed to the Tigrons, directing his attention to Cal first.

Cal raised a hand. 'Hello, Galdra. Thank you for coming.'

Galdra sat down. 'No need to thank me. You have news about Loki?'

'No,' Cal said.

Pellaz was grateful that Cal appeared to have assumed control. He was almost incapable of speech himself. Tharmifex too seemed content to let Cal do the talking. He sat down next to Galdra and folded his hands on the table.

Galdra frowned. 'Then why am I here?'

'After discussion,' Cal began, 'the Hegemony has concluded that it's essential communication is re-established with Lileem Sarestes. We have already made attempts to do that, without success. We believe that only you and Pellaz can create the specific conditions necessary for such communication. Would you be agreeable to participating in an experiment to do this?'

Galdra did not attempt to hide his surprise, or his consternation. He allowed himself one brief glance at Pellaz, laughed, put a hand over his mouth, then stared at the table.

'Well?' Cal asked. 'What are your thoughts on this?'

'This is a shock,' Galdra said. 'The last thing I expected to hear.'

'I understand that,' Cal said. 'We wouldn't be asking you if we didn't think it was essential.'

Pellaz noticed that now Galdra's gaze did not leave Cal's face. Pellaz might as well not have been present.

'I don't know,' Galdra said. 'I confess I find it difficult to discuss this with you, Tiahaar.'

'I understand that too. Perhaps we should be speaking alone, but please be assured that everyhar present has only Loki's interests at heart. I'm prepared to do anything to find him. I trust you feel the same.'

Galdra nodded. 'Of course. I'll do what it takes, although I must admit I'm sceptical this will work.' Now, he glanced at Pellaz. 'Circumstances are very different to those surrounding the events at Fulminir.'

Pellaz addressed Tharmifex. 'When do you suggest we should make the attempt?'

Tharmifex appeared surprised he'd been asked that question. 'When you feel ready,' he said. 'That's hardly up to me.'

'We must talk, Pellaz,' Galdra said. 'This isn't something we can just go away and do. We need to discuss the matter.'

Pellaz and Galdra went out into the garden and walked around its perimeter. Silence hung heavily between them, but at first it appeared Galdra was content to remain quiet until Pellaz felt ready to speak. As they reached the lawn that looked out over the ocean, a line of ships could be seen, sailing into dock. Here, Galdra paused. 'Takes me back,' he said, staring out to sea. 'It seems centuries ago I first came here.'

Pellaz nodded. 'Mmm.'

There was another short silence, then Galdra asked abruptly, 'Whose idea was this?'

Pellaz didn't hesitate. 'Cal's.'

'You could have refused.'

'Unfortunately, I couldn't. Cal's probably right.'

Galdra shook his head. 'He continually astounds me. I would never have expected him to behave like this.'

'He is Tigron,' Pellaz said. 'Don't be astounded. Put aside your prejudices.'

'I think you'll have more difficulty doing that than me,' Galdra said. 'What did I ever do to you that was so bad? I went into that final Grissecon virtually as your chesnari, and woke from it to find I was an outcast. Is there something I've forgotten? Or was it simply that once Cal returned to you, I was an embarrassment to be discarded?'

'The reason we have not talked for so long is because I never wanted to have this conversation,' Pellaz said.

'I deserve an explanation,' Galdra said. 'You owe me that much, surely.'

Pellaz turned away and began to walk once more along the edge of the lawn. With one hand, he brushed the heads of the flowers that grew in the border beyond the grass. Galdra followed him. 'We... we should not have become so close,' Pellaz said. 'I allowed it to happen and I wish I hadn't. But you were a force, Galdra, a very strong force. You were determined to get your own way, and you got it. Now, you must live with the consequences. I'm not totally to blame. I did try to tell you once.'

Galdra pulled a sprig from a rosemary tree, twirled it beneath his nose. 'You tried to tell me many things. You once implied that you were ready to let me take Cal's place. If I recall correctly, it was me who stopped that discussion. You did feel the same as I did, Pell. I think you hate yourself for it. You have very strange concepts of loyalty and betrayal. I expect it's some leftover of once being human.' He crumpled up the fragrant leaves and threw them away.

Pellaz laughed bitterly. 'How long you've waited to say these things. You must have rehearsed them many times in your head.'

'Too many times to count,' Galdra said. 'I can't go through the whole script; it would take too long, which is a shame because there are some choice lines in it.'

'And now you have your moment. Come on, give me the best line.'

Galdra put his head to one side. 'Ah, a breakthrough. You're smiling. Smiles are not your best expressions. You are most at ease with sneers of withering contempt.'

'And yet you adore me. How touching.'

Galdra's expression became sober. 'Pell, there's something I want to say and it is this: you won't break apart if you let go. You know what I mean. The love you and Cal have for one another is too strong. It's safe. I've always known that. It seems strange to me that you don't.'

Pellaz sat down on the grass, while Galdra remained standing. 'I know it,' Pellaz said. 'I think you might be right – it's something to do with a tiny flame of humanity inside me. I can never be totally Wraeththu like you. There are boundaries inside me you don't have, which is why you can't understand me. As a righteous and arrogant newly-incepted har, I thought I knew it all. I thought it would be simple to give of myself and to take, beyond the restrictions of petty jealousies and fears. Perhaps we were all idealistic like that, and our young philosophers infected us with the idea that we were different from how we'd been. But we weren't different enough. We had yet to learn that only our sons could be truly free.' He rubbed his hands over his face. 'Sons... Only the truly doomed souls are condemned to be born into *my* family. It seems I'm forever losing them, in one way or another.'

'We'll get Loki back,' Galdra said, hunkering down beside Pellaz. 'I feel that we will.'

Pellaz nodded and for a while there was again silence between them; strangely, an easy silence. Then Pellaz said, 'Galdra...'

'What?'

'Respect me, don't swamp me.'

'What do you mean?'

'I think you know. If you're tempted to exact some kind of revenge, please don't. I'll do this with you, but it has to be for Loki, not for you.

Do you understand?'

'You mean you don't want me to enjoy it? That might be difficult, for both of us. It doesn't work that way. You know it.'

'I didn't mean that. Just don't... *gloat*.'

Galdra expelled a short burst of laughter, but he didn't sound amused. 'Thanks!'

'You were always good at gloating. Whenever I opened up to you, you puffed up with delight and smugness.'

'Pellaz!'

'Well, it's true. The amount of gloating that would have gone on, should we have remained close after Cal came back, would have been unendurable.'

'Seems like you've had your script waiting too,' Galdra said dryly.

'You got to me when I was vulnerable. We were actually quite vile to one another. Pureborn, you're not as emotionally adjusted as you like to believe.'

'OK, I'll accept that. Can we agree on the fact that physically we find each other irresistible?'

'*Found*,' Pellaz said. 'If there's new ground, it starts here, not in the past.'

Chapter Twelve

Soft golden light spilled out over the white buildings of Immanion, into the dark blue night. In his apartment in Phaonica, Pellaz prepared himself as if for battle. Caeru came to the Tigron's rooms, quietly sympathetic, talking about inconsequential things, but Cal kept away.

Pellaz sat before his mirror, which seemed dark and foggy. It was as if his image was fading away. 'I should move rooms,' he said abruptly.

'What?' Caeru laid a hand on top of Pell's head. 'Why?'

'I've sat here too many times in my life, looking at my own face, before having to do something unpleasant. This place reeks of my own stupidity and mistakes.'

Caeru laughed. 'Pell, what you're about to do… *unpleasant*?'

'Cal should be here. He should be part of it. He says he's fine with all this, but he isn't here.' Pellaz sighed. 'Nothing unusual about that, I suppose! He's never here when I need him.'

'He isn't here for your sake,' Caeru said carefully.

'You've discussed it with him?'

'Er…' Caeru appeared shifty. 'Yes.'

Pellaz expelled a bitter laugh. 'You must feel this is all quite ironic. The way things end up. One of the times I sat here cursing was the day I bonded in blood with you.'

Caeru withdrew his hand, and his voice became cold. 'Is there any har in this world, with whom you've been intimate, who you haven't resented? Have you ever taken aruna, with a har other than Cal, without regret? Sometimes, I think you're more messed up than Cal ever was.'

'Rue…'

'And you can snipe at me all you like. The bullets bounce off now, trust me.' He went to the wardrobe and pulled out some of Pell's clothes. 'Here, wear these. Black for mourning.'

Pellaz stood up, took the garments offered to him. 'You're right; I *am* a mess. If I was still human, I'd be more than halfway through my life, and yet I feel like an addled teenager. Black. Yes. Most appropriate.' He took off his robe and began to dress.

Caeru folded his arms. 'You know, half your problem has always been pride. It won't make you any less of a har if you give in for once.'

'It was your fault I ended up with Galdra in the first place.'

'Probably, and it was the best thing for you. I have no regrets about that. For Aru's sake, Pell, get a grip of yourself. It's becoming tedious. Add self-pity to pride. Not a palatable dish.' Caeru put his hands on Pell's shoulders and leaned forward to kiss his brow. 'Come on, get ready and go. It's not that much of a trial.'

'It *is*, Rue,' Pellaz said. 'Even if I was going to attempt this with you or Cal, it'd be a trial. I don't think I can do what everyhar wants of me. Not anymore. It's nohar's fault. It's just what is.'

'You can only try,' Caeru said. 'I'll be with you in spirit, as will Cal. We're strong together now. We'll help you.'

Pellaz pulled Caeru into his embrace. 'Hold me for just a minute. I feel like I'm going to the scaffold.'

It had been agreed that Pellaz would meet with Galdra in the neutral territory of Tharmifex's house. Tharmifex and his chesnari vacated the premises and gave their staff the night off. When Pellaz arrived, the house felt strange, too empty. Dim lamps in the entrance hall did little to dispel the heavy breath of night, and the scent of flowers from the garden outside was overpowering, as if the blooms themselves were aroused by what was to come. There was no moon in the sky, which seemed appropriate – times such as this should occur in the dark of the moon – but the stars were achingly bright.

Galdra was sitting in the dark in the main salon, drinking costly wine that the Calvels had left out for the occasion. His hair was luminous in the starlight. Pellaz came silently into the room and stood at the threshold for a few moments. Galdra was so wrapped up in his thoughts, he didn't realise somehar was watching him. He looked young and unsure of himself; an image he'd never betray consciously. The sight touched Pellaz, made him remember how much older he was than the har here waiting for him. This was a trial for Galdra too. He just didn't want to admit it. Pellaz moved the door a little to make a noise and Galdra's mask of confidence slipped back over his face. He straightened his spine, as if bracing himself for conflict.

'We should be honoured,' Pellaz said lightly. He walked across the room. 'Tharmifex is notoriously mean with his wines. He goes to great trouble to import them from every obscure corner of the world and consumes them greedily in private. I doubt his chesnari even gets a taste.'

'Well, he did leave only one bottle.' Galdra risked a smile.

'Fortunately, I know the cellar is never locked,' Pellaz said. 'And I dare him to complain if we take more.'

'Will it help if you're drunk?'

Pellaz sat down on the couch two feet away from Galdra and poured himself a drink. 'It always helps if I'm drunk!' He took a sip and was taken back instantly to the time in Imbrilim, when he'd met secretly with Galdra at one of the inns. They'd drunk red wine then, too. 'This taste reminds me of you.'

Galdra was silent.

Pellaz scraped a hand through his hair. 'There's no guarantee this will work. I wonder whether Lileem is lost to us. That realm she inhabits, it's a dangerous place. It guards its inhabitants jealously.'

'We visited the dehara, Pell,' Galdra said. 'What we saw... experienced... I can hardly believe it happened. I too wonder what will happen now. It's as if the planets aren't in the right alignment or something. I don't know.'

'Perhaps we should concentrate on Loki. He is part of us. To me, that seems the best course.'

'I'll follow your lead. I've not done anything like this before or since we were last together.'

'I've tried with Cal, and managed to get inside myself, as it were, but not beyond.'

Galdra winced a little at those words, and Pellaz knew they were somewhat cruel, but he didn't want Galdra thinking what they'd done was unique to them.

'We need information,' Galdra said. 'It's not just about Loki, is it? At Fulminir, we made things difficult for something... or somehar... but we didn't stop them or discourage them. What are we really taking on?'

'I don't know,' Pellaz replied. 'But Lileem must help us now. I want you to try and remain conscious, come with me. I know that's difficult after so long without practice, but I confess that, if we succeed, I don't want to do this alone.'

'And how exactly *do* we do this?' Galdra asked. 'How do we get from this moment to that of intimacy? I feel a world apart from you.'

Pellaz drew in his breath. 'We perform our own private Grissecon,' he said. 'In the garden. If it's ritualised, it'll be easier.'

Galdra nodded. 'As you wish.'

'First we finish the wine.'

Pellaz knew it was important to remain focused. He must keep Loki in his mind, and also Lileem. As he threw back his head to down the last dregs from his glass, he called silently upon the dehar Aruhani. *Now is the time I need you more than ever.* He put the glass down on the low table in front of him. The wine had affected him pleasantly; he felt far mellower than when he'd arrived. He glanced at Galdra and then stood up.

The doors to the garden were open, and beyond them all was still. Galdra followed Pellaz out onto the lawn. It felt too exposed there to Pellaz; he needed to feel more enclosed. A gazebo covered in climbing jasmine stood a short distance off, screened by cypresses. *It must be there.* Nearby, a fountain in the shape of a rearing horse spat crystal streams into a wide marble half shell. Pellaz knelt here to take a mouthful of water. He was conscious of Galdra standing behind him. Now it had to be done.

When he rose to his feet again, Galdra put his hands on Pell's arms and turned him round. Nothing was said. They shared breath in the starlight, cautiously recalling the past; how it had felt, what they had done. Was it possible to recapture that time as if the intervening years had never been? Galdra's voice was a murmur in Pell's head. *No, it isn't possible. This is now. Live it.*

I think it was the feeling that got us there, not the act, Pell told him.

Perhaps, but what you can't see is that Loki was the reward for that work, not a punishment. He's our responsibility and we must help him, whatever our feelings. And – as you said earlier – we must help him in the here and now, not the past.

Pellaz drew away from Galdra. 'You're right,' he said. 'We *will* reach Lileem, I swear it, by all the dehara.'

Galdra smiled and put a hand against Pell's face. 'I know.'

They went into the gazebo, where the delicate flowers hung over them, occasionally dropping down, as if Aruhani was shaking the slender branches. The smell of jasmine was very strong, almost narcotic. Pellaz surrendered himself as a sacrifice to the dehar of aruna. It was both Grissecon and personal; a balm over a wound perhaps, but ultimately not difficult at all. Pellaz knew this body beside him. They shared a skill and a history. Cal had been right: there was no other way.

It seemed that Aruhani had heard the Tigron's prayer. He was present in his most benevolent aspect, as the guide and protector. Very quickly, Pellaz slipped inside his own being, feeling calm and centred. He found himself in the cauldron of creation, and Galdra was with him as a separate form. Previously, they had always visited this place as a combined creature; perhaps this new development was evidence of the way things were between them now.

The cauldron could take many forms, but the way it appeared to them on this occasion was as a jetty that poked out over an ocean of sky; a terminal for travel. Pellaz could not see Aruhani, but could sense him strongly. He was an invisible giant hanging before them, haloed by and comprised of stars.

Pellaz knew he should summon transport and sent out a strong call. Presently, a beautiful ship came towards them, trailing a sparkling cosmic mist. Its sails were silver and its figurehead was a smiling carving of Aruhani. Just by willing it so, Pellaz and Galdra boarded the ship, and it turned in a graceful circle, heading back the way it had come.

This is... different, Galdra said.

For me too, Pellaz said. *Think of Lileem, Galdra. Think of the realm of the library. I have been there before. I'll give you images.* He paused. *This journey is not without risk. The last time I went to that place it was very difficult to leave, but that was with the sedim. This might be different.*

We'll make it so.

Ahead was an immense shimmering portal of purple cloud, which hung in the firmament like a nebula. The ship headed directly towards it.

This is it, Pellaz said. He took Galdra's hand. It felt warm, alive and solid in his grasp, amazingly real. Pellaz had no sense of what was happening to their bodies in reality. The experience was entirely objective. Perhaps they had never left their flesh this completely before. *We should have posted guards,* he said. *We've left ourselves too vulnerable in the realm of earth.*

Galdra squeezed his fingers. *We're safe. Don't worry. Aruhani watches over us.*

They were enfolded by the purple glow, which eclipsed all other impressions. Pellaz tasted honey and oranges in the back of his throat. He smelled baking bread. Then the purple light was something else: a gigantic sun surrounded by a red nimbus and he was looking up at it. He stood naked upon the shifting silvery sands of an alien realm, his hand still held in Galdra's. They were in a wide canyon, surrounded by high cliffs that glittered with white and violet points, in the light of the strange sun. Overhead, myriad heavenly bodies soared and danced. Pellaz was sure that if he listened hard enough, he'd hear their ecstatic song. This was Lileem's realm, he was sure of it. There was no protective bubble around him, as there had been when the sedim had brought him here before. He and Galdra were simply standing there, and there was no ship. Did this mean they were trapped?

'Well, I think we made it,' Pellaz said. 'I don't want to worry you, but it appears our transport has vanished.'

'I had noticed that,' Galdra said. 'I hope Lileem doesn't stand on ceremony; we're both naked.'

'Considering that aruna gets hara and parazha here, that's one of the hazards.' Pellaz laughed. 'Well, I don't think that's the case for Lileem now, so we'll have to hope she can help us to leave her realm, when the time comes.'

Galdra turned round in a circle. 'I can't believe I'm here. It's the most amazing place. It doesn't feel like a vision, but totally real.'

'That's because it *is* real,' Pellaz said. 'We're technically in two places at once.' He grabbed Galdra's arm. 'Something's just occurred to me. The last time I came here, it was even more physically, since I didn't leave my earthly form behind. Also, when Lileem and Terez came, they did the same thing. Perhaps that's why we all found it difficult to leave. I hope I'm right, but I think that visiting here astrally might make it easier to escape.'

'A good theory,' Galdra said. 'I hope you're right too. Let's trust to our superior wills and believe it.' He pursed his lips. 'So... do you recognise this location?'

Pellaz gazed around himself. 'No, but then I was here for only minutes last time. Aruhani will have brought us to somewhere near Lileem, I'm sure.'

'Call her.'

'Yes...' Pellaz considered projecting a mind call, but then decided that in this place it probably wasn't necessary. He simply opened his lungs and yelled: 'Lileem!'

The call flew from cliff to cliff, echoing around them. It mutated into a cry like that of seagulls, flying off in all directions. 'If she doesn't hear that, she's not in this realm,' Pellaz said.

Gradually, the call ebbed away, occasionally becoming louder briefly, before dying out completely. Pellaz and Galdra waited. After some time, Galdra said, 'Perhaps you should call again.'

Pellaz was just about to do so, when he noticed an indistinct, shadowy form approaching them. He pointed. 'There, Galdra, do you see?'

'Yes!'

Pellaz raised both his arms and waved; a ridiculous thing to do, he thought wryly, since the approaching figure was clearly heading towards them and knew they were there. It grew taller as it drew near; a thin creature clad in a robe of deepest crimson, with long black hair hanging over the breast to the waist.

'That's not Lileem,' Galdra said, stating the obvious.

'No,' Pellaz said.

The figure halted a few feet away from them and bowed extravagantly. 'Tigron, you are *most* welcome.'

'Ponclast,' Pellaz said. For one terrible moment, he wondered whether the erstwhile Varr leader had somehow murdered his friend. 'Where's Lileem?'

'She's away on business, Tiahaar,' Ponclast replied. 'May I help you?'

'Away on business?' Pellaz couldn't keep the exasperation from his voice. 'That's absurd. Where is she? I must speak with her at once.'

Ponclast smiled graciously. 'I'm afraid that's quite impossible, Tiahaar. You will have to speak to me.'

Chapter Thirteen

At some point in her timeless existence, Lileem had come to the conclusion she was no longer parage. She rarely experienced self-awareness, except for those occasions when she ran across her captive guest in the labyrinth of the library. She had seized Ponclast from Fulminir, at Pellaz's request, without really thinking that afterwards she'd be sharing her private realm with another living being. Not that he was any trouble; her realm stultified emotions. Whatever rages had torn at Ponclast's soul were quelled now, but he still had memories of them. When Lileem looked into his eyes, she was reminded of what she'd been. She saw in his gaze a receding echo of all those hot troubled feelings that had plagued her life. It was good to be rid of them, to be so complete and sure.

Ponclast had adapted as well as any living creature could to existence in Lileem's realm. She called it hers, because she believed that in some way she had created it. As she roamed the library galleries beneath the silver sands, she felt affinity with the great stone tablets that contained all the knowledge of creation. She did not feel love, because emotions didn't exist for her.

The library could be entered by a vertical shaft that rose and fell through no apparent mechanism other than the intention of those who wished to visit the lower chambers. Above the library rose a magnificent pyramidal structure that was a warren of chambers and passages, with a central vault that contained an immense seated statue. This statue was so big it was impossible to see its face. The pyramid was empty but for the statue. Lileem had no idea what race had built the pyramid and the library, or when. Sometimes, she suspected they hadn't been built at all and she'd simply dreamed them into being. The library was a vast labyrinth filled with large stone tablets that were carved with words, pictures and hieroglyphs. These "books" were written in many different languages, not all of them of the earthly realm. Lileem was convinced that the secrets of how Wraeththu and Kamagrian came to be were hidden in the library. She had devoted her life to finding them.

Immediately after arriving in Lileem's realm, Ponclast had remained huddled in a tight ball, more like a harling than a grown har, which perhaps was only to be expected. Lileem didn't anticipate

Ponclast would share her enthusiasm, so didn't try to coerce him to help her search. She deposited him in a chamber of the pyramid, telling herself she was his jailer, not his caretaker. Anyway, she had work to do. Ponclast no longer had to eat and drink, of course, or even sleep. He had a lot of room either to go utterly mad or become more like Lileem. Ultimately, it appeared he opted for the latter choice. She knew he was confused by the fact that he didn't want to attack her: she was responsible for his incarceration in this realm, after all. But strong feeling, hope and desire had been left behind. It was difficult to become bored, but Ponclast was an intelligent har, and eventually, once madness no longer seemed an option, he became curious. Lileem had left him alone, but finally he had looked for her, and after a protracted search, found her in one of the galleries of the library.

His first question was: 'What are you?'

Lileem was surprised to see him, since it was the first time one of them had initiated an intentional meeting. She was sitting on the floor with one of the stone books in her hands. She had been running her fingers over the glyphs it contained, with her eyes closed, hoping the meaning would come to her as she felt the marks. 'What do you see?' she asked in return.

Ponclast loomed over her; a tall thin har, still clad in the deep crimson robe he'd worn when she'd taken him into her custody. His ragged black hair fell to his hips; his hands were beautiful. 'A har can call himself she,' he said, 'but I don't think you are har. You're wearing the garb of a woman, but neither are you female or human.' He gestured at her torn skirts.

Lileem touched the fabric. 'That's because I was wearing this when I first came here. There was a reason for it.'

'This is your landscape, you're part of it. That's what makes you not har.'

'I was Kamagrian,' Lileem explained. 'But not anymore.'

'What is this place?'

She gestured with one hand. 'A library.'

'Is there anyhar else here?'

'Not that I've seen.'

'Why am I here?'

'It's your prison, Ponclast. You're here so you don't cause trouble for hara.'

'Where is this place?'

'I think it's best described as another exit point of the Otherlanes. We must assume there are countless other realms, apart from earth.'

Ponclast frowned. 'You mean a different planet?'

'I don't know. Perhaps it's the same place, but in a different layer of reality. Things are not the same here. You already know this.'

'What must I do?'

Lileem shrugged. 'That's your choice. Do what you like. You won't be going home - ever - so I suggest you find something to occupy yourself. You could read the books, as I do.' She could tell Ponclast was yet too dazed to think straight. He wasn't normally the type to ask plaintive advice off anyhar. He hadn't yet accepted what had happened to him was real.

Although it was difficult to assess the passage of time in that realm, Lileem had accepted it did in some way exist, albeit perhaps slightly differently to what inhabitants of the earthly realm experienced. There were days, because different suns held sway in the sky at different times. When the violet sun rose, it was easier to find things that made sense to her in the library. At those times, she could read script that would otherwise be meaningless marks. Perhaps in an attempt to create some kind of routine, Ponclast began also to read the books, although he so far had only investigated those he could read. Some of these were just pictures. He had become childlike, in certain ways. Lileem did not question him about his life, and he didn't volunteer any information. Lileem realised that she enjoyed his presence, which was odd, because she'd never felt lonely.

Once, Ponclast said to her, 'Who built this place? Have you ever found the answer to that?'

'I think it builds itself,' she replied. 'It changes constantly. You can never find a book in the same place twice.'

'Have you ever found a book twice?'

'Yes. Sometimes, all I ever do is find the same book. The way to stop that is to look for it in places where you found it before. Then you'll get something new.'

'You're not a prisoner here, are you? Not in the same way I am.'

'It's my choice to be here,' Lileem said. 'I prefer it.'

'But you can leave. You came for me, so you can leave.'

'I went into a book, that's all,' she said. 'A book of Pellaz har Aralis. He spoke to me from the stone.'

'He's not that different from me.'

'Perhaps not,' Lileem said.

'I want to know what happened before I came here. That's what I'll look for.'

'Then it's what we're both looking for. I think the book with that information runs before us.'

Unlike Lileem, Ponclast was not eager to release the world of his birth. He was puzzled by his experiences, and wanted to know exactly what part he'd had in whatever it was that had occurred. Who were the Hashmallim, the strange otherworldly allies who had freed him from the Forest of Gebaddon? What did they really want? Had they been defeated at Fulminir? Ponclast didn't think so. He eventually told Lileem about Abrimel, the Tigron's son, and how they had once loved one another. He spoke of his own son, Geburael, and wondered what had happened to him.

In his words, however slight, was the implication he wished Lileem would try and find out for him. She never responded to this unspoken request. She couldn't try and communicate with Pellaz yet. She was still searching for something and she knew that when she found it, it would be time to go home. More than once, she wondered what would happen to Ponclast then. She didn't want to leave the library, but knew it was her destiny. It was possible that when she went back to the earthly realm, Pell's highchildren might be ruling Immanion in his place. Terez might be long dead.

'What exactly is it you're looking for?' Ponclast asked her once.

'The meaning behind Wraeththu and Kamagrian,' she replied. 'What caused us, how we are different, and what keeps us apart.'

'Explain,' Ponclast said. 'You've spoken of Kamagrian before. What is it?'

Of course, Ponclast had been confined in Gebaddon when the Kamagrian first made their existence known to Wraeththu. 'We're like Wraeththu in most respects,' Lileem said. 'In fact, I wonder whether we are the same thing, really, only at a different end of the scale. We're born to hara, only when we hatch, we appear primarily female. This changes as we mature. At first, Kamagrian believed they could not incept human females to be like them, but I incepted someone by accident, so we discovered it is possible, after all. Gender in humanity was never the black and white thing most people supposed - I've learned that much. I think it might be the same for us. Kamagrian identify more with the soume aspect than ouana, but perhaps this is simply a choice. I don't know. Some hara are very feminine, such as Terzian the Varr's erstwhile consort, Cobweb. And some Kamagrian are more like Terzian the warrior, so who's to say? Do you think that the reason you were so aggressive as a Varr was because the feminine aspect of your nature frightened you?'

It was the first time they had touched upon the more sensitive areas of his personal history. Ponclast considered her question. 'Savagery, in itself, can be a belief system. Youthful male humans are, or were, capable of terrible things. *I* did terrible things, and at the time it seemed right. There was a heady euphoria to doing the unspeakable, like being a god. I believed the Varrs should control Megalithica – I wouldn't go so far as to say I planned world domination. Uigenna were a mess, and the other tribes weak and fragmented. I could see that Wraeththu needed order. The Varrs were accused of many things; perhaps more than half of those accusations were justified. The rest were fictions. I was driven by resentment, frustration, scorn… other things… Fear. Yes. Perhaps you are right. But in Fulminir, the second time, I was a dark queen rather than an evil overlord. That was my choice. In Gebaddon, I accepted my nature, and embraced it. Gebaddon does strange things to the mind. Perhaps, if I'd not been confined there, I would have been different.'

'If you returned to the earthly realm, what would you do?' Lileem asked.

She sensed Ponclast seize upon this question with the most hope he could muster, which he carefully concealed. He shrugged. 'If I returned, I presume that would be under the grace of Tigron Pellaz. I expect he would choose my future for me.'

'And if *you* could choose it?'

Ponclast's eyes assumed a faraway expression. 'I would be like Wraxilan, who was once a great Uigenna leader. I would become ascetic, I think, and live in a cave on a mountain.' He smiled and turned his eyes once more to Lileem. 'This is all pointless. I won't be going back. We both know that.'

'I'll go back,' Lileem said. 'And when I do, I'll speak for you. It would be too cruel to leave you here alone for eternity. As cruel as anything you ever did.'

'How do you leave here, Lileem? You spoke of entering a book, but I think it's more than that.'

Lileem nodded. 'It is. When hara take aruna together, they're like lights coming on in the darkness. They're like stars, beacons to light the way. It's difficult to explain. Perhaps eventually you'll see for yourself. I choose not to extend my senses that way at present, because it isn't the time to leave.'

'Anything could have happened in earthly reality since we've been gone. Wraeththu and Kamagrian might no longer exist.'

'That's true,' Lileem said. 'However, I must do what I want to do, and that is search.'

Another time, Ponclast came to Lileem when she was outside the library, studying the pyramid. Sometimes, new carvings appeared in the outer walls, and Lileem tended to inspect them regularly. Once, she was sure she found a picture of herself.

'Lileem,' said Ponclast. 'How far have you travelled in this world? Have you even ventured beyond the library itself?'

Lileem pondered for a moment. 'When I first came here with Terez Cevarro, we walked a long way to get to this spot. Terez looked around, I think, but... he never found anything, if that's what you're getting at.'

'Someone or something built this library,' Ponclast said. 'We must suppose there is a librarian.'

Lileem, much to her surprise, shuddered at his words. It was like a breath of chill wind had brushed her skin. 'Perhaps they're already here,' she said, 'but we can't perceive them.'

'That's possible,' Ponclast said. 'I think I'll explore. I think you should come with me.'

'It doesn't interest me. There's nothing to see but black rock.'

'I wonder.' Ponclast gestured at her with one hand. 'I think you should come.'

Was it the conviction in his voice that swayed her, or something else? Lileem could not be sure, but she found she had agreed to accompany him.

They set off, walking around the edge of the gunmetal ocean that lay behind the pyramid. Neither sun was in the sky. When the white sun rose, it was impossible to walk around outside; it was so bright it blinded you. 'We could walk for eternity,' Lileem said. 'I've no idea how big this realm is.'

'But we don't get tired, hungry or thirsty, so what does it matter?' Ponclast said. The sands were glittery black and silver beneath their feet, shifting with a sound like the sucking of mud. 'In some ways, this is a hideous place. The way it numbs the senses, takes away from us all that makes us har - or parage in your case - is terrible. Pellaz has punished me beyond my imagination of severity.'

'In my opinion,' Lileem said, 'you're safer lacking sensitivity and emotion. Look what you did to the Parasilians, Aleeme and Azriel. That was the act of a lunatic, and a psychotic one at that.'

Ponclast trudged silently at her side for some moments. Then he said, 'Yes... yes it was.'

'You should be glad you're no longer so full of hate.'

'I can't be glad about it,' Ponclast said. 'That is, of course, the problem.'

'A figure of speech,' Lileem said. She pointed to where what looked like a pathway snaked between the dark dunes. 'Shall we go that way?'

'Have you been there before?'

'I don't think so.'

Ponclast sprinted to the top of dunes and Lileem followed him. He was staring at the sky. 'It's not all hideous here,' he said. 'Look at the wonders of the heavens against the starkness of this world. Despite its terrors, this place has its own beauty. It's so untouched; it dreams.' He smiled at Lileem. 'Its dreams are recorded in the library. Perhaps this realm itself is the creator god, imagining the future. I don't think we should be here. I think you were an interloper.'

'Others have thought that too,' Lileem said, 'but if it's true, I think we're too small for the world to notice us. We're little fleas on the back of a mammoth, and if a mammoth has only two fleas, how can it complain?'

Ponclast laughed, and the sound of it seemed to shake the sky. Laughter was never heard in this realm. It occurred to Lileem that something might hear it. She laughed in return, and it sounded like the baying of an alien beast; a new language.

At one point during their travels, the white sun rose. It came up over the horizon with a thundering roar, and where its rays touched, all colours and details were bleached away. Lileem and Ponclast could not be burned by it, and any blindness would only be temporary, but it was uncomfortable to travel. They kept colliding with rocks they could not see. 'We must find a cave and sit it out,' Lileem said.

She held out her arms and felt her way forward, her fingers running over sharp invisible rock that normally would be black. Eventually, she discerned a shadow, which as she'd suspected, indicated a narrow cave mouth. She crawled into it and Ponclast followed. 'Terez and I did this before,' she said, and they composed themselves in the relative darkness.

'You came here with a har, yes?' Ponclast said. 'You mentioned that before. How did you get here?'

'Through aruna,' Lileem replied. 'When Kamagrian and Wraeththu come together physically, it opens portals. It's why our leader prefers to keep her parazha separate from the harish world. Too much temptation!'

'Surely it should be investigated,' Ponclast said. 'It was a phenomenal discovery.'

'Yes,' Lileem said. 'That's what I'm doing, to the best of my ability. Unfortunately, Terez and I also discovered that we couldn't leave this place in the same way we found it. We couldn't take aruna in this realm. All such earthly pursuits are impossible here, like with the eating and sleeping. Our bodies must be in some kind of suspended state.'

'Then how do you leave? And don't say it's through the pages of a book!'

'I can't tell you that,' Lileem said, grinning. 'Remember why you're here.'

'That is becoming increasingly difficult.'

When the white sun began its descent and shadows once again appeared amidst the brightness, Lileem and Ponclast left their retreat and continued their journey. Lileem left small cairns and arrows of stone, so that they could retrace their steps. As far as she knew, such signs would remain for them to find again. However, she was aware of a slight twinge of anxiety about losing herself; the library was her reason for being. She did not want to be away too long. And yet she was compelled to keep walking, as Ponclast was. It seemed inevitable that they would reach some kind of destination. They found it in the time of the violet sun.

For some time, they'd been walking along a deep canyon, which appeared to have been carved by water. 'Perhaps this world wasn't always dead and barren,' Ponclast said.

'I'm not sure it's a world, in the sense we know the word,' Lileem said. 'There are no certainties.'

'Is *that* a certainty?' Ponclast asked. He pointed up to the right, and Lileem squinted to see what he meant. It looked like a stone doorway, high in the cliff face. A narrow path led up to it. Lileem stared at it for some moments, unsure of what she was seeing. Was that an oblong of carvings, or not?

'Why are you hesitating?' Ponclast said. He began to walk towards the path.

Strangely, Lileem felt short of breath after the climb. Rather than the physical exertion, it seemed to be because she was being faced with the astounding evidence of another created structure. The portal, as such it seemed to be, was around eight feet high and four feet wide. It was surrounded by a wide rectangular arch of carved stone. Its centre was a solid obsidian slab, which when she reached out and touched it was warm beneath her fingers. 'Astounding,' she murmured.

'Certainly,' Ponclast agreed. 'Now, how do we get in?'

Lileem glanced at him, pursed her lips, and pushed with both hands against the stone. It felt totally immoveable. 'Not easily is the answer,' she said.

Ponclast narrowed his eyes in thought. 'The answer, of course, is in the library.'

'Well... most probably. But it could take us forever to find it.'

'Hmm, to my mind we have forever,' Ponclast said dryly. 'Let's head back now and hope your way markers are still in place.'

The markers were exactly where Lileem had left them. It occurred to her as they walked that Ponclast's presence, and his different view of things, was affecting this realm, making it somehow more solid. Perhaps – and this was an exciting thought – he was the key to finding what really needed to be found within the library. Perhaps Ponclast could make the books settle down and behave, and reveal to them what they sought. They discussed this concept most of the way back, deciding upon different strategies to employ.

'I think the answer is to be found behind that portal,' Ponclast said. 'It's no coincidence we came upon it. I'm inclined to agree with you; I'm affecting this realm.'

'Maybe everything is preordained,' Lileem said, gazing up at the sky. 'Are you meant to be here?'

'It's a far preferable fate to that of finding myself in Gebaddon,' Ponclast said. 'I like the way this realm strips all the nonsense from my mind. I've never felt so full of clarity in my life. It's almost joyous.'

Lileem grimaced. 'Terez never felt that way. He hated it here.'

The immense pyramid appeared before them over the horizon. Ponclast stopped walking to admire it. 'It's an incredible edifice,' he said. 'And I don't believe it manifested here of its own accord. Someone or something built it.'

'Then, where are they?' Lileem asked.

Ponclast set his mouth into a firm line. 'I intend to find out. I've had enough of these confounding books. It's time we got answers.'

'I can see why you were a leader,' Lileem said, grinning. 'Maybe I should have tried to order this place about more!'

'You lived the life of an academic,' Ponclast said. 'I think you needed somehar like me here to remind you what else you can be. You were far too happy just pottering about your cyclopean shelves.'

'Now, I'm reminded,' Lileem said. 'Come on, let's get on with the job. *This* time, we're going to find something useful.'

They went directly to the shaft that led to the library proper, underground. But just before they stepped upon the circular dais that would lower them into the labyrinth, Ponclast paused. 'You know, I think I'll investigate the upper building while you search below.'

'Why?' Lileem asked. 'If we're right and you're the catalyst to finding things, I need you down there with me.'

'Just an instinct,' Ponclast said. 'Trust me.'

'All right. Come and get me if you find anything.'

Lileem hoped he was right, but didn't think the upper structure was much use to them. It was an empty shell, a network of stairs, chambers and corridors that, if they had once contained anything, were now empty.

Once down in the warren of the library, Lileem applied herself with determination to examining the stone books. 'Come on, come on,' she whispered under her breath, 'show me, damn it!' She realised that for the first time in ages she felt emotion; excitement, hope, also some irritation and frustration. In fact, she had been feeling these things ever since she and Ponclast had found the portal. As if in reaction to her state of mind, the books were more contrary than ever before. Glyphs seemed to sizzle and transform beneath her fingers, information changing its mind a thousand times a second. The library was agitated. 'As well you might be!' Lileem told it. 'Come on, I've given you years of my life. Who else cares about you but me? Give me something back.'

As she spoke these words, one hand flat against a cold slab of carvings, a shock jolted through her fingers and up her arm. 'You heard me!' she cried in amazement.

'Lileem!'

At first, Lileem thought this was the voice of the library itself answering her back, but then realised it belonged to Ponclast, who was running towards her. 'What is it?' she called.

He came to a halt several yards away from her, and beckoned. 'Come quickly!'

Lileem put the stone slab on the floor, not even bothering to put it back on its shelf. She ran after Ponclast, who was already hurrying back towards the elevator shaft.

When you enter the library from the outside, passing through open doors fifty feet high, you find yourself in a huge chamber, which contains only one thing: an immense seated statue of polished obsidian. Its head is invisible, high in the shadows of the chamber, while its feet are the size of small houses. It was the first thing that Lileem and Terez had seen in the library, all that time ago. Lileem had never seen its face. If you squint upwards for long enough, you might get the impression of the underside of a chin, far far overhead, but that is all. Even the dais upon which the statue sits towers feet overhead.

Ponclast led Lileem towards this statue. She saw at once, without him having to point it out, that there was something in the dais that most certainly hadn't been there before, either in the reign of the white sun, the violet sun or the realm of the night: there was a doorway leading into blackness.

'Have you been inside it?' Lileem asked.

'No,' Ponclast answered. 'I saw it and came for you.'

She glanced at him. 'Something has made this happen. Perhaps it was when I touched the stone of the portal.'

'This is the key,' Ponclast said. He gestured towards the dark silent opening. 'Shall we?'

Lileem went towards the doorway. She touched the sides of it. So strange. It was as if someone had come along and cut out an oblong of stone, then had taken it away. *Someone knows we're here...* The thought disquieted her, which was odd. Surely, if there was anything around to be aware of her presence, it had known about her for a long time. Unlike other entrances throughout the building, most of which were grandly immense, the doorway was only just over five feet high, so Lileem had to duck down to pass the threshold. To her, this indicated a secret, a revelation in a whisper. Ponclast bumped his head as he followed her, cursing softly.

A short corridor of only ten yards or so led to a chamber within the statue itself. Lileem emerged into it and found she could stand up. The ceiling was around ten feet above her head and the room was empty but for an altar-like plinth in its centre. Soft light glowed from the seam between walls and ceiling. The walls were covered in carvings, marks that resembled those Lileem had seen in the stone books. Different languages; some in hieroglyphs, some in dots and lines, others with characters that must be alphabets. 'This is another book,' she said softly.

'Yes,' Ponclast murmured. 'But if that's so, it's a book of one fairly short story.'

'What?'

'Look.' He indicated a section of the wall, and Lileem saw some letters around three inches high in Megalithican. Ponclast went to this place, touched the wall. 'Above it are other words in different languages of earth.'

'You know about languages?' Lileem asked.

He nodded. 'Once I did, many lifetimes ago, it seems. I know enough to guess that whatever is written on these walls is the same thing in many different tongues.'

Lileem was almost afraid to read it, yet so eager to discover the chamber's secret her vision blurred with the desire. She had to blink and lean closer to read the words:

'The ways to T'nteph are closed. The Towers of T'nril are silenced. The dance of creation has been disrupted. This chamber, and the chamber of the

Exile, were sealed in the Fifth Aeon, upon the order of the Light of Lights, foremost of the Hashmallim.

Child of Earth who stands before this testimony, be welcome here. I know not how you will come or when. I know only that, as you stand here, the records have opened themselves to you, beyond wards and deceits placed to conceal all truths. Through you, in this moment, I live again. Heed my words and carry out my wish. Take the tezarae to the high place in the mountain you have found. Through them, sing the song of creation. Then the bonds will break.

These are the words of Hagak, Codexia of T'nril, in the last days of the Aeon.'

Lileem stood back. Her head was pulsing with the beat of her own blood. She felt dizzy at what she had read, or rather at the thought of how they had come to be there.

'Each of these messages,' Ponclast said in a hushed voice, 'must say the same thing, but for one word; the one that addresses the reader's home realm. In our case, this word is earth.' He sighed, and the sound was shaky. 'I feel quite ill.'

'Mmm.' Spontaneously, Lileem put her arms about him, and after a moment he returned the embrace. Lileem wept. It was as if her heart had been sealed and now it had opened; a flood of feeling surged out. She knew this wouldn't be happening if Ponclast hadn't come to this realm.

They stood holding each other for a long time, knowing that once the embrace ended, they must face the fact that reality had changed. They would have to act on it.

Eventually, Lileem pulled away. She rubbed her face, scratched her scalp vigorously. 'Hashmallim,' she said. 'It seems some of your questions at least will be answered, Ponclast.'

He nodded slowly. 'Now, I'm afraid of what I might learn.'

'We have to face it.' Lileem touched the wall again. 'Tezarae? What can they be?' She turned around and scanned the chamber. The answer of course was obvious. They would lie upon the cubic plinth at the centre.

The tezarae stood upon a surface of glossy obsidian. They were three crystal stones; each was just the right size to fit into one of Lileem's hands. One was dull black and felt warm to the touch; its facets were blunted. Another was cold like frozen ice; transparent, with hints of white and blue fire flashing within it. Its facets were sharp and had to be handled with care. The last was red with threads of living fire in its centre. When Lileem touched it, a strange shock coursed up her arm, similar to electricity, if not exactly that.

She passed the stones to Ponclast, one at a time. He examined them in silence for some minutes.

'Have you seen anything like this before?' Lileem asked at last.

Ponclast put down the last of the stones on the plinth. 'No,' he said. 'Lileem… you know what the message implies.'

'Yes. Behind that portal we found… lies someone or something… The Exile.'

Ponclast fixed her with a stare. He looked shaken, somehow younger. Lileem saw in his face the har he had once been, perhaps in the first days following his inception, before rage, before fear, before bitterness had taken his youth and his soul. He swallowed with apparent difficulty. 'It might be we've found the Librarian,' he said.

Chapter Fourteen

When Lileem and Ponclast reached the portal in the cliffs for a second time, the violet sun ruled the heavens. Its strange fire picked out details in the carvings around the stone door, including more words, although none of them were readable. Lileem had carried the tezarae in the pockets of her skirt; the same ripped skirt she had worn on the day she'd left the gardens of *We Dwell in Forever*, the home of the Parasilians, in Galhea. She had shared breath with Tyson, the son of Cal, in the gardens of that house. They had slipped away from a feybraiha party, into the night. She had used Tyson, his essence, simply to return to this realm. Now, she could taste him again, and it seemed as if the air around her smelled of a summer garden.

Lileem arranged the stones in a line before the portal and squatted before them. 'Well, here we are. What in Aru's name do we do with them?'

'Strike them,' Ponclast suggested. 'The message said we have to sing a song. I think that means we have to make the tezarae sing.'

Lileem tapped one of them with the ends of her fingers, but it made no sound. She picked up a stone from the ground and used that. Still nothing. 'How?' she asked, thinking aloud.

Ponclast hunkered down beside her. He picked up the black stone and held it in both hands. After some moments, he began to hum beneath his breath.

'Yes,' Lileem murmured. 'Maybe...'

It reminded her of the humming bowls that they used in the temples of Shilalama, the capital city of the Kamagrian in Roselane. At first you don't think the sound is there, but then it builds up so much it begins to shake the teeth in your head. Ponclast sang to the stone without drawing breath, until he had to stop, but when he lowered the stone, it continued to hum on its own, in a low warm tone. Ponclast sent a message to Lileem in mind touch, presumably concerned that the sound of their voices might interfere with the tezar tone: *We must make each of them sing. You take the white stone, I'll take the red.*

Lileem picked up the white stone and sang to it. It responded more swiftly than the black tezar, and vibrated at a higher rate, like the cry of a songbird. A tingle went through her flesh. She grinned at Ponclast and he inclined his head to her. He picked up the red stone.

The song of the red tezar was piercing and raw. As Ponclast sang to it, the fire in the centre of the stone grew brighter. The three tones combined into one ringing note, all the time growing stronger and louder. Lileem was concerned it would bring down the cliff face. The sound reverberated before her eyes, and it was like looking at a heat haze. She could *see* the song with her physical sense. It filled her with a strong feeling of elation. Ponclast took her hand and pointed towards the portal. A shape had formed upon it, wavering through the shimmering air. As she stared at it, it became more definite: the shape of two hands indented in the stone.

Gradually, the tone died away, leaving a silence that now sounded unnatural, even though there was normally no sound in this realm – no birds singing, no music, only silent stillness. Lileem stood up and approached the portal. The prints were odd, because the thumbs were on the outer sides. She crossed her arms and placed her hands upon the indentations. Deep within the stone, she could feel a resonance still humming. But the portal remained closed. 'Ponclast,' she murmured.

He came to her side and she moved one of her hands, so he could place one of his in the empty space. At once, stronger vibrations coursed up her arm and it felt as if the very atoms of the stone were moving. She could no longer move her fingers.

After only a short time, Ponclast whipped his hand away and grabbed Lileem's wrist to prise her away also. It was fortunate that he did. Within seconds, the structure of the portal broke up and disappeared. Nothing was left of it, not even a single particle of dust.

Lileem nursed her numb hand with the other, which now felt hypersensitive. 'Thanks,' she said. 'How did you know?'

'I didn't.' Ponclast peered into the opening that had appeared before them, not that anything beyond the threshold was visible from the outside. 'Well, are you ready?'

Lileem nodded silently. They went into the dark.

They felt their way along a narrow, low-ceilinged stone corridor. The walls were smooth and felt undecorated beneath Lileem's fingers, but the air had a definite scent to it; sweet and dusty. As they progressed, dim light bloomed ahead of them, emanating from the fabric of the ceiling itself. After a few minutes, they came to the end of the corridor, which opened out into a small domed chamber. In the centre of this stood a huge open sarcophagus.

Lileem went to its side, hardly conscious of Ponclast beside her. She put her hands on the lip of the stone and stood on tiptoe to look within. *Oh, sweet dehara, a body. It's a body, Ponclast.*

Not human, Ponclast responded. *And not harish either.*

Lileem had to agree with his assessment. The body was covered in a grey shawl of shimmering material. It was extremely tall, maybe eight feet. Lileem knew she or Ponclast must remove the shroud, but now she was reluctant to see what lay beneath. She had accepted many strange and unbelievable things in her life, but the thought of gazing upon some being completely alien, even if it was dead, unnerved her greatly. Also, because the sarcophagus was so deep, one of them would have to climb inside to accomplish the task. Ponclast intuited Lileem's feelings even though she didn't even touch his mind. He patted her shoulder, hitched up his robe and climbed onto the wide lip of the stone.

Be careful, Lileem advised him.

He smiled down at her and then dropped lightly to the floor below. There was enough room for him to stand there without touching what lay within. Lileem put her fingers against her mouth. She held her breath. *Do it!*

With one final glance at her, perhaps for reassurance, Ponclast leaned down and took the shroud in his hands.

Lileem closed her eyes, then forced herself to open them again. Ponclast had already drawn the shroud down to the body's neck, no further. He was frozen in position, staring at what lay there. *Hashmal!*

Is it? The sight wasn't too dreadful, yet even so, Lileem felt slightly faint. The body appeared to be perfectly preserved. Its face was abnormally long with a high smooth brow. Its nose was straight, its mouth pale and sensual. The eyes were closed. Perhaps it was just a carving. But no statue would have hair like that, long and white. The whole thing was covered in a silvery patina of dust.

Ponclast removed the rest of the shroud. The body was clad in dark robes, its arms positioned crossed over the breast. The hands looked huge, with weirdly long fingers.

'I think it's all right to speak aloud,' Ponclast said, looking up at Lileem.

'Do you think he was walled up here alive?' Lileem asked.

'Could have been, but in that case he was either a willing sacrifice or was drugged.'

'He looks peaceful… Is he a Hashmal?'

'I can't say for certain. It was just a first impression. He has a look of the Hashmallim, the long face, the height. He looks similar to a human or a har, but there's something not quite right, something that marks him as "other".'

'What now?' Lileem said. 'We opened this place, but all we've found is a corpse.'

'What makes you think that?'

Lileem laughed. 'What?'

'I don't think this is a corpse.'

'Don't be ridiculous. Why not?'

'Because it's breathing.'

Lileem took a step back. 'Get out of there!' She was filled with an irrational fear, similar, she supposed, to how phobics feel when faced with the cause of their phobia. She had a gut instinct to flee. If that thing was alive…

'Lileem, it's all right. Really.'

Lileem forced her breathing to slow down, steeled herself. For whatever reason, Ponclast wasn't frightened, so neither was she. Taking a deep breath, she clambered up onto the top of the sarcophagus, then joined Ponclast inside. Close to, it was easier to discern the slight rise and fall of the body's breast.

'I suppose we should touch him,' she said, 'try to wake him.' She squatted down, holding herself together with the greatest of effort. The body gave off a strange scent, a more concentrated aroma of the sweet dusty smell that filled the air.

'It might be too much of a shock,' Ponclast said. 'Who knows how long he's been like this?'

Lileem extended her hand, intending to touch the body gently, simply to see if it was warm, but found she couldn't make herself do it. It was as if her physical self screamed in rebellion at what her mind demanded. 'I can't,' she said. 'It's too alien, too strange.' She was on the verge of hysteria, and couldn't help imagining those weird eyes snapping open to fix her with a gaze that would drive her insane. She had to get out.

'Fetch the tezarae,' Ponclast said. 'Perhaps we should activate them again, put them on or near to him.'

'Yes, good idea.' She stood up.

Ponclast gripped one of her shoulders. 'I thought I'd lose my mind the first time I met a Hashmal. It's something we're not meant to see, I think. But because of my experiences, this is easier for me than for you.'

Lileem nodded and went to fetch the stones. Once she had them in her hands, they seemed to soothe her. *This is the moment you've been waiting for. This is why you've been here. It's the answer. Don't be afraid.* By the time she returned to the domed chamber, she felt better, less disorientated.

Ponclast arranged the tezarae alongside the body, and then activated them in the same order as before: black, white, red. Lileem was content to remain outside the sarcophagus and observe, grateful for Ponclast's presence. She wasn't sure she could have done this alone, but then it was doubtful she'd have found the chamber if Ponclast hadn't been there.

Once the stones were singing, Ponclast climbed out and stood beside Lileem. He put an arm around her and she did likewise to him. They waited.

Later, Lileem could not remember what she expected to happen. Perhaps a shuddering sigh, the eyelids flickering open. Perhaps even a collapse to dust. What she did not expect was the scream.

It was the most terrible cry she had ever heard or could imagine. It was an expression of the ultimate torment and pain. Lileem and Ponclast hugged each other tightly, both aware the other was powerless to move or act, even when the most merciful thing to do seemed to be to break the neck of the creature emitting the sound.

Eventually, Ponclast released Lileem and jumped into the sarcophagus. Lileem cried, 'No!' and then hurled herself against the stone. 'Ponclast!' She saw that he had gathered the screaming creature to him, one arm about its shoulders, his free hand pressed against its face, which he held to his breast. The face looked huge, repulsive in its unnatural size, even though the features were handsome. The mouth was a yawning dark cave. Ponclast put his mouth against it, breathed into it. It was a horrible sight, and Lileem was afraid that huge maw would somehow suck Ponclast into it.

'Ponclast...' Lileem could speak normally now, because the screaming had stopped. The creature lay trembling and panting in Ponclast's arms, its eyes wide, its mouth now hanging only slightly open.

Ponclast glanced up at Lileem. 'It's all right.'

The pitiful state of the creature made it no longer an object of terror. Lileem climbed into the sarcophagus and knelt on the other side of the creature's body. She lifted one of its enormous hands in both her own, and the fingers clasped her, like bony serpents. She felt fear, but it didn't belong to her. 'You're safe,' she said. 'Can you understand us?'

The creature turned its head, looked directly at her. She shuddered. It was so ancient a gaze. 'Speak more,' it croaked. 'Need hear words. Learn.'

Lileem glanced at Ponclast, who shrugged. 'Tell him your story.'

'I am Lileem of the Kamagrian,' Lileem began. 'A creature of Earth.'

Chapter Fifteen

For some while after his initial meeting with the Thanax, Loki avoided them. He hoped that his presence, his living warmth, his sympathy, would somehow impel them to help him – plus the fact he had made an offer to some day help them in return. How he would do that exactly he had no idea, but he presumed, if he was reunited with his family, Pellaz and Cal would know what to do. Sometimes, he noticed the three Thanax trailing him as he ventured around the empty city of towers. He did not come across any of the hostile individuals that they had warned him about.

One time, Loki went over to Apanage for dinner and found that Diablo wished to communicate. 'Remain here,' he said. 'Someone wishes to speak with you.'

Diablo's choice of words did not escape Loki: "someone" not "somehar".

'Who and *what* is this individual?' Loki asked.

'He will tell you himself, no doubt,' Diablo replied gruffly. 'Don't wander off.'

Loki didn't like spending time in Apanage. It was full of noxious emanations, which he supposed seeped from Diablo's bitter soul. 'Where is Geburael?' he asked.

Diablo shrugged. 'Around.'

Loki sighed deeply. He went to the top of the tower, where to him the air felt cleaner. He didn't know who or what to expect, although he thought that if Ponclast himself appeared in a puff of smoke, he wouldn't be surprised.

He became aware he was not alone only when his skin prickled with the sensation of being watched. Loki jumped, and then noticed that a figure was sitting upon a stone seat set into the wall, regarding him intently. This individual appeared superficially harish, but also emanated "other". Loki had no doubt at all that this was the person Diablo wished him to meet. The stranger's long blue-black hair hung in two braids over his shoulders. His clothes, a plain robe with silver embroidery at the hem, covered by a wide sleeved open coat, were nearly the same colour as his hair. His skin was dead white, the face long and narrow, and his eyes... they weren't like eyes at all, but rather smoking holes of azure radiance.

'Loki,' said the stranger. 'Approach me.'

Loki remained where he was, some yards away. 'Who are you?'

'I am Zikael, amanuensis of the Hashmallim. Do not be afraid. I wish only to speak with you.'

Loki eyed the creature with trepidation. If a snarling, starving lion had said a similar thing to him, he would have been less afraid. Zikael was an embodiment of terror, albeit in a beautiful form. *I can trust nothing he says,* Loki thought, but forced his limbs to propel him forward.

Zikael inclined his head. 'You know of my people?' he asked.

Loki nodded. 'I've been told of the Hashmallim's involvement in the last war between the Wraeththu tribes.'

'You know you were conceived during that final battle?'

'Yes, I know that too.'

'Because of that circumstance, there is more of us in you than you realise. We look upon you as our son as much as your harish parents do.'

'I already have too many parents,' Loki said dryly.

Zikael laughed, and it was a free ringing sound; the laugh of a creature who knows neither fear nor pain in his life. 'Sometimes, individuals are created who are more than the sum of their parts. They are the beings of legends, remembered as the sons of gods for their exploits. You are such a har, Loki. It is your destiny to become a historical figure.'

'What is it you want of me?' Loki asked. Did this Hashmal think him so naïve and gullible as to be swayed by flattery?

'Those whom I serve wish you to be given all the information that has been kept from you. It is not our wish to fight against you and your kind, Loki har Aralis. Far from it. We are opposed to waste.'

'Who do you serve?'

'Among my people, there are many divisions, as there are among harakind. You mirror us in many ways. For example, as in the earthly realm, there are two main factions, with many smaller ones who affiliate themselves to their best advantage. The smaller ones are troops, essentially. It is like the Gelaming and the Varrs.'

'Except that the Varrs have been conquered in my realm,' Loki said. 'Who do you identify with: Gelaming or Varrs?' He smiled and felt his hostling's fire in his eyes.

Zikael did not react to this question. 'What we would like you to consider is that in any conflict, each side seeks power and believes their way to be right and the enemy's to be wrong. Both sides think this. The truth is that there is no "right" or "wrong", only viewpoints that oppose each other. We want you to know our viewpoint; that is all. You are currently biased against us, and for that we hold no grudge. You are young and uninformed. I am here to enlighten you.'

'Forgive me,' Loki said, sounding more courageous than he felt, 'I might be uninformed, but my instincts are acute. My instincts tell me you're full of deceit and cunning, and that I should not trust you. That has nothing to do with bias, but mere gut reaction.'

Zikael smiled. 'You are not wrong in your assumption, and as a future ruler, you should not accept someone's words as truth without checking the facts. I can tell you this: often, I act as an agent in precarious situations, and my ability to be cunning is essential for survival. I do not ask you to trust me, only to listen. Then you can make up your own mind.'

'If you admit to deceit, how can I believe what you say? It makes no sense.'

'Just listen. The creatures you know as *sedim* are agents like me, but for the faction that opposes the Hashmallim. For eons, they have made use of the resources of your realm, and to Wraeththu they have shown more of their true form, albeit disguising themselves as genial beasts of burden. The har Thiede delved too deep into the inner realms, and discovered their existence. They spun lies to beguile him, which he believed for a time.

'The fact is that our rivals have made free with your realm, and their agents have moved unseen among its peoples. They gave rise to the legends of gods and monsters, because sometimes, especially in the distant past, they interacted with humanity. The human race was more fearful and superstitious then, and was more inclined to believe in supernatural beings. Our rivals would say that they nurtured the sentient beings of the earth, as a protective mother; but that is a smothering protection. Not all of their own kind agreed with such methods.'

Zikael paused, as if in polite anticipation of questions. Loki merely said: 'Go on.'

Zikael inclined his head. 'Very well. Our way is different. We believe in rewarding those who serve us. We are not opposed to advancement. We see no benefit in stultifying the growth of lesser realms. If a realm becomes aware of us, we think it is then time to educate its peoples, not to keep them in ignorance. Essentially, both we and our rivals want the same thing. We are simply more open about it and seek to demonstrate the relationship can be symbiotic rather than parasitic.'

Zikael smiled, and gestured graciously with both hands. 'You don't have to like me, Loki, or even trust me, as I said. I just want you to think about the fact that the *sedim* have never been honest with Wraeththu, as we have. Even now, they hide their true identities and purpose. If you stood before one of them and told them what you know, they'd simply stare back at you like a dumb beast and pretend they could not understand.'

The information Loki had received dazed him. It was like a mythical history, and hard to credit as real. But Zikael clearly expected a response. Loki swallowed. His mouth felt too dry. 'If the *sedim* seek to confound us so much, why even give us access to the Otherlanes at all?'

Zikael hesitated, then said, 'Just a few crumbs from the table. Thiede encountered a *sedu* in one of his astral excursions. He caught and travelled with it, perhaps not even knowing why he did so. The *sedim* and their masters know that Wraeththu are far more than humanity ever was, and not so stupid and blind. If they don't give a little something, hara like Thiede would only keep delving. Then, there is the risk that more truth would be uncovered. The *sedim* do not want that.'

'Give me the names of these two main factions you talk about,' Loki said. 'You haven't done so yet. Why?'

'The names would mean little to you, but all right. In your tongue, my kind are the Aasp, founders of the great Aaspori empire that spans many realms. Our rivals are the Zehk. These words do not exist for us; they are merely labels for others to use. Our language is like music; it also involves the senses, such as the primitive ones of taste and smell. There are other senses, beyond what hara can comprehend, and these are involved also. Part of my profession is linguistics. I teach others of my kind how to communicate with lower beings, and how to adopt the forms that facilitate such things.'

Loki had moved from dazed terror and mistrust to fascination. He realised he was standing before what equated to an alien being, from a race far older than humanity or any other species on earth. 'I must know what you want of me exactly,' he said. 'What are your plans?'

'We wish only to end the dispute,' Zikael said. 'A good general knows that physical conflict should always be a last resort. The skirmish at Fulminir was unwise, initiated by an individual who acted too hastily. It is our Masters' wish to avoid such conflict. Any confrontation between the *teraphim* and the *sedim* is doomed to stalemate. They cannot destroy each other exactly, only expel. It is our wish for you to become an advocate for us with your kind.'

Loki wondered how he, a young and inexperienced har, could

really be of use to these creatures, other than as a gullible cat's paw. They were clearly far more advanced and powerful than Wraeththu, so why couldn't they just take what they wanted? 'What benefits would Wraeththu receive from co-operation?' he asked, aware that the diplomatic training he had received at home was asserting itself.

'We would give you more access to the Otherlanes. There are certain realms you could visit or even colonise, should you so wish. We have no objection to that. The Zehk would never allow that.'

'And what would the Zehk give us? Supposing you'll give me a true answer…'

'They regard themselves as protectors, but they do not believe that species such as Wraeththu should be given knowledge. They would say to you that it is up to your own kind to advance yourselves, yet at the same time they work to prevent that advancement. Ultimately, Loki, as far as mundane life is concerned, there would be no discernible difference to Wraeththu, whichever faction gained control. Some hara might even wish to let the matter resolve itself, without involvement. That too is your choice, but like I said, I'm here to give you information, so that the choice you make will be based on understanding, not ignorance.'

Loki hesitated. 'I would like the gift that Geburael and Diablo have – the ability to travel the Otherlanes without a *sedu*. Give me this, let me see these realms you speak of, then I'll be more disposed to make a choice.'

'At this stage, I am not permitted to allow you to return home,' Zikael said.

'I wasn't speaking of home,' Loki said. 'I want to understand this conflict. I want to know what it is your kind gets from our realm. I want to see other realms. I know that restraints can be put upon the *sedim*, so I presume you can do the same to me. Let me travel. You can keep the earthly realm off limits to me.'

Zikael considered. 'I will communicate with my Master about this,' he said. 'Your request is not unreasonable.'

'I would like to meet your Master.'

'You can't. He is one of the Faceless Ones.'

'And what are they?' Loki asked. He was struggling to ask the right questions, but what he was hearing was so beyond his experience, he wasn't sure how to deal with it.

'Beings you would find it very hard to perceive. They have no contact with lower species.'

Zikael stood up, and it was only then that Loki realised how tall the Hashmal was. It looked eerie, unnatural. 'I will leave you now,' Zikael said. 'Think about the matters we have discussed, formulate any further questions, and we will soon speak again.'

Zikael bowed politely, and then somehow the air swallowed him up, until all that remained was a pinprick of bright blue radiance, which disappeared with an audible pop. A faint breeze was left behind that smelled of a perfume Loki could not identify. The scent made him feel strange; excited, fearful and nostalgic.

For some minutes, Loki remained where he stood at the top of Apanage. He felt bewildered. The conversation with Zikael seemed like a dream; it couldn't have happened, could it? Loki tilted back his head and gazed at the starless sky. At home, stargazing made him think of the immensity of the universe, but here the empty blackness conveyed a greater kind of space. Loki had never been so conscious of how small and insignificant he was, yet at the same time he felt renewed and powerful.

He had no wish to speak with Geburael or Diablo; not yet. He sensed that Geburael was looking for him, so went back into the tower and began to descend the levels, his skin alert for Geburael's presence. Proximity to Zikael must have done something to him, because when he entered a chamber where Diablo and Geburael were talking, they did not notice him. Loki could slip past them, slinking along the wall of the room like a disembodied shadow.

Outside, Loki walked among the towers, mulling over what he'd learned. As far as he could see it, and he was still not totally convinced he knew the whole story, the Aasp simply wanted Wraeththu to change affiliation, and were prepared to make the deal sweet with privileges and gifts. But what was it exactly that the Aasp – and the Zehk, for that matter – took from the earthly realm? Did Wraeththu *have* to ally with one faction or the other? Was there perhaps a third way? He had to admit that didn't seem feasible. Wraeththu were harlings compared with these creatures. A politician would listen to both sides, and he was destined to be a politician. He would say this to Zikael next time they met up and see how the Aasp reacted.

Thinking about it all had given him a severe headache, or maybe Zikael had inadvertently affected him in that way too. He hadn't eaten anything either. The pain made him feel dizzy.

Loki was so deep in thought, he didn't notice at first that the three local Thanax were trailing him. Were they after his warmth again? He stopped and turned to face them. 'Go away,' he ordered.

The Thanax huddled together, their thin bodies dipping and swaying like serpents. They were sniffing the air and trembling, as if the warm scent of him was driving them mad. Loki was reminded of a pack of starving, loyal hounds, who were standing before fresh meat their master had forbidden them to eat. A pang of pity went through him. 'I can't give you warmth,' he said. 'I've already told you that.' He rubbed his temples, which were throbbing.

One of the Thanax detached himself from the group and sidled forward. 'Let us eat your pain,' he said.

'What?' Loki took some steps backward.

'Do not be afraid. I will not harm you. You see me as a parasite, I know, but there are some forms of heat you can do without. I can take it away.'

It took all of Loki's will not to flee as the Thanax approached him. 'Explain,' he said. 'You mean my headache?' He laughed, somewhat nervously.

The Thanax was very close to him now and had extended a skeletal arm. 'Let me touch you.'

'I don't think…'

The Thanax, however, was clearly too driven to be ignored. He'd got this close. Swiftly, he pressed the fingers of one hand against Loki's head. Loki tried to pull away, but a powerful magnetism held him to the spot. He felt a strange tearing sensation in his head, tried to cry out, and then the Thanax was backing away, staring at something he held in his bunched fingers. He licked his lips, and seemed about to devour it, but his companions leapt forward with a cry. For some moments, there was a scuffle. Loki watched in fascinated horror. The Thanax who had touched him held a small oily globe of light, which because of the assault, he was obliged to break into three parts and share with the others. Each Thanax devoured it with evident pleasure, then stood swaying, eyes closed. Loki thought he could hear them purring, or making a sound very like that. He also realised his headache had gone. *Pain is energy,* he thought. *And they have taken it from me.*

After a short while, the first Thanax opened his eyes and shook himself. The pain seemed to have done him good. 'It has been a long time for us,' he said.

'Well… thank you,' Loki said. 'That was… interesting. If pain is heat to you, it's a fire that any har would be happy to give you, I'm sure.'

'Heat brings clarity,' said the Thanax. 'We see you properly for the first time. What are you doing here?'

'I'm…' Loki paused. 'Listen, before that, do you have a name?'

The Thanax inclined his head. 'I am called Atoz, and these are my brothers, Sokh and Tur. These were names we had once. When we have clarity, we still use them. We think they came from a long time ago.'

'I am Loki. Loki har Aralis har Gelaming, to be precise. You know of the Gelaming?'

Atoz frowned and shook his head. 'No, we know very little. We can only feed in the spirit paths.'

'Then you must have met Gelaming,' Loki said, 'since very few hara of other tribes can use the Otherlanes.'

'Perhaps.' Loki could sense that Atoz was confused by his words.

'As to why I'm here,' Loki explained, 'let's say I'm a captive of sorts. The other hara brought me here, the ones in the towers. But I intend to leave very soon.'

'It is very difficult for entities to leave here,' said Atoz, 'owing to the barrier.'

'What barrier?'

Atoz pointed at the sky. 'The veil,' he said.

'Can you tell me about it?'

Atoz nodded. 'We can tell you what we know of this realm,' he said. 'It will be a gift in return for the heat you gave us.' He beckoned. 'Come, follow us.'

The Thanax went off in a single file towards the hills where Loki had first communicated with them. He followed behind them, and not once did they attempt to talk to him during the first part of the journey. Loki didn't know where they were taking him, or why, but neither did he feel threatened. They walked for what seemed like a long time, to areas that Loki had never visited before. When he looked back, he could still see the highest towers of Thannaril in the distance, so did not worry about becoming lost. They walked along a ridge, where a wide circular valley lay below. In the middle of this was a strange lumpy structure that looked partly like a natural rock formation and partly like some kind of castle. Here, Atoz paused and pointed downwards. 'That is Tenebrian, the place where the vengeful reside,' he said. 'They know things you don't want to know.'

'The vengeful?' Loki asked warily.

'Those like us who you must avoid. Come. We must not linger.'

'What do they know?' Loki asked as the line set off once more.

Atoz did not answer.

Eventually, the narrow path disgorged the travellers into what appeared to be a roofless cavern. The rock walls were pale and looked porous, pocked with many small holes. At one time, this realm must have been something other than a dry and arid place, because Loki had the strong impression these ancient rocks had been shaped by water. There were many natural caves, and here the group of Thanax had made their home, such as it was.

Atoz led Loki to one of the caves, and once he was inside it, Loki thought that the Thanax lived like animals. There were no decorations, no tools lying around, nothing at all, in fact, to suggest the cave was occupied by sentient beings. What did they do with their time? He couldn't believe they spent it in conversation, and it was evidently not spent in creative pursuits.

'Sit,' said Atoz.

There was no hearth, no central hub to this dwelling, just a dusty floor, worn smooth by many feet. Loki sat down against one of the walls. Sokh and Tur stood by a shadowed entrance to what appeared to be an inner chamber to the cave. They stared straight ahead, like guardians or mute beasts.

Atoz composed himself before Loki. 'We have brought no other here,' he said.

Loki inclined his head. 'I'm grateful for whatever you can tell me.'

There was no expression in Atoz's eyes; Loki suspected he could have none. How strange to be sitting here with this impossible being, talking about an impossible world. Loki reflected on how adaptable the harish mind must be, to accept these impossibilities without losing its reason. Could a human have coped so well? He had no idea.

'I remember being drawn here,' Atoz said. 'Before that was terrible pain, the pain of being lost, beyond all words. Those of us who come here take the history of this realm into our being as we are drawn through the veil, for the veil holds all memories of itself. There was once a time, many eons past, when the Thanadrim constructed the cities of towers. This was a different world then, a place of life and activity. Sometimes, if you are very still, the towers will relive their memories for you, and you will see. The Thanadrim had a duty. They regulated the currency of essence between realms, and the towers were the means they used to accomplish their task.'

'What is the currency of essence between realms?' Loki asked. He meant to ask many questions.

Atoz ducked his head. 'It is hard to describe. Even now, having seen it, I am unsure that what I have perceived is truth, or the whole story.' He closed his eyes for a moment, appearing then more like an ordinary har, thinking hard. 'Reality is composed of many different layers, and within those layers exist species of sentient creatures of varying degrees of awareness. Worlds, or realms, themselves are sentient creatures. They think very slowly, and in doing so, create.' He shook his head. 'I'm not sure…'

'It's all right,' Loki said. 'Go on.'

'I – and my brothers – would be half-formed creatures but for the towers. They gave us awareness and knowledge, even if we lack the other things that would make us har. From them, we learned that certain species worked with the essence of realms, taking the thoughts of the worlds, the dreams, and…' Atoz slapped one hand against the rocky floor. 'No! I cannot describe it. I cannot!'

'Please.' Loki reached out and gently laid his fingers on Atoz's shoulder. The creature was warm beneath his hand: alive. 'Try.'

Atoz sighed and blinked at the ceiling, which Loki now noticed was hung with a lacy curtain of dusty webs. He wondered whether spiders had spun them. He'd seen no spiders in the towers.

'The Thanadrim regulated the currency,' Atoz said. 'That's all I can say. They were a neutral race, and respected for their work. They created about Thanatep an obscuring veil, which served as both a protection and a filter for the power of their workings. That is why you can see no stars. There is but one sun, one world and one moon. The veil hides everything beyond.'

'The sun is very strange,' Loki said. 'It looks flat, and hardly gives light – not in the sense I know anyway.'

'You have not seen the sun,' Atoz said. 'The body in the sky is the moon. The days here are very long. They are like seasons, almost. When the sun rises, Thannaril is a different realm beneath its light.'

'That's amazing!' Loki said. 'Have you seen this, Atoz?'

'No, but I have learned of it.'

'What happened?' Loki asked. 'Where are the Thanadrim now?'

'Several races partook of the essence of the realms, and their activities were governed by the Thanadrim. The realms themselves had no interest in this commerce, since to them it was irrelevant, but to those who yearned for the essence, it was of prime importance and focus. However, some realms are more vulnerable and volatile than others; the Thanadrim officiated over which ones could be subject to the treaty of harvesting.

'The sorrow of the towers is that one faction wished to expand their influence, and objected to the Thanadrim's decree this must not be so. The outcome of this disagreement was something that had never happened before. This faction took it upon themselves to disempower the Thanadrim and banish them. The power matrix of the towers was disrupted and stilled. And now this realm lies dead, and is a home of the dead, such as us. The power still sighs in the winds and dust, but it is dormant. What you see around you is only the external workings. The Thanadrim built their cities deep beneath the ground; the towers are the conduits of their power. The place you live in is Thannaril Above; there is a Thannaril Below also.'

Loki felt overwhelmed with information, yet he was still curious. 'Was this because the time of the sun makes the realm uninhabitable?' Loki asked.

'No,' Atoz replied. 'It was because the world above had to be uncontaminated by sentient creatures; a virgin world, if you like, the province of beasts without thought, of untainted intention.'

'Some things are becoming clear to me,' Loki said. 'Atoz, was this faction you spoke of, who opposed the Thanadrim, called the Aasp?'

Atoz shook his head. 'I do not know their name. They have no name, not as you or I would know it. The towers can create shapes that are names, for lowly creatures such as ourselves to understand. Most of the towers are benevolent. Some are completely dead, others mad.'

'I've often communed with my tower,' Loki said. 'Well… it's not mine, exactly, but I live there. Its name is Ninzini. I feel now I should try to communicate further.'

Atoz nodded. 'You should do so. Ninzini is known to me. It is a female tower, and I think that once a female of the Thanadrim was responsible for it. Some of the ancient races are like humans, dualistic in gender, while others are like Wraeththu. There are yet more variations. One species that Ninzini told me about are comprised of three genders. Another has only one, hermaphrodite like hara, in some respects, but they need no other for reproduction.'

'I would like to learn more about these things,' Loki said. He hesitated. 'Atoz, a creature came to me recently, who I think is of the faction you described, which exiled the Thanadrim. He appeared harish. He was trying to persuade me to think kindly upon his people, to speak for them with my own kind. He talked about some kind of currency between realms. I think he was talking about what you've told me.'

'That is possible,' Atoz said. 'When the Opposers exiled the Thanadrim, things didn't turn out quite how they expected.'

'Why?'

'The information is vague, but I think that the Thanadrim managed to impose some kind of protection upon the realms before they were expelled. I believe they passed guardianship of each realm to the species that live within them.'

'But…' Loki rubbed his face. 'I don't get it. The Aasp are very powerful; Wraeththu are flies in comparison. What I don't understand is why they can't just take what they want. They obviously did so once. Why would they abide by the strictures of the Thanadrim?'

Atoz shrugged. 'I told you; I don't know everything, only fragments.'

'What you've told me is very helpful,' Loki said. 'I appreciate it, whether it's fragments or not. I knew nothing before.'

'You are welcome,' Atoz said. 'Being with you makes me feel more alive. It is like coming awake. My existence is mostly like a dream, or what I imagine a dream to be.'

'It is,' Loki said. 'You're right in that belief. If you don't harm me, I'd like to spend time talking to you. You're better company than the hara here, trust me.' Even as he said those words, Loki experienced the tiniest pang of guilt that he'd spoken ill of Geburael that way. He wasn't sure why. 'One of them is my sori,' he felt compelled to say – as if Atoz really needed the explanation. 'But he has betrayed my family.'

'He is not the twisted one,' Atoz said, in a matter of fact tone.

'No,' Loki said. 'That's Diablo. He's... different.'

'I would shrink from taking warmth from the twisted one. It would not bring warmth, but something else.'

'Probably,' Loki said. 'Tell me... do you know how to enter Thannaril Below?'

'No,' Atoz replied. 'The ways are sealed, perhaps destroyed.'

'But does it still exist?'

'I don't know. It was closed down a very long time ago.'

'Will you help me find it? You are more in tune with this realm than I am.'

Atoz visibly shuddered. 'We cannot approach the towers. They are as hungry as we are, though they mean no harm. We are...' He twisted his mouth to the side, again a very harish gesture. 'We are anomalies, we should not be. The towers' nature is to absorb us, even as they give us form. Our nature, as sentient creatures, is to survive. So, we are incompatible, if loosely allied through common sorrow. Do you understand?'

'Sort of. But perhaps you won't have to enter the towers to help me.'

'I don't know how I can help, but I will try, if it would please you.'

'Thank you. You spoke of a power matrix in this realm. Is there more than one city?'

'Thousands,' Atoz said. 'All like the one you know. You could walk for several lifetimes, I think, and not visit every corner of this realm. It is vast.'

'How far have you travelled?'

'Not very far. I know only what the towers have intimated to me. They feel the silence of their distant brethren keenly, for once they sang in unison.'

Loki considered for a moment, then said, 'In your opinion, what would it take to reactivate a tower?'

Atoz was also silent for a while. 'I have never looked for that knowledge, nor been shown it. I suggest you ask Ninzini that question.'

'I will. Would you guide me back now?'

Atoz got to his feet. 'As you wish.'

Loki stood up also. 'Why did you bring me here, Atoz? You could have told me everything where we were.'

'I had a wish, an instinct, to bring you to my home,' Atoz replied.

'It's a poor home,' Loki said. 'Perhaps you'd feel more alive if you made it different.'

'I understand,' Atoz said. He smiled sadly. 'One of our greatest dilemmas is listlessness. It is part of our torment.'

'You're a contradiction,' Loki said. 'Speaking to you now, I feel a personality before me. I've communicated with a thinking mind. Perhaps you're not as lost than you believe.'

'That is a glad thought,' Atoz said. 'It will warm me for a time, though once you are gone, all life will slip away. That is how it must be. Your presence… invokes me. Alone, I haven't the strength to cling to myself.'

'That's another currency of essence, I'm sure,' Loki said.

'We must leave now,' Atoz said. 'I sense that others of my kind are drawn to this place by your flame. I cannot guarantee they will respect you in the way that I do. I cannot guarantee your safety.'

Chapter Sixteen

Geburael was waiting in Ninzini when Loki returned to it. Loki came across him in the area he'd designated as his living room. He was amused to see that Geburael had made himself some Thannaril coffee. He was sitting on the floor drinking it. 'Where have you been?' Geburael demanded. 'You've been gone a long time!'

'I wanted time alone,' Loki replied. He hunkered down by the small fire Geburael had built in the middle of the room, where the brew was simmering, and helped himself to a cup of it. 'I had to think about things. I take it you know that the Hashmallim sent an envoy to me.'

Geburael nodded. 'Yes… What are your thoughts now?'

Loki managed a smile. 'He was similar to you. He was so *concerned* I got the whole story, so I could make up my own mind.'

'And have you?'

Loki hesitated for a moment, took a sip of his drink, then put down his cup. 'Geb, how much do you know of Thanatep, or rather of Thannaril in particular?'

'What do you mean?'

Loki sighed. 'One of us has to answer a question.' He smiled. 'OK. I've been talking to the Thanax, and have discovered a few things. I wondered if you knew these things too.'

'What?' Geburael visibly paled. 'You've gone near the Thanax, *communicated* with them? Loki, don't do that. Don't *ever* do that! It's too dangerous.'

'Actually, it's not,' Loki said. 'Perhaps that's another difference between Varr and Gelaming, Geb. I give others a chance before I want to kill them. In this instance, it's paid off well. Do you even know what the Thanax are?'

'They're parasites. Disgusting.'

'In some ways, yes,' Loki agreed, 'but they are *of* us, Geb. They told me they're the remains of failed inceptions.'

'What? Then what are they doing here?'

'I can't answer all the questions you'll have, because even the Thanax don't know all the answers. But they've given me interesting insight into this realm. It has bearing on why we're here.'

'Then you'd better tell me,' Geburael said coldly. 'Everything.'

Loki recounted his meetings with the Thanax, and saw no reason to omit any information, other than that he had a desire to reactivate a tower, simply to see what would happen. If the Hashmallim discovered that desire, Loki had a feeling he'd be removed from Thanatep before he could draw breath – should his suppositions about the Hashmallim be correct.

'Why didn't you tell me all this before?' Geburael asked.

Loki shrugged awkwardly. 'I wasn't sure it was in my best interests. I've changed my mind. I can't see the harm in it. If you wish to prove yourself to me, and I know part of you does, help me investigate Thannaril. Only a fool wouldn't want to know the truth about the Aasp, especially if the Hashmallim are affiliated to them, and I don't think you're a fool, Geb.' Loki presumed that last morsel of approval wouldn't go amiss.

Geburael put a hand to his chin. 'I expect you intend to keep Diablo ignorant of these *investigations*.'

Loki shrugged. 'He's no friend of mine, and to be honest, I don't think he'd give a damn if the Hashmallim were the Aasp, or if they'd obliterated and exiled half the races in the known universe. I wouldn't be surprised if he already knew what the Thanax have told me.'

'It's not easy to keep secrets from him.'

'This would be, because it wouldn't interest him. All he cares about is keeping me here.' Loki wasn't sure if that was the truth.

Geburael was silent for a moment; he stared at the walls of the room. 'I know the towers have voices, albeit small ones. What you've said makes sense. I suppose it wouldn't do any harm to try and establish better communication with these entities, although the idea of an edifice of stone having a mind is somewhat far-fetched, even to a har like me, who's travelled the Otherlanes and visited other realms.'

'Perhaps they are more like machines than empty stone,' Loki said. 'We have no idea what technology the Thanadrim possessed.'

'That *is* a possibility,' Geburael said. 'What do you want to do?'

'Let's just open ourselves up to Ninzini and see what we perceive.'

Geburael nodded. 'OK. Here?'

'At the top of the tower,' Loki said. 'To me, that's where its presence seems strongest.'

Geburael got to his feet. 'OK.'

Loki and Geburael climbed the spiralling stairs to the top of Ninzini and at the summit, they sat cross-legged on the floor, opposite one another.

'Do you know how to do this?' Loki asked.

Geburael grimaced. 'The same as any other mind touch, I assume.

Do you think I'm so uneducated?'

'Well, no, but....'

Geburael appeared to be affronted, even though Loki had not meant to imply he lacked education. 'I might not have undergone normal caste progression,' Geburael continued, 'but I'm very well trained.'

'I can tell,' Loki said. 'I didn't mean to imply anything. It's weird, because I often feel you're more educated than me, but that must be impossible. I learned from the best tutors in Immanion. Who taught you, Geb?'

'Diablo made sure I got knowledge,' Geburael said. 'He asked the Hashmallim to teach me. Zikael has always visited us. I learned a lot from him.'

'I'd like to know all the things he taught you.'

'You only have to ask,' Geburael said. His face took on an expression of deep longing that in some ways made Loki want to reach out and take Geburael in his arms. But another part of himself screamed in outrage at the very idea.

'Well,' he said, 'let's see what Ninzini can teach us.'

Geburael nodded and closed his eyes. Loki stared at his surakin's face for some moments before he also closed his eyes.

Loki began to breathe rhythmically and deeply, calming his mind and body. He projected a question: *Ninzini, will you communicate with us?*

For a few moments, his mind was empty, and then it was shocked by a blast of information from an intelligent source. Loki gasped and threw back his head. He braced himself to receive the information.

Communication with the tower was a peculiar experience. In some ways, the information Loki received was like hearing a gong being struck, then quickly silenced, or it was like an artist slathering paint of many colours onto a canvas with a broad knife, blurring images as much as creating them. Ninzini was not reluctant to communicate, but its ability was limited - at least with a harish mind. Rather than transmitting information in a linear way, it *pulsed* images. Pictures came like bubbles, bursting upon the surface of Loki's mind, but although they were incredibly detailed, they passed too quickly for him to discern very much.

When Loki ended the meditation, by calling Geburael back to mundane reality, Geburael reported a similar experience. 'I should have done this before,' he said. 'I'm mad at myself I never have. Why? I've lived here all my life, virtually.' He gestured emphatically at Loki with one hand. 'I get the feeling communication will get easier the more we attempt it. We need to learn to see Ninzini's way, to put ourselves in its space, as it were.'

Loki was pleased that Geburael was such a willing work partner in this venture. He also appeared to be a har who would actually be useful. 'I got a vague impression of the city beneath the ground. Did you?'

Geburael nodded. 'Yes, but I felt like I wanted to slow Ninzini down. It was too fast.' He grinned. 'I want to get down into that city, don't you?'

As this was precisely Loki's thought, he grinned also. 'It would be… at the very least, educational for Wraeththukind.'

'Who cares about Wraeththukind? I just want to see it for myself! The impressions I got…' Geburael shook his head. 'Almost impossible to describe, but vast, immense rooms, galleries, walkways and pits. How about you?'

'Similar. I felt it went very deep, level upon level upon level.'

'It's still there, isn't it?'

'I think so,' Loki said. 'Yes.'

Geburael got to his feet and began to pace the room. 'Have you ever been down to the lowest levels of Ninzini, Loki?'

Loki nodded. 'I have, but they're empty.'

Geburael cupped his chin with one hand. 'Hmm. I wonder just how empty though. We can only presume the entrances to Thannaril Below were at the bases of the towers.'

'You think we should go and look again?' He also stood up.

'That's exactly what I think,' Geburael said. 'Let's go.'

The floor to the lowest level appeared seamless, a sheet of stone. There were no indications of hidden doorways or of contraptions that might reveal such things. Loki and Geburael carefully investigated every inch of the room, tapping the walls and the floor, in an attempt to find evidence of a space behind or below them.

Eventually, Loki said, 'This is hopeless. Perhaps there is only one entrance, and it's somewhere else. We should be looking outside… maybe.'

Geburael sat down on the floor. 'No, it's here. I can *smell* it. It wants us to find it.' He raised his hands. 'Come on, now, Ninzini, give us something to work with!' He paused and held out his hands to Loki. 'Let's open up again. Here. We'll concentrate on what we desire. And this time we'll be linked physically.'

Loki sat down opposite Geburael, and took hold of his hands. He was surprised to find he did not flinch. Both he and Geburael shared a need. In that, they were united and beyond superficial differences or conflicts. The physical conjunction of their hands was electrifying. Loki could feel that their intention became condensed like a spear. He realised he was in a heightened state of awareness, and must have been ever since the last meditation. Every sense was hypersensitive. He closed his eyes. Geburael's breathing sounded very loud, echoing in a strange hissing resonance around the room, sighing like waves of water crashing upon a distant beach.

'Concentrate,' Geburael murmured, 'on a point in the air between us, before our faces. Into this point, we must direct our will, our purpose, our desire. It will become a spark of light.'

It was almost as if Loki could see this light with his physical eyes. It was a bright tiny star, revolving, emitting blades of intense radiance that sliced right into him.

Geburael slipped into mind touch. *Show us, Ninzini. Show us the way to the place below.*

For a few moments more, all Loki could hear was their combined breathing, but then, distantly, a tone. He wasn't sure if it was in his head or in reality.

Loki... Geburael's voice was a whisper in his mind. *We must make the tone. Aloud. Make it low in the throat, not the mouth. Do you understand what I mean by that?*

Yes... Resonate.

That's it.

The sound in Loki's head was so distant, he could barely make it out, and the moment his voice sounded aloud in the room, the tone disappeared completely. His voice combined with Geburael's, who appeared able to continue sounding the tone without stopping to draw breath. But then Loki found he was able to do that too. He could breathe deeply and evenly, and the tone did not falter. It seemed to operate independently of his body. The sound was beautiful; a song. But even though they seemed to continue making it for many minutes, there was no discernible change around them and no new information bloomed in Loki's mind.

Then Geburael told him: *Stop. Open your eyes.*

Loki did so. Geburael was smiling at him. He pressed Loki's fingers with his own. 'Look up,' he said softly.

Instead of the ceiling about seven feet overhead, Loki saw a yawning shaft that disappeared into infinity. The steps that should have led up to the next level ended abruptly at the place where the ceiling should have been. Behind Geburael was a dark doorway.

Loki's mouth went dry instantly and a strange shiver of heat, followed by an intense shiver of cold, passed through his flesh. 'The floor has sunk,' he said, stating the obvious.

Geburael laughed. 'It would seem so. I didn't feel a thing, did you?'

Loki shook his head. 'Nothing. We should have had some sense of descent, surely?'

Geburael got to his feet and gestured towards the doorway. 'Well, we're here, let's explore.'

Loki swallowed with difficulty. The doorway seemed sentient somehow, as if entities clustered in the thick shadows beyond it, watching and listening intently. Enough light to see by was coming from *somewhere*, but where? There was no obvious source; the light just *was*. He knew they had to cross that dark threshold. It was why they were there.

The chamber they left behind appeared to be in the centre of a circular building, since the passageway outside was curved to left and right. There were no windows and the light was a strange dark azure, which emanated from what looked like small blue crystals set into the walls. The walls were very smooth, made of a curious soapy-looking bluish stone, slightly veined like marble or – as Loki thought – the wonderful creamy blue cheese that the Freyhellans were so fond of. When he touched the walls they were warm, like a living creature is warm.

After only a short walk, Loki and Geburael came to a series of doorways, leading outwards. They chose one at random. There was another short passageway, of maybe twenty yards or so, that led into a chamber so immense that Loki at once felt dizzy. There was hardly anything within this room, if such a vast structure could be so termed. It was domed and softly-lit by the same azure radiance as in the corridors. It had the ambience of a Nayati, Loki thought, serene and full of the potential of gods. In the centre of the chamber, quite some distance away, was a dark cube, which looked as if it was made of stone. Loki had the strong impression that once a Thanad had sat upon that strange throne, and through it had communed with Ninzini.

Geburael whispered, 'This place, it looks sort of organic, but then not – too plain.' Plain was not a word entirely appropriate to the circumstances.

'Were the Thanadrim giants, do you suppose?' Loki said, a light-hearted question he hoped would establish some kind of normality, but which in essence was genuine.

'I've no idea,' Geburael replied, 'but the Hashmallim are, aren't they? I presume the Thanadrim were similar. If what the Thanax told you was true, then presumably the Thanadrim's structures would have to be large-scale, since they were supposed to regulate the entire farming of realms.' He paused and briefly touched Loki's shoulder. 'Well, now we're here... do we move on?'

Loki realised his heart was beating as fast as if he'd been running, and had been that way since he'd opened his eyes after the meditation. 'We must,' he said.

It took nearly fifteen minutes to cross the chamber; it was even bigger than it first appeared. When they reached the "throne" in the centre, it was at least seven feet high. Loki's flesh tingled as they passed it, almost as if someone, or something, was sitting on top of the cube, staring down at him.

Loki had assumed that Thannaril Below was simply a series of hollowed out chambers, albeit huge, but after he and Geburael had wandered through several long curving corridors and passed through other domed chambers - smaller than the first one - they finally reached the outside, and the scene made Loki light-headed. He took hold of Geburael's hand; he couldn't help it. 'We must have travelled down for miles,' he whispered hoarsely, unwilling to raise his voice in case something - *something* - heard it.

'Our trance was deeper than we thought,' Geburael murmured back.

Nothing else could explain the sheer immensity of what lay before them now. Loki's first thought was of the Sahale city of Sahen, in Jaddayoth, but really the only thing Thannaril Below shared with the place was the fact it was underground. Loki and Geburael had passed through a doorway, which led to a railed platform. What lay before them was a city so incomprehensibly vast, the senses could barely take it in. Domed buildings, some with cupolas and towers, rose all around them. When Loki looked over the rail, he saw the roofs of other buildings below.

'It's like coral,' he said. 'A reef.'

There were no perceivable limits to the city, just an endless vista of cyclopean buildings. Loki's first impression was that it was not dead, since there was light, but after only a couple of minutes' stunned observation, Loki realised that nothing moved along the maze of walkways. Some of the structures appeared to be made of glass or crystal, and were lit with the strange dark lights of blue and sometimes green, but no life was visible within. A myriad of walkways and paths intersected the city.

'It was just abandoned,' Geburael murmured. 'I bet if we could find living quarters, there'd be the remains of food on the tables. Don't you get that impression? It feels like it's holding its breath.'

'The Thanadrim were driven out,' Loki said. 'Strange that the Aasp didn't just destroy this place, though – and the thousands of similar places.' He was trembling; he couldn't help it. He felt light-headed, almost nauseous. It was fear, wonder and excitement, shaken together.

'It's just so incredible,' Geburael said, somewhat lamely, shaking his head. 'It makes me want to weep and laugh. Diablo should see this!'

'What?' Loki shared no such sentiment. 'He shouldn't! Don't tell him about this, Geb.' It occurred to Loki at that moment, that he had no idea how they could return to the surface – other than simply make another request in trance to Ninzini.

'If he saw this,' Geburael said, gesturing with one arm, 'I think it might change him. Nohar could stay the same after seeing it.'

Loki doubted Diablo was capable of any positive transformation. 'I think we should keep it secret for now. I believe the Hashmallim are enemies of Thanatep. Diablo would tell them about this. We shouldn't abuse the privilege we've been given. The place, after all, is – well – dormant. There's no need for anyone to know we've seen it.'

Geburael frowned at this. 'But why did Ninzini consent to us coming here? It must know who and what I am.'

'I don't think it has that much reasoning power,' Loki said hastily. 'We simply did the things that made certain events take place. I think we should try to return to the surface now, discuss what we've seen. It's too overwhelming. I need to get out.'

'I agree,' Geburael said. 'But this is a turning point. It means something.' He tilted back his head and squinted his eyes. 'Look,' he said. 'There must be shafts leading from all the towers.'

To Loki, they appeared like the pipes of an immense organ; he had seen such things in the remaining ancient human cathedrals that Cal had shown to him in various old cities around the world. Perhaps that analogy was apt; he imagined the tone of Ninzini and a thousand other tones harmonising with it. In such ways, perhaps, the Thanadrim had conducted their work.

'I miss my family,' Loki said. 'If it wasn't for you, Geb, I'd never have seen this, and for that I'm grateful, but I miss my home. I want my regular life back.'

'You were lucky ever to have had a regular life,' Geburael said, tartly. 'You're a son of the Aralisians. It had to stop. Whatever made you think you'd be able to live a simple life like a normal har?'

Loki sighed. 'I just can't imagine where it's going to go from here. It's bizarre, but having seen all this, I feel sort of hopeless.' Now he'd begun to voice his inner thoughts, he couldn't stop, even though he suspected he shouldn't be confiding in Geburael. 'My feelings are that, as an Aralisian, and a future member of the Hegemony, I should get the Zehk and the Aasp to sit round a table with the leaders of Wraeththu and discuss things. I know that's impossible, but I don't feel I can make an informed judgment any other way. I'm too young to make such big judgments. It's not right. I think it's the very fact of my youth that has made the Hashmallim contact me. They think I'm gullible and easy to manipulate. I'm not. But neither have I strength or the command of slippery words to match them.' He drew breath to say more, but decided against it. He could sense that Geburael had become a little tense beside him.

'What did the Hashmal ask of you?' Geburael asked.

'You don't know?'

'Well… what do you think? I just asked the question.'

'I think we should return to the surface, then we'll talk more. It's not appropriate to discuss it down here.'

It was fairly easy for Geburael and Loki to retrace their steps to Ninzini's entrance shaft, although on one occasion they took a wrong turn and, once they realised they were in completely new territory, Loki nearly gave in to hysteria. The thought of being lost in Thannaril Below terrified him. But Geburael remained calm and soon worked out where they'd gone wrong and got them back on track. He'd memorised some landmarks on the way.

Once they'd seated themselves once more at the base of Ninzini, the tower complied unhesitatingly to the request to ascend. This time both Loki and Geburael kept their eyes open, although they did link hands. Loki was grateful for the contact. He'd once congratulated himself on being able to tolerate completely alien and extraordinary experiences, but visiting Thannaril Below had left him light-headed and full of an inexplicable feeling of apprehension.

As before, there was no sense of movement as the floor rose, but the walls appeared to become fluid. The ascent seemed to go on forever, which Loki thought strange, because it had seemed so quick on the way down. He closed his eyes, and felt Geburael squeeze his fingers. 'Hey,' Geburael whispered.

Loki opened his eyes again. He saw at once that the walls had solidified once more, and when he looked up, the ceiling was reassuringly above his head. Perhaps closing his eyes, and changing his perception, had speeded up the process subjectively for him. It made his mind whirl.

'Are you OK?' Geburael asked.

'I'm exhausted,' Loki said. 'I don't feel good at all.'

'Mmm, it *was* rather overwhelming.' Geburael let go of Loki's hands and rubbed at his own hair.

Loki didn't think he sounded overwhelmed at all.

Geburael got to his feet. 'You should sleep. You'll be all right afterwards.'

Loki pressed his hands against his eyes. 'Yeah,' he said shakily. 'In fact, I need to sleep right now, this moment.' Unsteadily, he got to his feet. The room swam before his eyes and for a moment Loki thought he might vomit. He leaned against the wall with one hand; it felt solid and eternal beneath his palm.

Geburael came up behind him and wrapped his arms round Loki's waist. 'Breathe deeply,' he advised.

Loki did so, and eventually the feeling of nausea passed. 'Will you stay with me?' he asked. He leaned back against Geburael, feeling that he would disintegrate if he were left alone, untouched.

Geburael turned him round. 'Share my strength,' he said. 'Share breath with me.'

Loki did not resist. Geburael's calm strength grounded him, made him feel safe and sure again. He did not break the contact even once he felt better. Neither did he think of Diablo. His body began to respond to Geburael. He felt hot.

Geburael broke the kiss and leaned his forehead against Loki's own. He uttered a soft groan.

'Let's go upstairs,' Loki said.

They went to the chamber just below the summit, which was where Loki slept when he didn't sleep outside. Loki wasn't sure what he was doing or if he'd regret it bitterly later; all he knew was that he wanted aruna. It was more than want. He needed to be part of another har, if only temporarily. It would be like seeking sanctuary beneath a curtain of ivy, where nothing could find him.

He and Geburael shared breath again in the centre of the room and this time Geburael was more confident. He'd realised that Loki wasn't going to push him away. He ran his hands over Loki's body, then held him tight. Loki could feel Geburael's ouana-lim pressing against him, and his own body became soume. It seemed almost preordained.

'Undress me,' Loki murmured.

Geburael stepped back and began reverently to remove Loki's clothes. His touch was light; he did not caress Loki in any way. Loki found this deeply erotic. He wanted Geburael to stroke him and the fact that he didn't heightened Loki's desire.

Once he was naked, Loki lay down on top of his bed and watched Geburael disrobe himself. *There will be thorns,* he thought. At that moment, even the idea of this strange addition to aruna excited him.

Geburael's body was smooth; there was no sign of anything thornlike. Loki lay in anticipation of what would happen.

Geburael came to lie beside him and they shared breath once more. Now, Geburael began to caress Loki's body, at first with a tantalising, gentle touch, away from the more sensitive areas, but gradually moving towards them. Loki arched his body when Geburael touched his soume-lam. He felt he might faint. It had been too long since feybraiha, and he'd bullied his body by denying it this. He reached down and took Geburael's ouana-lim in his hand. It felt like it had a heartbeat.

Geburael moaned in delight and rolled Loki onto his back. Loki opened his legs in invitation and then Geburael was inside him. The feelings this conjured were exquisite. Loki had never known such physical pleasure. It did not feel contaminated or wrong.

The thorns, when they came, were etheric, Loki realised. He had expected some physical protrusions to burst from Geburael's torso, but it wasn't like that. They were part of the aruna vision, not physical at all. When they went into his astral flesh, it was as if they injected some kind of euphoric drug. The experience was so intense, Loki's corporeal body reacted as if the thorns were real. Blood welled from tiny cuts; his belly became slippery. Geburael cried out and took them both to the highest peak, which to Loki was like a mountain summit above the clouds. In this place, he could see what the clouds concealed from harish eyes below: angels dancing between the stars.

Loki had no idea how long he slept for, but when he awoke he had the sensation that a lot of time had passed. Beside him, Geburael slumbered on. Loki observed him. *The only time you can really look at a har is when he's asleep,* he thought. *How I wish Diablo had never touched you, Geb.*

Loki's body still reverberated from the wonderful sensations he'd experienced. He looked at his stomach and saw the triangular scars, which were already fading. Was it possible that what they'd done together had cleansed Geburael of what Loki regarded as an unclean feybraiha? He hoped he'd scoured every atom of that vile creature from Geburael's being. He was sure that Diablo would never share breath with anyhar; that was something new for Geburael. It was his and Loki's alone. Loki leaned over and touched Geburael's lips with his own, breathed into him a stream of clear light. Geburael mumbled in his sleep.

Loki intended to take this further, but then he shivered. The air in the room had become somehow hard. It was about to fracture: a portal was opening up. Loki rose from the bed and pulled on his trousers. He stared into a corner of the room that no longer looked wholly stable. Within moments an oval portal pushed reality apart and the Hashmal Zikael stepped through it.

Zikael glanced at the sleeping Geburael, smiled mordantly and then addressed Loki. 'It is time for your first lesson. You want to learn how to fly, Loki har Aralis?'

'You'll teach me to use the Otherlanes?' Loki asked. He started to put on the rest of his clothes.

'It's what you asked for, isn't it?' Zikael said.

Chapter Seventeen

After Lileem had told the Exile her story, he did not attempt to communicate for some time, but simply lay in his sarcophagus with his eyes open. Lileem and Ponclast kept watch over him. After all, there was nowhere else they had to be.

Lileem was sure that more than the Exile had awoken. She was conscious, on the edge of her perception, of a low vibration in the chamber around her, as if arcane mechanisms were secretly at work.

While Lileem had been speaking, the Exile had kept his eyes on her mouth the entire time. It seemed that the more he heard her speak, the more he understood her. But the effort of that understanding appeared to have exhausted him, or perhaps he was mulling it all over in his mind, working it out. Lileem had no idea; he was an alien being to her. Eventually, he expressed a sigh that made his entire body shudder. When he tried to sit up, both Lileem and Ponclast assisted him. The Exile smiled, slowly, as if he couldn't operate his facial muscles properly. 'I wish I wanted a drink,' he said, which was such a normal and therefore unlikely thing to say that Lileem laughed. It was also spoken perfectly in her own tongue and - she noticed - with her accent.

'Do you know how long you've been here?' she asked.

He frowned. 'No. Not yet. Too long. The Codexia Hagak hid me here. The rest of my people were taken to a far less accessible place. It feels like yesterday.'

'There's no one here,' Lileem said. 'You heard how I came to this realm, but the Codexia is long gone. It's just a barren place, but I think the library is still alive, in a way.'

He nodded, and then winced, raising a hand to his neck. 'This body is not made for such privation as it's endured. I would not have survived in any realm but this one. You can give me healing, yes?'

'Of course.'

'I will need this before anything else. The name you can use for me is Ta Ke. You could not comprehend my true name.' He lay down again and closed his eyes, carefully positioning his arms by his sides.

Lileem exchanged a glance with Ponclast, who shrugged. Together, they put their hands upon the Exile's torso.

Eventually, they took Ta Ke back to the library. His body was weak, so the journey took a long time, with many stops for rest. Lileem was convinced he would have been in a worse state in any other realm; in this instance, the quirks of the library's landscape were fortunate. Ta Ke towered over them, even though he was stooped with pain. His long feet, with their absurdly attenuated toes, dragged in the sand.

Lileem took him into the room that had opened within the statue. It was the closest she had to somewhere to take visitors. Really, the whole situation was bizarre.

Ta Ke examined the writing on the walls, and it seemed to sadden him. He touched some of the marks with his fingers.

'Can you read all the languages?' Lileem asked.

'Most,' he replied.

Lileem and Ponclast sat on the floor and waited patiently, assuming he would eventually offer them some kind of explanation. After he'd walked round the chamber several times, Ta Ke halted and sighed deeply. 'I am supposed to return to my home realm,' he said. 'I am supposed to right all that is wrong.' He shook his head. 'I said I would do that. I was obviously a fool. Where are my people?'

'Can we help?' Lileem asked.

Ta Ke stared down at her. He smiled. 'You are such a little thing,' he said.

Lileem grimaced. 'A little thing who came to this realm, and who's been able to read some of the words in the library. Tell us why you're here, and why you must return.'

Ta Ke inclined his head respectfully. 'The words that are written here were for you. I imagine you are right, and I should involve you, take advantage of your offer of assistance. Very well. In your tongue, my home is Thanatep. My people are the Thanadrim. We were banished from our home. Let me tell you of our great cities, and of their function.' He sat down. 'This will take time.'

Lileem and Ponclast learned all that Loki had learned, and more. Ta Ke spoke of the time when the Aasp breached the veil of security around Thanatep and poured out of the Otherlanes with their fearsome *teraphim* and their warrior Hashmallim.

'Hagak was our archivist here on Shaa Lemul,' Ta Ke said, thus revealing to Lileem her realm had a name. 'I sent a message to him when the invasion began. Others tried to reach the Zehk, but it appeared we were unable to contact them in time. You must understand, we did not wish to initiate a great conflict, but my people are not warriors. We could not defend ourselves, and at first we thought the Zehk would object strongly to the Aasp's actions. We sought their assistance, but the Aasp had planned too carefully. Thanatep was swamped, and their operation took very little time to complete. Hagak acted in the only way he could think of. He came for me swiftly and brought me here.'

'So Hagak was the librarian, then,' Lileem said, thinking aloud.

'He had a large staff also,' Ta Ke said. 'He was able to conceal me and this chamber, with only seconds to spare. The Hashmallim came here and took away the library staff. This realm was scoured, rendered dead, even though the library itself is a living organism. As you have gathered, it creates itself to a large degree, and this process was initiated by beings of such a high order not even the Hashmallim or the Aasp could close it down. But they did make it very difficult for others to come here, as you have discovered. The library remembers everything. It is a danger to all beings who seek to delude and conceal. There are no untruths in this place.'

'So, now you want to return to Thanatep,' Lileem said. 'Does that mean you'll try to reactivate the cities?'

'I am supposed to, I think,' Ta Ke said. 'But I fear it is too great a task for an individual to accomplish. Also, I have no idea what condition the cities were left in. But from what you have told me, it is clear that the regulation should be reinstated. Once I am free of this realm, and its restrictions, I will attempt to communicate with those who might assist me.'

'What I don't understand,' Ponclast said, 'is why the Aasp and the Zehk can't just take what they want. Why do they need the co-operation of Wraeththu, for example?'

'The Thanadrim emplaced several safeguards around the realms to which we had access,' Ta Ke said. 'We did this simply as a precaution, should anything happen to us or our cities. The physical guardians of a realm, be they good, bad or indifferent in their duties, have a certain amount of control over the commerce of essence. In most cases, they are unaware of it. When the denizens of a realm undergo advancement, this affects the essence, makes it - shall we say - more desirable to those who use it. The advent of Wraeththu and Kamagrian in the earthly realm has refreshed it. Traditionally, it is the territory of the Zehk, but the Aasp were continually contesting that claim. There have always been some realms that the Aasp and Zehk fought over. Ancient contracts were held to be erroneous or outdated. It is a complicated territorial dispute. However, it is interesting to me that the factions' imprudent and reckless action in your realm has inadvertently precipitated my awakening. They would not have counted on that.' He sighed. 'But I am only one. Also, I was never trained in Otherlanes travel. If I wished to do so, I would secure the assistance of a *sedu* or a *teraph*, back in the days when they were amenable to such services.'

'I can do it,' Lileem said. 'If you can at least give me some directions, I'll do my best to find your realm.'

Ta Ke observed her for some moments. 'You can do this without assistance?'

Lileem nodded. 'Yes. I wouldn't say I'm as skilled as a *sedu*, but I have a certain degree of mobility in the Otherlanes. Being in this realm for so long has changed me. I can do things few of my kind can do.'

'Then I will take advantage of your offer.' Ta Ke frowned. 'Of course, there is the risk that if I reach Thanatep, the Aasp will still be monitoring it. The moment they sense me, their creatures could come for me.'

Ponclast took the tezarae from a pocket of his robe and replaced them on their plinth. 'Do you think that the Zehk would want you to reinstate the regulation?' he asked. 'If so, it makes sense to try and contact them. Lileem could do that through the *sedim*, couldn't you, Lee?'

'Well…' Lileem began, but Ta Ke interrupted her.

'The Zehk did not respond to our call for help,' he said. 'Hagak and I wondered whether this was because in some ways they were happy to let the Aasp do what they did. After all, they benefited from it too. Both factions are now free to squabble with each other over territory. Before, they were allocated realms under strict controls. No, at this stage, I would not wish to try and contact the Zehk. I will ponder upon how best to protect myself and you, too, Lileem.' He paused a moment, considering matters. 'It would be preferable for us to enter Thanatep through the deepest heart of my home city. This might be perilous, but in other ways safer. I would prefer to wait until I feel stronger, but it concerns me that my awakening might have been registered by agents of the Aasp. We should leave as soon as possible.'

'What I'd like to know,' Ponclast said, 'is what the threat actually is to our home realm. Does it make any difference to us whether the Aasp or the Zehk are in control? And if so, what?'

Ta Ke considered these questions for some moments. Eventually he said, 'There are certain things about the Zehk you do not know. It has always been the rule that the inhabitants of a realm should develop at their own pace unmolested, however tempting it might be to advance them. There has also been continual debate about this rule. Some think that it is a perfectly legitimate -- indeed proper -- thing to share higher knowledge with a lower species and thereby advance them. In the distant past, a group of renegade Zehk came to your realm and took on earthly forms. It was their intention to share their knowledge and interact totally, with the idea of creating a hybrid race. This precipitated a host of problems. The Zehk sought to destroy the rebels and their offspring, but were not entirely successful. That act alone was regarded as inappropriate. The Zehk now feel a sense of responsibility to your realm, because in their opinion most of humanity's problems were caused by the contamination of their gene pool.'

'Stop!' Lileem said. She felt as if a dire ghost stood at her shoulder.

Ta Ke raised his eyebrows, clearly not used to having "lower species" interrupt him when he was talking.

'Answer me this,' she said. 'In your opinion, could Wraeththu and Kamagrian have been created deliberately, in order to replace the human race?'

Ta Ke regarded her thoughtfully. 'I have been asleep for a long time. I cannot answer that.'

'An educated guess would do.'

He closed his eyes briefly. 'It is not beyond the realms of possibility.'

Lileem rubbed her hands over her face. 'It's like putting together an immense, universe-sized jigsaw puzzle.' She glanced at Ponclast. 'I feel we've just found an important piece, don't you?'

Ponclast shrugged. 'Perhaps the picture is becoming clearer.'

'But in that case, were we created by the Aasp, who favour advancement, or the Zehk, who wanted to clear up an ancient mess?'

'Neither faction could simply manifest in your realm and start creating new species,' Ta Ke said. 'It would have to be more complicated than that. Essentially, they'd have had to work through humans.'

'A breakthrough in knowledge,' Lileem said softly. Her voice became more excited. 'A human, or humans, working on a brilliant ground-breaking project that was in fact the seed of their own destruction.'

'Now you are making assumptions,' Ta Ke said. 'Before vaulting to conclusions, you should gather more information.'

'I've spent years of earthly time doing that,' Lileem said. 'Your words are the closest I've come to finding anything out.'

Ponclast fixed Ta Ke with a narrow-eyed stare. 'You still haven't answered my original question,' he said. 'Well?'

Ta Ke gestured languidly. 'Of course it will affect you. It all depends on who created you, doesn't it? But be aware of what happened to humanity when they received the gifts of the rebel Zehk. They became monstrous hybrids really. To use an analogy of your world, they became half angel, half beast, capable of the greatest compassion and nobility but also the basest brutality. Their natures were constantly at war with one another. Your kind should think carefully before accepting tempting offers from higher powers.'

'We already travel the Otherlanes,' Ponclast said. 'Do you think that should be curtailed?'

Ta Ke shrugged. 'That is not my decision to make. I suspect it is too late for that gift to be revoked, in any case.'

'I'll take you to Thanatep, or at least will try to,' Lileem said, 'on the understanding you'll help us discover our origins. Are you agreeable to that?'

Ta Ke inclined his head. 'It is a reasonable request.'

'Can we work in mind touch?' she asked.

'That should not present a problem,' Ta Ke replied.

'Good.' Lileem turned to Ponclast. 'I'll have to leave you alone… perhaps for some time.'

Ponclast raised a hand. 'You must do it. Don't concern yourself with me.'

Lileem hesitated. 'I won't forget you, Ponclast. Remember that.'

He closed his eyes briefly. 'I know…'

Lileem braced her shoulders and addressed Ta Ke. 'Well, there's no point in delay. Let's get started, shall we?'

Ta Ke nodded. 'I agree.' He held out his spidery hands to her. 'Join with me, and open your mind to me.'

Lileem did as he asked. The experience of touching his hands was unsettling enough because they enfolded her own completely, but the moment she touched his mind it unnerved her utterly. His essence was totally unfamiliar. She had to steel herself to withstand it.

Open a portal, Ta Ke instructed. *Project us into it, and I will then take control.*

Lileem did this by focusing inwardly on her own cauldron of creation. She visualised it as a doorway within her, through which she could step into other realities.

Interesting, Ta Ke observed.

Generally, when hara do this, they have to be engaged in aruna, sexual activity, Lileem told him. *I'm able to accomplish this purely by my own will.*

A useful skill, Ta Ke said. *Now, surrender your will to me. I can direct us from this point.*

Ta Ke effortlessly took control of Lileem's ability. He might have been physically impaired, but the strength of his mind and his will was volcanic. He used her as he would use a *sedu,* she thought. She was a vehicle he could direct.

As they neared Thanatep, the first thing that Lileem became aware of was that the realm contained harish life force. It was unmistakable because it was what she had often used to guide her in her travels. It was faint, just a trace. But what were hara, or creatures like hara, doing in that realm?

She communicated her findings to Ta Ke, and he was firm in his response. *If there are hara in Thanatep, it's likely they have been taken there by the Aasp. From what you have told me, they could be individuals taken from the battle of Fulminir. Do not attempt communication.*

Lileem was impressed Ta Ke had remembered such detail of her narrative, since at the time she'd related it, he'd still been learning her language.

But we're drawing closer to them.

Unavoidable. This is our exit point. It might be uncomfortable, because generally the opening of portals within Thannaril itself is prevented. But the wards have decayed enough for me to breach them. They will identify my life force and permit me entrance, but they might try to resist you.

If Lileem had been a horse, Ta Ke would have put spurs to her flanks to encourage her to jump. As it was, his psychic directive had the same effect and Lileem burst from the Otherlanes involuntarily. She hit the ground with a bone-shaking crack, and for some moments lay there, dazed, barely able to draw breath into her aching lungs. She felt as if an invisible force had tried to squeeze the life from her.

Ta Ke towered over her. 'Forgive me, that exit was rougher than I thought it would be. It is different with you than with a *sedu*. They are more adept.'

Lileem dragged herself into a sitting position. She clawed her hair from her face and gazed about herself. They were in a huge domed chamber that was lit with a beautiful dark blue radiance. The light was dim but bright enough to see by. Lileem and Ta Ke had manifested close to the circular wall. The chamber spread out in front of them, so large Lileem's perceptions had difficulty in taking in its details. 'Where exactly are we?' she asked.

'We are in my work area in Thannaril Below,' Ta Ke said. He surveyed his domain, hands on hips. 'I am relieved to see it does not appear to have been touched since I left it.'

Shakily, Lileem got to her feet. 'Why didn't the Aasp destroy it?'

Ta Ke had begun to walk along the wall, touching various glyphs of light there, which appeared to respond to his touch, since some of them brightened while others faded. Lileem followed him. 'The Aasp would not be so stupid,' Ta Ke said scornfully. 'To destroy Thannaril Below could have had catastrophic effects upon the fabric of the realms. The cities of Thanatep are inextricably wound with the different realms, although it is likely the Aasp disabled the surface areas of the city quite drastically. As far as the lower city is concerned, it is clear to me that the Aasp simply let things lie, go dormant. It must have been the only way for them. Thannaril and her sister cities are useless without the Thanadrim to manipulate them.' Ta Ke smiled at Lileem, clearly excited and pleased to be home. 'We must hope that the underground farms are still operational. Now, of course, free from Shaa Lemul, we will feel hunger and thirst. We will have to sleep.'

'Or I could fetch food from the earthly realm,' Lileem suggested.

Ta Ke sniffed fastidiously. 'I would prefer to see what's left here first. Also, I doubt you would find it easy to enter Thanatep again without me to guide you. It is well secured against intruders.'

'Then I hope the farms are still working,' Lileem said, 'or otherwise we'll starve.'

Ta Ke made no comment to this, but continued to examine his arcane equipment.

'What exactly do you plan to do?' Lileem asked him.

Ta Ke paused in his work. 'Inspect my tower, Mutandis,' he said. 'It rises above the surface of Thanatep, as do countless others, and is my tool of regulation. If I can wake it, it might be able to wake others. But it has been exposed to the elements for a long time, so I expect it will have suffered damage. I have to investigate the feasibility of repairing it.'

Lileem folded her arms. 'Ta Ke, there are other beings above us here. Perhaps we should go to a different city, somewhere isolated.'

Ta Ke shook his head. 'I can only work with my own tower. We are attuned.'

'Are you sure? Have you ever tried?'

Ta Ke regarded Lileem disapprovingly. 'Feel free to explore. If you go through that doorway over there and keep heading straight on, you should come to the farms. They are unmistakable.'

Lileem stood her ground. 'I question the wisdom of waking a tower when there might be agents of the Aasp around it. It doesn't make sense.'

Ta Ke sighed; it was clear his patience was wearing thin. 'Lileem, you speak in ignorance. It will take me some time to reactivate the tower, and I intend to be discreet. I know my job.'

'And if you succeed, what then?'

'I will use it to try and track down others of my kind, or seek alternative aid. It is possible a higher power might assist me, although they usually regard the antics of lesser beings as inconsequential.'

'You don't say!' Lileem shook her head. 'I'll go and look for food.'

Lileem found the farms quite easily, as they were recognisable by their glass exteriors. They looked in fact like enormous greenhouses. At first, Lileem was concerned she'd find only a barren desert of dried-up stalks within them, but was relieved to discover the opposite was true. The farms had been neglected, but the mechanisms that provided light and nutrients had obviously remained functional since, inside, the greenhouses resembled impenetrable jungle.

Lileem had to force her way in, and it took several tries, with different greenhouses, before she found one where she had the strength to push the door against the tangled growth within. She clawed her way through the vegetation and was pleased to discover large, pale-yellow fruits hanging amid enormous wide leaves. There was a strong smell of over-ripeness in the air, like sickly sweet honey. But for the first time in ages, her stomach growled in anticipation of food.

The plants had originally grown in raised beds between wide aisles, but now grew rampantly all over the place. Lileem progressed down one of the aisles, picking fruit as she did so, and laying them on the floor in piles. Although the smell the fruit left on her hands was strong, it was not unpleasant, and this indicated to her that they were unlikely to be toxic to her body. Back in the earthly realm, Lileem had often used her heightened senses to identify consumable foods in this way, but she decided to err on the side of caution and take everything she found back to Ta Ke before sampling it. Her body had waited years to feed; it could wait a short while longer now.

As she pulled the fruits down, she let her mind drift over pleasant memories: living with Flick, Ulaume and Mima on the riverboat *Esmeraldarine*; her first days in Shilalama; her love for Terez har Aralis. When she got to that part, Lileem decided she'd gathered enough to eat. She'd come to a work station, where panniers were stacked in a pile, just visible but mostly covered by leaves. She dragged one of the panniers free and retraced her steps up the aisle gathering the fruits she'd left on the floor. She supposed that different fruits and vegetables might grow in the other aisles; another time she'd investigate further.

When she returned to Ta Ke, he was not at all happy. She'd been gone for longer than she'd realised because he'd had time not only to inspect his tower on the surface, but also to scan the ethers for traces of his people.

'They are gone,' he told Lileem in bewilderment. 'I cannot find any sign of them. They have either died out or have been hidden somewhere so distant they might as well be dead.'

Lileem put down her basket. Ta Ke barely glanced at it. 'I'm sorry,' Lileem said. 'Can you do this alone?'

Ta Ke sighed heavily. 'The towers are badly damaged,' he said. 'Time has taken its toll on them. I do not even think the Aasp harmed them. Natural dissolution has gnawed at their fabric.'

'Does that mean you can't do anything here?'

Ta Ke's eyes took on a fierce expression. 'I will attempt to rebuild Mutandis. It will be a start. As to whether one tower is enough, I cannot yet say. I have no choice but to try.'

'Eat something,' Lileem said. 'This fruit smells edible.'

'They are goyani, yes,' Ta Ke said, in a wistful tone. He bent to take a fruit from the pannier, then held it to his nose. 'Once, I feasted on this delight with my loved ones.'

'I really am sorry,' Lileem said. 'It must be terrible for you. You said it felt like you only went to sleep yesterday. The grief…' She shook her head.

'In some ways, yes, there is much grief,' Ta Ke said, 'but in others, I am numb. I feel as if I lost everything a long time ago, even though it also feels recent. Strange. It must be an effect of what Hagak did to me.' He was silent for a moment, then bit into the fruit he held, chewed it slowly. He swallowed, blinked a few times and sighed. Then, almost sadly, he smiled. 'Try the goyani, Lileem. Enjoy this experience for the new and rare thing it is for you, and I will enjoy it for the happy memories it invokes. There are many other delights to be found in the farms.'

'You haven't seen the state of the farms,' Lileem said dryly. 'They are jungles now.'

'But still fertile,' Ta Ke said. 'We must be thankful for that. You will need something to occupy your time as I am working. You can concentrate on clearing an area in the farms for us.'

Lileem laughed. 'All right. It'll be like old times for me. But if there's anything I can do to help you with your work, please let me assist.'

Ta Ke inclined his head. 'I will bear that in mind.'

Lileem could tell he didn't think a lower being of her type could do anything to help him. She sighed. She had a feeling she'd be in this place for a long time.

Chapter Eighteen

Ookami set up his black pavilion in the field opposite Phade's Tower. It appeared overnight, and Darq first saw it when he rose from his bed and looked out of his window. Ground mist swirled around the graceful folds of fabric; it looked somehow mystical, as if a magician lived within. There was no sign of life, because Ookami wasn't in it. He was elsewhere, breathing in the morning. Darq did not yet know the name of this har but nonetheless was aware that his fate had come to meet him. His time at Samway was nearly over.

A fleeting twinge of wistfulness nibbled at his heart, and he turned to face the bed where Thiede lay sleeping. For two weeks since Darq's feybraiha, he and Thiede had been together almost constantly. They had kept themselves apart from other hara, either walking in the woods where they had long conversations, or else exploring the delights of aruna. Darq had accepted this exotic lover, as if it was a privilege he'd earned or deserved. It seemed he'd always known Thiede, deep in his blood, and maybe he had.

Since they'd been physically close, Darq had noticed that his own abilities had strengthened. He knew it would take very little to extend a seeking tendril now and insert it into Thiede's mind. Was the har so deeply asleep he wouldn't notice? Thiede knew everything. Darq was impatient with the notion that ignorance was protection. He wanted to know everything too.

But don't you realise? his own conscience whispered, *once you're away from here and away from Thiede, you'll have more freedom. You'll be free to explore in your own way. Whatever har they've sent to train you doesn't matter. Pretend, as you've always pretended. You know there are other creatures and hara out there who have the information you need.*

As if these thoughts were too loud and had roused him, Thiede awoke, and stretched. Then he fixed Darq with a stare. 'Your new mentor is here,' he said. 'I can feel it. His name is Ookami.'

'There's a black pavilion in the field opposite,' Darq said. 'I suppose that's his.'

Thiede narrowed his eyes. 'He will not be what you expect, Darq.' Which could have meant anything.

Darq shrugged. He didn't care.

Thiede clearly thought Darq should care. 'Don't you want to know how I found him?'

Again, Darq shrugged. 'How did you find him?' he asked, deadpan.

'His master is known to me, a Nahir-Nuri of the Far East. I know his students are particularly useful as both bodyguards and teachers. I communicated with him, and he told me Ookami was fairly close to us here. He recommended this har as of exceptional talent.'

'I'm sure,' Darq said.

The new mentor did not appear at breakfast, as Darq had expected. Phade seemed almost forlorn, now that he truly realised that Darq would soon be leaving. Darq winced as Phade attempted a farewell speech. 'I haven't always been the best guardian to you. But know that Samway is always home for you, Darq. If you ever need to, come back, or call to me.'

Darq had no intention of doing any such thing. He supposed that, in a dim way, he was slightly fond of Phade, but now that Amelza had gone, and her family was cut off from him, there was little to keep him in Samway. There would be other landscapes, other forests. The world was full of them.

After breakfast, Thiede went to find Ookami, which Darq thought was rather unusual. Surely, this har should have presented himself to Phade before anything else, and Thiede was important and shouldn't have to go looking for anyhar. For the first time, Darq felt a worm of trepidation concerning this individual.

Thiede told Darq to wait for him in the tower, and thus Darq was forced to endure further attempts by Phade to say goodbye. Clearly, the har felt guilty that Darq's removal was necessary.

'I hope in some measure what you've learned here will help protect you,' Phade said, and then drew in his breath, as if a weightier speech was about to emerge.

'Will you excuse me?' Darq interrupted. 'I'd like to take a bath.' He wasn't sure which of them was the more relieved when he left the room.

Darq looked up and down the empty corridor beyond the dining room. He closed his eyes briefly and scanned for living presences with his senses. Everyhar was engaged in morning work. In the yard, a few guards discussed another, who wasn't present. It seemed this har had offended them. Darq listened to their rather heated exchange for a few moments, then got bored of it. He thought himself into a quiet space and went outside the tower. In the yard, he walked right past the guards who did not see or even sense him. Darq headed towards the fields.

The pavilion was still empty. Darq could perceive that wards had been placed about its entrance to deter intruders. He could also tell that the har who owned the tent travelled light. A well-bred black horse was tethered nearby. It was not a large creature, but very beautiful. Darq went up to the horse and stroked its long nose. It sniffed him in a skittish manner, whites showing around the edges of its eyes, ears flicking back and forth. 'So where is your master, hey?' Darq whispered to it.

Thiede had left a shimmering trail, visible only to Darq. It was easy to follow. The trail led into the forest beyond the fields, lying like sparkling mist over the damp grass. It wound between the trees, beckoning Darq onward. Eventually, it led to a glade, where Darq could see Thiede standing in the shadows of the oaks and birches that surrounded it. Thiede was in a quiet place too, silently observing the har who moved upon the grass. Darq skirted the glade and took up a similar position some distance from Thiede. He took care to wrap himself in deceits, to blend in with the surroundings. He was sure Thiede could not sense him.

A har, clad in trousers and shirt of loose black silk, danced a ballet of swords in the early sun. His dark hair hung like a sheet of unravelled silk also, swinging with his movements. His feet were bare and the two swords he brandished flashed like silver fire. Darq considered that this har knew perfectly well he was being watched. He expected the performance would end with one of the blades being flung, perhaps to spear a tree at Darq or Thiede's shoulder. It might be best to leave now, to deny the har this final flourish. But the dance was hypnotic and Darq was reluctant to leave, without being consciously aware of it.

'He could teach you this art,' murmured a voice. 'The dance… and the death that goes with it.'

Darq wheeled round, and all his concealing devices evaporated.

Thiede stood smiling behind him. 'I thought I told you to wait for me.'

'You did. I was curious.'

The dancing har had ceased his practice and now stood in the centre of the glade, staring expressionlessly. His eyes were slanted. He looked nothing like any har that Darq had seen before.

'Ookami,' Thiede said, his voice louder. 'This is Darquiel, who is impatient to meet you.'

The har bowed to Thiede and approached. He still held the silver blades in each hand. Darq had the distinct impression Ookami was offended that he had been interrupted. He would not show it, though. Darq was sure this har rarely showed anything that lay inside him. That was something Darq could admire.

The har inclined his head to Darq, his eyes full of an expression that implied he understood what Darq was about, all too clearly. 'I am honoured to serve you, Tiahaar,' he said to Thiede. Could he possibly mean that?

Darq laughed aloud, and the sound fractured the morning air harshly. He regretted it at once.

'The exuberance of youth,' Thiede said airily, as if by apology, and now he seemed distant, an adult far removed from Darq's life, not the har Darq had lain with for two weeks. Darq felt stung and moved to rebellion. He pushed past Thiede and ran back towards the tower. He felt young again; this was the morning he had woken up to a strange feeling, and later he would notice Amelza for the first time.

Back in his room, Darq lay on his back on the bed, blinking at the ceiling. He would go so far into himself, nohar would find him. And then there was a voice in his head that said, *Not even me, sweet thing?*

Not even you, Darq answered at once, although he had a feeling that wasn't true.

Very shortly, Phade knocked on Darq's door and entered the room without waiting for a response. 'You should come and meet this har, Ookami,' he said.

Darq propped himself up on his elbows. 'I *have* met him,' he said.

'Properly, Darq. Formally.'

'He looks different.'

'He's from a tribe that lives far away,' Phade said. 'From the Orientis. Thiede has chosen him to be your new guardian, because he has the skills to protect you, and also to teach you. Your caste training must begin at once.'

Darq knew vaguely about this training, and that he was supposed to aim for progression through the various levels. Privately, he scorned the concept. He knew what he had to know and would teach himself more. It was just a question of application and attention. 'Where will he take me?'

'I won't be informed of that, for obvious reasons. Somewhere safe. Come along, now. Be polite.'

Darq stood up. He felt as if his life had become a series of unconnected present moments.

Phade had installed Ookami in a formal reception room on the first floor of the tower. Househara had brought to him a late breakfast, and he now sat drinking tea with Thiede. When Darq entered the room, their conversation ceased. *Thiede has told him I am trouble,* Darq thought.

'Darquiel,' Thiede said in a cool greeting. 'You'll be leaving today, after you've prepared what items you wish to take with you. It would be best if you were stern with yourself about that. Too much luggage will be awkward.'

'I have nothing to take with me,' Darq said, 'apart from clothes.'

'Choose a horse for yourself from the stables,' Phade said. 'Take your pick, apart from my own.'

'*I* will choose a mount for him,' said Ookami, in a serene yet commanding tone.

'Of course,' Phade said hurriedly. 'My staff can walk the best ones out for you.'

Ookami inclined his head, sipped tea. So far, he had not yet glanced at Darq, which Darq knew was deliberate. He was being treated like an animal that needed careful handling to be tamed. Perhaps, if he was ignored, Ookami expected Darq ultimately to edge forward and sniff the taming hand. It would be best for now to let him believe such a ploy might work.

'Look on this as an adventure,' Thiede said.

Darq gave him a withering look, hoping also to inject a small measure of disappointment in the expression. *Don't treat me like a harling. I'm not stupid.*

Thiede held Darq's gaze, but let no information slip from his eyes. 'We'll meet again, Darquiel. Trust my judgment for now.'

Darq said nothing. He felt nothing.

The Olopade occupied a myth-soaked landscape. Darq had seen little of it, because Phade had kept him close to home, and the Olopade had little contact with other hara in the country. Soon, Darq would see that the forests appeared to go on forever, that the mountains were full of silent, brooding power. The remains of ancient castles had been taken over by various Wraeththu factions, comprising the indigenous incepted, known collectively as the Anakhai, which was also the name by which the region was now known, with many sub-tribes and groups within it and, in the western territories at least, also hara who had travelled east from Megalithica during the Gelaming purge of the Uigenna/Varr alliance. Phade's Tower itself was one of these structures, and had undergone radical reconstruction once Phade had been installed there by Thiede, long before Pellaz had been taken to

Immanion. Many of the towns and cities of Anakhai had fallen to ruin, yet a few had been claimed by Wraeththu. Ookami intended to avoid these settlements. Humans had badly polluted much of the landscape, but since their demise the world had tidied up the debris of human depredation. Anakhai was a wild and beautiful place. Most of the old roads had long gone, but it was still possible to ride along the overgrown railway tracks in places. Not that Ookami intended to take any such risks; he preferred to follow the deer trails.

On the first afternoon of their journey, neither Ookami nor Darq spoke much at all. Darq was content simply to drink in the sights that unfolded along their path. He could feel the power of the landscape rising around him like green-gold steam. He fancied the spectral hunters of the forest observed their progress from the shadows; weak ghosts in the afternoon. Ookami had chosen a fleet yet sturdy mount for Darq: a bay, gelded colt named Follet. Darq was pleased, because he especially liked the creature. Follet was known for his stubbornness, which suited Darq perfectly. Sometimes, the colt was filled with an urge to run, when there was no stopping him, save by breaking his knees. Like Darq, Follet had learned early the advantages of taking the bit between his teeth. But today, the colt was calm, his head hung low, as they ambled along the forest path, with sunlight coming down in hot yet narrow cascades through the canopy of foliage.

Late in the afternoon, Ookami chose a place to pitch his black tent. He did not ask Darq to help him, so Darq went for a walk. They had camped near to a woodland stream; Darq took off his boots and sat on the bank, dangling his feet in the water. It was so cold, it hurt at first, but then his flesh numbed and the sensation was pleasurable. Sunlight warmed his hair and the back of his neck where the locks parted. The only things he could hear were birdsong, the ripple of the water over stones and the dull knocking sound of Ookami hammering tent pegs into the soft earth. Darq felt light of spirit, as if he could dissolve into his surroundings. These were the physical pleasures of leaving Samway behind.

Presently, the knocking died down, and Darq became aware that Ookami had crept up behind him. He turned his head. 'Did you expect me to help you?' Darq asked. He felt he ought to know. Perhaps a "sorry" was in order.

'You can prepare our meal,' Ookami said.

'I don't know how to cook.'

'Then learn.'

Darq could see how this skill was useful to survival. 'Teach me,' he said.

'Can you hunt?' Ookami asked.

'You'll need to teach me that too.'

Darq had also to learn what local fungi and plants were edible. As he cut up roots and put them into a pot, Ookami began to instruct him in the various options available to hara on the road. Darq enjoyed the education, being fond of facts. Ookami was patient. In fact, in some ways, he was like a statue brought to life. He did his job and that was that.

Later, as they ate beside their fire, Ookami questioned Darq about his natural abilities, and his understanding of being Aralid, the first of the caste levels. Darq explained to Ookami that he didn't really think such distinctions applied to him, and braced himself to defend his position.

Ookami merely nodded. 'It will still be useful if you learn about the system,' he said, 'to understand where your abilities fit within it.'

'What tribe are you from?' Darq asked.

'Ikutama,' Ookami replied.

'You look different to other hara I've seen. I don't mean that rudely; you're what hara call beautiful, I suppose.'

'You've seen very little,' Ookami said. 'Your book is at its first page.'

Darq liked those words. He smiled, and Ookami smiled back, slightly.

'The most important aspect of magic is silence,' Ookami said. 'When your mind, soul and body are quiet, you have clarity to move energy.'

'I know that,' Darq said. 'I've been experimenting with it recently. It allows me to move among hara unseen.'

Ookami nodded. 'That's one aspect. You can also use it for far-seeing, for non-local communication and many other things.'

'Is that part of Ara?'

Again, Ookami smiled. 'Perhaps awareness of it is part of Ara, but as you have rightly deduced, some of your skills transcend the lowest levels.'

'How can you tell? I might be exaggerating.'

'I can tell,' Ookami said.

'Can I begin to learn about the swords?'

'In time. For now, you should concentrate on journeying inward, listening to your own silence. Transcend impatience. I can see that's a trait you have.'

Darq knew immediately that Ookami was right, even though he'd never considered that before. He realised that working with this har would not be as annoying as he'd thought it would be. He appreciated

Ookami's reserve, the way he didn't appear to think a silence was something that should be filled with inane chatter.

When they had finished eating, Ookami said, 'We can begin your training now, if you're ready.'

'I'm ready,' Darq said.

Ookami nodded and took out some incense from one of his leather satchels. He threw some grains of the sweet-smelling resin into their campfire and instructed Darq to compose himself for meditation. He led Darq on an inner journey, through wondrous landscapes, which he described in a soft voice. Darq's mind expanded. He felt as if he were nothing but a spark of consciousness in an endless vista of wonders. He did not feel disorientated or disturbed. He felt at peace.

After the meditation, Ookami did not ask Darq to describe his experiences, but simply said, 'Reflect on what you've seen. The landscapes you saw are part of yourself, and there will be messages within them for you.'

'It was interesting,' Darq said.

'It was a start.' Ookami smiled. 'Now, we should sleep.'

Darq had his own bedroll, which he laid out in the surprisingly spacious pavilion next to Ookami. Before they went to sleep, Darq asked, 'Are you taking me anywhere in particular? You don't have to tell me where. I'm just curious.'

'We'll go where our trail leads,' Ookami replied. 'That's not a deliberately obscure answer; it's what will be.'

'So, the answer really is no,' Darq said. 'How much do you know about me?'

Ookami raised himself from his bed, propping himself on one elbow, his head resting against his hand. 'My hienama gave me this task. I was told where to come, and that I'd be entrusted with the care of a young har. Your guardians informed me you might be in danger, from factions who wish to use you. That's the sum total of my knowledge. Is there anything you'd care to add to that?'

'No, I was hoping you could enlighten me.' Darq paused. 'I think my parents were important... or are. I don't know who they are, but I'm sure my lineage is significant.'

'That seems a sensible deduction,' Ookami said.

Darq considered, at this point, telling Ookami about the voice he sometimes heard in his head, but for some reason felt reluctant. He knew that Ookami would tell him to block it out, and Darq also knew that would be the right thing to do, and yet part of him welcomed the messages. He did not feel particularly threatened by them, and once Ookami had trained him in the manner Thiede had suggested, surely

Darq could look after himself?

'Sleep now,' Ookami said, lying down again. 'We'll head towards the east tomorrow.'

'How long for?' Darq asked. 'There must be an end to this.'

'There will be,' Ookami said, 'and when it reveals itself, we must be prepared.'

After a few days' travel, Darq realised that the desires Thiede had awoken in him were not something to be confined to a few nights' pleasure after feybraiha. He was astounded to discover his body had physical demands, which appeared to override many other considerations. Ookami, for all his reserve, became an object of desire that Darq wished to touch and taste. However, the har did not appear to share these needs. He was utterly self-contained. Darq had no idea what the etiquette of such things might be, so he wrestled with how the subject should be broached. Eventually, he decided a direct approach was best, so he announced over their evening meal one night, 'My body needs aruna.'

'That's natural,' Ookami replied. 'We'll enter one of the villages tomorrow. There, you can attend to your physical needs.'

This was not quite the answer Darq had anticipated. 'Won't that be dangerous? I thought we had to stay away from other hara.'

'These are isolated communities,' Ookami said. 'My instincts tell me you'll be quite safe.'

'You speak as if I must go alone,' Darq said. He didn't welcome the idea of that. How did hara initiate physical contact? He foresaw difficult moments.

'I can't take part in such activities,' Ookami said. 'I'm preparing for a Grissecon and must abstain for a while.'

'Isn't that… problematical?'

Ookami twitched one side of his mouth into a smile. 'It can be borne,' he said.

'That's another thing you must teach me,' Darq said. 'I find this whole aruna thing very inconvenient. It's worse than having to eliminate waste!'

Ookami laughed aloud. 'You're an unusual har, Darquiel.'

'So I've been told. Well? Will you teach me that?'

'I'll teach you how to prevent discomfort,' Ookami said, 'but really you should not deny yourself aruna unless it's unavoidable. It is a pleasurable activity, as well as refreshing in both a spiritual and physical sense.'

'I do enjoy it,' Darq said, 'but the fact that it's a need rather than a choice is irksome.'

'You haven't truly enjoyed it yet,' Ookami said. 'If you had, you wouldn't speak like that.'

'So, what must I do? Just go up to somehar? I really don't know.'

'I'll come with you to socialise, if necessary,' Ookami said. 'You'll be pleasantly surprised. It's not that difficult, and you too are what hara call beautiful, though in truth you meet few who aren't.'

'So, if everyhar's beautiful, then nohar is more desirable than any other?'

'It doesn't work quite like that. We all have our individual preferences. You'll eventually discover yours.'

'I find it difficult to look at hara in that way,' Darq said. He sighed deeply. 'I'm swiftly coming to the conclusion this might be an aberration.'

Ookami grinned. 'Trust me, there will be certain hara who you *do* look at in that way. Start tomorrow. I'm sure you'll see what I mean.'

'I already see what you mean,' Darq said, 'but it just seems to me my preferences are narrow, and sometimes you can't always have what you want.'

Ookami observed him inscrutably for some moments. Then he inclined his head in silent acknowledgment. Darq's heart turned over.

Chapter Nineteen

The following day, they came to a valley with a river running through it. A small town clung to both sides of the valley, which had a relatively small community of hara who called themselves the Nemodilkii. They did not speak a language either Darq or Ookami could understand, and the only way communication could take place was through mind touch. The language spoken predominantly in Samway was Megalithican, since the Olopade were not originally native to this land. Although the mountain phyles of the tribe spoke other languages, Darq had never learned them. Phade had made it a requirement that all his hara could speak Megalithican too. Darq quickly found himself wishing he'd learned Anakhai before, but of course he'd never thought he'd have a need to know it. Mind touch was immensely useful, and in many ways eliminated the need to learn other tongues, but there was something in speaking aloud, face to face, that could not be replaced by any communication of the mind.

Darq and Ookami rode into the town square, which flanked both sides of the river. The water ran wide and shallow in that place and could be crossed on foot, although there were numerous bridges for carts and those who wished to keep their boots dry. Hara went about their business, and most made a gesture of greeting to the two strangers. In mind touch, Ookami asked a har for directions to the Nayati. He'd told Darq it was well thought of by hara if newcomers went to pay their respects at the community sacred building on arrival.

The buildings of the town were very old and apparently lovingly tended. The Nayati was actually the original church, once used by humans, and many of the ancient icons remained, now decked with the garlands of a gentler religion. Ookami said he also wanted to visit the place in order to acknowledge his gods, the dehara of Ikutama. He missed them when travelling in lands beyond their immediate influence. It was possible to speak with any dehar in a working Nayati.

While Ookami sat cross-legged on the worn stone floor, and composed himself for votive meditation, Darq wandered around the building, taking in details. The Nayati was empty but for its two visitors, and the atmosphere was peaceful, the air smelling of lilies. Darq stared at the brightly coloured windows, depicting bearded men who raised admonishing fingers and looked stern. Every single one of them appeared about to give someone a severe telling off. Darq came upon a realistic life-size statue of a man hanging upon a wooden cross, and thought he looked quite beautiful, but for his hairy face. So sad a god, though. And how cruel of humans to have kept him like that. Darq thought that those who had worshipped the hanging god should have cut him down from his torment centuries ago. Darq was compelled to pick up a handful of flowers and twine them around the statue's head and shoulders. It made the whole thing look more cheerful.

The town was sleepy in the afternoon. Dogs lay sunning themselves on doorsteps, and the distant sounds of hara at work came from the fields. Ookami considered it safe for Darq to wander around on his own for a while, perhaps thinking this would give his charge the opportunity to strike up friendships. So, while Ookami pitched the tent in a meadow outside town, Darq ambled into an area where pottery was made. Here, looking into the open workshops, he made polite and guarded greetings to the hara working within. All were cordial, if reserved. Some tried to sell him wares, others sent him images of places where he could find a good meal. Visitors were few in this area, but hara clearly perceived he was no threat.

Life appeared to move at a very slow pace here; slower even than Samway, which was hardly a maelstrom of hectic activity itself. Darq could feel himself slowing down, as if falling into a dream. He came upon a young potter working a clay pot on a turning wheel. Noticing he was being observed, this har beckoned for Darq to approach. He took Darq's hands in his own and pressed them to the wet clay. Darq laughed, enjoying the silky feel of the forming vessel beneath his fingers. The other har laughed too, even when Darq's clumsy pressing reduced the pot to a misshapen mass.

You are just passing through, the har said to him in mind touch.

Yes… a short visit. I like it here.

Where are you travelling to?

I don't know.

The har raised his eyebrows, 'Darzu,' he said, and placed a hand against his own chest.

'Darq.' Darquiel indicated himself.

I will finish work soon. Would you like me to show you the best place to eat?

That is kind of you, though I probably don't have any of your currency.

Darzu grinned. *I can stretch to buying roasted roots for a hungry stranger.*

Darq inclined his head in gratitude, realising he was probably looking at the second har with whom he'd take aruna. Darzu had a wide, high-cheekboned face, and dark auburn hair, which he wore in three plaits, two of which hung over his shoulders, the other down his back. In sunlight, his eyes were almost orange. His hands were long and sensitive, the hands of an artist. Darq knew he should probably inform Ookami about this development and indicated as much to his new friend. *I'm travelling with my teacher. I should tell him my plans, otherwise he would worry.* Or rather, Darq thought, Ookami would look for him, which could be inconvenient.

If you return in an hour, I'll be finished, Darzu told him.

Darq walked to the meadow where Ookami had erected their tent. 'I have an assignation,' Darq said.

Ookami smiled. 'Efficient work, my friend!'

'I'm going to eat with him. Will you excuse me?'

'Of course.' Ookami hesitated. 'Be careful in the tides, Darquiel. Let nothing slip through the water. The hara here are not your foes, but others might pass through later, who are.'

'I understand. My mind is sealed.'

Darzu took Darquiel to a small inn, which was full of workers relaxing after a day's toil. It appeared hara in this area did not believe in working long hours, since they took their dinner fairly early by Samway standards.

We do what is necessary, Darzu explained when Darq questioned him. *Life is for more than toil, don't you agree? We produce enough to fulfil our needs and a little over for the late summer markets. All hara of Nemodilkii believe in the celebration of life, and all of its subtle pleasures.*

It sounds excellent, Darq agreed.

Friends of Darzu's came to join them, and for some time Darq was able to observe his companions in silence, since they were all chattering in their native tongue. He did not feel excluded, however. He drank the heavy red wine that Darzu had bought for him, which further enhanced his general feelings of torpor. A har with a fiddle began to play, and another young har, with long rags of black hair, jumped onto a table to dance. His trousers came to just below his knees and he wore beaded bracelets around his ankles. Other hara clapped and sang. Perhaps it was wonderful to lead so simple and joyous a life. These hara appeared to have no cares; they lived fully in the moment. Darq found it impossible to imagine any of them lying awake at night, full of inexpressible thoughts and desires, yearning for something they'd never heard of.

Darq was quite drunk by the time Darzu suggested they leave the inn. The Nemodilkii had unbound his hair; it hung in a rippling dark red cloud down his chest and back. Darq could smell its perfume. Outside the inn, it was very dark, as there were no lamps or torches to light the narrow streets. Darzu took one of Darq's hands in his own. His palm was powdery with clay. Sometime during the evening an unspoken agreement had been reached.

Darquiel expected to be taken to Darzu's home, but perhaps that was not the custom with strangers in Nemodilkii. They went out of town and into the forest meadows, where sheep cropped the sweet grass; ghostly shapes in the darkness. Overhead, the sky blazed with stars, although there was no moon. At the top of one of the hills was a hollow, surrounded by trees. At the bottom of the hollow was a pool, and the earth around it had been churned to mud by sheep and wild deer. Ferns grew high around the pool, and Darzu took Darquiel into them.

There are spirits of the ferns, he said. *They live in the smell of the green. They are powerful and sometimes cruel, but to them aruna is an offering. They will give you favour.*

Nothing had so far been mentioned about any such intimacy. Clearly, Darzu had simply assumed Darquiel would be compliant, as indeed he was. How strange though that these things were taken for granted.

Darzu drew Darq into an embrace and leaned forward to share breath with him. Darq was slightly reticent; he knew how information could leak in the wisps of swirling breath. Behind the physical warmth of Darzu's lips lay the story of his life; images of his harlinghood, snatches of conversation with colleagues, an argument with a dear friend. Darq was alarmed. How could he tell what might be pouring from himself?

Darzu perceived his hesitation. *You're not long past feybraiha, I can tell. Are you afraid of me?*

No, I'm not used to intimate sharing, that's all. It discomforts me a little.

Forgive me. I have nothing to hide, and yet I hardly know you. I didn't mean to embarrass you.

I'm not embarrassed, just surprised you would show me so much. I'm not used to strangers.

Darzu seemed a little crestfallen, for which Darq felt contrite. He took Darzu's face in his hands and kissed him, at the same time letting flow a few harmless images of his life in Samway; the moon on the waters of the lake, looking up through a forest of tall pines, hearing the cry of birds. Nothing more. Darzu's breath seeped right into him, in pinkish-yellow tendrils of light. They coiled like warm steam in his chest, down his limbs. They settled as little flames in the pit of his stomach.

Darzu gently touched Darq's ouana-lim through his trousers, indicating his preference. Darq acknowledged this signal and let all of his sensual energy pour into his masculine aspect. Darzu uttered a soft gasp. He drew away and undressed himself, soume in starlight. Darq did likewise, thinking that what they were about to do was like a magical ritual. He felt like an ancient priapic god of the forest, who would honour a deity of the living breathing earth, digging into the soil, planting nourishment. Darzu knelt before him, and for several minutes pleasured Darq expertly with his mouth, something Thiede had never done. Sometimes it was almost painful, because the petal folds were hypersensitive, but it enlivened the organ in a way Darq hadn't experienced before either. He was trembling, and eventually had to pull away, sink to his knees. He felt as if his ouana-lim was about to tear free of his body and scuttle off about its own business. The rest of him was merely a tiresome appendage. He was light-headed, in agony, yet ecstatic. He could barely move.

Darzu drew him down among the ferns, and guided Darq into him, which Darq was incapable of doing by himself. He let Darzu do most of the work, swooning upon his body, wholly unsure if he was in pleasure or pain. He wanted it to end, or else go on forever. It was impossible to tell. The tide was building up within him, bringing clarity. Gradually, the uncomfortable feelings were washed away. Darq uttered a cry; his movements became furious, and Darzu moaned beneath him. They were moving towards a shining pinnacle, when the universe would shower them in light. It was incredible. Sensations and images crashed through Darq's mind. He couldn't help what flowed from himself, but there was nothing to fear. Those images meant nothing to Darzu; he was beyond noticing them. Darq's upper body reared up, just at the moment when they reached the eye of the storm, the moment of stillness before release. He felt triumphant, powerful, joyous...

Then darkness slammed into his body between his shoulder blades.

He shuddered, feeling blue-black light flood throughout his flesh. Darzu screamed in pleasure, releasing fluids that were burning hot. Darq was paralyzed. He felt his own release, but another entity controlled it. A dark fist closed about his heart.

Mine!

Darq passed out for some moments. When he came to, Darzu was still moving weakly beneath him, his soume-lam contracting with the last dying waves of orgasm. Whatever had possessed Darq had either departed or gone into hiding. It did not seem as if Darzu had noticed anything amiss. He took Darq's face in his damp hands, kissed him, squeezed him. He spoke words aloud Darq couldn't understand, though Darq intuited their meaning. Darzu was more than pleased with their union. Darq touched the har's face and rolled off him. He realised at that moment his heart was beating so fast it was painful. He felt as if he'd been punched in the back, a blow that had reached right through his chest. Darzu settled himself along Darq's side, placed a hand on Darq's breast. Darq wound an arm around Darzu's shoulders.

You're dazed… Darzu laughed aloud. *Perhaps I drank too deep of you.*

Darq squeezed Darzu's shoulder. *Yes… I think perhaps you did. It was overwhelming, amazing.* Now was a time Darq wished he could speak aloud. It was too much effort to concentrate on mind touch, difficult to keep his confusion and fear from his thoughts.

I can teach you many things. I like to teach this way. Doesn't your teacher do that for you?

No, he can't. He has to abstain for some reason. It's partly why we came here.

Then I'm glad to have helped you. I can see you know very little.

Darq was thinking on two levels: on one he was trying to communicate affably with Darzu, on another his mind was screaming in panic about what had happened. He knew enough about aruna to realise that the blue-black light was not natural. It was not part of him. But what was it? And why had it come at that moment like that?

Darzu sighed languorously and took a lock of Darq's hair in his hand. *I saw in the sunlight the threads of gold in your hair, like the most expensive fabric; black silk threaded with gold. Your eyes are the same, dark with motes of gold. You looked so serious, standing there in the doorway, and yet full of promise and magic. From the very first moment I saw you, this is where I wanted to be.*

Darq didn't know how to react to these disclosures. He supposed it was a fancier way of intimating what he'd felt himself. *This one will do.* But it could be more than that for Darzu. *Perhaps,* Darq thought, *I can never feel that way.* And perhaps there was no outside entity flooding his body with dark light. It might be wholly part of himself, after all.

You seem wistful, beauty… Darzu's fingers traced the line of Darquiel's jaw. *Muscles so tight. Will you not let me in? Can I not help?*

I'm fine… really. To shut Darzu up, to distract him, Darquiel guided Darzu's lips to his own. In his breath, there was only summertime, the warmth of the day seeping from the hills, a soft cry from a night bird like a song of love.

They slept for some time, naked in the ferns. Darquiel's dreams were empty of fear. He dreamed he was riding with Ookami, and they were talking about making fire from a waterfall they would come to, which even in the dream seemed odd. Ookami was different, more like Darzu in manner. He kept leaning over from his horse to touch Darq's hair and once said, 'You must stop being so beautiful. It has blinded me in one eye.' In the dream, Darq experienced an unusual volt of personal power. He felt very happy.

He awoke to Darzu nuzzling the back of his neck. They were lying side by side, curled into each other' bodies. Darzu's breath was heavy in Darq's ear and he could feel the slightly pulsing hardness of Darzu's ouana-lim against his spine. Was this wise? Even as Darq was mulling over the possibility in his head, his body responded. Darzu's right hand slid over his hip, between his legs. Darq felt his breath come faster. He put his own hand on top of Darzu's, uttered a sigh. Darzu gently bit his ear and slowly withdrew his hand. Darq began to turn over, but Darzu stopped him. *No...Lie like this. It is another way. Open to me, Darq.* He pushed into Darq very slowly; it was the most blissful feeling. Darq put his own hand between his legs again, stroked the slippery hardness sliding into him and out. This was very different to how it had been with Thiede. Not that it had been bad, just different, somehow less intimate. Darq realised then that Thiede had difficulty letting go. Aruna with him was more clinical, less elemental.

It's very good... Darq told Darzu. *Make it last.*

I will.

Darzu stopped moving. *Listen to the night. Be still. Feel it all around us.*

Darq did so. The darkness was full of sounds; rustling, animal squeaks, the mysterious call of an owl. He could hear the sheep, their comforting calls to one another. This night was magical.

Darzu expelled a strange coughing sound, and for a moment his body shuddered. Darq thought there was something wrong with the har, but then he began moving again, powerfully now, faster. Darq couldn't keep quiet. He felt as if stars were exploding inside him, one after the other.

Slow, Darzu... I can't...

Darzu ignored this request. Instead, he reached forward with one hand and touched the bunched chrysanthemum of Darq's quiescent ouana-lim. He pushed his fingers into it, which was uncomfortable.

'No,' Darq said aloud. He struggled a little. 'Don't, that hurts.' It was as if Darzu were reaching right inside him, trying to stimulate his masculine aspect, but surely that was impossible. 'Darzu!'

Darq attempted to pull away and a voice said in his ear, 'Don't look round.'

Darq froze. Could Darzu speak his language after all? If so, why had he kept quiet before? This thought was swiftly followed by: *It's not Darzu.*

'Don't you know me, Darquiel? Don't be afraid. I can only come to you this way.'

'Who are you?'

'We have spoken, haven't we? You know me.'

Darquiel realised that, in whatever bizarre way, the har moving inside him at that moment was the owner of the voice that had spoken in his head. 'How?' he said. 'How are you doing this?'

'It's very easy, especially with a simple soul like your new friend. You felt me earlier. I know you did. Don't be afraid. I wish you no harm.'

'What *do* you wish me?' Darq asked. The har's hand was still caressing him in a disturbingly invasive manner.

'Let go of yourself. I want to give you something. Trust me.'

'Trust you?' Darq almost laughed. 'I don't know who or what you are, and this situation is grotesque. Get off me!'

'I can't do that and neither do you want me to. Let me show you something. Relax. Give in. You won't regret it. We are kin, in a way.'

'Kin?'

'I know you want your kin, Darquiel. And soon I will speak to you of this matter. For now, enjoy what I can give you. It will help if you push a little.'

'What are you doing to me?'

'Showing you the ultimate androgyny, my lovely. The experience makes ordinary aruna seem like puddle water. This is the finest of wines.'

'Ouana and soume? Is that what you're saying?'

'Yes. Come to my hand. And relinquish yourself to physical sensation.'

Darq could feel then that inside his body, his ouana-lim was waking up. It was a peculiar stretched feeling, as if his body was confused. It seemed like the organ didn't know whether to emerge or not. But the massaging fingers were persuasive, and Darq found it was possible to push against them, into them. Presently, he was hard, flowing into his unknown lover's hands. On another level, he was wholly soume. It was a weird experience, like being two hara at the same time. The sensations were entirely different, yet somehow joined by a taut silver cord; that was the image in Darq's mind. He closed his eyes, gave into it, and his conscious mind sank deep. It was like dreaming, ultimately. He was no longer aware of flesh, but simply expressions of feeling he had no terms for. The ouana-lim inside him was the same as the one outside of him, moving forward like a vehicle into unimaginable territory. They became one har, desiring more than hands around them.

And then the black, star-studded sky turned purple and the stars began to disappear. A monstrous shape appeared, first as a silhouette, then gradually taking form. It was a gigantic har, hanging in the sky, whose skin was the night. His hair was snakes of darkness and his beauty was terrible. This vision drew closer, becoming smaller as it did so, until it hung before Darq's streaming eyes the size of an ordinary har. He rolled onto his back, unable to feel the har beneath him. All he knew was that he wanted to bury himself in that wondrous vision. Darkness engulfed him; hot, scented darkness. His entire body was squeezed, every atom of him crying aloud. He could feel his own release, and it was as if he expelled a torrent of new worlds, exploding stars and sparkling cosmic clouds. All of which were absorbed by the entity squatting over him. Darq screamed. He couldn't help it. He saw the vision creature in perfect detail as it drank his essence. It was not a living har. It was something otherworldly, in the form of a har. A god, a dehar that smelled of blood and incense.

Some moments later, Darq was lying on his stomach, retching into the ferns. Cool hands were laid against his shoulders, comforting as he heaved. Eventually, he managed to croak, 'What was that?'

And there were no hands upon him, no voice in his ears; only in his mind. *That, my Darq, was the dehar Aruhani, the devourer, the ruler of aruna. You have sacrificed to him. You are now his priest.*

Darq sat up, looked around himself. He saw Darzu lying on his back some feet away, his hair over his face. For one awful moment, Darq feared the har was dead. He crawled over to him, brushed away the strands of hair. Darzu groaned, expelled a sigh. He smiled and turned on to his side. He was asleep.

Darq sat there stunned, hugging his knees. His whole body was throbbing, as if he'd run madly for an hour. Every particle of him was hot, emitting powerful energy. Something very big had just happened to him. It had changed him, and he was afraid, because he didn't know in what way he was changed.

In the morning, Darzu was cheerfully oblivious to any of the previous night's stranger events. He sat in the ferns, clothed only in his hair, which he began to rebraid. *I must have drunk more than I thought last night. The only thing I can remember is that whatever we did together was wonderful.*

Darq managed a convincing laugh. *It was. Thank you, Darzu. You gave me quite an education.*

Darzu held out a hand. *Come here. I don't have to be at work that early.*

Darq went cold. He stared at Darzu's fingers, unable to grab hold of them, not because he didn't want to take aruna again, because he did. It was what might come with it. Darzu frowned and lowered his hand.

I wish I could stay, Darq told him, *but my teacher will be waiting for me.* He pulled what he hoped looked like a rueful face.

Ah, that's a shame. Darzu hesitated. *How long are you staying in Nemodilkii?*

I think we'll have to move on today.

That's even more of a shame. I would have enjoyed spending more time with you.

Me too… Darq looked down upon this attractive and friendly creature. He was angry that an uninvited intruder had perverted their simple enjoyment. Ookami would have allowed Darq to stay an extra night, Darq was sure. They had nowhere urgent to be. Instead, they'd have to move on, because Darq was afraid of what might happen if he spent another night in Darzu's arms. *Never again!* Darq thought hotly, hoping the owner of his mysterious inner voice would hear it. *I'm sad to leave,* Darq told Darzu.

Return one day, Darzu suggested. *I'll light a lamp to guide your way, because I can feel you have a long journey ahead of you. Part of you is very sad.*

Darq felt a pang of genuine emotion. He leaned down and kissed the top of Darzu's head. 'You're a good har,' he said aloud. 'In another life, I might have been allowed to love you.'

Darzu took one of Darq's hand, pressed it to his cheek, kissed it. *Be safe, my friend.*

Darq walked to Ookami's tent in a sombre mood. He debated what he should reveal to his teacher and what should be kept secret from him. He was desperate to share his thoughts with somehar, but also shrank from doing so. It occurred to him that the interloping entity might be swaying his feelings in that regard.

Ookami was exercising beside the tent, observed by the horses, who seemed particularly intent on his movements. Darq sat down between them, drawing comfort from their familiar scent, their huffing breath as they nosed his hair. He watched Ookami's graceful turns and thought: *Nothing could take possession of him.*

Perhaps Ookami sensed something was wrong, because he appeared to end his practice before he'd really finished. He saluted the sun with his swords, then came towards Darq. 'Pleasant night?' he asked.

Darq nodded. 'I begin to see what you meant about aruna. It was certainly... well, certainly not like eliminating waste.'

Ookami smiled, then put his head to one side. 'You're not entirely happy. What's bothering you?'

Darq hesitated. 'I think...' He ran both hands through his hair. 'I'm not like other hara, Ookami. I know it. There's something wrong with me.'

Ookami squatted down and carefully replaced his swords into the black sheaths that lay beside the tent. 'What do you mean?' he asked at last.

Darq shook his head. 'I can't explain. Perhaps it's just that... my visions are darker than other hara's. Last night, I saw a dehar named Aruhani. He was not exactly a god of sweet little creatures and skipping harlings.'

Ookami's mouth twitched, although he did not laugh. 'I know of Aruhani. You were taught about dehara, then?'

'A little,' Darq lied. In Samway, he'd simply known that hara elsewhere had created and believed in these entities. He'd never bothered with them himself.

'Aruhani is the dehar of aruna, life and death,' Ookami said. 'He has many parallels in the old human belief systems. He's sometimes the devourer, sometimes the benefactor. He represents the cycles of the cosmos, creation and destruction. He's also very sexual. It's not that surprising you should see him in an aruna vision.'

'It was rather more than that.'

Ookami didn't even blink. 'That too is not unusual in the spiritually inclined.'

'I'm not that spiritual.'

'You think so?' Ookami stood up. 'Take time to get to know yourself, Darquiel. Anyway, I'm sure you're hungry after your night's exertions. Let's see to breakfast.'

'OK.' Darq stood up. 'It helps to talk with you. Thank you.'

Ookami inclined his head. 'It's my job.'

As they prepared the food, Ookami said, 'How long would you like to stay here?'

Darquiel responded without thinking. 'I want to leave today.'

'Oh? Is that wise? I think perhaps you should revisit the thing that worries you, banish it. Make a friend of Aruhani, Darquiel. I'm told he makes a superb benefactor. You could do worse than to honour him.'

'It's not just that. The har I was with likes me too much. I've said goodbye to him, and in my mind it would be cruel to see him again, because I can give him nothing but brief union. Also, it would be equally cruel to take aruna with somehar else in this town.'

'I see,' Ookami said. 'In that case, we'll move on. There will be plenty of other small towns where it's safe for us to linger.'

I would feel safe with you, Darq thought, and deliberately took little care to shield it. But if Ookami picked up on it, he gave no sign.

Chapter Twenty

Years later, Darquiel would look back upon the months he spent travelling with Ookami as some of the best of his life. They wandered through a mythic landscape, heading east, pausing at small settlements occasionally, but generally keeping to themselves, self-sufficient. Ookami was an easy companion, and Darq never got irritated with him. His guardian shared his knowledge generously, if not his body. As time went on, Darq became more and more curious about the Grissecon Ookami was preparing for, although he sensed it would be importunate to ask about it.

After leaving Nemodilkii, Darq had received no further communication from the mysterious entity that had hijacked his aruna with Darzu. As time went on, he became increasingly convinced he'd hallucinated the whole thing. With some trepidation, he initiated aruna with other hara he met and nothing untoward occurred, although none of it was as explosive and overwhelming as that time with Darzu had been. Without mentioning the more bizarre aspects of that occasion, Darq discussed it with Ookami as they rode along an empty road. Fields spread away to either side, and beyond them were mountain forests.

'It was like the experience with Darzu was my first,' Darq said, 'even though Thiede had taken me through feybraiha. I wonder if I'll ever experience anything like that again.'

Ookami nodded thoughtfully. 'There's no doubt that sometimes the chemistry between hara is very strong. If I were you, I wouldn't shut myself off to the possibility it can't be recaptured though. There will be others, Darq. That is the way of life.'

Darq liked to talk about aruna with Ookami, because he could see it was the closest he could get to touching the har. Occasionally, once the training with the swords began, Ookami would hold Darq's body to position his limbs correctly, and once Darq couldn't help sinking back against him. Ookami was still for a moment, then gently pushed Darq away. But Darq had registered that stillness, so felt neither embarrassed nor upset. In some ways, it was enough. He could lose himself in the dance of the blades, moving energy around him in the way that Ookami taught him. He hoped one day to have swords of his own.

Although Ookami had never pushed the matter of caste ascension, leaving Darq to make up his own mind, Darq eventually decided he'd like to go through the initiations, if Ookami was willing to officiate. Ookami said he'd be happy to do this, and they agreed that the first ceremony would take place on the summer festival of Reaptide, this being a significant time for such activities. At Ookami's gentle yet repeated suggestion – the closest he ever got to insistence – Darq had begun to pay his respects to Aruhani whenever he meditated or trained with the swords. The dehar did not seem disposed to make another spectacular appearance, even in visualisation, but Darq took care to dedicate whatever aruna he took to Aruhani. Ookami said it was the offering that the dehar preferred.

On the eve of Reaptide, Darq and Ookami made camp in an isolated mountain meadow. On the way up the trail, they had spotted an inhabited farmstead, so once the tent was erected, Ookami told Darq to begin his meditations for the ascension to come. Ookami would ride back down the rough road to ask if the farmsteaders had any milk, cheese or eggs they could spare to travellers. It was his intention to provide Darq with a small feast after the ceremony.

Warmed by this consideration, Darq climbed sun-heated rocks to a high vantage point. From here, the world stretched away in a cascading tapestry of a thousand different greens. The wind blew Darq's hair across his face and pressed his shirt to his back. Sitting cross-legged on the rock, Darq raised his arms to the sky, feeling life surge in every atom of his being. The disciplines of mind and body that Ookami had taught him appeared to have silenced the sly inner voice, if indeed it had ever existed outside of himself. Perhaps inevitably, this calm and satisfied thought invoked it.

Darquiel, my Darq, you disappoint me. Would you deny that I exist?

Darquiel froze. *Get out of my head!*

Very well…

And it was gone.

Darq pressed his fingertips against his temples. He felt faintly sick, remembering all too clearly the last time he had heard that voice. But by the time he'd climbed back down to the camp, the nausea had subsided, and Darq had convinced himself the voice had been his own. It must be part of his inner self, perhaps the darker part.

At sundown, Ookami lit small lamps and hung them in the trees about their campsite. Darquiel bathed in the icy water of a mountain stream and bound up his hair. It was a solemn and intimate occasion. Darq sat in a circle of softly glowing lights, while Ookami stood before him and called upon various dehara and spirits in his own tongue. His voice was a song, barely more than a whisper, yet containing all the power of the loudest invocation.

When the preliminaries were over, Ookami said, 'I'll conduct the rest of the ceremony in Megalithican… I just prefer to speak to the dehara in my own words.'

'I know,' Darq said. 'Please keep doing it. I feel the words inside me. I don't have to hear them.'

He closed his eyes, concentrating on sensations within his body, the pulse and rush of his own energy. He could sense Ookami stirring him up, raising his frequency to a higher level. It was most astounding. Darq was glad he'd decided to opt for the caste ascensions.

Then Ookami fell quiet. As Darq had undergone no previous ceremonies, he thought at first this silence was simply a part of it, and would have continued to think that, if he'd not heard a strange coughing splutter.

Darq opened his eyes. Ookami stood rigid, his eyes staring madly, straight ahead, as if he was looking at something hideous. Darq glanced over his shoulder, but saw nothing. 'Ookami?' he murmured. 'Are you…'

Ookami began to shudder, as if in a fit. Darq leapt to his feet. 'No! Don't touch him! No!' He knew what was happening. He knew it. An image was forming over Ookami's body, like a ghost, transparent and wavering. It was an image of the entity that sought to control him, that was torturing his flesh. Ookami was no simple soul. He wouldn't surrender himself without a fight. Darq saw a creature taller than the har it sought to inhabit. Details were indistinct, but he got an impression of very long pale hair and a light-coloured robe. The only things that were easily perceived were two smoking holes of burning blue light. He could not call them eyes.

'Get out of him!' Darq yelled. 'I command you.'

The image shimmered and then settled over Ookami like a shroud. It sank right into him. Ookami shuddered, jerked his head to the side, and then smoothed his face with his hands. 'Ah,' he said, 'that's much better.' The voice was not his own.

'In the name of Aruhani, I exorcise you!' Darq said.

Ookami laughed. 'You call upon *him* to dismiss *me*? How little you know, my Darq.'

'Who are you?' Darq shouted. 'I'm not *yours*! Who *are* you?'

Ookami extended his hands in a gesture of appeasement. 'Calm down. There's nothing to fear. I'm here to conduct your ascension.'

'I already have somehar to conduct it,' Darq said. 'I don't want you.'

'You have no choice,' said Ookami. 'It's my wish to do it.' His voice hardened. 'Now sit down.' He raised a hand, and Darq found himself flung back to the ground. Ookami's eyes were a dark velvety brown; the har before him now had blazing blue eyes, as cold and dangerous as the eternal flames that might burn upon the altars of damned temples. Darq could see the entity meant business; to defy it might put Ookami in danger.

'All right,' he said, displaying his palms. 'Finish the ascension.'

'It's all but done.'

Darq closed his eyes as Ookami approached him. He didn't know what to expect, but didn't think it would be good. The har placed a hand flat on Darq's chest and held it there for over a minute. At the end of that time, a bolt of scalding energy shot from his palm into Darq's body. It took Darq's breath away, and he was afraid it was the first of many excruciating experiences, but then he heard the har move away. He opened his eyes.

'It's done,' said Ookami, rubbing his hands together. 'A very simple process.'

Darq placed a hand upon his chest. The skin beneath his shirt still felt unnaturally hot. 'I suppose it's pointless to ask what you've done to me?'

Ookami gestured with both hands. 'Not at all. I've simply done what your mentor would have done, only much more efficiently and in a shorter space of time.'

Darq continued to rub at his chest. He felt burned inside, even his throat. It was as if he'd swallowed a drink that was too hot and it now lay boiling in his stomach. 'Why?' he asked. 'Why are you interested in me? Who are you?'

Ookami folded his arms. 'Don't you think you should ask the question you really want to know the answer to?'

'I have! Tell me!'

'No, what you really want to know is who *you* are.'

Darq blinked, swallowed. 'Who… who am I, then?'

Ookami laughed and the blue eyes blazed brighter for a moment. 'Not yet,' he said. 'As for the other questions, let's just say that I'm your true teacher. I recognise and respect your potential. I can't stand by and allow lesser beings to meddle with your development.'

'Are you har?'

Ookami shrugged. 'This world… all that you see in it, my Darq, will one day be yours.'

'What?' Darq had to laugh. The creature, har, whatever it was, must be insane.

'Laugh as much as you like,' Ookami said coldly. 'It's true. There's a war going on, of which you are completely unaware. In this war are two main factions, one of which considers Wraeththu to be their disposable allies. The other faction had a stab at controlling hara of their own, through Ponclast har Varr before you were born. This failed, and they realised they couldn't fight their battles in the earthly realm. Now, they seek other ways to infiltrate and manipulate.'

'And where do you stand?' Darq demanded. What he'd heard was similar to things Thiede had told him.

Ookami pulled a sour face. 'I stand for neither of these factions, as I abhor them both. Or rather, I stand for Wraeththu. I object to lesser species being exploited.'

Darq narrowed his eyes. 'Come out of that body. Show yourself to me.'

'Not yet. Make use of this time. I know you desire your mentor and I'm happy to accommodate you in that regard.'

'You disgust me,' Darq said. 'It's Ookami himself I desire, not an empty shell.'

Ookami shrugged. 'Suit yourself, my Darq.'

Darq stood up. It was disorientating to think that he was talking to an unknown entity inside the body of a har he knew fairly well. 'I don't like what you did to me. It was beyond my control.'

'Next time you do that, it will be utterly in your control.'

Darq sliced the air with one hand. 'There won't be a next time. I think what you did was unnatural.'

Ookami laughed. 'What an innocent you are. Hara do that all the time.'

'I don't believe you.'

'It's true. Well, certain hara are aware of the procedure, hara with vision who can see beyond mere physical gratification and a bit of simpering spirituality. Your mentor could have taught you that, but has chosen not to. You have no idea what his plans are. I know everything in his mind. Shall I tell you?'

'Don't do that,' Darq said. 'It's wrong.'

Ookami walked in a circle around Darq. 'Wrong? But you do it, Darq, you know you do. How many times were you chastised for it?'

Darq hesitated, then said, 'I don't want to talk with you anymore. Go away. I don't want anything to do with you, or this war that doesn't exist, or factions, or anything like that.'

Ookami stopped pacing and faced Darq again. 'Don't be ridiculous! Why do you think Thiede hid you away in Samway and is now extremely concerned for your well-being? You have no choice in the matter, Darq. You can't escape your heritage. Ookami is training you to defend yourself, but your ultimate purpose is to defend others.'

Darq was silent for a moment. 'Who are my parents? Tell me! If I'm to be part of this thing, I have to know.'

Ookami put his head to one side, and smiled in an infuriating manner. The expression didn't resemble Ookami's natural smile at all. 'Thiede is right to keep that information from you,' he said, 'because knowing it could make you a beacon to undesirable attention. Thiede is wise to hide you. I have no issue with that. But one day you'll thank me for my intervention in your life. It just doesn't seem feasible now, because your life has barely begun.'

Darq's hands had bunched into fists at his side. He wondered what would happen if he tried to attack this entity. Would it hit back? 'Tell me your name,' he said.

Ookami glanced at Darq's hands. 'No. I don't think so. Names are dangerous. Think up your own name for me, if you must use one.' He laughed again. 'Relax your fingers, my dear. If you attempt to attack me, I'd have to prevent it, and I've no wish to hurt you.'

Darq unbunched his fists self-consciously. 'So, what happens next?' he asked in a dull voice. He felt as if the weight of the sky rested on his shoulders now.

Ookami's voice became gentle. 'You travel, you learn, you wait for what will come. I will be with you.' He reached out and briefly touched Darq on the shoulder. 'Befriend the dehara, Darq. Aruhani is a powerful ally, and he was created by Wraeththu. He's an expression of harish potential. Use him when you need to.'

'I need to know the history,' Darq said. 'I need to know what I'm involved in.'

'You will. Now, I'll leave you, but I'll never be far away. If you ever wish to call me, go to a high place. Swing a weighted cord above your head and intend for me to hear it. Call to me through the winds.'

Without warning, Darq was filled with a feeling of panic. It was as if reality suddenly expanded out from him swiftly in all directions, full of threats. 'Will you protect me?' he asked hurriedly. He wished at once he hadn't said those words. He still didn't know what this creature was.

'As much as is possible,' Ookami replied softly.

Darq bowed his head. Here, in the beautiful summer night, he knew that everything he'd heard was true. Ookami laid a hand upon Darq's head. 'Don't be in sorrow, my Darq. These days will be happy ones for you. Enjoy them while you can.'

Darq looked into the unfamiliar eyes in the very familiar face.

'Before you go,' he said. 'Share breath with me.'

Ookami inclined his head. He said nothing but put his lips against Darq's own. Darq saw visions of mighty wings, thousands and thousands of them. He was carried upon them.

A voice came faintly in Darq's head. *I am gone…*

Yet the sharing continued. Presently, Ookami drew away and then pressed his forehead against Darq's own, one hand still cupping the back of Darq's neck. 'I am dishonoured,' he said. 'I could do nothing. I've failed you and those who placed you in my care.'

'You're *not* dishonoured,' Darq murmured. 'That creature is very strong. You had no chance. I saw you fight.'

Ookami exhaled a shuddering breath.

'We both need to learn how to deal with him,' Darq said. 'And we will.'

Chapter Twenty-One

For some reason, on the Uigenna's flight from the Gelaming into the eastern territories beyond Almagabra, they had not settled in Anakhai, other than in the extreme west. This was unusual, because most areas on the Almagabran continent supported small groups of erstwhile Uigenna and Varrs, even if they chose not to remember their history. Most had fled to Jaddayoth, sustained by the rumours that their great leaders had fled before them. Many ended up in Maudrah, where the har who had once styled himself as Wraxilan, the Lion of Oomar, now lived in a semblance of ascetic nobility as Ariaric, the archon of that tribe. Ariaric, now the Lion of Oomadrah, strove to be a just ruler, although the customs of his tribe were peculiar, involving a bewildering array of abstemious restrictions concerning behaviour and etiquette. Some said Ariaric was actually mad, as he'd had strange visions in the past that had prompted him to abandon the wild, hedonistic ways of the Uigenna and live like an austere, nomadic monk for years. Whatever the truth of that was, like all hara, the first generation Uigenna had had to grow up; there were few now who would boast of their youthful exploits, or even cared to remember what kind of humans they'd been, which in many cases had been violent and anti-social to say the least.

As Darquiel and Ookami travelled through Anakhai towards the east, Ookami gave his protégé lessons in Wraeththu history. He too remarked upon the fact that no Uigenna were to be found as they ventured deeper into that country. 'I've heard that the hara here in the heart of Anakhai prevented any settlement from what they considered to be undesirable elements from the west,' he said. He and Darq were following a wide track that led through a forest. Mellow sunlight fell upon them. 'They used the mists of the land to obscure their villages and towns,' Ookami continued. 'They cloaked themselves well, and sent out their local elemental spirits to discourage strangers. It's different now, but at one time, it was supposed to be perilous for anyhar other than the Anakhai to travel these lands.'

'I like the hara here,' Darq said. 'I like the way they're so complete unto themselves.'

'They are on the whole affable,' Ookami agreed. 'It's because they know they have the power to deal with threats. This allows them to be less defensive than hara in some other territories.'

'Have you travelled far, Ookami?'

Ookami nodded. 'I have visited many lands, yes. It interests me to observe how Wraeththu is developing. I think it's commendable that in some places the best elements of human civilisation have been retained, while all that was worthless has been discarded. I'm not talking of building and technology, but the components of the psyche.'

'You think hara are perfect, then?' Darquiel couldn't help laughing at the idea.

'Of course not. What I see is the dream of perfection, like a ghost image over the trees and the mountains, and the ancient spires. I see happy spirits, who are perhaps less bitter than they were before.'

'Human spirits?'

'Maybe.' A long black and white feather drifted down from the treetops overhead. Ookami caught it, twisted it in his fingers. 'The most important aspect of being har is to be awake to the world. You should constantly be on your guard against the baser side of your nature. It will manifest at times, because we're still essentially animals, but we should not make the mistake that humanity did and succumb to greed and indolence. We must never let our leaders fool us, although there are some hara who would say that is already happening.' He handed the feather to Darq, who put it into his hair.

'What do you think?' Darq asked.

'I think we're still in a stage of transition. Those who hold power were once human; there are few second-generation leaders of any great status. Our leaders remember human ways and what appeared to work. They're not always right in their assumptions.'

Darq considered this. 'The one who… the one who came to me says I am to be a leader.'

'This is my thought also,' Ookami said.

Darq was surprised by this frank admission. As they'd travelled, they'd not really discussed the episode at Reaptide. Darq kept quiet, even when he was bursting with questions he knew Ookami might be able to answer, simply because he was aware Ookami felt deeply shamed by being possessed. Darq didn't want to add to the har's discomfort. 'He hasn't come back,' Darq said.

'I know,' Ookami said. 'I would have known if he had.'

'Can we talk about it now?'

'We could always have talked about it. I've left it to you to introduce the subject.'

'What or who do you think he is?'

Ookami's face took on a strange expressionless rigor. Darq could tell then that Ookami was still furious about what had happened, and fully intended to wreak thorough revenge should the opportunity present itself. 'When he violated my being, I received some impressions, but they weren't very clear. He could be a very powerful har, who has trained for a long time, and can therefore project himself as something *other*.'

'Is that what you think he is?'

'Yes. I don't think he will come to you again, at least not in the same way. He could never abuse me again like that. I would die before that happened. Now, I'm prepared.'

'I know,' Darq said. 'He surprised us both, at a time when we were very open. But what does he want with me?'

Ookami frowned. 'Obviously, he seeks to use you for his own ends. I've made that difficult for him. He's no doubt just one of the many individuals that Thiede believes are out there, having heard your cry in the ethers.'

'He says he's a teacher of mine,' Darq said scornfully. He rolled his eyes.

'I remember that,' Ookami said. 'It's what he wants you to believe.'

'And also that we are partly kin.'

'We are *all* partly kin,' Ookami said dryly.

Darq's strange visitor never again attempted to possess Ookami, but that did not mean he did not continue to make his presence felt. It seemed to Darq that the entity, which for convenience's sake he now called Zu, was waiting for Darq to call to him. Sometimes, when Darq took aruna with the hara he met on his travels, he sensed that Zu was present, hovering at the boundaries of Darq's activities, but he did not manifest more overtly than that. The mere fact that Zu was no longer such an invasive presence softened Darq's attitude towards him. He realised this might simply be a tactic on Zu's part, so remained aware, but more than once he was tempted to find himself a high place and swing a weighted cord above his head.

Darq was not convinced that Ookami's deductions were correct; he believed they were coloured by the Ikutama's fury and shame. He had not revealed much to Ookami of what Zu had said, because he knew Ookami would at the very least disapprove and disagree. Darq knew that Ookami would be right to do so too, which threatened to shatter the rather fond fantasies he had begun to concoct in his head. As they rode though these ancient lands, which breathed in relief and spread their glory in the wake of human passing, Darq found it hard to credit that shadowy factions were competing to control Wraeththu. Perhaps it was true in places like Almagabra and Megalithica, but here...? It seemed unlikely. Still, it was pleasant to imagine himself a king, issuing wise decrees and having hara look up to him. He felt slightly perplexed about these daydreams, since he didn't usually much care for idealism.

In the days of human occupation, Anakhai had been a landlocked country, some of whose sister lands to the east were next to the coast of an inland body of water now known as the Sea of Shadows. The lands around this sea formed Jaddayoth. Between Jaddayoth and Anakhai lay the land of Thaine in the north, Florinada in the southwest, and Huldah in the southeast; the boundaries between these lands were vague. Some hara, living on what could be regarded as the borders, spoke of themselves as Thainish in one village, then Anakhai in a village two miles down the road. The Anakhai had phyles and phylarchs, like any other tribe, but it seemed their government was loose. Each local phylarch operated a benevolent kind of feudalism within his territory.

Ookami intimated to Darq it would be best if they skirted Jaddayoth, since the harish populations were higher there, and many were in contact with, if not allies of, Almagabra. Although Darq was interested to see what Jaddayoth might be like, he also enjoyed travelling through Anakhai - which in itself was a vast country - so did not object. 'We'll visit the Carvanzya Range of Thaine,' Ookami said. 'They're haunted mountains and you'll like them. Humans believed that paranormal creatures lived there, like vampires and werewolves.'

'Sounds great,' Darq agreed. He wondered if there was any possibility he could come face to face with a vampire.

The further east they travelled, so the more primal the land seemed to become. Darq felt it had a definite personality, watchful and brooding, but given to occasional spurts of exuberance. He began to sense once more shadow riders among the trees in the dense forests they rode through. He was unsure if they were the same ones from back home in Samway, or just of the same type. They did not show themselves to him but were flickering presences at the edge of his perception, and Darq was well aware how Zu had once used them to try and summon him.

Summer had faded into autumn, bringing with it that wild, hopeful yet melancholy aspect that is the spirit of the season. Darq and Ookami had celebrated Smoketide with a local community, and now as Shadetide approached and the weather drew in its limbs, Ookami wondered whether they should consider settling in one place for the winter.

'We're far from what hara would call civilisation here,' he said. 'These are the forgotten lands, and are all the better for it.'

'If you think it's safe to stay somewhere, then it will be,' Darq said. 'I'd like to stay in the mountains.'

Ookami laughed. 'The weather will be harsh.'

'I don't mind.'

Darq and Ookami came upon Nezreka late one afternoon. They were following a fairly well-defined if little-used thoroughfare through a mountain forest, close to the border with Thaine. Dusk was stealing in and orange leaves swirled in the air. The road beneath the horses' hooves was treacherous and slippery with sodden leaves, and the air smelled tartly of the harsh season to come; a scent of frost and pine drifted down from the higher slopes. Darq and Ookami were riding in silence, Darq almost dozing in his saddle. Soon, they would find a place to camp for the night. Perhaps they would knock upon the door of an isolated cottage where lamps burned inside; the archetypal symbol of welcome and respite for travellers.

Darq was brought to full wakefulness by the fact that Ookami had brought his horse to a halt. He was staring intently at the trees to their right.

'What is it?' Darq asked.

'There are wards in the trees,' Ookami replied. He dismounted and went to the side of the road, peering intently into the shadowy depths of the forest.

Darq walked Follet over to him. 'Wards? What against?'

'Wards of concealment,' Ookami replied. He turned to Darq and smiled. 'And there's a hidden track leading up the mountain here. I believe there's a settlement nearby, but a veiled one.'

'Perfect,' Darq said, grinning. 'Let's find it.'

'We could take a look,' Ookami said. 'I like the idea of a hidden settlement. It'd be a good place for us – if the hara there are welcoming. That depends on their reasons for hiding their home, I suppose.' He remounted his horse and urged it into what appeared to be dense foliage, but it was merely a screen of ferns that parted like a curtain before him. Beyond lay a narrow trail, heading into darkness.

'Like a ghost story,' Darq said. 'We're going to find something intriguing, I sense it.'

Darq and Ookami followed the trail, which led upwards between broad-leaf trees. After half an hour or so, they came to a deep pass, where dark cliffs loomed over the path. Here, the horses' hoof-beats echoed eerily. There was no sign of life and all was silent. Darq's flesh prickled in a pleasurable way. The idea of a hidden settlement was appealing to him. He sensed a secret, a feeling that built in him slowly as he and Ookami ventured further from the road they'd left behind.

At the end of the pass, the path opened out slightly to reveal a high wooden wall, constructed of split pine trunks, the tips of which were carved into points. Ookami and Darq had come across a few Anakhai settlements that were walled. The thick wooden gates were covered in stylised carvings of what appeared to be animal totems. Upon it was inscribed the word Nezreka. Atop the wooden palisades, guards could be seen, none of whom, Darq thought, would be able to speak Megalithican. He and Ookami had picked up a smattering of Anakhai but, as once they'd been told by a Megalithican har they'd met, who had lived in Anakhai for over a decade, the language was so complex it was very difficult to speak it fluently. It might take a lifetime to learn it. The guards stood motionless and stared down with stern expressions.

Ookami called up to them, repeating the simple phrases he had learned concerning the availability of food and lodging. The only word he received in response was 'no'. He turned to Darq. 'The sun has all but set. I think we should go back down the pass. There were homesteads some miles back on the main track. We're wasting our time here.'

'This is where I want to stay,' Darq said. He urged Follet forward and gazed up at the guards. He saw only their expressionless faces shadowed by wide-brimmed hats. The guards carried spears with strangely ornate steel blades at their tips. They were quite beautiful weapons, in fact. 'Tiahaara,' Darq called. 'We wish to speak with your phylarch. We carry news.'

Ookami sighed deeply. 'Darq...'

Darq ignored him. He projected with all of his will a sense of curiosity into the guards, so that when they looked down at him they would see a secret as delicious as the one they no doubt concealed behind their walls. For some moments, the guards stared at him silently, then they conferred. One called down a word that Darq recognised as 'wait'. He glanced at Ookami, who raised his eyebrows.

The word 'wait' was not an exaggeration, since it took over twenty minutes for any further exchange to take place, by which time it was dark. Ookami tried to suggest that perhaps they should leave, but after Darq's insistent refusal, held his tongue. Darq felt a brush of mind touch and was warmed by it; Ookami trusted Darq's instincts. The Ikutama too felt there was something significant about this place.

Eventually Darq felt a shiver of scrutiny steal through his skin. It was like a fan of light coursing down his body and he guessed that somehar of considerable psychic ability within Nezreka was scanning them. Eventually, a har wearing a dark, hooded cloak appeared on the palisade. He called down, 'You!' in Megalithican.

'You speak our language?' Darq called back.

'We do not welcome strangers here,' said the har.

'We wish to speak to your phylarch,' Darq said. 'We pose no threat, as you know, since you scanned us.'

The har said nothing to this but disappeared from view. Presently, the gates creaked open a short way and he came through them. 'What do you want with us?' he asked. He wore a long indigo-coloured robe and many glittering rings upon his hands, where the fingernails were long. His face was also long, as well as bony, and strangely weathered for a har. Dusty-looking, fair plaits hung over his chest to his waist.

'I wish to speak with your phylarch,' Darq said.

'Our phylarch doesn't receive visits from strangers,' said the har. 'That is my function. What do you want?'

Darq was now completely at a loss. He'd said they had news, but what could he make up that might possibly interest these reclusive hara? While his mind worked frantically to formulate a plan, Ookami urged his horse forward.

'Tiahaar, there are strange processes in motion, which will affect even these faraway corners of the world,' Ookami said. 'It would be best to arm yourself with knowledge.'

'And you have taken it upon yourself to impart this knowledge,' said the Nezreka sourly. He folded his arms. 'Which tribe do you represent? Who seeks our allegiance?'

'Many would no doubt seek your allegiance,' Ookami said, 'but we represent none of them. We're travellers, and to be honest with you, we seek a safe haven for the winter, but we're willing to barter with what we know for lodging.'

The har smiled a little and inclined his head. 'If that is truth, I respect your honesty, Tiahaar. But we're a private community. There are many settlements - woodshara and trappers - who would offer you shelter. I'd be happy to give you directions to find them.'

Now Darq spoke up. 'It's important I have security,' he said. 'That's why we wish to stay here, since it's obvious this settlement is secure.'

The Nezreka raised his eyebrows. 'Indeed? And will you be so honest as to tell me why you need that?'

Darq knew he should perhaps glance at Ookami to find out what he thought of that request, or even attempt a brief deep mind touch, but he felt sure the Nezreka would sense that, and any hesitation on his part would look suspicious. He took a breath. 'I don't know my parentage,' he said, 'but it's been made known to me that certain factions have an interest in me. I'm interested only in remaining apart from such matters. This is why we're travelling.'

Darq could see he had pricked the Nezreka's curiosity now, but perhaps not in the best way. 'If that is so, I sympathise with your predicament,' the Nezreka said, 'but it's not our way to attract attention to ourselves. In my view, you would be equally safe among the forest phyles.'

'I know this is where I'm supposed to be,' Darq insisted. 'I won't leave until you let me speak to your phylarch.'

The Nezreka laughed. 'You are young,' he said, 'and autocratic. What are you; some by-blow of Maudrah? You have no authority here, Tiahaar. Our phylarch would not be interested in you.'

'Shouldn't you let him be the judge of that?' Darq said. By now, he could feel Ookami's attention, focused like a dart, warning him to be cautious. The Nezreka was being friendly, to the extent of actually having this conversation, but he still had an unknown number of armed hara stationed upon the walls behind him, and if his tolerance of the situation wore thin, things could get sticky.

'Tiahaar,' Ookami said, 'we respectfully request you ask your phylarch if he would speak to us, and grant us shelter until Bloomtide, perhaps sooner than that. It's all we ask. If he himself says no, we will depart.'

'You have great faith he'll grant you an audience,' said the Nezreka, and there was a tone in his voice that suggested perhaps they weren't wrong.

'Please, Tiahaar,' Darq said, projecting into the words every shred of intention he possessed, as well as a sense of helplessness and need.

'Very well,' said the Nezreka. 'Wait here. I'll have refreshment sent out to you. We might be a private community, but we're not inhospitable to those in need.'

'Thank you,' Darq said. 'Really… thank you.'

The Nezreka went back into the settlement and the gates closed behind him. Ookami chuckled.

'What?' Darq asked.

Ookami shook his head. 'Sometimes, my friend, it pays to be different, and for that difference to shine from your face.'

'What do you mean?'

'He fell beneath your enchantment, that's all. I can say for certain that normally that Nezreka we met takes pleasure in turning hara away from here, whatever their reason for calling. It's one of the joys of his job.'

Presently, two hara wearing loose trousers and long embroidered tunics of russet cloth came out of the gates carrying baskets. These contained a fairly sumptuous meal of dried sausage, dark bread, hard-boiled eggs, a slab of butter so hard it was like set wax, and a covered jug of sweet milk. The hara could not speak Megalithican, and were clearly reluctant to communicate in mind touch, but stood to the side and observed Darq and Ookami consuming the food. Like the spokeshar, their hair was long and fair, but somehow dusty, as if they put some substance into it to make it look that way. Darq liked their appearance. Their mouths were wide and thin-lipped, but when they smiled at each other, it made lines in their cheeks. They weren't innocent, like the other hara of Anakhai had seemed so far. They were wry, cautious, and wiry like wolves. As Darq chewed his food, the image of wolves came to him more strongly. He knew then without question: this was one of the secrets of the tribe. The carvings on the gates were of lupine faces, and these hara were like wolves; slinking, suspicious, alert, yet as close as brothers in a pack would be. Weren't these mountains soaked in folklore about wolves who were really men? Could there be such a thing as were-hara? The thought made him smile. He wished it could be true, although he knew the explanation would be far more prosaic than that.

'They're going to let us in, aren't they?' Darq said to Ookami.

The Ikutama nodded. 'Without a doubt.' He took his swords from his saddle and strapped them round his waist.

The food had been devoured and the hara who'd brought it had retreated back beyond the walls by the time the original spokeshar reappeared. He seemed to be more affable than before. 'Our phylarch has consented to hear you,' he said. 'You are honoured.'

'I know we have you to thank for that,' Darq said. 'It won't be forgotten.'

'Bring your horses,' said the har. 'They'll be cared for during your audience.'

Darq and Ookami followed the har beneath the arch of the gates. The guards stared down at them sternly, and once they were in the small square beyond, every har in the area stopped what they were doing to stare also. Visitors were clearly rare in these parts. Huge torches illuminated the settlement, so that Darq could see the buildings in Nezreka were made of stone, with low brooding eaves; they appeared to be very old. It was not a large community and it huddled beneath an enormous cliff. From what Darq could see, it consisted of the central square, with a well in the middle of it, and a large building, presumably the office or home of the phylarch, directly beneath the cliff. Other streets led off the square, but they were little more than alleys. These were lined by leaning dwellings.

The Nezreka paused before the shallow flight of steps that led to the official-looking building. 'I must ask you to surrender your weapons as a matter of courtesy,' he said.

Ookami, naturally, was unhappy about that, but reluctantly complied. Darq knew his reluctance was not so much because he wanted to remain armed, but that the swords were very valuable to him, both in terms of cost and emotional attachment.

The Nezreka took them with due reverence. 'Have no fear you will be robbed, Tiahaar,' he said, bowing. 'I can see the value of these weapons, and we are an honourable tribe.'

It seemed he had sensed the right words to flatter or at least mollify Ookami.

'Give me your names,' said the Nezreka, 'and you'll be announced.'

'May we have your name?' Ookami asked.

'I am Jezinki har Nezreka. I am drudehar to our phylarch, who is Tava'edzen, Lord of the High Forests and leader of all our runners.'

Darq was intrigued by all the epithets and resolved to ask questions later. He bowed his head and touched his chest lightly with the fingers of one hand. 'I am Darquiel har Olopade.'

Ookami made a similar gesture of respect. 'Ookami har Ikutama.'

Jezinki indicated for them to follow him into the building.

'You're not Anakhai, or weren't originally, were you?' Darq asked Jezinki, hoping that was not importunate. 'I mean, you speak Megalithican so well, and… there's no accent.'

'That's true,' Jezinki conceded. He opened the wide double doors ahead of them with a flourish. Beyond was a dark entrance hall that smelled of smoke and polished wood. Darq glanced round before Jezinki closed the doors and he saw that flakes of snow had begun to fall outside; huge soft things that would cover the world in white without much effort and certainly no care.

Jezinki led the way down a corridor, which was lined by several closed doors. On a table stood a vase filled with ferns and delicate white flowers with a strong scent. Next to the vase lay a pair of leather gloves. Further along, a series of heavy coats hung upon the walls and there were boots lined up beneath. This was definitely a home.

Darq expected they would be taken to some kind of audience chamber, where Jezinki would do most of the speaking, and the phylarch would sit in splendid isolation, listening, and later pronouncing judgments. Instead, they were led to a fairly small room that overlooked a yard where washing hung, now acquiring a layer of snow. In this place was a hearth and a table set before it, surrounded by five chairs. Upon the table were documents, ink, pens, and parts of what looked like a horse's bridle. Standing before the hearth was a har with hair the colour of beechnuts, which fell over his shoulders in thick waves. It did not look remotely dusty.

Jezinki bowed, 'Tiahaar, may I present Darquiel har Olopade and Ookami har Ikutama.'

The har came forward. Darquiel had to resist an urge to step back. Tava'edzen was first generation, clearly, and possessed such composure and charisma, it was dazzling. He moved and exuded the kind of confidence all young hara would wish to possess. His eyes were strangely pale, almost yellow, and although he emanated the ambience of a warrior, it was not at the expense of his feminine side. He was both gracious and fierce, beautiful and commanding, sensitive and powerful. Darq sensed all these things in an instant and it took his breath away. How could such a har be hidden away here, in this lonely spot, when he clearly should be running a tribe like the Gelaming? Unless, of course, he really was a were-har. That might explain the strange eyes.

'You are welcome,' Tava'edzen said, and his voice too was beautiful, low-pitched and clear. It was also unaccented, perhaps an adjusted Megalithican. 'Jezinki tells me you wish to remain in Nezreka for the winter.'

Darq bowed his head. 'That is true, Tiahaar. We do not wish to continue travelling in the harsh weather.'

'Understandable,' said the phylarch. 'But Jezinki also tells me you were most insistent upon Nezreka over all other options, and also concerning your desire to speak with me. Why is this?'

'Just... just a feeling,' Darq said, which was the truth. He noticed that so far Tava'edzen had barely acknowledged Ookami, even though the Ikutama was obviously the older of the two of them and therefore in charge.

'You know that we discourage visitors.'

'Yes.'

Tava'edzen picked up the bridle from the table, ran the leather straps between his fingers. 'It's my choice to live apart from the world. I've seen too much of it in my life. Those who live here with me feel the same. We prefer a simple existence, closeness to these mountains and forests. The politics of Jaddayoth and beyond hold no interest for us.'

'We know nothing of Jaddayoth politics,' Darq said. 'I want to remain here because it feels safe, and sometimes I don't feel that. I'll in no way compromise your security, I promise you, but if my presence here ever does, I'll leave.'

'You are being followed?'

'Not exactly.'

Tava'edzen put his head to one side and raised his eyebrows. 'Please explain what that means.'

'Tiahaar.' Ookami stepped forward. 'I've been appointed as guardian to Darquiel. All I can tell you is that I believe his parentage to be of high status, which for some reason has been kept secret. I've been told that certain factions have an interest in Darquiel, which is why we're travelling, keeping on the move. At some future stage, I believe his destiny will be revealed, but for now he's a simple traveller, at the mercy of your judgment.'

Tava'edzen smiled and put the bridle back on the table. 'And what a privileged young traveller, whatever his status, to be protected by such an obviously noble warrior like yourself.'

Ookami was clearly uncomfortable with that. He inclined his head.

'Very well,' Tava'edzen said. 'I pay attention to significant events, and last night I had a dream that foretold of your coming. You may remain here for the winter, unless you break the rules of our tribe.'

'Tell them to me and I won't break them,' Darquiel said.

Tava'edzen nodded. 'Respect the privacy of others. Do not raise your hand in violence. Venture only where you're invited. You'll also be expected to work for the community during your stay. Nohar here shirks his duty.'

'That is acceptable,' Ookami said, before Darq could utter anything else.

Tava'edzen gestured to Jezinki. 'Find them accommodation within this house.'

Jezinki bowed. 'As you wish, Tiahaar.'

'Good.' Tava'edzen smiled and clasped his hands together. 'In an hour, I'll eat my dinner and you will join me to tell me of your travels.'

Chapter Twenty-Two

Although Tava'edzen was phylarch of Nezreka, which was technically a phyle of the Anakhai, the settlement was also administered by a council of elder hara. The phylarch's house, known as the Drudehall, served as his palace, the council offices and the town Nayati. The councillors, known as the Laukumati, lived elsewhere in the town. Darquiel quickly discovered that the term drudehar, which Jezinki had given as his title, was the local variant of hienama, or a magical adept who served the phylarch.

Darq made a lot of suppositions during his first days in Nezreka, not least that Tava'edzen had most likely come from Megalithica originally, as Phade had done, and Jezinki had come with him. The phylarch did not appear to have an official consort, but Darq pondered whether Tava'edzen's relationship with Jezinki was more than simply hienama and leader. He found that this thought filled him with perplexing anxieties.

Many times, Darq lamented the fact that he now appeared to care what other hara thought of him. His childhood in Samway, free of such considerations, seemed like an idyll. He hated what feybraiha had done to him, and resolved to try and recapture his initial neutral stance. Surely, it should have been the other way around: a harling should seek favour because he wants to be loved, but an adult har should be in control of himself and removed from such manifestations of insecurity. He observed the harlings in Nezreka, of which there appeared to be about a dozen, and they seemed more like human children to him than the way he'd been as a harling. They were quicksilver, their attention flitting this way and that, endlessly fascinated by everything they came across, eager to learn and understand. They feared chastisement and responded well to approval. Not one of them, it seemed to Darq, had ever thought to themselves about the mechanics behind the word "sorry". If they did apologise, it was genuine. All of it puzzled Darq endlessly, but he didn't feel he could mention the subject to Ookami.

There was no school in Nezreka, since every family taught their own harlings, but Tava'edzen did request Ookami to teach some of his younger hara the eastern way with the swords. Darquiel ended up helping, and eventually it was more than harlings who came to learn.

Apart from this activity, Ookami and Darq went hunting, and also sometimes worked in the tannery and the butcher's workshop. The thing that pleased and intrigued Darq the most, though, was the fact that when they hunted, the Nezreka became wolves. This was not literal, as he'd once hoped, but they wore the pelts of wolves over their heads, with the limbs and tails trailing down their backs and the death mask snarling above their faces. When they took on the pelt of the wolf, they took on the quality of the animal. They could move without sound and anticipate each other's moves.

Few of the Nezreka could speak Megalithican, and most refused to mind touch with strangers, but a couple had clearly once come from the west, perhaps with Tava'edzen himself. Darquiel decided to befriend one of these hara, in order to get information.

Nohar ever suggested that Ookami or Darq should wear a wolf pelt, so one morning, with the snow falling all around them as they prepared to leave for the hunt, Darq cornered a har named Bithi and asked him, 'Must I catch my own wolf to wear him?'

Bithi gave him a stare, then said, 'It's more than that.'

Gazing at Bithi, with his dusty hair falling from beneath the mask of the wolf, Darq considered it would be pleasant to take aruna with a har wearing this costume. He dismissed the thought. 'What, then?'

'Only the Weavers may bestow the mark of the wolf,' Bithi said. 'It's tribal lore. You can never wear the wolf, because you're not of our tribe.'

'But if I should stay here…?'

'You won't.' Bithi mounted his horse, a strong pony with a thick winter coat. He gathered up the reins, clucked to it, then said, 'Come on. The days are short now.'

The Nezreka rode their tough ponies to the locations where they began to hunt, and then left their mounts behind, hobbled. Darq did wonder why he'd ever been invited to participate, since doing so meant he had to be treated as "pack". Surely, if the Nezreka were so against outsiders knowing their lore, they'd have made Ookami and Darq simply work in the town? He decided to ask Bithi directly. The response was interesting: 'Tava'edzen requested we bring you with us.'

'Why?'

Bithi shrugged. They had reached the place where the horses would remain. 'He will have his reasons.'

Ookami, naturally, was very good at hunting, even though he was more like a lone mountain lion than a wolf. The Nezreka worked in a team, seeking deer, and the wild sheep and goats that had once belonged to humans but had gone feral. Never once did Darq see wolves, at least not at first.

It did not escape Darq's notice that Zu was absent, as if his influence couldn't penetrate Nezreka's walls, either the physical or etheric variety. Perhaps this was why Darq's instincts had been so strong about the place, but he thought it must be more than that. He wanted to talk with Tava'edzen, to know how he'd come here, and why. He must have been some high-ranking har in Megalithica. He had a story and a history, and the tantalising scent of it tugged at Darq's senses. He wanted to know Tava'edzen's secrets, which were sure to be plentiful and wondrous. He wanted to know about the wolves. However, apart from the first evening, when Tava'edzen had wanted to hear their stories, the phylarch thereafter paid little attention to his visitors. Perhaps he was wary of his secrets being uncovered. Darq wondered what he did with himself all day, since he did not appear to go hunting or indeed take part in any other communal activity.

Darq asked Jezinki, who he also seldom saw, if it would be possible to have another audience with the phylarch, but Jezinki only said, 'Perhaps. He's busy at the moment.'

'Doing what?' Darq wanted to ask, but kept silent.

He explored the Drudehall, but found nothing to suggest a sinister or romantic wolf cult, a mysterious history, or anything else remotely of interest. There were wolf pelts hanging in the Council Chamber, and lots of decorative carvings, but nothing more. The Laukumati, although admirable hara in their own way, did not possess the same astounding appeal as Tava'edzen. Darq had met a few of them, and had experienced a mutual lack of interest.

Tava'edzen became Darq's obsession. On the rare occasions he came across the phylarch, and Tava'edzen's gaze fell upon him, Darq felt a jolt within his flesh. The phylarch's eyes were so wise, so *there*; they could see right into a har. But nohar would give Darq information about Tava'edzen, so after Darq had been in Nezreka for around two weeks, he decided to undertake some clandestine research of his own.

The best time to conduct investigations was the hour after breakfast, since most hara were then engaged in the first of their daily activities. Because Nezreka was small, it was difficult to get away from others, but fortune threw a coin in Darq's direction. One morning, Nezreka's chief butcher asked Darq if he'd mind taking a delivery of meat to a har who lived alone some miles down the mountain. Apparently, this har was some kind of hermit, who had once been part of the community, but now preferred to live alone, for whatever reason. Darq agreed to the task, realising he now had free time and, most importantly, time alone.

He rode Follet like a maniac down the perilous mountain road, so that he skidded and stumbled. The colt didn't appear to mind, being of a somewhat manic nature anyway. Darq followed the instructions he'd been given on how to find the recluse's cottage. Here, Darq virtually threw the parcel of meat at the rather astonished har who responded to his shouted summons. Without further pause, Darq took off again, this time, not up the main track, but along a path that would take him round the side of Nezreka. The one area where the hunters did not venture was the cliff top behind the town. Darq decided this was the place he would start nosing around. He was sure he'd find something of interest there.

The forest, shrouded in snow, was silent. Darq was aware of excitement building within him. He trotted Follet along the edge of the trees, where a narrow path skirted the precipice from which the land swept downwards to his right, in a tumble of cliffs and rocks. He kept in view the skeins of smoke rising from Nezreka's chimneys. It would not aid his purpose if he got lost. He could feel the season changing around him, the indefinable frisson in the air that spoke of the approach of Natalia, the winter solstice. It was only three weeks away. At that moment, he decided that by Natalia things would be different. Exactly how they would be so, he'd yet to calculate, but he knew it would be good.

A creature that at first Darq took to be a large dog stepped out onto the path some yards ahead of him. He quickly realised it was a wolf. But didn't wolves travel in packs? Darq reined Follet to a halt, even though the colt didn't appear to be that concerned about the predator ahead of them. The wolf stared at Darq and Darq stared back. Then the creature yawned and loped off along the path. It seemed like an invitation. Darq chuckled to himself. At last! Something would be revealed to him now; he was sure of it.

At the top of the path, the trees had been cleared in a circle, and here there was a low round building with a thatched roof. It was quite large, and a plait of smoke curled lazily from a chimney in the centre of the roof. At the top of a short flight of steps was a narrow doorway, lined by wooden pillars and topped by a carved lintel. Beside the steps were piles of logs. The glazed windows, which were also round, had shutters over them that were open. Somehar lived here. Another hermit?

Darq dismounted and led Follet forward. There was no sign of life outside the building, but as he drew nearer, he saw there were outbuildings to the far side. One was a stable, and a pony stood looking out of the top half of the door. When it caught sight or scent of Follet, its head went up and its ears pricked. It uttered a whinny; a greeting or a warning. Follet responded with a grunt.

The wolf had climbed the steps to the front door and now stood in front of it, staring back at Darq. In front of the building was a rail, presumably for tethering horses, so Darq tied Follet's reins to it. He was filled with a wild kind of bravado, almost driven. He ascended the steps and reached down to stroke the wolf's head. It opened its mouth and its tongue lolled out, as if it was smiling. Darq knocked on the door. There was no response, but he was sure that somehar inside had heard him and was listening. He knocked again. 'Hello?' he called.

He did not expect to get an answer, and was considering trying to open the door himself, when it slipped ajar with a creak. He saw part of a face, a dark eye, looking out at him.

'Hello,' Darq said again. 'I'm from Nezreka. Can I come in?'

The door opened wider. 'You're early,' said the har who now stood revealed at the threshold. As Jezinki and Tava'edzen did, he spoke Megalithican like a westerner, with no local accent. He had a strong feminine aspect, which immediately suggested to Darq this was another drudehar of some kind. The har's hair was loose and dark, hanging to his waist, and he wore a black robe with dark blue embroidery at the hem and cuffs. Around his forehead was a string hung with coins and acorns, and his eyes were lined faintly with kohl. He was pale-skinned and beautiful, exuding an enticing air of magical power; without doubt an adept.

'Apologies,' said Darq. He eased himself past this har into the building, following the wolf who clearly regarded this place as home. The room beyond the door was a segment of a circle, narrowing almost to a point, but not quite, suggesting there was an inner chamber. Doors led off to either side, presumably to different segments. The room Darq stood in was a kitchen. The wolf had gone directly to a black iron stove set into the right-hand wall of the room and now lay down in front of it to lick his paws.

The dark-haired har closed the door. 'Well?' he said.

'What time was I supposed to come?' Darq asked.

'I think in a week's time.'

Darq shrugged. 'Oh well, I decided to come now.' He wondered who he'd been mistaken for, and how long this charade could continue before the har realised his mistake and threw Darq out. It was important to make a good impression in that time. He took care to guard his thoughts.

'You'd better sit down,' said the har. 'You don't know who I am, of course. I am Slinque.' He indicated a chair next to the stove.

Darq sat down. He wasn't sure what to say now.

Slinque knelt down before him on a brightly-patterned rug and pushed his fingers deep into the wolf's thick pelt. He observed Darq for some moments, then laughed. 'It's quite all right, Darquiel. I know who *you* are!'

Darq blinked. 'You were expecting *me*?'

Slinque nodded. 'Yes. We should also have expected you early. An oversight.'

'Who are you?'

'I'm a Weaver, as are my brothers Shayd and Stelph. You'll meet them soon.'

'A Weaver.... Somehar spoke to me of you.' Darq glanced down at the animal at his feet. 'About the wolves.'

'We know. You wish to take on the wolf. Perhaps you will. Perhaps you already have.' Slinque stood up. 'Would you like tea?'

'Yes... thank you.'

There was a black kettle keeping warm on the stove. Slinque picked up a cloth to lift it. 'I know why you're here,' he said.

'You do?' Darq smiled uncertainly. 'I'm not sure *I* do.'

Again, Slinque laughed. It was a free, ringing sound, like bells announcing the birth of the sun. He set about pouring Darq a mug of tea and shovelled into it a large spoon of sugar. 'Here, take this. It'll warm your spirit.'

Darq accepted the crude pottery mug Slinque offered to him. 'Thank you.' The tea was so strong, Darq was sure the spoon could stand up in it. When he sipped it, he tasted wood smoke and cut pine, a strangely resinous tang. It was also very hot and scalded his tongue. 'Why am I here?' Darq asked.

'We've been waiting for you,' said Slinque, 'from the moment of your birth, terrible though it was.'

'You know me,' Darq breathed, and he was filled with both relief and anxiety, which felt very odd.

Slinque sat down opposite him in a chair, and arranged his robes fastidiously over his knees. 'Yes, we know you. Tava'edzen knows you, much though it pains him. That is, he knows you're significant to him. We've always told him his day would come. He denies it, but part of him mourns all he has lost.'

Darq now felt dizzy. He was so full of questions he didn't know which to ask first. 'You're an oracle,' he said.

Slinque inclined his head. 'Yes. That's one of our functions. All leaders of merit need an oracle, don't you think?'

'You're not Anakhai.'

Slinque shook his head. 'No. Sulh. In the early days of Megalithica, hara of our tribe were much prized by the Uigenna and the Varrs for our abilities as seers. Many of us found ourselves places close to the phylarchs and archons. My brothers and I came with Tava from the west.'

'I thought as much.' Darq couldn't believe these revelations, so utter and so clear, had been this easy to acquire. 'Tava'edzen was Varr or Uigenna. Which?'

Slinque rested his chin on one hand. 'Well, technically all tribes came from the Uigenna. Tava did not survive Megalithica long enough to see that. He was one of the first.'

'Who was he, Slinque?'

The Sulh was silent for a moment. 'The name will mean nothing to you. Anyway, it's his privilege to tell you that. He doesn't know who you are, by the way, and for now you shouldn't tell him.'

Darq smiled sourly. 'He doesn't speak to me, so it's not likely. Also, I don't know myself who I am.'

'I can tell you.'

'I know. I sense that. But I've been told it's dangerous for me to know. I think that once I do, all hell will let loose.'

Slinque appeared to be amused. 'Not here, it won't.'

'You *want* to tell me, don't you?'

'And now, after all your wondering, you're afraid. That's understandable.' Slinque leaned forward, put his hands together and pointed at Darq with them. 'We want what is best for Tava. You're part of his destiny, and he can be part of yours. You want that.'

'Don't tell me who I am,' Darq said abruptly. 'It's not the right time.' At that moment, he felt it was the last thing he wanted to know. He wasn't sure why.

'You're right,' said Slinque. 'I'm glad you're wise, because you could have been stupid.' He leaned back again. 'You're here for many reasons, but only one of them really concerns us. When the time comes, you'll help Tava'edzen, because he was displaced. He was meant to be a great leader, but another was envious and betrayed him. We believe that the history of Megalithica would have turned out very differently if this betrayal hadn't happened. The Uigenna and the Varrs ended up being controlled by hara who had not left their humanity far enough behind. If Tava had still been in control, he would have grown as the Gelaming grew, as the Unneah, the Colurastes, the Sulh and the Kakkahaar grew. His chance was stolen, and the result was... chaos.

All hara were beasts in the beginning, well, most of them.' Slinque gestured with both hands. 'Tava would have died, but for my brothers and I. We found him. We brought him here. The greatest punishment we bestowed upon his enemy was awareness. We opened his mind, gave him visions of what is and what will be. But still…' He shrugged. 'That enemy is still in power. Our punishment advanced him, which is ironic, really. It was meant to destroy him. We underestimated him. It's interesting to us that this seems to be a trait of Wraeththu. The har Ponclast, once reviled as the most evil in the world, was given a similar awareness and now flourishes. His star will rise again, though many would say he doesn't deserve it. That says something, doesn't it?'

Darq nodded. 'Yes, although I don't know all of what you speak. I'm aware of some of the history, but not all of it. I agree with you about Tava'edzen, though. His qualities shine out from him.'

'He berates himself,' Slinque said airily. 'He has too good a memory. But it's very easy for hara to look back now and be annoyed with themselves for being what they were. The point is that they *had* to begin that way. We believe hara had to learn to advance themselves. If they'd simply been created perfect, it would have meant nothing. Still, Tava will not listen to us. He looks at his hands and sees blood, in the same way that his enemy does.' Slinque made another two-handed gesture. 'Oh, they're no longer enemies, of course. It means nothing now.'

'Who is his enemy?' Darq asked. 'I know hardly anything, so it won't hurt to tell me.'

Slinque paused. 'Very well. He is the archon of Maudrah, Ariaric, the Lion of Oomadrah.'

Darq shrugged. 'See… Means nothing. I've heard of Maudrah, of course.'

'Strange, isn't it,' Slinque said pensively. 'All that history meant so much, but to a second generation har raised in Anakhai, it means nothing. The names are meaningless. It's how it should be.'

'Yet you want Tava'edzen to regain power.'

'Yes. He was meant to have it, for the good of his kind. He knows this.'

Darq took another mouthful of the strange tea. 'He had a dream about me coming here.'

'He did. It is no doubt recorded, and laid alongside the sheaf of papers that comprise the letters he's never sent to Maudrah.'

'Perhaps if he had sent them, the archon would have had him killed.'

Slinque laughed. 'That's unlikely. Ariaric has a shrine to Tava. He has shrines to many hara he wronged or loved in vain. His memory too is very good. But Tava should not rise again through Ariaric. The Lion shouldn't be given that privilege, which he would dearly love to have. If Ariaric knew Tava was alive and well, he could partly forgive himself, and personally I don't think that should be allowed. Not yet. Anyway, Tava should rise by himself, or rather with the support of those who are not part of his history.'

Darq put down his mug on the floor. His lips had become slightly numbed. 'Then it's true that I'm destined to be a leader?' he asked.

Slinque nodded. 'I'm afraid you can't avoid it, Darquiel. But it *will* be contested.'

Darq frowned. 'By these strange factions I've heard about?'

Slinque grimaced. 'They're the least of your worries in a worldly sense. No, by your own kin, mostly.'

Darq was surprised by these words. 'My parents?' he snapped.

'No,' Slinque replied, 'your brothers.'

Darq put his hands against his face. His skin felt hot. 'When?' His voice felt small in his throat.

'Soon,' Slinque said. 'I'm sorry. We'll help you as much as we can. As you rightly said, all hell might break loose.'

Darq took a shuddering breath. 'I have three brothers, right?'

Slinque appeared puzzled by the question. 'No. To my knowledge, only two. Why?'

'A prophecy I once heard. There are four of you. That's what I heard.'

Slinque shrugged. 'Then perhaps there are things that even we know nothing of. But one thing is certain: your brothers have been, and are being, influenced by somehar or something. We haven't picked up much information on this subject, but can feel the potential for trouble is there. If you agree to help Tava, then we agree to help you.'

Darq shook his head. It was all too much to think about. He remembered something Zu had said, something about hara messing with his development. 'What of my voice?' Darq asked.

'Your voice?' Slinque frowned.

'The one who visits me and speaks in my head. He says he is of neither faction. I'm not sure who or what he is, even whether he's har or not.'

'I know nothing of that,' Slinque said, and there was a tone to his words indicating that if he didn't know about it, it could only be meaningless and unimportant.

At that moment, the door to the house opened and two other hara came into the room, bringing with them the cold. They shook out their hair and stamped the snow from their boots. In appearance, they were almost identical to Slinque.

'You are here!' one of them said to Darq.

'Early!' said the other.

'This is Shayd and Stelph,' Slinque said. 'My brothers.' He smiled at his kin. 'I've been giving Darquiel a history lesson.'

'Have you told him yet?' Shayd asked.

'No,' Slinque replied. 'Not yet. It isn't the time.'

Darq stood up. He felt nauseous. He had to get away. 'I must go,' he said. 'I'll be missed.' The room appeared to be swaying slightly. He hoped he could cling to his stomach and his consciousness until he got outside. The power of the Weavers seemed to swirl around him, like a century's worth of spider webs in an old house, caught in a hurricane. Slinque must have put some kind of potion in the tea, but why?

Slinque took hold of one of Darq's arms. 'Yes. Go. And think. You'll return to us when you're ready.'

Darq tried to stagger towards the door, but his limbs felt restricted.

'One thing,' Slinque said. 'Before you go.' He pulled Darq to face him, holding onto his shoulders. Darq could feel how powerful the har's fingers were. They might gouge though flesh if they had a mind to try. 'You mustn't confide in your mentor, the Ikutama, about our meeting.'

'Why not?'

'Because although he's loyal to you, and would no doubt die to defend you, he's still employed by Thiede har Gelaming. If you tell him what you've learned, he'll feel obliged to report it, and it's not in Tava's interests for Almagabra to know he's alive and where he is. Not yet.'

'I won't say anything,' Darq mumbled. He really wanted to get outside, breathe cold air.

'No, you won't,' Slinque agreed. 'I've put a binding on your tongue. Apologies. It was necessary. There's only one you may speak to, and that is Tava. You'll do this when the time is right.'

Darq swallowed with difficulty. His mouth was full of the bitter taste of pine. 'I have to go now.' He pulled away from Slinque and somehow managed to grope his way outside.

Below the steps, Follet raised his head, ears forward. Darq stumbled to the pony's side and leaned against him. Follet sighed. Darq looked up at the round house. It was impossible to see what was going on inside. It was very quiet. No har might live there after all.

Chapter Twenty-Three

Darq could not remember how he got through the rest of that day. All he could recall was feeling feverish and the phrase repeating in his head: *I have brothers.* He wished now he had not been so squeamish about asking who his family was. It was odd, most unlike him. He thought perhaps that when he knew, he would be disappointed, even disgusted. At least he could spend the day savagely chopping up meat, which provided some small comfort and outlet for his feelings. Everyhar left him alone. It was as if they knew where he'd been, and now he was off limits. The Weavers had touched him. It could be visible on his face.

When he finished work for the day he returned to Tava'edzen's house and made his way to the small bedroom he shared with Ookami on the top floor. Ookami, who had been engaged in other tasks in the town, was already there. He roused himself from meditation when Darq entered the room. 'You look ill,' Ookami said. 'What's wrong?'

'Something's going to happen,' Darq said. He threw himself face down on his bed.

Ookami came to stand over him. 'What makes you think this?'

'I just know. I feel it. I need to sleep.'

'Is it the voice again?'

'No. The voice has gone. Please, Ookami. We'll talk tomorrow.'

'You must eat.'

'No. Tomorrow.'

Ookami remained where he was for some seconds, then withdrew. He would perhaps communicate with Thiede now.

There were no significant dreams for Darq that night, nor for the nights that followed. Several times, during the next few days, he considered returning to the round house, but then changed his mind. He felt contaminated somehow. He didn't think the Weavers had his interests at heart. They were concerned only about Tava'edzen. He also considered talking to Ookami, but as Slinque had warned him, the words stuck in his throat. The Weavers had bound his tongue. As for Tava'edzen, the har was nowhere to be found. Also, Darq wasn't sure what he could say to the phylarch. He felt that Tava'edzen would think that Darq's fate was none of his business. In the end, cut off from any other recourse, there was only one thing Darq could do.

A week after his visit to the cliff top, he waited one night for Ookami to fall asleep. Moving himself into a quiet space, he slipped from his bed and dressed. He slid through the silent Drudehall like a ghost and crept outside. He went to a high place, but not the one where the round house stood.

It was very cold, and the snow was frozen hard beneath his boots. When he took off his gloves to swing the weighted cord, his fingers pained him with cold. He realised there were tears on his face. He had lost himself entirely. He was alone in a place he barely knew, calling upon the one entity who should not be trusted. The cord sang in the cruel air; an ancient, shamanic sound. *Come to me,* Darq thought, as loudly as he could.

The movement of his arm became hypnotic. He could not stop. It felt as if his whole essence was being tugged into the whirlpool of air, and he would disappear from this world. Where would he go then?

A hand folded over his own. Warm fingers clasped his frozen ones. 'Be still, Darq.'

Now Darq could barely move; he was frozen into place. 'Zu,' he said. 'Is that you?'

A tall figure glided in front of him. It looked har, very beautiful, clad in close-fitting yet draped clothes of pale fabric, long white hair hanging over the chest. His face was quite long and the eyes slightly slanted, though not as much as Ookami's were. Darq knew those eyes were blue, but in the dark they looked black. 'Is that what you call me?' Zu said. 'Why have you brought me to this place? Your need is very strong.'

'Tell me who I am,' Darq said.

'You are Darquiel har Aralis,' Zu told him.

It meant nothing. 'Is that all?'

'That's all. To others, it would have great meaning. You're the second son of a celebrated family. Most hara believe you're dead. Your pearl was excised from your hostling's body before term. You were taken into the Otherlanes, and from there eventually to Samway.'

Darq choked on a sob. 'Why?'

Zu moved closer, but did not touch Darq. 'Because you're like no other har. Your fathers are Tigrons of Wraeththu. Do you know what that means?'

Darq hugged himself, wishing that Zu would do it. 'No.'

'They rule the Gelaming, along with your hostling, who is the Tigrina.'

Darq swallowed painfully. 'Who cut me from him?'

'An enemy of your family. The plan was for you to be devoured before you came forth from the pearl. Devoured alive.'

Darq dropped to his knees, hugging himself tighter. 'Who?'

'Ponclast har Varr. You have heard of him?'

'Yes.' Darq put both hands flat against the snow. It made his skin look very dark. 'His star will rise again.'

'Fortunately, you were rescued,' Zu said. 'Thiede has kept you safe ever since.'

Darq uttered a sobbing laugh.

Zu hunkered down beside Darq and at last put an arm around his shoulders. Zu was warm, even though the clothing he wore appeared flimsy, designed for a hot climate. 'You asked, and it was time to tell you.'

Darq leaned against him. 'Thank you. I knew I was Gelaming. Do my parents know I'm alive?'

Zu stroked Darq's hair. 'Pellaz and Calanthe do. Your fathers. You know you have two fathers?'

Darq wiped his nose. 'Thiede told me I was created by three hara. I don't really know what that means, or how it was done. When Thiede told me, I didn't care about it. How did they do it?'

'I wasn't there,' Zu said. 'Some things aren't meant to be observed, but it's obvious that the aren of two hara mingled with the yaloe of the third. It summoned you into being.'

Darq shivered. He saw in his mind's eye an image of shadowy hara taking aruna together. 'These names,' he said, 'Pellaz... Calanthe... they are strangers. I can't think of them as family. What is my hostling's name?'

'Caeru.'

'And my brothers?'

'Loki and Abrimel.'

Darq uttered a short laugh. 'Instant family. How will they feel about me? Perhaps my brothers might resent me.' He remembered what the Weavers had told him.

'That's possible,' Zu said. 'When you finally return to your family, you might well encounter jealousy.'

'Just that?' Darq pulled away from Zu. 'Who are *you*? Will you tell me now?'

Zu got to his feet. 'My true name would mean nothing to you, Darq. All you need to know is that I'm not your enemy.'

Darq looked up at him. 'Will they come for me now, enemies and factions?'

'Here? No. The hara here are very strong, but then they have had help.'

Darq too stood up again. 'Who helped them?'

'Those who were once my people.'

'*Your* people?'

Zu nodded. 'Yes. Darq, there's something you must understand. When the plagues came, the madness, the zealotry, and the aggression that destroyed the human race, it was sent deliberately, but not aimed at them. They were merely a casualty. The human world was destroyed to kill my kind.'

'Who *are* your kind? Are you human? I don't understand.'

'You will,' Zu said. 'You've had enough revelations to deal with for one evening.'

'I feel like I know less than before,' Darq said. 'What am I supposed to do, now that I know who I am? I'm confused. I think I should be doing something, formulating a plan, but what? My head's spinning.'

Zu smiled. 'You're strong. What you feel now is a growing pain, that's all. It's the moment of awakening, like feybraiha, when nothing can be the same again.'

'Can I trust the hara here? There are some, called the Weavers...' Darq was surprised he could even speak their name. 'I'm not supposed to be able to talk about them. They have bound my tongue.'

'Not against me, they haven't!' Zu said. 'I know of these hara. Tell me what they've said to you.'

Darq told Zu what had occurred. 'It was why I had to call to you. I felt bewildered. I couldn't think of anyone else to turn to.' He laughed bleakly. 'Even to me, that seems insane.'

'I'm glad you feel you can trust me a little.'

'I'm not sure it's that, Zu! It seems to me more like desperation than trust.'

Zu did not appear offended. 'Well, whatever the case, I'm glad you called to me. I'm confident the Weavers will try to protect you, because they see you as useful. Tava'edzen was wronged, but then many hara were wronged. His part is up to him, not you. But if you want him, Darq, then take him. You could do worse.'

Darq sat back in the snow. He laughed. He felt drunk. 'I can't believe I'm doing this, talking to you here.' He paused, and Zu let the silence stretch. Darq stared at him. Zu couldn't be a human. He was har, and a supremely attractive specimen, even if he was full of mysteries and deceits. Darq wondered if the information he'd received would somehow feel more real if he lived it again through Zu's breath and inner vision. He made a decision. 'Zu, I feel disorientated, almost out of my body. Can we take aruna together?'

Zu raised his eyebrows, then grinned. 'No, much as I'd like to. It would not be… appropriate. Not at this time.'

Darq gestured wildly. 'Then possess Tava'edzen. We could do it that way.'

Zu shook his head. 'Darq, that is *not* what you want.'

Darq scowled. 'Darzu wasn't what I wanted either, nor what you did to Ookami. You needn't start acting all moral on me. You don't care.'

'*They* didn't matter.'

Darq rubbed his face with both hands. 'I don't know what to do next. I don't want to be waiting like this, unarmed and ignorant. If you know what's going to happen, you must tell me.'

'Part of it is beyond your control, and mine. We have to wait for events to synchronise. The Weavers think they have you, but let them wait too. Show them your mettle, and when you do face them again, tell them who you are. Command them to take you to those who were my people.'

Darq considered this for a moment. 'Will the Weavers obey what I say? They are powerful.'

Zu nodded. 'Yes, they are, but not as powerful as you will be. They're simply older and more experienced. They are also Sulh, who often think highly of themselves.'

Darq sighed. 'Well… I can only try.' He paused. 'Zu…'

'Yes.'

'This is completely unrelated, and I don't know why I thought of it, but do you know I tried to incept a human female?'

Zu hunkered down once more. He seemed more at ease again. Darq realised the har had been unnerved by Darq's request for aruna. This was odd, given their previous encounters. 'Yes,' Zu said. 'I know about the girl. I had… agents observing you during that time. I heard about most of what happened.'

Darq experienced a surge of relief and asked hurriedly, 'Do you know what happened to Amelza. Did she live?'

Zu nodded. 'She did. I was interested in the outcome myself. You didn't kill her, Darq. You're different to any other har.'

'Where is she?'

'In Roselane, which is a country of Jaddayoth.'

'Is she angry with me?'

'I have no idea, but seeing as you have given her the greatest gift, I doubt it.'

'Could you bring her to me some time?'

Zu laughed softly. 'Does Darq the Invincible, who stands alone, miss his friend?'

Darq pulled a sour face. 'Yes. I miss everything, not least ignorance. Well?'

'Not yet, Darq,' Zu said softly. 'You'll find your solace in other ways. When you meet Amelza again, it will be because you've summoned her or found her.'

'But she is safe?'

'Yes.' Zu stood up again. 'Return to your bed. Sleep. You'll feel better now. We'll talk again, but our meetings must be secret for now.'

'So many secrets,' Darq said. 'I'm used to them. Thank you for telling me the truth.'

'You had only to ask,' Zu said. 'I wouldn't tell you until you summoned me.'

'Be with me again some time. You know when. I miss you too.'

Zu laughed. 'Next time, Darq, the last person you'll be thinking of is me.' He leaned down and kissed Darq's head. 'Now go. It's cold out here. Look forward to Natalia, for that is the time of rebirth.'

Darquiel walked slowly back down the hill. He couldn't think of anything other than a new mantra: *I am Darquiel har Aralis.* His parents were great rulers, greater than hara like Tava'edzen. It was too much to take in.

Just outside the town walls, he saw an amazing thing. At first, he thought it was a trick of the starlight, a sifting of powdery snow falling down from a high tree branch, but then he really saw what it was: the most beautiful white horse. Its eyes were dark and intelligent, its mane falling thick as a har's hair down its neck, and over its brow. It was watching him. Was it wild?

Darq approached the horse slowly. It didn't appear to be afraid. He held out his hand to it and the animal stepped forward daintily, placed its soft nose in his outstretched palm. Darq ran his free hand up the horse's neck, beneath its mane. Like Zu, it was very warm, as if it had just travelled to this spot from a hot country. 'Beauty,' Darq said to it. 'Whose are you?'

I could be yours, if you desire me.

'Zu?' Darq said aloud, glancing round. The voice had been in his head. The horse stood motionless, its nose hovering just above Darq's hand. Then it raised its head and kissed him on the cheek.

Darq took a step back. Horses don't kiss, and yet it had been unmistakable. Had somehar trained it to do that?

You know me, Darquiel. You met a brother of mine once, who carried Thiede to your side. We did not know you, then, for he shrouded you well.

Darq laughed and said in mind touch. *Am I talking to a horse?*

It would seem so. If that is what you see. The senses of creatures of earth are primitive, after all, yet you are superior to most.

You're a sedu.

The creature tossed its head. *Yes. I'm a leader of* sedim. *You may call me Lurlei. Nohar travels with me, but I will take you travelling, Darquiel, if you desire it.*

Why?

The *sedu* studied him for a moment before answering. *Because I wish to work with you. I can show you many wonders, bestow many gifts upon you. I can take you to Immanion, to your kin. I can take you to other realms. Whatever you wish is available to you.*

Darq couldn't help but feel sceptical about this apparently generous offer. *In what way do you want to work with me? What do you want in return?*

The *sedu* snorted. *The* sedim *have cared for Wraeththu since the beginning. It is our wish to protect you now.*

Darquiel rubbed his face, wondering if he had dreamed the entire night's events and would soon wake up. He was talking to a horse! This was ridiculous. And yet not. *If I've learned one thing, Lurlei, it's that nothing is without a cost. Why have you come to me now? Is it because I've come into myself, and claimed my identity?*

The *sedu* stamped a front foot and turned its head to the side, regarding Darq with what appeared to be some amusement. *Perhaps it could be that. A perfume came to me through the ethers, which was your awareness. I came to you at once.*

You're from one of the factions, then. I've been warned of you. You want Wraeththu, through me, to take your side.

Naturally. It's the best way for you. If our rivals took control, things would change. There's nothing wrong with the way things are. If you pledge your allegiance to me, you'll ensure the future safety of your kind, for we can protect you.

Darq uttered a scornful laugh. *If you're that powerful, you don't need me. I might be potential, Lurlei, but that potential is yet unknown, even to me.*

Climb on to me, Darquiel. Let me show you wondrous things.

Darq considered. The temptation was great. But first, he felt he should discuss this development with Zu, if he could. Zu had said no faction would be able to reach him here, which had now been proved wrong, but Darq was sure that the *sedim* couldn't coerce him. They could only attempt to seduce him. Also, Lurlei hadn't mentioned Zu, which surely it would have done if it had known about him, if only to try and discredit him. *I will think about your offer,* Darq said at last.

The *sedu* bowed its head. *Think wisely. If you wish to communicate with me, do so beyond the walls of the Nezreka. And do so only when we can be alone. You should know that the Nezreka are not impartial. Be careful among them.*

I am always very careful.

Others might come to you, Darquiel. Their offers no doubt will be appealing, but remember who are the friends of Wraeththu. We will speak further.

Darq felt a strange shudder throughout his flesh and then he was staring at an empty space, where once the *sedu* had stood. For some moments, he continued to stare. Then he laughed. 'I am Darquiel har Aralis,' he said aloud.

When Darq returned to his bedroom, he found that Ookami was awake. 'Where have you been?' Ookami asked.

Darq sat down on Ookami's bed. 'I know who I am,' he said. 'And I've spoken to a representative of one of the factions interested in me.'

Ookami sat up. 'What? Tell me.'

So Darq told him. He didn't mention Zu, but implied the *sedu* had told him his identity. 'So, I'm a kind of prince,' Darquiel said. 'That's insane. What do you think?'

'I think you should *not* wander about on your own at night,' Ookami said dryly, 'although this is an interesting development and wouldn't have happened if I'd been there. At least the *sedu* didn't attempt to harm you.'

'I don't think he can,' Darq said. 'He needs my co-operation. So, now I know who I am, what should we do?'

Ookami looked thoughtful. 'I must try to communicate with Thiede. The *sedim* are his allies.'

'I know, but I don't think he trusts them entirely.'

'Perhaps the time has come for our travels to end,' Ookami said. He stared at a point on the wall beyond Darq's shoulder. There was a strange fire in his eyes.

'It seems a bit of an anti-climax,' Darq said. 'I want to stay here until after Natalia. I think that's important.'

'Why?' Ookami's tone was sharp.

Darq shrugged. 'I don't know. But tell Thiede that. Tell him I *know* it's important.'

'It could be dangerous for you to stay here. If the *sedim* have become aware of you, so will others. Thiede might want you to go to Immanion now.'

'Yes, well, I also have my own opinions, and I won't let Thiede make all my decisions for me. Or you, for that matter. Or anyhar else.' Darq sighed. 'There's something that's meant to happen to me. I know it. I'm not quite ready to become who I'm meant to be. And I'm not scared of the *sedim* or anything else that might manifest in front of me. They can all put their cases forward. It's amusing.'

Ookami appeared sceptical. 'Thiede wouldn't have gone to all this trouble with you if there wasn't the potential for danger,' he said. 'We know the *sedim* are benevolent - apparently. Others might not be so cordial with you. You mustn't go out alone. If you wish to speak to the *sedu* again, I'll go with you.'

'Fair enough. You are my bodyguard, after all.' Darq flopped back on the bed, lying across Ookami's legs, his arms outflung. 'I feel different,' he said. 'It feels good.'

'Don't become drunk on it,' Ookami said, then softened. 'Enjoy this heady feeling now, but tomorrow forget who you are again. I'll get information for us as soon as I can. Get off my legs. I need to get up now.'

Darq sat up. 'You're going to talk to Thiede now? Can't it wait?'

'No. Go to bed. Give me silence.'

The last thing that Darq wanted was for Thiede to show up in Nezreka, not least because it would complicate his communication with Zu, but first thing the following morning, Thiede arrived without the agency of a *sedu*, right in the middle of Nezreka. He didn't bother with a polite request outside the town for an audience with the phylarch. His appearance naturally sent hara into a state of panic. It was the noise of this that drew Darquiel and Ookami outside. Jezinki was there also, shouting demands at Thiede, who was apparently unaware of the commotion going on around him. He spotted Darquiel on the steps to the Drudehall and brushed past Jezinki to approach him. 'Well, well,' he said. 'Events have moved along!'

Jezinki followed Thiede up the steps. 'You know this har?' he snapped at Darquiel. 'This is an affront. You know we guard our privacy.'

'Be at peace,' Thiede said to him mildly before Darq could answer. 'I'm no threat to you. I've come to speak with my protégé here. It is none of your business.'

'Who is this?' Jezinki demanded of Darquiel.

Darquiel couldn't resist saying, 'It's the Aghama, Jezinki. Don't worry about it.'

Jezinki made a kind of gibbering sound and swept back into the Drudehall, no doubt to speak with Tava'edzen.

Thiede laughed. 'That was uncalled for. He won't believe you, anyway.'

Darquiel folded his arms. 'I know. That's why I said it. You'd better come inside.'

Darquiel thought it would be best to introduce Thiede to Tava'edzen. He was pleased this gave him a genuine reason to speak to the phylarch. Ookami made his excuses and left, saying he had tasks to attend to. Darq knew the har removed himself because he sensed that Thiede wished to speak to Darq alone. Thiede certainly didn't insist that the Ikutama should remain with them.

'He was a good choice,' Darq said, once Ookami had left. 'He's cared for me well, and has taught me much.'

'I know,' Thiede said. 'He'll be with you for as long as you wish him to be. Darq, I felt it when you became aware of who you are. What I need to know is: who told you?'

'I'll tell you everything soon,' Darq said. 'Let's just talk to Tava'edzen first.'

Thiede gave him a caustic glance, but did not pursue the matter.

As Darq led Thiede through the passages of the Drudehall, he wondered what the Weavers had made of the tremors of Thiede's arrival. He had no doubt they had sensed it.

'Is this really necessary?' Thiede asked as they paused before the door to Tava'edzen's private office. 'We have a lot to discuss, you and I. I can't be bothered with all this petty ego-pandering to little phylarchs.'

'Tava'edzen is our host,' Darq said. 'He's been good to us. Please be courteous to him.'

Thiede sighed. 'Oh, if you insist. I take it he's on your list?'

'What do you mean?'

'You know very well.'

Darquiel laughed. He knocked on the door, and could hear voices inside the room. He waited for permission to enter. Eventually, Jezinki opened the door. His expression was grim. 'You will have to leave,' he said. 'You have abused the hospitality of Nezreka.'

Darquiel ignored this. He saw Tava'edzen sitting in one of the chairs before the hearth. He looked hunted, or haunted, or perhaps both. When Darquiel came into the room, he stood up.

'Tiahaar, please excuse what has happened,' Darq said hurriedly. 'Something occurred, and it was vital I speak to my mentor. His arrival was unconventional, I know, but he means no harm to you or your hara. We will depart, if that's what you wish.'

Tava'edzen made a gesture. 'Come in. Both of you.'

It was at this point that Darquiel saw Thiede staring intently at Tava'edzen. His expression hovered between a frown and a smile.

Thiede knew the phylarch, then. Darq hadn't thought of that, but if Thiede was the first Wraeththu, he must have known all of the other early leaders. He probably made them.

'Now, this is a surprise,' Thiede said.

Tava'edzen smiled somewhat grimly. 'I've concealed myself from every har for a great many years. Now you turn up in my sanctuary. I knew it was you, Thiede, even before Jezinki told me *the Aghama* was here.' He rolled his eyes.

Thiede shook his head. 'So, here you are, alive and well. I can appreciate why you let the Uigenna think you were dead, rather than simply vanquished. An embarrassing business. Still, I really did think Wraxilan killed you.'

'He nearly did kill me,' Tava'edzen said. 'Fortunately, or unfortunately, my Sulh Weavers saved my life. I'm still unsure whether to thank or damn them for that.'

'I commend you on your powers of concealment,' Thiede said. 'Some time ago, I made a concerted effort to locate all the erstwhile phylarchs and archons. Most are dead. You know what became of Wraxilan, of course?'

Tava'edzen grimaced. 'Yes. I don't care about it.'

'But you incepted him, made him what he was. He was an ungrateful pup.' Thiede stepped forward and embraced Tava'edzen. 'I am glad to find you alive, Manticker. Very glad. And age has refined you.'

'You too,' Tava'edzen said. He returned the embrace stiffly.

Thiede drew away from him. 'Thank you for extending hospitality to Darquiel and Ookami. I'll reward you for it.'

'No need,' Tava'edzen said. 'I could see Darquiel was… It was no problem.'

Thiede gestured at Darq. 'You see, I did far better with my protégés than you did with yours. Pellaz har Aralis sired this splendid young thing you see before you, and he has never turned on me.'

'Few would dare,' Tava'edzen said. He glanced at Darquiel, and it occurred to Darq then that Tava'edzen actually found it difficult to look at him. 'If there's no problem with your Tigron, why have you concealed his son?'

Thiede sighed. 'It's a long story. We'll speak of it. First, I would like to confer with Darq in private.'

Tava'edzen inclined his head. 'Of course. Make use of this room. I have tasks to attend to. Would you like refreshment?'

Thiede nodded. 'That's courteous of you. Yes.'

Tava'edzen turned to Jezinki, who still appeared greatly displeased.

'Would you?'

Jezinki also inclined his head and said through gritted teeth. 'Of course, Tiahaar.' He left the room.

'Your hara love you,' Thiede observed, 'but then they always did. Even Wraxilan. What happened – it was a great pity.'

'I was no better than him, Thiede,' Tava'edzen said.

'Oh, you were,' Thiede said. 'You *are*. You should have been part of the Hegemony. I thought of you often.'

Tava'edzen uttered a snort. 'The har I was could never have been part of your dream for Wraeththu. You left Megalithica in disgust at us, you know you did. You were right to. You brought to us the greatest gift. It was so fragile and new, so beautiful. And what did we do? We just tore it apart and ruined it. We were animals, no better than humans, unworthy of your care. We never listened to you. We didn't even think. We just took what we wanted, whatever the cost. And the cost to me was my power. I created Wraxilan as the young wolf who would eventually fight and conquer me. I deserved it.'

'These coals are long cold,' Thiede said gently. 'Don't rake them. It's a different world now.'

Tava'edzen nodded thoughtfully. 'I'll leave you now.' He clasped Thiede's shoulder briefly as he departed.

Thiede was silent for a moment, gazing at the floor, then he gave himself a visible shake. 'So then, Darquiel. Tell me everything.'

Darquiel did not tell Thiede about Zu. Also, because of the binding Slinque had put upon him, he couldn't speak about the Weavers either. But he could talk about Lurlei. He implied that Lurlei had revealed his identity to him, and hoped that by the time, if ever, Thiede found out that was misleading information, it would no longer matter.

'Hmm,' Thiede murmured, when the tale was out. 'I admit I'm somewhat confused about all this. Your identity was kept secret in order to hide you from entities like the *sedim*. How did they find out about you?'

'I don't know,' Darq said, expending a large amount of energy shielding his guilty thoughts. 'Lurlei didn't tell me. I suppose, maybe, it could have been the *sedu* you were riding when you first met me?'

Thiede wrinkled his nose. 'I doubt it. Azure is a placid beast and easy to fool. I chose him deliberately for that reason. Didn't you think to ask Lurlei about it?'

Darq shrugged. 'At the time, I was too stunned. There are lots of things I wish I'd asked him, but I felt I should be cautious. I didn't take advantage of his offer.'

'Wise,' Thiede said. 'Still, the *sedim* must take you seriously. Lurlei is their king, or one of their kings. I have never met him.'

'I presume the *sedim's* rivals will also contact me,' Darquiel said. 'What's your advice on that?'

'If it should occur, listen to them,' Thiede said. 'Talking is good, especially if it is endless. It makes time for you.'

Darq narrowed his eyes. 'You have no idea what to do, do you?'

Thiede pulled down the corners of his mouth. 'Well, this is all rather sudden. I'd hoped to keep you a secret for longer. I've a feeling the *sedim* will now do rather a lot to conceal you from their rivals. I've been in touch with Tigron Calanthe. I've not yet told him about you, but I'll do so very soon. There's a lot going on, and it's all going to come together in one way or another. Your brother, Loki, has been abducted, and your father Pellaz is working hard to find him.'

'One of my brothers has been abducted?' Darq asked sharply. 'By who or what?'

Thiede frowned a little. 'It's too big a tale. Wait.' He tapped his chin with the fingers of one hand. 'I suppose you should go to Cal and Caeru. Now that your identity is known, it's pointless keeping you in hiding out here in the wilderness, and Immanion is as safe a place as any other. But bear in mind that your brother was taken. I wouldn't say the *sedim* are more benevolent than their rivals; they just use different methods.'

Darq shuddered. 'You think that the *sedim's* enemies took my brother, then?'

'It's likely. You were believed to be dead. Loki has his own potential, so he's of interest to the factions too. Abrimel is out of the picture, since he's a political prisoner.'

'Why? What did he do?'

Thiede put his head to one side. 'Let's just say he made some unwise choices, owing to the fact he didn't get on with your father, Pellaz. He became the consort of Ponclast. You know of him?'

'Yes, I've heard of him. Wonderful.'

Thiede touched Darq on the shoulder. 'You don't realise how important you are. The mere fact of your existence has made it safer for me to return to this realm. Attention is directed upon you, and I'm regarded as inconsequential. This is uncommon for me, trust me.' Thiede paused. 'Darq, this story really is very long and it needs telling properly. I have to start at the beginning. I want to tell you all about your family.'

Darq sat down. 'I'm listening.'

Darquiel reached the point of information overload about halfway through the story. His head began to ache with facts. He drank some of the tea that Jezinki had brought for them, then wished he could drink something stronger. At the end of the tale, Thiede said, 'You should go to Immanion now. I think it would be best.'

'Not yet,' Darq said.

'Why?'

Darq avoided Thiede's eyes. 'I want to stay here for Natalia. It might be the last festival I can enjoy as a simple har. I feel it's important. There's unfinished business here. Also, I need to think about meeting all these hara who are my family, yet strangers to me. It's daunting.' He looked Thiede full in the face. 'I want to delay going to Immanion for a while. Please don't insist otherwise, Thiede. Will a couple of weeks make that much difference?'

Thiede laughed. 'Dear har, a *minute* might make a difference, but if you feel that strongly, then we'll stay.'

'We?'

Thiede shrugged. 'I haven't attended a festival for a long time, Darq. And believe me, I have no intention of leaving your side now, efficient though Ookami might be.'

'You said you'd made the decision to leave this world. Are you back now simply because of me?'

Thiede grinned. 'Partly. The truth is: I miss this realm. At one time, I thought I'd never come back, and then for a while, I couldn't. I thought I'd be Aghama, remote and all-powerful. I'm not ready for that. I love life as a har, and realise that my job in this realm isn't finished. The Aghama has been created, and he came from me, but he is apart from me also.'

Thiede made an airy gesture with one hand. 'Anyway, I'll be here to guide you, but not meddle too much. Meddling isn't always good, as I've learned. You must speak with your parents. Loki must be reclaimed. We need information about what really is going on around us and what your destiny truly is. Perhaps the only way is for Wraeththu to confer with both the *sedim* and their rivals. I don't know. You've changed things. You might simply be the first of many, and I don't think the *sedim* would quite approve of that. You incepted a woman, for a start. It's a shame you came to the world so late.'

'How is Amelza? Do you know?'

'I can tell you little other than that she survived. When I took her to Roselane, she was simply going through althaia, albeit rather a traumatic one. There are immense implications in what you did, Darq.'

Darq nodded. Those events seemed so far away now. He felt as if the whole world, the one he knew so little about, was surging towards him like a tidal wave.

Thiede stretched and yawned. 'I need a bath and a sleep. Care to join me?'

Darq inclined his head. 'I would, but...' He smiled. 'I want to stay here now to sort out my list.'

Thiede narrowed his eyes. 'He's old enough to be your grand-high-father, at least!'

'Age has refined him. You said so. Also…' Darq gestured towards Thiede. 'In that case, *you* are positively decrepit!'

'Thank you, Darq. Your tongue drips silver. But your point is taken.'

'What was his name again?'

'Manticker the Seventy. Ask him how he earned that epithet. He might tell you.'

'I will.'

Darq wasn't sure quite how long he'd have to wait, but resolved not to leave the room until he'd spoken with Tava'edzen. Jezinki came in and took away the refreshments tray. He said nothing, and only gave Darq a sharp, unfriendly glance. Darq said nothing either. He sat slouched in a chair before the fire, his legs stretched out. His mind was boiling. He thought about this brother called Loki, who had been abducted. He remembered what the Weavers had told him. A cold worm of suspicion wriggled in his heart. Was it possible that Loki would ally with one of the factions against him? Darq was utterly frustrated with the fact that he didn't know what his purpose in life was. Others spoke of his 'potential' and 'difference,' but he couldn't feel anything like that within him. Given the choice, he'd spend his life exploring the world, as he'd done with Ookami. He didn't relish the thought of Immanion, and the brief daydreams he'd once had of being some kind of king were distasteful to him now.

Tava'edzen returned around an hour after Thiede had left Darq alone. He did not seem particularly surprised to find Darq was still in his office. He went to a cupboard and took out a bottle and two glasses. 'Do you want some?' he asked Darq.

Darq straightened up in his chair. 'Yes please.'

Tava'edzen handed him a glass. 'I think we both need this.'

Darq nodded and drained the glass. The liquor was fiery, faintly perfumed. Darq held out the glass and Tava'edzen refilled it. 'I met the Weavers,' Darq said. He was not surprised to find he could speak of this to the phylarch, since Slinque had told him he'd be able to, when the time was right. He felt that time had come.

'Uh huh.' Tava'edzen sat down in a chair opposite Darq's.

'They think I can help you. Do you want that help?'

Tava'edzen twisted his mouth to the side. 'That's difficult for me to answer. I need time. I think perhaps I've become too fond of this isolation. I'm not sure what role there is for me now, beyond this land.'

'Well, if you need help, I'll give it gladly. And if I ever need your help, can I count on it?'

Tava'edzen smiled. He really was unbearably beautiful. 'And what help could I give you, Darquiel?'

'I am Darquiel har Aralis, son of the Tigrons in Immanion. I think the Weavers know that. Didn't they tell you?'

Tava'edzen laughed in apparently genuine amusement. 'No! So, you discovered your heritage. And now you're seeking an ally for your tribe. Manticker might well be an appealing gift to take to Immanion. There are many who would no doubt like to stare at what's left of the legend.'

'It's not like that,' Darq said, suddenly feeling young and stupid.

'No?'

'I meant… oh, it doesn't matter. Forget it.'

Tava'edzen leaned forward and patted Darquiel's knee. 'You have my help, if you need it. *You* do, but not your tribe. Do you understand?'

'Yes. Thank you.' Darq paused. 'I wasn't trying to recruit you as a Gelaming ally. I have a name, but that's all. The Gelaming and their rulers are strangers to me.'

'I was wrong to assume otherwise,' Tava'edzen said. 'It seems we're both somewhat prickly about what might be required of us.'

Darq nodded. 'So, who *was* Manticker the Seventy?'

Tava'edzen leaned back in his chair. 'A good question. As he spent most of the time drunk, it's difficult to recall.'

'How did he get his name?'

'He slew seventy humans in one insane burst of temper. Well, that is the legend. I don't think anyhar actually did an accurate head count. But it was a mess, believe me.'

'I can't see you doing that.'

'Be thankful for that. You were lucky to be born so much later. The early days were ugly, Darq, and cruel, as were we.'

'You were never ugly.'

'Well, that is a matter of opinion.'

Darq paused for a few moments, then said, 'Do you mind if we stay for Natalia; Thiede, Ookami and I?'

Tava'edzen narrowed his eyes. He looked stern. 'Hmm. You wish to partake of our festival?'

'Yes.'

The phylarch didn't respond immediately. Darq wondered what he was thinking. 'It might not be what you expect,' he said at last.

'I want to stay.' Darq held Tava'edzen's gaze. It burned him. He wondered if he'd lose control and throw himself at the phylarch's body. What would Tava'edzen do then?

As if he'd read Darq's thought, Tava'edzen smiled. 'Stay if you wish. I'd like to talk with Thiede anyway.'

Chapter Twenty-Four

On the first floor of the Drudehall was a large room where the ceiling was supported by thick wooden pillars covered in stylised carvings of wolves and the hara who ran with them. For Natalia, this room was decorated with boughs of evergreen; pine, holly and ivy. The air itself smelled of green. Ribbons of red and gold were hung from the boughs, and long trestle tables were set up around the edge of the room. There was a dais at one end, where the phylarch would sit, and also his honoured guests, as well as the highest-ranking members of the Elder Council. A feast was to be held on Natalia eve, which is a customary event for all tribes. There might be local variations to the actual procedure, but the winter solstice is significant to every har. It is the day when the year turns, and the days become longer from thereon. It is the feast to herald the return of the light. Solarisel, the dehar of the season, drops the pearl of the deharling Elisin two weeks before the solstice. On Natalia eve, the pearl gives up its treasure and the light comes back to the world in the form of a shining dehar.

Darq saw these symbols as particularly significant. Two weeks before Natalia, he too had been born as a pearl. Now, it was his time to come forth and shine.

He went to visit the Weavers again, to inform them of things that Tava'edzen had no doubt told them already. He did not mention anything about Zu's people, because he sensed he had to get Natalia out of the way first. He hoped that during the festivities, which would last several days, he'd find time alone to try and communicate with Zu. The Weavers were pleased for him, and wanted to meet Thiede. They removed the binding from his tongue.

'I've offered Tava'edzen my help,' Darq told them, 'but I'm not sure he wants it.'

'He wants it,' said Slinque. 'He just doesn't know it yet.'

Stelph touched his brother on the shoulder. 'Do you think we should tell Darq about what happens at Natalia here?'

Slinque pursed his lips. 'What purpose would there be in that?'

'Forewarning?' said Shayd, smiling slyly.

'What do you mean?' Darq asked.

'The rites of Natalia are different here,' Slinque said. 'It's the festival of the hunt too, and the hunters enjoy certain privileges. You have run with the hunt, Darquiel. I'd be surprised if you weren't offered the same thing.'

'What thing?'

The Weavers laughed together. 'Don't get too drunk,' said Stelph.

At sundown, all the hara of the town gathered in the room that smelled green. Candles burned everywhere and the light was magical. There was enough room for everyhar to sit down, and presently Tava'edzen's staff began to bring out the feast. Whole roasted pigs and birds, every conceivable variety of vegetable cooked in delicious sauces, mounds of freshly cooked bread, wines, ales and fiery liqueurs. The Nezreka set about the serious business of eating and drinking to excess.

That evening, Darq purposefully put all matters from his mind, other than the one he felt was currently most important to him. It was as if he had only a few moments in which to accomplish his heart's desire: the future was uncertain and nebulous. He intended to seduce Tava'edzen. There might be only this one chance.

Throughout the feast, he maintained a covert observation of Tava'edzen and noticed the phylarch didn't drink or eat much, although he was in a convivial mood. He and Thiede had appeared to have renewed their friendship, as if they'd never been parted, and Darq did wonder whether this might interfere with his plans. It was difficult to attract the phylarch's attention for long, since so many others wanted to talk to him, although Darq was aware that Tava'edzen was watching him covertly too. The signs were there. He was sure of it. It hung in the atmosphere like perfume; hot and potent. It made his mouth dry and his loins tingle. His heart ached with a longing he'd never felt before. The air was charged with potential.

By around ten o'clock, nearly everyhar was very drunk. Musicians came into the room, having previously left the feast to fetch their instruments. They played drums, and stringed and wind instruments of a design unfamiliar to Darq. Ookami, sitting beside Darq, said the music sounded eastern, like something from Huldah. 'I like it,' Darq said. 'It makes you want to dance.'

And inevitably, there were dancers. They came into the room, dressed as wolves, wearing very little other than the silvery pelts. Darq was entranced by them. The whole gathering began to sing, a strange lilting song, voices of different timbres melding seamlessly together into a plait of sound. Darq's skin prickled. He glanced over to Tava'edzen, but then saw the phylarch's seat was empty. Darq hadn't seen him leave, but it must simply be that he'd had to obey a call of nature. He'd be back. Darq played over scenarios in his mind; what he'd say to the phylarch, how the moment would come. They would leave this place together, and afterwards Darq would discover something new. He could feel it in his bones. Their union was preordained and sacred.

Now, the music started to die down, and so did the voices, until eventually a single drum was being played, its rhythm slowing down. The dancers had slunk away. Tava'edzen's staff moved quietly around the room, snuffing a lot of the candles, so that the light became much dimmer. A new mood sizzled through the gathering. Darq sat upright in his chair. He licked his lips, almost whined.

From the shadows, a shape emerged. It moved slowly to the centre of room and then crouched down, its arms stretched forward. It was a har wearing a magnificent wolf skin. The head was set with glass eyes, which Darq felt looked at him directly. Moving to the slow rhythm of the drum, the har got to his feet, swaying this way and that. Darq swallowed thickly. The dancer was Tava'edzen.

Apart from the wolf pelt down his back and over his head, he wore a long skirt of what looked like multiple strands of rope weighted with coins. There were gold bracelets around his ankles and up his arms. His chest was bare. Around his hips hung a huge golden disk that concealed his groin: it clearly represented the sun. But for this apparel, he was naked. As he turned, the strings of his skirt swung out in a circle. His arms coiled like smoke. Now the other instruments came back in, one by one, and voices began softly to sing once more. It was hypnotic, rhythmic, tribal. Tava'edzen was the epitome of a har, both gracefully feminine and fiercely masculine. As he rotated his hips, so the candlelight danced in the sun disk. It was as if he were weaving light, creating it, radiating it. His body seemed boneless, moving in complicated steps, swaying, undulating. Darq was consumed by desire. If he didn't touch this har, he'd die.

The dance became faster, wilder, and Tava'edzen was simply a streak of movement in the room. He was both the king and queen of all wolves. He leapt up and it seemed as if his body hung in the air for several seconds. He landed in a crouch, leapt up again. The sound of howling filled the room, and then the hunters came back, leaping and yelling, circling their leader, who spun in their midst, the coins of his skirt throwing off sparks. One of the dancers caught hold of him, and he lashed out with clawed hands, leapt away. The hunters pursued him round the room, and yet the dance was still graceful. Then came the boom of an enormous gong. Its brazen sound echoed to the blackened rafters, and then there was silence.

Tava'edzen padded, almost limped, to the centre of the chamber, and the hunters formed a circle around him. The phylarch knelt down, his hands against the floor, his head lowered. He was a wolf then. All that could be seen was the shining pelt, the legs dangling down his sides, the tail between his legs. All that could be heard was panting breath. A different kind of charge came into the atmosphere. It had a smell to it.

Darquiel picked up his goblet and drained it of wine. He needed a refill. He knew what would happen. He wasn't sure he could bear to witness it, and yet he must. Tava'edzen had granted him permission to attend. Perhaps the message being given was: see me for what I am, then decide.

Slinque appeared at Darquiel's shoulder and handed him a full glass. Darq sipped it, and only the dehara knew what secret ingredients the Weaver had slipped into the potent liquor. Darq didn't care. Slinque's left hand was on his shoulder and he clasped it.

It will be fine, Slinque told him.

Stelph or Shayd, it was difficult to tell which, had entered the circle of hunters. He raised his arms and spoke words in Anakhai, which were clearly part of a ritual. Those gathered around the edge of the room murmured responses.

Then the first hunter went down on his knees behind the king/queen wolf. He put his hands on Tava'edzen's hips, lifted aside the wolf pelt.

Darq turned his head away, but Slinque said: *No, this is sacred. It is his power and his time. Do not turn from it, Darquiel. You wish to know him? Then give him your eyes.*

There were twenty hunters, and what they did seemed to take forever. Darq had a foul sour taste in his mouth; he was stripped of desire. This was the rite of the wolf, when the leader submitted to his pack, became soume for them all, gave himself willingly. It had nothing remotely to do with Darq's plans for the evening. There would be no private, meaningful communion. He felt sick.

When the final hunter rose to his feet, he turned towards the dais and gestured.

'They mean for you to take your turn,' Slinque said.

Darq stood up. He couldn't see properly, because he'd given his eyes, as Slinque had suggested. All other eyes were upon him, waiting. He moved away from the table, and perhaps in that moment, the briefest lightest mind touch reached him; a thread of longing. He couldn't, wouldn't respond to it. He was aware that Thiede was staring at him speculatively, but he wouldn't meet the har's eyes. Ookami was also watching Darq carefully. Somehow, without speaking to anyhar, Darq found his way outside.

In the snow, Darq vomited hot liquor. He sat on the steps of the house and threw up between his feet. He didn't care. He'd drunk too much, and even a har can drink himself to the point of nausea. *Immanion, then,* he thought. He was incapable of thinking about Zu. He knew he should move, because somehar would come to find him; maybe Thiede, or Ookami or one of the Weavers. He couldn't face talk. He'd made a fool of himself. He should have smiled at the hunter and done what was expected of him. It was, after all, the only thing he could expect. He'd broken custom, the rules of the tribe. His dream of Tava'edzen had been only that: unreal. It was time to leave. Had Ookami taken a turn?

Darq groaned and staggered to his feet. He stumbled back into the Drudehall, his flesh shrinking against his bones, because he didn't want to be seen. Bumping from wall to wall, falling upon the stairways, he made his way to his room, where he felt sick again. He needed to drink something other than alcohol. In the adjoining bathroom, he plunged his head entire into a sink full of cold water. He drank from it, tempted to breathe it in. *You are pathetic!* he told himself. *No, you are in love. Oh, for the love of Aru, get a grip!*

He went back to his bed and sat on it, hands dangling between his knees. 'Aruhani, I make a poor priest for you,' he said. 'Sleep, that's what I need. It'll make it all go away. Yes. Sleep.'

It took him some time to get his clothes off, because the fastenings for some reason seemed too complicated to deal with. Eventually, he crawled beneath the quilt and curled up in the dark. He closed his eyes and was assailed by images of what he'd witnessed. It would have been worse if Tava'edzen had been facing him, if they'd had to look at each other. Be thankful for small mercies. *Stop it and sleep!* Darq told himself.

Some hours later, he only realised he'd been dozing when he was shaken back to a wakeful state. He peered outside the quilt and saw Tava'edzen standing beside the bed. 'I'm sorry,' Tava'edzen said.

'I know that word,' Darq said. 'I know how it works, and that it means nothing.' He put his head back beneath the quilt. There was silence, so he re-emerged briefly and said. 'Anyway, you have nothing to apologise for. I'm just a stupid harling. Good night.'

Tava'edzen laughed. 'Darquiel, come out. We must talk. I'm sorry you weren't warned, that's all. What on earth possessed us to think a young outsider could join in our customs like that, I have no idea.

Blame Slinque. He thought it was right.'

Darquiel squirmed into a sitting position, the quilt held tight around him. 'I didn't wreck your ceremony, did I?'

'No. Your virtuous companion obeyed the summons, and everyhar assumed he was the one who'd been invited.'

'Ookami?'

Tava'edzen nodded.

Darq groaned. 'He wasn't supposed to… oh, that's bad. He was being celibate for a Grissecon.'

'Well, you could say he performed his Grissecon. It was a sacrificial act, I could tell that much.' Tava'edzen sat down on the bed. 'Darq, what you must learn is that any leader, whether a lowly phylarch or a great Tigron, has responsibilities to his hara. In some ways, you are denied a private life. You have to make sacrifices, do what's expected of you. If, for example, the phylarch of the Nezreka would have dearly loved to leave that feast tonight, alone with a wondrous young har, so that they could spend the night together, just the two of them, and nohar else in the whole world, he couldn't do it.'

'I understand,' Darq said. 'Thank you for saying that.'

'Among the Uigenna, such practices were very common,' Tava'edzen said. 'Initiation into an inner cabal of any phyle usually involved some kind of group aruna. It was a mark of trust, of submission, but also reverence. Tonight, when those hara came to me, one by one, it was not violation. It was an act of honour. And it was my honour to receive them, these hara who hunt for our tribe. On this night, I give myself to them, and the light returns.'

'Thanks for explaining. I'm young, Tava… can I call you, Tava?'

'Of course.'

'I'm young, and my lack of experience is sometimes inconvenient. Slinque should have told me. You should have told me.'

'I know.'

Darq picked at a loose thread on the quilt. 'It's really embarrassing, but I think I've fallen in love for the first time. I expect it'll pass eventually. It's a peculiar thing, like being struck by a stone. I never thought it would happen, because, really, I tend to objective all the time. But…'

'Ssh'. Tava'edzen put a finger to Darq's lips. 'There is one other rite. Shall I tell you of it?'

Darq nodded. He didn't want Tava'edzen to take his finger away.

'I've given of myself, as is the way, but at the end of the feast, the wolf selects for himself the har who will accept a similar gift to the one he received. Do you know what I mean?'

Darq nodded again. Without taking his eyes from Tava'edzen's face, he pulled back the quilt. 'In that case, you have to do it twenty times,' he said.

Tava'edzen laughed. 'Well, that might be a record.' He stood up and began to unfasten the wolf pelt from his head.

'No,' Darq said. 'Don't. Leave it on. Just... not the metal disk. That might get in the way. Let me help.'

Tava'edzen stood before him and with shaking fingers, Darq undid the belt that held on the skirt. It dropped to the floor in a clatter of coins. Darq did what Darzu had taught him and Tava'edzen sighed in pleasure. He bloomed in Darq's mouth, tasting of musk and pine, the smell of the wolf pelt all around him.

Tava'edzen might not have possessed the stamina to do what Darq had suggested, but he did know the twenty ways of delight, perhaps more. Darq hovered in a kind of delirium that was partly sorrowful. He wondered what a har was supposed to do when he met somehar else who seemed to have been designed by the universe specifically for himself. Darq would have to leave Nezreka soon. He knew Tava'edzen would not leave with him.

'Don't think of tomorrows,' Tava'edzen said to him, intuiting in Darq's breath his wistful thoughts.

Before dawn, Darq told Tava'edzen about Zu. He didn't know why he did it, but perhaps he hoped the phylarch would know what he was talking about, especially the mention of Zu's people.

'We'll visit the Weavers later,' Tava'edzen said, and Darq was warmed because he had suggested they would go together.

Darq was lying with his head on Tava'edzen's chest, his whole body relaxed and sated. 'I want to try and contact Zu first.' He propped himself up on his elbow. 'Will you come with me?'

Tava'edzen reached up and ran a hand over Darq's exposed shoulder. His hair was spread out over the pillow, his arm beneath his head. Darq felt he would never tire of this sight. 'He might not manifest if I'm there,' Tava'edzen said.

'I'm sure he will. He knew...'

'Knew what?'

Darq shook his head. 'Just... things. Well? Will you come? We should go now, before the town wakes.'

'I doubt if all of it is asleep yet,' said Tava'edzen, 'but all right.'

Darq realised that part of the reason he wanted to take Tava'edzen with him was to show him off to Zu. And perhaps also vice versa. He wasn't sure himself if Zu would comply and turn up.

They went to the hill that Darq had visited before. A line of pale light showed on the horizon; the birth of the sun. It didn't feel cold at all, yet Darq's breath steamed from his mouth in thick clouds. 'Hold me,' Darq said.

Tava'edzen's pressed his warm body against Darq's back as he swung the weighted cord above his head. The phylarch added his own voice to the song of the cord. It was a gentle, lilting sound that made Darq's skin tingle. Shadowy black wolves came padding from the trees and stood around them in a circle, their eyes as softly brilliant as moonstones. 'Look,' Tava'edzen breathed into Darq's ear. 'The black brothers have heard your song. They honour you.'

'I'll remember this moment for ever,' Darq murmured.

Then Zu was walking towards him through the snow-covered trees, and the wolves slunk back into the undergrowth. It was as if Zu had simply arrived in a conventional way: a horse might be tethered further down the path. Yet Darq knew that just out of sight, Zu had manifested from the Otherlanes. Today, he wore clothes for travelling; a silvery hooded cloak covered him almost entirely. His hands were gloved and there were small pearls stitched into the backs of them.

Zu came to a halt a few feet away and regarded Tava'edzen inscrutably.

'I had to call you,' Darq said. 'Something has happened.'

Zu came forward a few more steps. 'I told you our meetings were to be secret,' he said coldly.

'This is Tava'edzen,' Darq said, hoping Zu would intuit the deeper meaning behind the words.

Zu ducked his head respectfully to the phylarch. 'An honour,' he said. 'I've heard flattering things about you.'

Tava'edzen was still standing behind Darq, and Darq felt the phylarch's body shaking slightly with suppressed laughter. 'Indeed? I've heard things about you too.'

'No doubt.' Zu's voice seemed hung with icicles.

'Zu,' Darq said firmly, 'the reason I brought you here is because the *sedim* came to me. You said they couldn't reach me here.'

Zu frowned. 'That *is* unusual. I underestimated them.'

'I'm no longer a secret,' Darq said. 'Thiede is in Nezreka. I'll be leaving here soon, I expect.'

Zu sucked his upper lip for a moment. 'Hmm.'

'Perhaps it's time for you to be honest too,' Darq suggested.

Zu didn't respond to this, but addressed Tava'edzen. 'Please take Darquiel to my people, Tiahaar. He must go to them before he leaves this country.'

'Do I know them?' the phylarch asked.

Zu appeared surprised by Tava'edzen's words. 'You know *of* them, surely. The Krim Sri.'

Tava'edzen let go of Darq and went closer to Zu, perhaps to read his expression more clearly. 'Our seers, the Weavers, have spoken of these beings,' he said. 'I believed them to be spiritual entities, creatures of the land in this place. You're telling me they're real people? By that, I mean human?'

'Not exactly,' Zu replied. 'They're an ancient race that has walked among humanity for thousands of years.'

'The Weavers know this?' Tava'edzen sounded sharp.

'I can't answer that,' Zu said. 'I don't know how much they've revealed to the Weavers.'

'Well perhaps you should be talking to them,' Tava'edzen said. 'How can *I* take Darq to these Krim Sri? Why can't you take him yourself?'

Zu smoothed wrinkles from his gloves. 'I would take him myself, but at this time I don't wish to make myself known to the Krim Sri. They would demand too much of me. The Weavers will help you, I'm sure, and it's vital Darq goes to them.'

'What's the purpose of it?' Darq asked. 'Why should I meet them?'

'You can help each other,' Zu said, 'but mainly, Darq, I want you to protect them. The Krim Sri who reside here in Anakhai are all that remain of my kind in earthly form. They've had to hide from humans, hara and other entities alike.'

'So, you're like the Weavers, really,' Darq said. 'You'll help me if I help those you care for.'

Zu pulled a rueful face. 'That sounds harsh, but it's an accurate assessment.'

Darq blew out his breath forcefully in exasperation. 'Then why didn't you just tell me from the start?'

'Nothing is certain. I needed to make sure you reached this place first. There's a limit to my capabilities.'

'So, you are Krim Sri, too.'

'Was,' Zu said. 'I am, I think, the only incepted Krim Sri.'

Darq frowned. 'What exactly are they?'

'Humanoid, but inhuman, as you are. They are in fact hybrids. At one time, they were androgynous, as Wraeththu are, but when they came to this realm and took on a more corporeal form, they became as men and women. This was to blend in, naturally.'

Darq glanced at Tava'edzen, who merely shrugged. 'So how do the Krim Sri relate to the *sedim* and the other faction?' Darq asked.

Zu pulled his cloak more closely around him. It was the first time Darq had seen him be affected by the temperature. It was strange, but each time he encountered Zu the har became more real somehow. 'Originally,' Zu said, 'my people came from the same source as the *sedim*. Controversially, and against the wishes of their rulers, they mingled with humanity. There have been several unsuccessful attempts to get rid of them over the millennia, but they learned to blend in well. The *sedim* have always feared the Krim Sri would go to their enemies, because of all the creatures in this world, the Krim Sri know the truth of what goes on in the upper ethers. They can't blend in with Wraeththu, not yet. It would take them many lifetimes. Wraeththu must extend protection to the Krim Sri.'

'If you required help and protection, why leave it until now - until Darq - to make that known?' Tava'edzen asked.

'Fear,' answered Zu. 'My erstwhile people have never been under greater threat. Darq will soon come to power. I want him to be aware of my people's plight.'

'Why do you care?' Tava'edzen said. 'The majority of hara choose to turn their back on their unhar origins.'

Zu drew himself taller and spoke haughtily. 'I'm not like most Wraeththu: I can't forget from where I came or those who originally gave me birth. The Weavers discovered the sanctuary of the Krim Sri many years ago. They've been my people's contact with the world, and have kept their secrets. The Weavers might have spoken to you of spiritual beings, but the Krim Sri are rather more than that.' Zu appealed to Darq. 'Go to them now. Speak with their leaders. It is time.'

Darq was in fact fascinated by the idea of this unknown race. He would have wanted to see them despite Zu's request for help. 'Very well,' he said, then paused. 'Is there a war coming, Zu?'

Zu sighed. 'I hope not. My hope is that you'll avert it. Do as I ask, and return here tonight to tell me what you learn.' He bowed and turned around. 'I'll leave you now.'

'Zu, wait,' Darq said, but the har ignored him. He walked back the way he'd come.

For some moments, both Darq and Tava'edzen were silent, then Tava'edzen said, 'That was somewhat astonishing.'

'Do you believe him?' Darq asked.

Tava'edzen took Darq in his arms, kissed his brow. 'As I said, I've heard of the Krim Sri. The Weavers have mentioned them as what I took to be local nature spirits.' He exhaled through his nose. 'Slinque and his dear brothers have some explaining to do.'

'If I go to the Krim Sri, will you come with me?' Darq asked.

'Gladly,' Tava'edzen replied. 'I'm as curious about them as you no doubt are.' He kissed Darq again. 'Right. Let's go to the Weavers now. I hope we wake them from peaceful slumbers. They're as tricky as foxes, those three!'

Chapter Twenty-Five

Darq and Tava'edzen arrived at the round house to find the Weavers sitting in their kitchen, drinking tea. Darq suspected they hadn't been to bed, because they still wore the ornate robes they'd put on for the previous night's ceremony. When Shayd opened the door, Darq said to him, 'You must know why we're here?'

Shayd indicated that Darq and Tava'edzen should come in. 'Perhaps you should tell us, all the same.'

Slinque and Stelph immediately became wary when they saw who had arrived. Their bodies went utterly still. 'What is it, Tava?' Slinque asked tightly.

'Darq can explain,' Tava'edzen replied.

Shayd went to stand behind his brothers, who both remained seated. Darq approached them. 'Take me to the Krim Sri,' he said.

Slinque put down his tea mug carefully by the stove. 'I see,' he said. 'Who has told you of them?'

'A har who was once one of them,' Darq replied. 'He's been with me since Samway. I only learned his identity very recently.'

Slinque sniffed. 'Interesting you didn't mention this to us.'

'I did,' Darq snapped. 'You dismissed it. The voice in my head, remember?'

'Hmm, careless of me,' Slinque said, 'although the last thing any of us would have expected was for one of the Sri to be har.'

Stelph nodded. 'Yes. They were decimated in the early years of the destruction of human civilisation, and the survivors fled long before Wraeththu took a hold. As you must know, they are full of fear.'

'I know,' Darq said. 'Zu doesn't want to go to them himself.'

Shayd folded his arms; somewhat defensively, Darq thought. 'Why do you wish to see them?' Slinque asked.

'The har who was once Krim Sri feels his people need protection and that Wraeththu can provide it. Whether this is true or not, I don't yet know. In order to assess the situation, I want to speak to their leaders.'

The Weavers exchanged glances.

'Well,' said Stelph, 'we can certainly ask if they'll see you.'

'That's not good enough,' said Tava'edzen mildly, although there was a hard edge to his voice. 'You'll take us to them now. No requests, no delays. Now! Understood?'

'Yes, Tava,' said the Weavers in unison.

'You'll have to go beneath the mountains,' said Slinque. 'We must forewarn the Sri of our approach.'

'And how long will that take?' Tava'edzen demanded.

Slinque sighed. 'We'll be as quick as we can. It's unavoidable, Tava. They have to know they'll be having visitors, otherwise their traps and wards could kill us.'

'Very well,' said Tava'edzen, 'but be quick about it.'

'Shall we return to Nezreka first?' Darq asked.

Tava'edzen shook his head. 'No.'

'They'll search for us. Thiede will think I've been abducted.'

'I'll send a message to Jezinki,' Tava'edzen said. 'He can tell your hara what he likes. I'll make sure he knows to keep everyhar away from here.'

Slinque bowed a little and beckoned to his brothers. 'If you'll excuse us, we'll communicate with the Sri and dress ourselves for the trip. Please, sit down and take some tea while you wait.'

'I'm not sure I want more of *your* tea,' Darq said.

Slinque smiled. 'It *is* only tea, Darquiel, but suit yourself.' He and his brothers went into the central room, closing the door firmly behind them.

In the centre of the kitchen, Darq took Tava'edzen in his arms. 'Today is Natalia,' he said. 'Happy festival to you, Tava.'

Tava'edzen kissed Darq on the mouth. 'My blood beats for you, Darq. We are of one heart. May the radiance behind the sun light your path.'

'Is that Uigenna talk?' Darq asked. 'Those sound like ritual phrases or something.'

Tava'edzen nodded. 'Those are a couple of the things we used to say to one another when we felt a little civilised.'

Darq pulled Tava'edzen closer to him. 'I think I'll love you always,' he said. 'It would be good if we could have a future together, of some kind. Otherwise it will be painful.'

'Whatever happens, I'm here for you,' Tava'edzen said. 'Perhaps we should hope the *sedim* win the conflict. It'll make it more convenient for you to travel to me.'

'If things turn out right, I don't think we'll need *sedim*,' Darq said. 'You're adamant, though? You'll remain here, whatever happens?'

Again, Tava'edzen nodded, and his expression was somewhat sorrowful. 'I think so, yes. The prospect of other leaders tires me. They'd irritate me into a state of violence, I'm sure. Manticker would never bow to anyhar, and there's too much of him left in me.'

Darq expected that the journey to the Krim Sri would take a long time, at least a day, but the entrance to their hidden kingdom was actually fairly close to the Weavers' home. Along the way, Slinque said to Darq: 'At first, we thought it was a wonderful coincidence that we settled in this place, so close to the Krim Sri. Now, we wonder whether fate took a hand, or the Krim Sri influenced us in some subtle way.'

'If they're anything like Zu,' Darq said, 'then I expect they had some influence!'

The Weavers led the way to a cliff face that was covered in hanging ivy. Darq assumed the ivy would be lifted aside and a doorway would be revealed, but the Weavers didn't attempt any such thing.

Slinque and Stelph went to the rock and put their hands flat upon it.

'This is going to feel strange,' Shayd said to Darq and Tava'edzen, 'but you must trust us. Part of the wall before you is an illusion. If you intend to pass through it, you will.'

'How did you find this place?' Tava'edzen asked. 'It looks just like rock to me, and not even my inner sight can detect a doorway.'

'Very occasionally, a Sri will come to the surface,' Shayd said. 'They hide themselves well, but when the portal has just been used it becomes more visible for a short while. You'd sense it yourself then, Tava.' Shayd indicated his brothers. 'We came across it by accident and investigated it. We were surprised by a Sri named Hannael, who was returning to her home. Or rather we surprised each other!'

'Was she hostile?' Tava'edzen asked.

Shayd shook his head. 'No, not at all. She could see what we were and was fascinated by us, as we were with her. Her people had fled here long before Wraeththu had taken a hold, so we were the first hara she'd met. Generally, Sri who come to the surface avoid both hara and humans. But anyway, Hannael and we became friends. For some time, we met with her to talk, and after a while she began to visit us at the round house. Eventually, her leaders discovered she had befriended us, and we were asked to visit Helek Sah, the city in the mountain. It was then we were taught how to use the doorway.'

'Why didn't you tell me?' Tava'edzen said, his voice puzzled. 'Didn't you trust me with this secret?'

Shayd bowed to the phylarch. 'Forgive us, Tava. We had to vow we would keep silent.'

'Did they put a binding on your tongue?' Darq asked sarcastically.

Shayd smiled thinly. 'No. There was no need.' He turned away and looked at his brothers, who had taken their hands from the rock. 'The doorway is primed,' Shayd said and gestured towards the cliff. 'Are you ready?'

Darq and Tava'edzen exchanged a glance, then the phylarch took hold of one of Darq's hands. 'We *intend* to pass,' he said to Shayd. 'That's all?'

Shayd nodded.

Darq squeezed Tava'edzen's fingers. They approached the cliff face where together, they took a deep breath and stepped forward.

Darq imagined that once they had crossed the threshold, they would find themselves in a cavern or passageway on the other side of the rock. This was not the case. On the one occasion he opened his eyes, he nearly panicked. They were passing through what appeared to be solid stone. There was pressure against his skin, and an unpleasant squeezing sensation in his head. *Keep your eyes closed,* Slinque advised behind him. The experience seemed endless, as it lasted for a couple of uncomfortable minutes. Eventually, the rock expelled them and Darq and Tava'edzen staggered forward. They had emerged into a narrow passageway, with a very low ceiling. Tava'edzen was obliged to stoop, since he was taller than the others. Darq watched as the Weavers emerged from the rock. It looked as if the stone was actually made of some kind of fluid. Was this magic or extremely advanced science? Ultimately, perhaps it was both.

'That was probably one of the weirdest and most discomforting things I have ever done,' Tava'edzen said. He laughed. 'And as you know, my Weavers, my colourful history includes a number of weird and discomforting events.'

'How did the Krim Sri create that boundary?' Darq asked. He had to keep opening and closing his mouth because his jaw felt oddly stiff.

'It's the work of many minds,' Stelph said. 'Come. They're waiting for us.'

The Weavers led the way along the path, which gradually descended, and grew narrower as they progressed. The ceiling also became lower and the air was almost unbreathable.

'This is vile,' Darq said.

Slinque looked back. He was bent nearly double; his hair touched the floor. 'The Sri have made the journey as unpleasant as possible,' he said. 'It's part of their security system.'

'I can't breathe!' Darq said. 'How much longer will this take?'

'Not far,' Slinque said. 'You'll be fine. Try to breathe deeply and evenly.'

Just when Darq thought he'd pass out from lack of oxygen, the passageway disgorged them into a cavern. Darq took a great gulp of air in relief. The scene before him was lit, somewhat inadequately, by a single enormous torch that rested upon a tall black metal stand. As far as Darq could see, the cave before him was full of water, with only a narrow beach. Silvery-grey damp sand shifted beneath his feet. The beach extended only a few feet; beyond it black water stretched out into a void. Darq could not see the other shore, if there was one. The air in that place was humid. His breath steamed, yet he did not feel cold.

'Now what?' Darq asked.

'Do we have to swim?' Tava'edzen enquired with some distaste.

'No, Tava,' Slinque said. 'Be patient.'

The Weavers stood in a line upon the narrow shore and put their fingers into their mouths. They blew a series of piercing whistles of different notes.

Presently a dark shape came gliding across the dark waters. It was a long, narrow boat. At prow and stern were carvings of what looked like a cross between eagle, horse and fish. Darq saw that the pilot was a tall, thin figure robed in black. He stood at the stern, using a single large oar to propel the boat forward. Eventually, the boat came to rest near the water's edge.

'Come,' Slinque said. 'You'll have to get your feet wet.'

Darq followed the others into the water. It was not as cold as he expected, and its consistency seemed thicker than water should be. Slinque murmured a few words in a strange tongue to the pilot, who neither moved nor spoke. Darq had the uncomfortable feeling that whatever lay hidden beneath the hooded cloak would be some kind of monster.

Once they'd all embarked, the pilot turned the boat and it slid smoothly and silently into the darkness. Darq was aware of immense space around him, even though he couldn't see it. He sat on a narrow bench with Tava'edzen at his side. A single lantern at the prow cast a small pool of radiance over the water.

On the far shore, a corridor of torches on tall metal stands lined a sandy path leading to a rock face. The flames of the torches were blue. At the end of the path, covering an arched entrance in the rock, was a wall of roaring red flames. Darq studied this with some trepidation as he disembarked from the boat. 'Don't tell me,' he said to Slinque. 'We have to *intend* to walk through that as well.'

'Don't be absurd,' said Slinque. 'You'd burn to death in an instant. Here, we wait. From this point on, we must be escorted.'

Darq was uncomfortably aware of the silent pilot, who still remained motionless in the boat behind them. Other than the initial words Slinque had spoken, the Weavers had made no attempt to communicate with the pilot and now they ignored him.

Darquiel linked an arm through one of Tava'edzen's elbows. For a brief stultifying moment, he became painfully aware of how vulnerable they all were. If the Krim Sri had any sinister motive in getting Darq to their hidden city, he had complied with them willingly and perhaps too hastily.

Tava'edzen drew Darq away from the Weavers a little, to speak in private. 'You're tense,' he murmured. 'Be at rest.'

'We were too quick to come here,' Darq said. 'I should have told the Sri their leaders would have to come to the round house.'

'I don't sense anything dangerous,' Tava'edzen said. 'Really, I think we'll be fine.'

The waiting took far too long for Darq's liking, but after only a few minutes, the wall of flames ahead of him drew back like curtains, and an extremely tall, thin figure walked beneath the arch. It was what appeared to be a woman, clad in a dark robe with a high collar that rose behind her neck in a stiff fan. Her hair was confined in a strange and complicated metal headdress, a mass of spikes and waving tines. Locks of hair gushed forth from apertures in this peculiar crown. Her neck was swathed in close-fitting necklaces of dark jewels, so that no patch of skin could be seen. She carried a long black staff that was tipped with an ornament of gold; it appeared to represent a bird of prey.

'You are privileged,' Slinque murmured to Darq. 'That is Tiy, the Eye Priestess of the Krim Sri. She has come to meet you personally.'

'And has dressed herself quite dramatically for the occasion!' Stelph added.

The priestess paused some feet away from the hara and bowed. Ornaments on her headdress tinkled. But for her height, she looked like a human woman in her forties, and yet at the same time appeared ageless. Her pale underworld skin was not lined or sagging, but there was an air almost of antiquity about her. She was not beautiful exactly, but striking. Her hair was very black. Darq guessed she must be extremely old, older than Thiede or any other har.

'Welcome to Helek Sah, Darquiel har Aralis,' Tiy said, then turned to Tava'edzen and inclined her head. 'And the phylarch of the Nezreka is also most welcome. I am Tiy. I'll escort you to the city.'

'You know why I'm here?' Darq asked her.

Tiy smiled. 'To discuss *my* future, I would imagine. Follow me. You must pass through the seven gates to Helek Sah. The Gate of Fire is open now. Come quickly, before it closes.' She turned swiftly and went back towards the curtains of flame.

Darq felt no more than gentle heat as he passed beneath the rocky archway. Beyond the gate, he found himself in a deep gorge. The rock here was bare and occasionally running with damp. The air smelled of earth. Looking up, Darq could see no ceiling, only darkness. The torches that lined the walls did not offer enough light to see too much detail.

Tiy did not speak but led the way quickly. Within minutes, they'd reached the second gate, which was a violent cataract of water across the path. 'The Gate of Water,' Tiy said. She raised her arms before it, and drew a few complicated symbols in the air with her staff. Finally, she uttered a tone, and the water drew back like the fire had done, as if it were merely curtains of fabric.

As Darq passed through the gate, a piercing chill went through his flesh. For a moment, it felt as if he was swimming, which was absurd, but then the gate was behind him and he stood once more upon the stony ground of the gorge.

'It gets better,' Slinque said to him.

'Better?' Darq pantomimed a double-take.

'You'll see,' said Stelph. He gestured towards Tiy, who was standing impatiently some feet ahead of them. 'Let's go. She doesn't like to be kept waiting.'

The third gate across the gorge was of stone, and this was covered in carved bas-reliefs of tall winged figures. 'The Gate of Earth,' Tiy announced. She opened it simply by knocking upon it with her staff. Beyond this gate, a perilous walkway of stone arced maybe fifty feet across a deep chasm. Darq thought he heard water rushing, far below. Although the path was fairly wide, the fact that it hung over so deep a drop and didn't possess any kind of wall or railing made Darq feel as if he'd plummet over the side at any minute. Weirdly, he was afraid he'd be driven to throw himself over. He'd never been bothered by heights before.

On the other side of the walkway, the party entered another chasm lit by flickering torchlight. Here, after a hundred yards or so, they came across the next gate, which was constructed entirely of dark metal. 'The Gate of Iron,' Tiy said. Again, she employed her staff to open it. She turned to address Darq before they passed through. 'The next two gates will no doubt intrigue you,' she said.

Darq managed a weak laugh. 'Believe me, the others have intrigued me immensely!'

Tiy smiled. 'You've not experienced the best yet. Have you travelled the Otherlanes at all, Darquiel?'

Darq shook his head. 'No.'

Tiy smiled. 'Then I think you'll enjoy this.'

She led the party onwards until they reached a place where the path seemed blocked by what Darq could only describe as "nothingness". He peered into endless darkness that felt more than simply absence of light.

'This is the Gate of Trackless Void,' Tiy said. 'It is part in this world, part in the Otherlanes. Have no fear of being lost within it. When it's open, you simply walk through it.'

'This is a very... *elaborate* security system,' Tava'edzen said.

Tiy raised an eyebrow. 'You think so? You have no idea what we have to protect ourselves against!'

Tava'edzen bowed. 'Excuse me, I meant no insult.'

Tiy turned away from him and raised her arms before the gate. She spoke a few words in a guttural unknown tongue, perhaps the same one, Darq thought, that Slinque had spoken to the boat pilot. Tiy then uttered some musical tones in a low humming voice. After this, she stood motionless for some moments, perhaps projecting intention into the gateway before her. She then beckoned with her staff. 'Come, it is open.'

Darq took a deep breath, again took hold of one of Tava'edzen's hands, and stepped into the void. He felt as if he was crossing the universe with a single step. There were few impressions other than that of unimaginable immensity. This generated a strange feeling of euphoria, as if a secret of life had been revealed. He was inside the gate for only a couple of seconds, yet time stretched to eternity. When he stepped onto the firm path beyond, it felt as if he'd woken from a long sleep. 'That was...' he said to Tiy, then shook his head, unable to describe what he felt.

She smiled at him. 'Interesting, yes?'

He nodded. 'At least that!' He glanced at Tava'edzen, who appeared dazed.

'The first time we came here,' Shayd said, 'we went back and forth through that gate four times. We couldn't get enough of it.'

'*You* couldn't,' Stelph said. He grinned at Darq. 'Shayd likes strange experiences!'

'Come along,' Tiy said. 'You won't be doing *that* again!'

The path turned a corner to the right, and here the sixth gate was revealed. It appeared as whirling nebulae of sparkling light. 'This is the Gate of Stars,' Tiy said. 'I think it's the most beautiful of all.' As before, she uttered sounds to open the gate. When Darq stepped through it, he felt as if his entire being filled with light. It was like becoming a star himself. On the other side of it, he felt refreshed, full of energy.

'Thank the Aghama there's only one more,' Tava'edzen said softly to Darq. 'I don't think I can take much more of this disorientation.'

The last obstacle was the Gate of Bones. It was a reminder to Darq that he was in the earthly realm, after the heady experiences of the previous two gates, since this final portal was made entirely of the bones of animals, or at least Darq thought they were animals. To open it, Tiy simply pulled a key from a pocket of her robe and unlocked it. Darq supposed the Krim Sri to have a sense of humour. Keys and locks seemed far too prosaic after the gates of Trackless Void and Stars.

Beyond the final gate, the path they followed became much wider. The rock walls to either side were smooth and set with globes of soft yellow radiance.

'It's not far now,' Tiy said. She smiled archly at Tava'edzen. 'You'll no doubt be glad of that, Tiahaar.'

Tava'edzen merely smiled at her. Darq could tell the phylarch had been far more disturbed by the experiences of the gates than he had himself. As they undertook the last stage of their journey, Darq said to Tava'edzen. 'I want to walk beside Tiy, speak to her alone. Do you mind?'

Tava'edzen shook his head. 'Of course not. I think you should.'

'I appreciate you coming here with me...'

Tava'edzen pushed Darq's shoulder. 'Hush, go and speak to her.'

Darq increased his pace to catch up with the Eye Priestess. 'Thank you for bringing us to your home,' he said. 'I have many questions.'

'I'm sure,' Tiy said. 'Soon, we'll speak in depth.'

'How much do you know about me?'

Tiy touched him briefly on the arm. 'Quite a lot; well, perhaps more than you'd expect.'

Darq shivered. '*How* do you know?

Tiy tossed her staff from one hand to the other; a playful gesture. 'Well, let me see.' She threw back her head and narrowed her eyes. 'When your soul entered your hostling's body, it was as if a special light came on in the world. We couldn't help but notice it. It was a light that attracted a lot of attention, and not all of it was well disposed towards you.'

'Did you hear my cry into the ethers too, not so long ago?'

Tiy nodded. 'A scream, yes! We knew where you were, then. To me, becoming aware of your being was like watching a star in the distant heavens. Sometimes, the star would glow brighter, but mostly it was a faint gleam. We were often very worried for you, because we knew your light was important, not just for us but for this whole realm of earth.'

Darq shook his head in bewilderment. 'It's still all very new for me, this idea of destiny and so on. It's overwhelming.'

'I understand,' Tiy said. 'You were kept in ignorance to protect you, we knew that. We felt the trauma when your pearl was taken from your hostling; it was terrible. After that, even though we knew you'd been rescued in some way, we often discussed finding you and bringing you here, simply to keep you safe. If things had ever got really dangerous for you, we would have tried to intervene. Fortunately, you've had good guardians, so our interference wasn't needed.'

For a few moments, Darq wondered what it would have been like to have lived in this place instead of Samway. He had to admit the idea had appeal. 'It's so strange to think that others have had an interest in me over the years,' he said, 'and that they've been *watching* me. It still doesn't feel quite real.'

Tiy tapped his shoulder with her staff. 'It *is* real, Darquiel. You must get used to the idea.'

Darq glanced at her. 'Do you ever miss the surface?'

Tiy sighed. 'Of course I do. I miss the sky particularly, but the day will come when we can emerge once more. I have to believe this. Are you willing to be an ally of the Krim Sri, Darquiel?'

Darq shrugged. 'Well, I've not yet seen or heard anything that sets me against the idea. I just can't imagine how I'll have that much influence to help you.'

Again, Tiy tapped him with her staff. 'Here we are, my friend. Helek Sah, last city of the Krim Sri.'

The path had turned another corner to reveal an immense cave. Helek Sah was a city of many levels, lit by flame. Tiy told Darq that around two thousand individuals lived there, all that remained of the Krim Sri. She led the way into the maze of streets and buildings. Much to Darq's surprise, it was a place full of life. The Krim Sri went about their daily business, pausing only to bow their heads to Tiy as she walked among them. The hara attracted many curious stares. Like Tiy, the populace was very tall and carried themselves with grace. Both males and females could be mistaken for hara, since they were androgynous in appearance. The men had no beards and the faces of the women were strong.

The buildings were tall and narrow, fashioned of obsidian. The pavements beneath Darq's feet were like black glass, yet not slippery. Tiy led the way along these glossy thoroughfares, between the looming crags of the buildings to a place where black stairs led upwards. At the top was a terrace, and here a villa stood. Ornamental fungi grew in decorative pots before the arched doorway. The sight made Darq wistful; the Krim Sri could never have green plants at their thresholds.

Tiy did not knock upon the closed door – a strangely beautiful artefact of dark red wood covered in stylised carvings of winged beasts – but opened it and walked directly into the hall beyond. She gestured for the visitors to follow her.

'Is this your home?' Darq asked.

'No,' Tiy answered. 'It's the home of our leader, Nimron. I'm taking you to him.'

Inside the villa, a narrow hallway was lit by softly glowing lamps upon the walls. It was not a homely place; the walls inside were unplastered and gleamed as if wet. Tiy led the way down a short corridor to an arched doorway. Here, she opened double doors and went into the room beyond. It was cramped and airless, every wall covered in shelves crammed with books, many shoved on sideways. The books looked very old. In this claustrophobic chamber, a large table took up most of the available space. It was cluttered with manuscripts and peculiar bits of metal apparatus, whose functions Darq could not fathom.

At the table, in an uncomfortable-looking high-backed chair was a tall man – or what appeared to be a man – who had long white hair. Apart from that, he did not appear old, but shared with Tiy an ambience of antiquity. His long hands looked delicate, as if made of a friable pale stone. His eyes, which were very dark, held a melancholy expression. His mouth was surrounded by faint lines suggesting humour, but if so it was wistful. He stood up as the visitors entered the room, and inclined his head.

'My lord,' said Tiy, taking hold of one of Darq's arms, 'this is the har Darquiel har Aralis.'

The tall man fixed Darq with a stare that reminded him very much of Zu. 'I am Nimron, Guardian of the Krim Sri, Lord of Helek Sah, such as it is.'

Darquiel inclined his head also. 'Thank you for permitting us to come here. My companions are of the Nezreka; Tava'edzen, who is phylarch, and I expect you already know Shayd, Slinque and Stelph.'

'Yes.' Nimron barely glanced at the others. He came from behind the table. 'You asked for entrance,' he said. 'We've been waiting for you, or one like you, but often I thought it was in vain. What brought you here? How did you discover us?'

Darq saw no point in concealing the truth. 'A har came to me, who was once one of you. I call him Zu, though he's never told me his true name.'

Nimron stepped back abruptly and leaned against the table top. It was clear this information had surprised him. 'Zu…?'

'Yes.' Darq frowned. 'I made the name up. I don't know his real name.'

'Forgive me.' Nimron collected himself. 'The pet name I used for my son was Zu. He disappeared… a long time ago. I believed him dead, and perhaps I'm foolish now to believe otherwise.'

'I'm sorry,' Darq said, 'I don't know about that. All Zu did was tell me about the Krim Sri and asked me to speak with you. He believes we might assist each other.'

Nimron nodded. 'Do you understand why we're concealed here?'

'Yes,' Darq replied. 'Tiy and Zu have told me nearly everything, I think. Tiy told me how you know about me.'

Nimron took a step forward. 'Yes, you're unique among your kind. Like us, you've been concealed. Sometimes, I confess, I feared you were dead.' He smiled. 'Tiy never lost faith. She always told me you'd find us, but we had no inkling about this har called Zu. I only hope it's my son.'

'I'll find out for you,' Darq said. 'The Weavers can tell you what I discover.'

'I'd appreciate that,' Nimron said.

'So how can I help you?' Darq asked. 'I have no power. I'm told I have it, but I don't feel it. My family is powerful, but I've never met them, well, not since I was taken from them.'

'Come to me,' Nimron said.

Hesitating for only a moment, Darq did so. The Lord of Helek Sah put his long cool hands on Darq's face and closed his eyes. He drew in a deep breath. Darq could feel a soft, unobtrusive presence brushing through his being. It was not invasive, but merely something deeper than a glance, a way of gathering information. He was not offended by it.

Nimron took his hands away, and even though his flesh had not been warm, Darq's face felt cold once the fingers had lifted. 'Would you like to know and experience your potential?' Nimron asked.

Darq merely stared at him.

'I can help you become acquainted with it, if you wish.'

'Of course I'd like that, but how?'

Nimron smiled. 'Darquiel, we might be disempowered in many ways, but we still have a few last tricks up our sleeves! Enter trance with Tiy and myself and let us act as guides for you. There's an important meeting you should have, which in my opinion is long overdue. Well? Will you do this?'

The request had come suddenly; yet another change of plans. Darq turned to Tava'edzen and the Weavers, who had been silent all this time. Tava'edzen blinked at him slowly, a subtle show of support. Slinque, Shayd and Stelph nodded in encouragement. Darq turned back to Nimron. 'Yes,' he said. 'Show me everything you can.'

'Then we'll do so immediately,' Nimron said. 'Are you ready?'

'I think so,' Darq replied, hoping that was true.

Tiy addressed the Nezreka. 'Servitors will be here presently to take you to a place of rest. Refresh yourselves. Darquiel will be brought back to you shortly.'

Tava'edzen gave Darq another long stare and said, 'Thank you. Please take care of him.'

'We will,' Tiy said. 'Have no fears about that.'

'Good luck, Darq,' Slinque said. The Weavers gathered around Darq and held him close for a moment. Darq wondered whether they were scared for him in some way; their thoughts were shielded against him.

Tiy and Nimron took Darquiel to a room at the top of the house. The chamber was empty of furniture and its ceiling was low. The floorboards were painted with a large circle of symbols; a place to work magic. 'This is my workroom,' Nimron said. 'As you've no doubt deduced, the only tool I use here is my mind.'

Tiy gestured at the floor within the circle. 'Please sit down, Darquiel.'

Darq did so. Tiy and Nimron sat before and behind him.

'What exactly are we going to do?' Darq asked.

'Simply be open,' Tiy said, her voice gentle. 'Be who you really are. Step into yourself.'

Darq frowned. 'I'm not sure I know what you mean.'

'You'll see,' Nimron said. 'Just open your mind to any possibility. It's sometimes difficult to achieve at first, but ultimately it's the simplest procedure. You just have to get used to it.'

'OK.' Darq settled himself more comfortably. 'I'll do my best.'

'That's more than enough,' Nimron said.

Tiy put her hands upon Darq's shoulders from behind him. 'Close your eyes now,' she said. 'Just relax.'

The moment Darq closed his eyes it was as if the room grew immense around him. He felt as if he was sitting in a vast cavern, and the walls were breathing. It was disorientating, and for a moment he nearly opened his eyes, but he managed to keep them closed. The suddenness of it all convinced him: this was what he'd come for. This would hopefully be the end of his search, the answer to all questions.

Tiy and Nimron began to vibrate low tones, deep in the cavities of their chests. Darq imagined these sounds weaving into the air like twin serpents of vapor. They wound around each other, forming a double helix, until it was one serpent eating its own tail. Darq did not know what he saw, but a thought came to him that it was a representation of the building block of life. The serpent was all around him. He was part of it, as was everything else upon earth. The sounds wove visions in his head; the song of creation. He was melting into it, becoming sound himself, a sigh upon the air.

He sensed a mighty presence become aware of him. It was almost impossible to describe, but he felt it throughout his being and beyond. He sank back into a vast sentience that had been with him all along, yet he'd been unaware of it. Sometimes he'd glimpsed it in the ecstasies of aruna, felt it stirring his soul in the forest around Samway, tasted it in spring air, but this was far more intense. He was filled with an immense feeling that was part joy, part awe, part fear. He was sinking into the earth itself, falling back, supported and known.

And the earth spoke to him. This was not in words, but in impressions. The world had known that eventually a being would come who would initiate something previously unknown in this realm. It was the moment when the tiny parasite becomes aware of the creature upon and from which it lives. It realises that the sweet blood it sups is alive, and part of something greater. And the host itself realises that the smallest nuisance - one is but an irritant, a multitude an agony - has become aware.

Darq was flooded with impressions. He saw the spread of humanity across the world, hastened by the actions of the rebel Zehk. Humanity became aware in some respects, self-aware at least, but like parasites, they ravaged their host. There was no symbiotic contract, merely a voracious swell. If it had continued, the world would have had to take action, but then something else occurred, something unexpected. Humanity was devastated.

The most enlightened humans believed the earth had taken its revenge, because they were unaware of the higher powers. They prayed too late and pointlessly. They did not know that in eons past they had been made guardians of the very thing they abused. If they had taken more care, it might all have ended very differently. The earth might have flexed itself and repelled the invisible invasion. How humans would have felt, had they known their destruction was merely a by-product of a greater purge, Darq could only imagine.

Wraeththu had been created as part of this purge, an attempt to forge guardians who would not abuse their home realm. Instilled within them, hidden beneath the initial wildness, was the imperative not to lay waste, nor to choke, use up and make barren. Through their superior mental powers, not yet come to full bloom, they would have no need for the industries that ravaged the world.

Then Darq's perception was guided outwards, through the multi-layers of the realms. The earth was with him and now he sensed it as female; an intelligence. He learned of the silencing of Thanatep and the rivalry between the Aasp and the Zehk. He saw that the Zehk, though critical of what the Aasp did to the Thanadrim, decided ultimately not to intervene, for the resulting situation could be exploited by themselves also. The earth knew this, because she communed with fellow entities throughout the Otherlanes. Messages came to her, images from far worlds. She watched and listened as the Zehk considered what should be done with her. Their own rebel sons and daughters had damaged this jewel of realms. Action must be taken to restore her health.

The rebel Zehk, known by many names throughout history, were considered by their superiors to be the authors of the earth's troubles. It was vital that their monstrous hybrid offspring finally be removed. Really, it was very simple. All it took was visions and dreams sent to the right fanatics and inventors. Certain natural calamities were easily nudged into being, because they had been waiting to happen for a long time. Humanity was scourged by its hatred of itself, and the germ of Wraeththu took root in the ruins. The face of the world could be changed, without any overt interference on behalf of the Zehk. They merely had to implant the right stimuli for events to initiate a chain reaction. And the Krim Sri, so long hidden within the human population, were nearly destroyed. Only two thousand or so escaped and had fled to the ancient underground realm of Helek Sah, which was a refuge from the times when the Zehk had first tried to expunge their rebel children.

Darquiel saw all this in a rapid succession of impressions and images, swooning in the barrage of information, but it ceased as quickly as it had begun. He opened his eyes and found himself standing upon a high hilltop beneath the light of the moon. His consciousness had moved from his physical body.

A grove of trees surrounded the brow of the hill: birch and oak. Darq heard the song of night birds and the trill of crickets in the summer grasses. Below and around him, an endless landscape spread out, lush and untouched: the earth as it should be, as it was coming to be again. Something pale moved at the edge of Darq's vision and he turned his head. A woman was walking to him across the soft grass of the hill. She was barefoot, clad in close-fitting trousers and tunic that appeared to be made entirely of leaves and feathers. Her long hair was red, its colour visible even in the moonlight. Darq felt he should sink to his knees, because he knew she was a goddess. He knew in his heart, as if he'd known her all his life, that she was the spirit of the world itself.

She paused some feet away from him and he heard the voice of the world for the first time. 'Welcome, Darquiel. You may know me as Divozenky.'

Darq bowed. He wasn't sure how to react. 'You are… the *mind* of the world?'

Divozenky laughed. 'I am the mind, body and soul that all earthly creatures inhabit. I'm your guardian, but you are my sentinel now. You're the shepherd of my skin, who can hear the words of my soul. You're beyond all others, for no har or human has ever communed with me this way. Not even the Krim Sri can come to me so *intimately*. Many beings have dreamed and wished, and worked magic to know me, but you are the first who has reached me. It might be that others will follow.'

'Tell me,' Darq said, 'what must I do?'

Divozenky came closer to him and linked an arm through one of his. She indicated they should walk down the hill. Darq was astonished. She felt real to him, as real as Amelza had been. He could smell the perfume of her; cut grass, pine needles, ripe fruit and summer flowers.

'Humans could never manipulate my essence,' Divozenky said, 'and neither can hara, not in the way that other powers can. Wraeththu is not yet ready to wield this power. However, despite this, I give you custody of it.'

Darq sucked his upper lip for a moment. 'I don't understand what your essence really is. How can I be its custodian?'

Divozenky patted his arm. 'I'll put it simply. The essence of a realm is what nourishes evolution and advancement for creatures throughout the many layers of reality. You can't see it, and the subtle energies Wraeththu work with are of lower frequency than essence - I'm talking about the energy hara use for healing and to affect reality, what they call Agmara. Really, you don't need to know any more than that.'

Darq nodded slowly. 'I think I see. So, in your opinion, who should hara favour: the Aasp or the Zehk?'

Divozenky guided Darq towards a path that had appeared nearby. They had nearly reached the bottom of the hill. 'All I'll say is that both factions would like to control Wraeththu, and hence earthly essence, but because of you, they can't do that - well, not easily. You should discover what they have to offer and make your choice.'

'What if I should choose neither?'

Divozenky laughed. 'They'll both be very upset! There's no reason, though, why you can't make a deal with these factions. It's not as if I don't have essence to spare. Strike a hard bargain.'

'Such as guaranteed protection for the Krim Sri?'

Divozenky nodded. 'It would only be fair if that was part of the deal. The time of the Krim Sri is past, but rare animals, if husbanded properly, may thrive in captivity.'

Darq was quite shocked by these words. 'That seems a cruel way to look at it.'

Divozenky shrugged. 'Just a simple observation. As for whatever else you asked for...' She gestured widely with her free arm. 'Ask for what you like.'

Darq sighed. 'This is insane. It all sounds so… so easy.'

Divozenky clasped his shoulder. 'Easy? Oh, Darquiel, child, not yet, not yet. You *are* unique, but in some ways you're also a great wrongness, come before her time.'

They now followed a fairly wide road made of marble slabs. In the distance, Darq saw shadowy shapes that might be the spire of a city. 'Do you see me as female, then?' he asked.

Divozenky considered. 'I suppose I do see you that way, because my creatures have formed for me a female image, and I regard you as an avatar of mine. But my view is of no consequence.'

'It's of consequence to me, Divozenky,' Darq said.

Even though they had covered a great deal of ground - the hill was far behind them - the city ahead was drawing no closer. But a forest had appeared to the left of the road. A herd of white deer came out of it and ran across the path.

'What else would you like to ask me?' Divozenky said.

Darq shook his head. 'Too many things, and my mind's a blank! OK, one thing: do you know about Zu? Who is he?'

'Ah, Zu,' said Divozenky, smiling. 'Let's just say he's a har who hasn't forgotten the past. He's a skein of smoke that has swirled through the corridors of power in Immanion. He has been many things to many hara, but not one of them was aware of his origins, not even Thiede.'

Darq laughed. 'Is there nothing you can't tell me?'

Divozenky ducked her head. 'Very little, Darquiel. The things I don't know are far from this realm.'

'I can't believe I'm here talking to you like this,' Darq said. He screwed up his face. 'It feels so… well, right, I suppose. I'm glad you're so willing to interact with me. I appreciate it's a great privilege.'

Divozenky stopped walking and pulled Darq round to face her. 'You must understand, it's not a case of me being willing, but being *able*. I've never done this before with one of my own creatures. Sometimes, I've had to scratch my skin and rid myself of a few of them, and sometimes in dreams and visions I came near to certain individuals, but that's all. I'm not simply a benevolent mother entity, as people have always thought me to be. I'm far more than that. You'll be as useful to me as I can be to you. You can be a tool for me, a mediator, and many other things.'

Darq stared into her eyes. They glowed with blue and green light. 'I've thought of something else to ask,' he said. 'Will you teach me to travel the Otherlanes as the *sedu* king, Lurlei, promised me?'

'No,' Divozenky said and for a moment, Darq's heart contracted. 'Don't look so disappointed!' she continued. 'I won't teach you, simply because there's no need for me to do so. You'll find your teacher on my skin.'

Darq nodded. 'OK. I also want to ask what I should do next. Should I go to Immanion?'

'That's your decision,' Divozenky replied. 'It's not my job to tell you what to do. You have free will, Darquiel! However, you should be aware that certain issues need to be resolved so that balance can be restored. The realm of Thanatep must be reawakened. We must hope the individuals involved in this task will succeed.'

Darq frowned. 'And if they don't?'

'Then we can speak again on the matter.'

'How?' Darq asked. 'How do I come here without the aid of the Krim Sri?'

Divozenky's eyes were the colour of the sea, and then the colour of the sky. She smiled and it was like the sun rising over her body. 'Think yourself into me,' she said. 'Do it alone, or during the throes of delight with another. We know each other now. Come, let's continue our walk.'

They now ambled beside a wide river, on the other side of which was spreading heathland. The spires were still visible in the distance. 'Where exactly are we?' Darq asked. 'Is this real or a dream vision?'

'This is my home,' said Divozenky. 'It's a realm within a realm. There are many other beings here, but not in this spot. I've kept us away from them, because I didn't want them to be curious about you.'

'What others?'

Divozenky put her head to one side, 'Oh, gods, dehara… all the entities dreamed up by humans and hara throughout history.'

'Amazing!' Darq grinned. 'Do you sometimes have lunch with Aruhani?'

Divozenky threw back her head and laughed gustily, 'Oh, *much* more than that, Darquiel!'

'Can I meet them one day, the dehara, I mean?'

'You've already met Aruhani, I know, but yes, if you wish for a less visionary meeting, you may come here for it.'

Darq knew that the idea of meeting a dehar should seem at the very least like fantasy, but in that place, it seemed merely appropriate. 'There's something else I'd like to know,' Darq said. 'It's for my mentor, Thiede.'

'Aha!' said Divozenky. 'You want to know how Wraeththu began, how it all really started. You want to know who created you. I think you already know why.'

'Yes,' Darq said. 'I want to know those things.'

Divozenky gestured towards a willow tree that hung over the water. Its trunk was surrounded by a wooden bench. 'Let's sit down,' she said. 'I'll tell you what you want to know, and more.' She sat down and crossed her legs, clasping one knee with her hands. 'I once sent a message to you. Do you remember?'

Darq sat down beside her and shook his head. 'I don't know… what message?'

Divozenky grinned at him. 'There are four of you?'

'That was you?' Darq was astounded. 'I thought it must have been Zu.'

'No, I sent a message to you from the lunar sphere.'

'What did it mean? Was it about my parents?'

Divozenky swung one of her legs like a carefree girl. 'I just felt that because it was a special moment, and I *could* make tenuous contact, then I should. It was meant to make you aware you were part of something. There will come a time when four hara of the second generation will work together and you will be one of them. I have visions too, you know.'

'Who are they?'

Divozenky put a finger to her lips, then said, 'I won't reveal that. Some things you must find out for yourself. Life would be tedious if you knew everything, don't you think?'

Darq was dubious about that. 'I don't know. It might be helpful for me to know.'

'There are important things I can tell you, which you can later tell Thiede. I also think it's right I tell you certain things about the Kamagrian. When this is done, you must return to your body. We'll have time for more conversation in the future.' She patted Darq's knee. 'Remember everything I say to you now.'

'I won't forget,' Darq said.

When Darq came out of his trance, the first thing he did was open his eyes to stare at Nimron and say: 'Do you think you were right to influence humanity's development?'

Nimron stared at him without expression for some moments. Then he said, 'We too are hybrid, Darquiel. We're closer to the Zehk than humans are, but it wasn't us who interfered in human development. We're merely part of the interference. It was our forebears who made those decisions. In the light of all that has followed, I think yes, the rebel Zehk were wrong. This could have been a different world.'

Darq nodded slowly. He was conscious of Tiy's hands upon his shoulders. 'I met the earth herself,' Darq said. 'That's what you wanted me to do, wasn't it?'

Nimron smiled gently. 'Yes. Your ability to commune with her is your unique talent.'

Darq rubbed his face. 'She told me so many things. It was incredible. It all felt so real.' He lowered his hands. 'She's not a goddess, though. Humans were wrong about that. She's just a living creature, like we are, only much bigger.'

Tiy let go of Darq's shoulders and moved round so she could look into his face. 'To primitive beings, she is a goddess,' she said, 'as is the sun, the moon and the stars. It's because they are often misunderstood.'

'Are all heavenly bodies *alive* and thinking creatures?' Darq asked.

Nimron shook his head. 'Not all, no. Some are dead.'

Darq pressed his fingers against his temples. His head was pounding. 'It's so much to take in.'

'Do you need to rest?' Tiy asked. 'You can do that before you return to your friends, if you wish.'

'No,' Darq said. 'I'll be fine in a minute. It's just all so very strange. I've recently undergone an unbelievable experience and yet it felt so... *normal*.' He shrugged. 'I don't know what else to say.'

'It felt that way because to you it *is* normal,' Tiy said.

'Did you receive information concerning the Krim Sri?' Nimron asked.

Darq flexed his jaw. His whole face felt stiff. 'Yes. I'll negotiate for you to guarantee your safety. I know now I've got bargaining power! I don't know when or how I'm going to do it, but I'll do what I can at the right moment.'

Tiy leaned forward and kissed his cheek. 'I trust you,' she said.

Darq took her hand. 'You've given me so much. I think we were meant to meet. Helping keep your people safe is the least I can do.'

'We've not given you that much,' Tiy said. 'Simply a helping hand, that's all.'

Chapter Twenty-Six

In the realm of Shaa Lemul, Ponclast and Pellaz stood together on a balcony that jutted out from the Black Library over the silvery sea. They had talked for a long time, and Pellaz had no idea how many days might have passed in his home realm. Lileem had not returned, but then Pellaz expected it would take some time for her and Ta Ke to accomplish their task. In the meantime, Ponclast had proved most informative. Galdra had prudently left them alone, and had gone to investigate the stone books beneath the sands.

Pellaz considered that the realm was changing, even as he observed it. One era had come to an end; another was beginning. He had a feeling that life was starting to pulse beneath the metallic surface of the ocean that spread away beneath the pyramid. This realm might have been asleep for a long time, or in stasis, but now it must wake. From what Lileem had told him, it occurred to Pell that certain changes might cause difficulty for any earthly creature living here, who had to eat and sleep and so on. The white sun, for example.

And Ponclast was sentenced to remain. He and Pellaz had talked in depth. Ponclast seemed hungry for it. He had told the Tigron everything that had happened since he'd arrived at the Library. His excitement, which seemed strangely youthful, was infectious. He also talked of the past, wistfully sometimes, but not with bitterness. He was not the har Pellaz had ever expected him to be. How different things might have been if this conversation had taken place a long time ago, perhaps between Thiede and Ponclast. A common ground might have been reached, who could tell?

Pell realised his mind was drifting. Ponclast was staring at him in a way to suggest he expected a response, yet for the past few moments Pellaz had been barely listening.

'You see, Pellaz,' Ponclast was saying, 'we're not so different, you and I.'

Pellaz smiled somewhat thinly, and narrowed his eyes. 'I've never committed pelki or murder, nor sought to intimidate the hara of my tribe into obeying me. To me, those are big differences.'

Ponclast leaned backwards on the balcony rail. 'Have you never had a despising for your own kind, a fury at the stupidity of beings who are supposed to be superior?'

Pellaz grimaced. 'Sometimes, yes, I have, but it has never impelled me to commit atrocities.' He fixed Ponclast with a stare. 'If you seek to sway my opinion about releasing you from this place, so far your effort hasn't been very successful.'

'I know you won't release me,' Ponclast said. 'I'm simply interested in talking with you. Previously, I would have delighted only in killing you as quickly as possible.' He paused. 'I could be a resource to you, Tigron. If you're wise, you'll admit that.'

'Is that so? In what way, a resource?'

Ponclast gestured with one hand. 'I have first-hand experience of the Hashmallim. I have ruled hara, as you do. I know the dark underbelly of Wraeththu, things a ruler should know, even if he disapproves. There are many ways I could be of use.'

Pellaz shook his head. 'You amaze me! Very well. Here's a question. I'm interested in your response. In my position, would you ally with the Hashmallim?'

Ponclast considered. 'No. I dislike the way both the Hashmallim and the *sedim* conduct themselves. Now, of course, we know they are merely agents of greater powers: the Aasp and the Zehk. They are the thugs of angels. Quite amusing, really.'

'So, what would you do, if you were in my place?'

Ponclast grinned mordantly. 'I think I'd wait to see what our new friend Ta Ke can do for us. If Thanatep is reactivated, the Aasp and the Zehk will have no choice but to toe the line, hopefully.'

Pellaz slapped his hands against the balcony rail. 'But that might mean we'd risk losing Otherlanes travel. I wonder whether even those of us who have learned how to do it without *sedim* might find the ability would be taken away. Is that the best course for Wraeththu and Kamagrian?'

'I think you have some bargaining power,' Ponclast said. 'There'll no doubt be places off limits to hara, but I can't see why the Thanadrim would object to them using the Otherlanes to facilitate travel within their own realm. It *is* better for the world, since most of the vessels of travel used by humans used to pollute it.'

'There's a risk Ta Ke will fail,' Pellaz said. 'You know that. Then what?'

'To my mind, we – or rather you – have no choice but to stand back and let the Hashmallim and the *sedim* fight it out. You can't stand against them. You either make a choice to ally with one, or withdraw completely. Of course, the *sedim* would not be pleased about that. Do I take it your instinct is to ally with them?'

Pellaz pulled a sour face. 'In view of the Fulminir incident, yes.'

'Understandable. But perhaps you should find out what the Hashmallim are prepared to offer.' Ponclast drew himself up straight. 'You might not think me impartial, Pellaz, but I am. The Hashmallim made no attempt to help me or rescue me from this place. They used and discarded me as an experiment that didn't work. I have no loyalty to them. I don't think the *sedim* have been entirely honest with you either, which is why you should perhaps consider the alternative.'

'Your counsel is noted,' Pellaz said. 'However, I would really like to speak with Ta Ke. Will he return here from Thanatep if he reactivates the towers?'

Ponclast shrugged. 'I have no idea.'

Pellaz sighed. 'If you can't be helpful with that, how about being useful regarding my son, Loki? As I said to you before, we believe Diablo has taken him.'

'That's likely,' Ponclast said. 'I certainly wouldn't put it past him. All I can suggest is that you ask Abrimel to try and contact our son, Geburael. We have to suppose Geburael and Diablo are still together.'

Pellaz frowned. 'I doubt that Geburael would co-operate with me. Why should he? Surely, he'll take the side of his brother?'

Ponclast shook his head, smiled. 'Pellaz, as I said to you, we're more alike than you know. Think about this, and its implications. Abrimel loves me. Go to him. Tell him you've seen me. Tell him that even in this forsaken realm, I think of him and miss him. He should be happy, Pellaz. Release him. Let him have a life. Can't you find it in your heart to forgive your oldest son? Perhaps that is the way to have all of them back. If Abrimel is reconciled with you, there's more chance Geburael will co-operate. Surely you can see this?'

'I *will* talk to Abrimel,' Pellaz said.

'He was very kind to me,' Ponclast said. 'He gave wise counsel.' He leaned back upon the rail and let his hair hang down over it. 'I expect your Loki is a fine young har,' he said, 'but what about the son who was taken from you some years ago?'

'The one you tried to steal, you mean?' Pellaz snapped.

Ponclast closed his eyes briefly. 'Yes. That one. The Hashmallim were very interested in *him*. They feared him and wanted him dead. If I were you, I'd be concentrating my efforts on finding him.'

'Do you know anything about him?' Pellaz demanded. 'Such as his whereabouts?'

'No,' Ponclast said. 'But I have a strong intuition about him. When and if Lileem returns here, I'll tell her we've spoken. She'll be in touch with you, no doubt. Perhaps more than that. I think she knows her time here is nearly at an end.'

Pellaz hesitated. 'Then, you will be alone.'

'Perhaps. I'm resigned to my fate.' Ponclast turned to face the ocean. He sighed deeply. 'I don't want to be part of a Wraeththu world that's designed by Gelaming.'

'We all came from the same source,' Pellaz said gently.

Ponclast uttered a bitter laugh. 'Are you finding pity in your heart for me?'

'Mercy. That's different.'

'I don't want to go back, but neither do I want to be alone. Think on this, if you think of mercy, Tigron. That's all I'll say.'

Pellaz nodded. 'Very well.' He rubbed his arms. 'Strange, I feel a chill. Do you feel it?'

'Things are changing here – swiftly,' Ponclast said. 'You should return to your home realm.' He smiled. 'And put some clothes on!' He paused. 'Just how do you plan to return home?'

Pellaz put his head to one side. 'As you said, things are changing here. I can feel it. I'll return the way I came.'

'You're lucky to work with such a powerful har as Galdra,' Ponclast said. 'He is magnificent and very much like Calanthe. Why *are* you working with him and not your beloved Cal?'

Pellaz managed to keep his voice level. 'Galdra and I have a special relationship that means we work together well, that's all.'

'How fortunate you are!'

'Indeed.' Pellaz put out a mind call to Galdra, to meet him outside the pyramid, but before he left the balcony he reached out and clasped one of Ponclast's arms. 'Goodbye. It's been useful talking to you.'

Ponclast returned the clasp. 'Goodbye, Pellaz. In spite of everything, I wish you luck.'

Pellaz opened his eyes and found himself lying beneath Galdra in Tharmifex's garden. Galdra was a dead weight and for several terrifying seconds Pellaz thought that the Freyhellan hadn't survived the journey from Shaa Lemul. Then Galdra uttered a groaning sigh and rolled from Pell's body to lie on his back. 'A dream,' he said. 'Was it real?'

'Yes.' Pellaz leaned over and kissed Galdra's brow. 'Thanks for your help.'

Galdra took a lock of Pell's hair in his hand. 'But we didn't find Lileem. I didn't help that much.'

'Oh, you did. I wouldn't have got to that realm without you and now we've got more information. The talk with Ponclast was useful. I know we could go there again, you and I.' Pellaz pulled away from

Galdra, who let him go reluctantly.

Pellaz stood up and began to dress himself. 'We should go back inside. It's cold.'

'Only an hour or so has passed,' Galdra said, indicating the sky. As a sailor, he knew the movements of the stars. 'Yet it felt like we spent days, if not weeks, in that realm.'

Pellaz nodded. 'Time, I think, is a matter of perspective. We travelled without *sedim.* We know we can do that now. All we used was aruna and our intention. I think we're beginning to stretch our muscles, magically. This is just the beginning.'

'What will you do now?'

Pellaz smiled without humour. 'Face something I don't want to face,' he said.

Pellaz travelled to the prison house, which was located an hour's ride from Immanion. He did not ride a sedu, but a bay horse that was kept in the stables at Phaonica. For now, he would keep away from the *sedim*, even Peridot, whom he loved.

He had felt uneasy when he had discovered that Cal was no longer in Immanion. This news had come from Caeru, who had been waiting for Pellaz in the Tigron's private apartment. He had slept there and from what he said, it was clear he hadn't been alone. Pellaz didn't know whether to feel warmed or slightly annoyed by the fact his consorts had been together in his own bed.

'Cal received communication from Thiede,' Caeru said. 'I don't know exactly what was said, but Cal left here quickly. He wouldn't speak to me, but he was agitated. He couldn't hide that. And no, before you even think it, it's nothing to do with the fact you were with Galdra last night. Are you going to tell me about it?'

'Yes, but not yet,' Pellaz said. 'I've an urgent task to attend to. I'll speak to you later about it.'

Caeru frowned. 'You look… odd. Just tell me one thing. Did things go well?'

'They went productively,' Pellaz answered. He took Caeru's hands in his own. 'I'll be back as soon as I can, then we'll talk.'

The prison house was surrounded by a high wall and there were iron gates across the entrance to the drive. Once, it had been a rich man's house, a place where a family had lived, but now its rooms never echoed with voices or laughter. There were ten guards always on duty, and two hara who worked to keep the house clean and to cook. Then there was Abrimel, son of the Tigron. He was a har without a soul, or so the staff said to their friends. He had betrayed his family and his tribe, and felt no remorse. He painted pictures of a thin har with black hair and a red robe. He wrote a lot; all the things he had never written before, which he could remember.

When Pellaz arrived at the tall iron gates to the estate, the hour was still early, and the househara had only just risen from their beds. Pellaz had to ring the brass bell for several minutes, before the guards who lived in the gate lodge, and who slept longer than the househara, woke up. One of them came to answer the summons. 'All right, all right!' the guard snapped irritably, only half dressed. He went pale when he saw who stood on the other side of the iron bars. He bowed his head. 'Forgive me, Tiahaar.'

'Just open the gate,' Pellaz said.

He rode the bay horse up the driveway, which was an avenue of cherry trees, barely cared for now. The house was locked up, of course, so Pellaz had to hammer on the door for entrance. He no longer felt like himself. It was as if the realm he and Galdra had returned to was not quite the one they had left. Things were slightly askew. In this realm, Pellaz had been able to spend all night in the arms of a har he had to admit he really did love, and not feel guilty about it. In this realm, perhaps, Cal had never been mad, and certain hara hadn't died, and there was a son who did not hate his father. Was it possible this was just a house in the country beyond the city, and a har who liked to write about Wraeththu history simply lived here, because he preferred solitude?

The cook came to answer the door. He bowed. 'Tiahaar, you are here to see the prisoner?'

'I'm here to see my son,' Pellaz said. Suddenly, he felt old. He could smell the jasmine that had grown outside the window of the inn in Ferelithia where Abrimel had been conceived. 'Take me to him at once.'

It was really pointless to lock all the doors in this house, since Abrimel had no intention of going anywhere. He had lost his love, his harling, his life. He had lost the ability to feel. He had told Caeru not to visit him, because his hostling's concern only annoyed him. When Caeru sent gifts, they went to the guards, because Abrimel had no interest in luxuries. He didn't speak to anyhar much, other than what was required. He wrote about all the tribes he had studied. He wrote about Wraeththu, which he viewed as being as pointless as the locks on the doors. He was not denied aruna, and different hara were often sent to him for this purpose. Some just did what they had to do, and weren't interested in talking. Others wanted to help him. Abrimel treated them all the same. He slaked the need in his body and that was all. He needed a clear mind to write, to paint. All of his pictures were of Ponclast.

Abrimel always rose at dawn and went to the walled garden he had access to. He did this whatever the weather. There, he would sit for an hour, thinking about words, then he'd have his breakfast, if it was ready. He wondered how long he would have to wait to die, sure it would be a very long time. He wished he wanted to kill himself.

Pellaz stood at the door to the garden and observed this har who had come from him. He had not visited Abrimel before. This son had grown up, become har, without Pellaz even noticing. He was a living thing, full of opinions and pain. *I made him,* Pellaz thought, and for the first time in his life, sensed the connection. A ghost of Caeru lived in the fine features of Abrimel's face, and the pale cast to his skin, but his hair was black Cevarro hair. For the first time in many years, Pellaz thought of his own father. He remembered himself, as he'd been, before the world changed. 'Bree,' he said.

Abrimel turned at the sound of this affectionate form of his name. His expression was blank. He showed neither surprise nor anger when he saw who stood at the threshold to his garden.

Pellaz walked across the grass. 'I'd like to talk to you.'

Abrimel shrugged.

Pellaz sat down in a chair opposite his son. There was a wrought iron table between them with some papers on it. Pellaz could not read the handwriting on them. It was spidery and sloping. 'I've visited your chesnari,' he said.

Abrimel's eyes widened slightly at that. He shifted on his chair.

'He asked me to tell you he thinks of you often and misses you. He is well. We talked for quite a while.'

Abrimel closed his eyes briefly. He nodded his head once.

'I'm here mainly to talk about Geburael. You know that he was taken by Diablo after the fall of Fulminir?'

'Yes,' Abrimel said. 'He at least got away.'

Pellaz clasped his hands together on the table. 'Are you in contact with him?'

Abrimel laughed harshly. 'No.'

'Would you try to contact him? Ponclast thinks you should do this.'

Abrimel glanced coldly at his father. 'Why? Wherever he is, he's safer there.'

Pellaz strove to keep his tone even and friendly. 'His safety is assured in Immanion, I promise you.'

Abrimel appeared suspicious. 'Why do you want him?'

'OK, I'll be honest with you. It's about your brother, Loki.'

Abrimel sneered. 'Half-brother,' he corrected. 'The golden child I've never met. What of him?'

Pellaz wished this interview could be easier. He found it difficult not to get annoyed with Abrimel. He always had. 'Loki's not long past feybraiha,' he said. 'Unfortunately, he's been abducted, perhaps in a way similar to how your hostling's pearl was taken all those years ago. We think Diablo is responsible. Ponclast has advised me to try and make contact with Geburael to see if he knows anything about this. I think perhaps that Ponclast would really like news of your son, too.'

Abrimel's stare was narrow. 'You're lying to me. Ponclast would never advise you.'

'He's not the same, Bree,' Pellaz said. 'He's no longer full of anger. He's resigned to what is.'

Abrimel scowled. 'Then he's lost his mind!'

'Far from it,' Pellaz said. 'Anyway, he pleaded on your behalf. He asked me to give you your freedom.'

Abrimel flicked another glance at his father. Some of the hostility had waned in his expression. 'In return for the advice he gave you?'

Pellaz nodded. 'Perhaps. Yes.'

Abrimel smoothed his trousers with both hands. 'The question is; will you comply with this request?'

Pellaz leaned back in his chair. 'If you help me locate Geburael, then yes.'

'I don't believe you. You can't risk freeing me.'

Pellaz found himself saying something he'd only just thought of. 'I could - if you went to the same place where Ponclast is.'

Abrimel's expression became more animated. 'You'd allow that?'

'Yes. If that's what you want.' Pellaz was surprised to find that this was true.

'It *is* what I want. I thought I'd never see him again. You know that, of course.' Abrimel frowned and shook his head. 'No. I can't trust you. You're deceiving me.'

Pellaz reached out and briefly stroked one of Abrimel's arms. Abrimel flinched away, and Pell's hand closed on empty air. 'I'm your father, Bree,' Pellaz said gently. He closed his eyes for a moment, took a deep breath. 'I know I failed you. I wish we could go back, but we can't. I'm not here to make amends, because the past can't be undone. I know that. You betrayed your tribe and went to our enemies. That's a difficult thing to forgive and forget, as are all the things I did to you, or rather that I didn't do. We can't be family, and I doubt we can even be friends, but I ask you now, as an Aralisian, and as father to Geburael, to allow your son his place in this world. If he doesn't want it, I'll respect his decision, but I do think he should be given the choice.'

Abrimel rubbed one hand over his face. He wouldn't look at Pellaz. 'If he's with Diablo, he won't want anything to do with you.'

'That is possible. We won't know until we've spoken to him.'

'He might be dead.'

'No,' Pellaz said. 'He isn't. You or Ponclast would feel it, if that were so.' He leaned forward. 'Bree, you know Diablo. Cal has told me of him and I experienced him first-hand in Fulminir. Is this really the har you want to be an influence over your son?'

Abrimel uttered a wordless, angry sound. 'No! What I wanted for our son was a life with me, with his hostling.' He thumped his own chest. 'For a short time, I had happiness I'd never known. You took it from me, as you took everything else from me. I despise you and your world utterly. You live a lie.'

Pellaz had to lean away from the hostile energy streaming from his son's body. He had to break through it somehow, keep his voice level, and his heart open to all that Abrimel needed to say. 'Bree, I'm not perfect, but I don't live a lie. Our differences as father and son aside, you must know that Ponclast, as he was, should never have been allowed to have power. You might hate what the Gelaming stand for, but I don't believe you'd countenance the sort of abuses that the Varrs were famed for either. I know you're a har of integrity. You weren't drawn to Ponclast because your shared his ideals. You went to him because I let you down and because I treated your hostling badly. You went to him to punish Cal, Caeru and myself. And you went to him, because he was strong and he loved you. But in your heart, I believe you knew the truth, even in the midst of that happiness you speak of.'

Abrimel stared at Pellaz for several long moments, then he sighed. 'I tried to change him,' he said bleakly. 'He was so bitter. You have no idea. If he'd ever come to power, it would have been different. I would have made it so.'

'Perhaps you would have done,' Pellaz said.

Abrimel rubbed his face hard with both hands. 'You've brought life here with you,' he said. 'As ever, you are cruel. I don't want to be grateful to you, but if I can be with the har I love, I'll assist you. There's one other condition. If I do as you ask and I'm successful, if Geburael comes here, I would like to see him.'

Pellaz nodded. 'I understand that.'

Abrimel drew in his breath through his nose, smoothed his hair.

'Did my chesnari give any indication as to how I should attempt this contact?'

'No, but I can send Listeners to assist you.'

Abrimel sneered sarcastically. 'What about the ones you have constantly scanning my thoughts? They know me pretty well.'

Pellaz shifted uncomfortably on his seat, cleared his throat. 'Do you think you could work with them?'

Abrimel made a dismissive gesture. 'It makes no difference. I have no friends in this land.'

Pellaz hesitated, considered. 'Of course, you could work with Caeru and me.'

Abrimel adopted an expression of revulsion. 'To touch your mind so intimately? You think I want that? And Rue is an imbecile. He loves you, despite the way you've kicked him relentlessly for years. He fawns over your insane Calanthe and lets you both into his bed. He's a hopeless case. I have cast him off. You're all sick.'

'Is that a no, then?'

Abrimel pursed his lips. 'You know as well as I do that three hara of Geburael's blood would stand a better chance of reaching him.' He paused for a moment, clearly thinking things over. 'Oh, very well! Bring Rue here, but advise him to keep his mouth shut. I have nothing to say to him.'

Pellaz was flooded with relief. 'Thank you. I'll stand by my word. Whether we succeed or not, you can go to Ponclast.' He stood up. 'One thing I have to say to you: Rue loves you, Bree. All harlings should know that they can't dictate the way their parents live. You might disagree with Rue's choices, as he disagreed with yours, but he respected that you're an adult who should make his own decisions. It hasn't affected the way he feels for you. When Rue loves, he simply loves. In that, he is quite unshakeable. You should think about that.' Pellaz leaned over and clasped his son's shoulder. 'I'll leave you now and return later.'

This time Abrimel didn't flinch away. He stared down at his hands, which were tightly clasped in his lap. 'Ponclast was wrong about the pearl, very wrong,' he said. 'But it wasn't his idea. It was what the Hashmallim wanted.'

'You couldn't have changed things, Bree.'

'I know.' Abrimel looked up at his father. 'Unfortunately, as you know, we cannot choose the ones we love. It just happens.'

Chapter Twenty-Seven

Loki had learned how to fly. That was how he thought of Otherlanes travel; a dream that was real. The Hashmal, Zikael, had come to him again and this time, it was to teach. 'I've been granted permission by my Master to take you to a certain realm,' he said. 'I've created it for training purposes.'

'You can create realms?' Loki had not imagined the Hashmal possessed such powers.

Zikael smiled. 'It's not that difficult. One day, you might be able to do the same, to a certain extent. You should be able to build limited locations. It's like making visualisation real, or virtually real.'

Loki was sure the *sedim* would not approve of such advanced education. He was nervous at first, because he couldn't imagine how anyhar could negotiate the Otherlanes without an experienced *sedu* to help him. He had no idea how to open a portal, or how to walk into it, or then how to use the confusing pathways beyond to get somewhere else.

Zikael conducted the first lesson at the summit of Ninzini, at Loki's request. They sat together on the floor while Zikael explained some of the basics of Otherlanes travel. 'The portal is a symbol you pull out of yourself and then make real,' Zikael said; rather unhelpfully, Loki thought.

'You'll look between the spaces in a realm,' Zikael continued, 'and see the potential for others there. You'll widen those spaces so you can step through. It's as simple as that, for a creature with the capability to do it.'

'What makes a creature that capable?' Loki asked.

'Desire and intention,' Zikael answered. 'Intelligence and awareness. If you can see ghosts in the sunset, if you believe that trees have thoughts, and that all the realms are full of things you cannot see, you can become an Otherlanes traveller. In essence, it's a willingness to accept there's more to life than what the limited senses of the earthly realm perceive. It's the capability to transcend your limits.'

'How do your people put blocks on certain areas, then?' Loki asked. He had begun to warm to Zikael, not least because the Hashmal appeared so open to sharing his knowledge.

Zikael wove his hands gracefully, drawing pictures upon the air, his body swaying slightly. 'We can create wards, illusions and side tracks. Wraeththu are a primitive species, so it's not difficult to curtail their movements.' He lowered his hands. 'Are you ready to make your first attempt?'

Loki nodded. He wasn't sure if he was ready, but thought he might as well try. He wasn't too happy that Zikael thought he was a primitive creature and wanted to impress him. He thought of Geburael, who still slept in the room below. It would have been reassuring if Geb could have been included in this lesson, but Loki had already sensed Zikael preferred it to involve just the two of them. He had guessed that the Hashmal was a proud being; he wanted to be Loki's one and only teacher.

'It helps if you have an idea of your desired destination in mind,' Zikael said. 'We'll go to a kind of training area I've created. It's a semblance of the earthly realm, though not very extensive. I'll send you its symbol, its sign, and you'll look out for this in the Otherlanes, since that signals the exit point.'

'You'll be with me, won't you?' Loki asked.

Zikael smiled. 'Yes. I won't risk you getting lost.' He held out his hands, which Loki took hold of. The long fingers completely enfolded him, as if Loki's hands were those of a tiny harling. 'Now, lower the barriers around your thoughts and open your mind to me,' Zikael said. 'I'll send you the image you need.'

Later, Loki considered that learning to open Otherlanes portals and then travel through them was the same as learning how to swim or to ride a horse. It was a skill that seemed impossible at first, but then suddenly you could just do it, as if you'd done it all your life. The knack, when it finally came, was instant and complete. Loki could peer between the spaces in the air before him and intend for a portal to open. He had some control over how the lanes beyond appeared to him. The *sedim* had no interest in making things easier for harish sensibilities, so journeys with them were often mind-numbingly surreal, through stupefying voids and vortexes of energy, but now Loki could turn the lanes into branching corridors of light, or passageways of stone. The energy parasites that inhabited the lanes could be perceived as bats or insects, or monsters. But he could carry a flaming torch to ward them off.

Zikael told him he would be allowed to use the training realm as much as he liked, and that for now Loki must concentrate on this short and fairly simple journey. Loki really liked the way Zikael had designed the realm. It was predominantly constructed in shades of greenish-blue and very beautiful. Its landscape was a tumbling vista of wide lakes and hazy mountains. The foliage on the trees was azure, the sky a soft lilac. There were a few creatures there that looked real enough; pigeons and thrushes, dark red squirrels, different kinds of fish in the waters, and drowsily humming insects. When Loki questioned Zikael about the reality of these creatures, Zikael merely shrugged and said, 'They aren't illusions, Loki. I pulled these creatures from your memories.'

'So, they could breed, die, and so on?' Loki persisted.

'If you want them to. The realm is yours to play in.'

So, Loki resolved to do just that. He would come to understand the limits of this "creation" through experience. He would look upon it as his personal realm, a place he could go to sit and calm himself, find the centre of his being. When he visited it alone, he *felt* for the way he had to go, and willed himself there. There was always a moment of panic when he perceived the exit portal, because every time he wondered how he would get through it. It was like daring himself to jump off a high wall repeatedly, thinking that next time he could land on his head or break both his ankles.

Sometimes, Zikael would meet him there. Often, they wouldn't say anything to one another, but would sit quietly together, in a wooden gazebo hung with wind chimes that stood on an island in the middle of a dark blue lake. Here, they would listen to the music of the chimes, and the soporific rustle of leaves from the lakeshore.

One time, Zikael was disposed to converse. 'Soon,' he said, 'things must change for you.'

'What do you mean?' Loki asked.

Zikael was sitting cross-legged, his hair hanging to the floor. He rested his chin on his hands. 'What will it take to persuade you to be our avatar, Loki?'

Loki shrugged awkwardly. 'I'm… I'm not sure yet.'

Zikael's gaze was unwavering. Loki felt the Hashmal could see every thought in his head. 'Events are moving along quite swiftly,' Zikael said. 'We've been warned that the *sedim* have put their case to Wraeththu. The moment hara ally with either them or us is the moment the matter is decided. If the *sedim* prevail, then Wraeththu can say farewell to any promise of advancement, perhaps for millennia.' He drew in his breath. 'Loki, you have a rival.'

Loki frowned. 'I don't know what you mean.'

'You have a brother.'

Loki felt a flutter of fear in his breast; a presentiment. 'Yes, Abrimel.'

Zikael's expression darkened. 'No, not Abrimel. Another.'

Loki glanced away. He remembered when Geburael had heard that strange yet familiar call in the ethers. He remembered the story of the pearl snatched from Caeru's body. 'I know... I know that's possible,' he said softly.

Zikael leaned forward and grabbed Loki's chin firmly. 'Look at me! We believe that the *sedim* have made overtures to this brother. Our agents suggest that they wish for him to rule all Wraeththu, to supplant his parents and Thiede, to supplant you.'

Loki uttered a small sound of pain, since Zikael was hurting him. The Hashmal released him, leaned back. 'This brother of yours has had no contact with your family, ever, so has no concept of loyalty to the House of Aralis. Perhaps Thiede sought to keep him as some kind of secret weapon, or a commodity to bargain with, but that secrecy has backfired. The *sedim* will know he has the potential for great power, because he *is* a har of greatness, Loki. In time, he will be five times more powerful than you could ever hope to be. He could squash you flat, along with whatever armies you could raise. But with our help, you can thwart his ambitions and secure your family's future.'

Loki stared at Zikael, wide-eyed. He tried to keep his dealings with the Hashmal business-like, so that he would earn respect, but now he felt out of his depth, and he could not hide it. 'Have the Hashmallim approached him too?'

Zikael's expression became tinged with distaste. 'No. We'd never do that. We wanted to destroy him before he was born, because we know he's an aberration, a har born thousands of years before his time. Wraeththu isn't equipped to deal with him, and eventually he'll become a tyrant.'

'You made Diablo steal the pearl from Caeru's body,' Loki said, and was unable to keep the revulsion he felt from his voice.

Zikael closed his eyes briefly. 'Yes, that's so. I know it seems barbaric and cruel to you, but we're above sentiment, Loki. We do things for the greater good, and you should cultivate a similar attitude. We weren't wrong in what we did, only in that we failed.'

Loki swallowed with difficulty. 'Are you saying he should be killed?'

Zikael stroked Loki's face, softly. His fingers left a tingling trail. 'Please appreciate how honest I'm being with you,' he said. 'I know that ethically your species is inclined to disagree with our ways, but...' He took a breath. 'It would be best to destroy the body this soul currently inhabits, yes. Let Wraeththu mature for some time before he comes back to them. It's not really death, Loki, because you don't understand death. Souls can only be moved around, never destroyed.'

Loki didn't want to hear this. He felt cornered, shadowed by an invisible threat. 'How can I know you're telling the truth? Asking me to condone the killing of my own kin is no small thing.'

Zikael ducked his head. 'I know that. Do you know how he was created?'

In truth, Loki had no desire to know such details about his family. 'Only that he was made by three hara, but not the mechanics of it, no.'

Zikael's gaze had taken on an intense gleam. 'You *should* know,' he said. 'Don't shy away from it, Loki. We wonder whether Pellaz was given an order to do what he did, but if so, we don't know who gave it. He combined the essence of three hara to create this pearl. He opened the cauldron of creation in Caeru, and kept it open so that Calanthe could expel aren into it also. He did this by…'

'Stop!' Loki exclaimed. Instinctively, he'd put his hands over his ears. 'I don't want to know any more.'

Zikael smiled faintly. 'Well, perhaps you now know enough. The fact remains that such a thing has never been done before, and shouldn't have been done then. A soul that would normally not be part of the Wraeththu matrix sniffed out the event and homed in on it. You should not look upon the fruit of that unnatural union as a brother. It's something different. When you face him, you'll know. You'll sense it. You won't need my words to convince you.' He paused. 'Loki, it's *you* who has to kill this creature.'

Suddenly, the beautiful realm around Loki seemed flat, like a badly coloured painting. The wind in the trees was the rattle of bones. 'Me?'

Zikael nodded. His expression was bleak. 'If there was any other way, I wouldn't ask it of you. I'd do it myself. But I can't. It has to be you. We know this for sure.'

'*Why?*'

Zikael regarded Loki steadily. 'Because of the way he was made, we can't touch him. He doesn't know this, and he mustn't know, but he's protected from beings like us. Because of the way you are, and the time of your creation… well, you could be his nemesis, if such a thing exists.'

Loki swallowed. 'Where is he, Zikael?'

'He's in Anakhai, east of Almagabra. You know that land?'

Loki nodded. 'Yes. I've visited most lands on our continent. The hara there are very independent. Has he made allies among them?'

'Unfortunately, yes. As you know, the Gelaming are not always regarded favourably by other tribes, who resent their superior development.'

Loki pressed his eyes for a moment with the fingers of one hand.

'I'd like to discuss this with Geburael.'

'We've no objection to that,' Zikael said. 'Diablo and Geburael have been loyal to us. Diablo will help you.'

'I don't want *his* help,' Loki snapped. 'I need to see this brother of mine, this *creature*. If what you say about him is true, then I'll do as you ask, but for Wraeththu, not for the Hashmallim. If I have any doubt, I'll not do it.'

'That's more than acceptable,' Zikael said. 'I'm sure that when you see him, you'll know I've spoken honestly to you.'

'Will your masters let me return to the earthly realm to see this creature?' Loki asked.

'I'm sure it can be arranged,' Zikael said, somewhat vaguely.

After this unsettling conversation, Loki returned to Ninzini and called Geburael to him via mind touch. While he was waiting for his surakin to arrive, Loki paced around the top of the tower. He knew that in some ways he'd been seduced by the Aasp and by Zikael in particular, who had swiftly come to feel more like a friend than a threat. Loki enjoyed Otherlanes travel, and wanted to learn more. He wanted to take all this knowledge back to the earthly realm and be recognised for his achievements. He wanted to solve the dilemma that faced the world. But if murder was the cost, surely that was far too high to pay, whatever this unknown brother might or might not be.

Ninzini, can you advise me? Loki asked desperately, but the tower was quiet. It might have been his imagination, but Loki felt he detected a faint air of disapproval emanating from the silent stones.

When Geburael came through the doorway to Ninzini's summit, Loki said, 'I need you to hold me, Geb.'

Geburael was not reluctant to comply. His arms were warm and strong and Loki was soothed by the contact. He could barely remember the time when he'd felt repulsed by Geburael. Now, the thought of not being with him was like trying to imagine life without his senses.

Geburael was silent for some moments. Loki knew he wasn't completely comfortable with the idea that Loki trained only with Zikael. He'd not said anything aloud, but Loki had picked up traces of this discomfort during aruna. Eventually, Geburael said: 'What is it, Loki?'

Loki sighed, and rested his face against Geburael's neck. 'Zikael has told me something. I feel confused about it.'

'*What* has he told you?' Geburael asked sharply.

Loki took a deep breath, and then related his recent conversation with the Hashmal. At the end of it, he said, 'I need to know your thoughts about this, Geb. Is this brother of mine the evil thing I've been told he is?'

Geburael grimaced. 'Well, we know the Aasp fear him, otherwise they wouldn't have wanted to destroy his pearl.'

Loki gripped Geburael's shirt in both his hands. '*They* might fear him, but are *we* right to?'

Geburael exhaled through his nose, stared Loki in the eye. 'I don't know - yet.'

'You felt empathy for him when you heard his cry,' Loki said. 'Do you still feel that?'

Geburael considered this, then released Loki from his embrace and stepped back. His expression was troubled. 'I think that we should see him before we draw any conclusions. The Aasp wouldn't order the excision and destruction of a pearl on a whim. He must be powerful for them to be that concerned about him.'

'Remember what you felt, though. You didn't want to tell Diablo.'

Geburael drew a hand over his mouth, considered. 'He reminded me of you. I felt part of you in him. That doesn't mean he's not what Zikael says he is. I'd know if I saw him, like I knew about you.'

'Zikael said he'll visit us later,' Loki said. 'We'll insist that we're shown this har. There's no other way.'

Geburael nodded thoughtfully. 'Supposing they *can* show him to us. Zikael fobbed you off with a vague promise. If all he said was true, it might be dangerous to get close to this har - especially for you. Five times stronger than you?' Geburael shook his head slowly. 'If that's the truth, we might be up against more than we know.'

Loki paused, then said, 'I know. But the Aasp might be more willing to allow you to get close to him, rather than me.'

Geburael laughed. 'The Aasp have never restricted *my* movements! It's not a case of "allow". All I'll need is a few precise clues as to his whereabouts.' Geburael reached out and clasped Loki's shoulders. 'And if it comes to having to kill him, I will do it, not you.'

Loki pushed Geburael's hands away. 'I can't ask you to do that!' he exclaimed. 'If blood has to be on somehar's hands, it should be mine.'

Geburael closed his eyes briefly. 'Loki, Loki,' he said softly, 'have you no idea how much I love you? I won't let you do this thing. You'll return to your home realm one day. I don't want this act to haunt your conscience. I'm a lost cause. I *will* do it. Don't argue. A Tigron shouldn't have the blood of his kin on his hands.'

Loki stared into Geburael's unflinching gaze. 'Thank you,' he said. 'Can I ask you to do something else?'

'Anything.'

'Don't let Diablo touch you again.'

Geburael ducked his head, uttered a half laugh, but it was a sound of discomfort. 'He hasn't touched me, Loki, not since we were first together. I'm not sure how long I can keep that up, though. He'll become suspicious.'

'It's nearly over,' Loki said firmly. 'Us being here, I mean. I really believe that. Please try, Geb. It won't be for long.'

'How do you see our future?' Geburael asked, and now his voice was wistful. 'Back in Immanion, will you still want me, or am I simply a comfort here, because it's convenient?'

Loki took Geburael's face in his hands and kissed him. 'We are close in blood,' he said, 'and I'm not sure what our family will think of us being together, but I'd be proud to have you by my side in Immanion.'

'Perhaps it would only be a problem if we wanted a harling,' Geburael said.

Loki found these words shocked him, but not in an altogether unpleasant way. 'Would we be inbreeding? Is that what you mean?'

Geburael shrugged. 'I don't know much about Wraeththu biology, except for the basics.'

Loki sighed. 'Such considerations are a long way away, in both space and time.' He gripped Geburael's arms briefly. 'Let's cross that bridge if we're fortunate enough to get to it.' He backed away, rubbing his arms and then began to pace around the tiled floor. 'For now, it seems like a dream. There are monsters in front of us: that's what it feels like.'

'Calm down,' Geburael said. 'There's no point worrying about the future until it happens.'

Loki threw up his arms. 'I feel so restless, like I should be doing something. I can't just sit around waiting for Zikael to come back.'

'We could investigate Thannaril Below again,' Geburael suggested hopefully.

Loki shook his head. 'No. I don't want to go there.' He pursed his lips. 'I think I'll keep practicing entering the Otherlanes. It'll occupy my mind.'

'I'll come with you…'

'No!' Loki said, then softened his tone. 'Thanks, but I won't be gone long.'

'What are you thinking of doing?' Geburael asked, suspicious.

Loki scratched at his hair. His whole body felt uncomfortable. 'Nothing. I just want time on my own, that's all. Also, I want to be proficient in the Otherlanes, not an amateur. I want to strengthen my skills. If I'm to go up against a har who's potentially five times more powerful than I am, I want to be prepared. That includes having the ability to make a quick getaway!'

Geburael laughed softly. 'All right, but don't brood alone. We're in this together.'

Loki couldn't help grimacing. 'You brought me into this, yes.'

'I'll wait here,' Geburael said dryly.

Loki went directly to his private realm and found himself a comfortable spot at the edge of his favourite lake. Perfumed breezes caressed the high branches of the trees. Blossom fell upon him like snow. He felt secure there, removed from all that was troubling. It was easier to think rationally in this place, without hot waves of apprehension washing over him. If his brother had to die, it must be accomplished without Loki's family ever finding out. How could he think such a thing? Had he lost himself? And yet he was sure that Zikael had spoken the truth. The pearl had been created by three hara, which was surely unnatural. What had lived inside it was not strictly har. It was an opportunistic and greedy soul, like a cuckoo. Bigger than the nest.

Loki opened his eyes and stared out over the water. It was so much simpler to exist here. He could walk forever, creating his path ahead of him; new vistas, new wonders. There might be a tower at the end of his journey, at the end of time, and at the top of that tower was Geburael, cleansed of all taint. He wondered how feasible it was to invent that, in so elastic a realm as this. Would the Hashmal let him keep it as his sanctuary forever? A breeze brushed over his skin and he shivered.

Loki turned quickly, sure that someone was standing behind him. He perceived a shadow, a dark flicker on the edge of his vision. At once, he jumped to his feet, every hair on his body erect. A breath of chill wind flowed over him and harried the placid surface of the lake. The trees were not shedding blossoms now, but leaves. They came down in drifts, dried up and lifeless. Loki was flooded with the imperative to flee. *Create a portal; get out!* Something had invaded his realm, and it wasn't Zikael.

Loki's vision blurred; it was as if the realm itself was disintegrating. He tried to form the portal symbol in his mind, concentrate on the particular type of seeing that facilitated opening it, but it was as if he'd lost the ability to focus.

A disturbing shape had begun to manifest in front of him: a nebulous figure of a murky green colour. Its eyes glowed yellow, sulphurous. Loki was filled with the urge to destroy it, an innate animal desire that eclipsed all instincts for survival. He was beyond controlling this feeling; it possessed him utterly.

Expelling a roar of rage, Loki lunged towards the invasive presence. He had become, in an instant, furious hatred incarnate. He lashed out with clawed hands, grabbing handfuls of cold viscous material that was neither gas nor flesh, but something of both. The apparition hissed, and it was the sound of a thousand enraged serpents about to strike. An amorphous limb shot out from the roiling mass and gripped Loki by the throat. It was so strong. Biting, kicking, Loki fought desperately, but the creature was too powerful. It pushed him towards the ground. He couldn't breathe. For the first time in a long time, Loki screamed in his mind for Cal. That too was instinctive.

And the cry was heard, wasn't it?

Loki could barely see, but was aware of another form that hurtled overhead, kicking out. The image swam into focus and Loki saw that it was Geburael, his face set into a furious snarl. It all happened so quickly. Geburael's attack on Loki's assailant somehow managed to loosen its grip. Loki sucked in a lungful of air, spluttered. Something wet rained down onto him, but it wasn't blood.

Geburael yelled at Loki: 'Get out! Get out!' The invader was twining itself around him.

Loki once again tried to form the portal, thinking that somehow he must drag Geburael with him, but it was still so hard to concentrate. The image of Geburael was only half visible through the seething mist of murky green. Spears of invisible energy were shooting in from all directions. There was a sound like thunder, a great crack, and the sky disappeared. Loki saw what looked like an immense *sedu* manifest, its nostrils and eyes flaming red. It was no gentle beautiful creature, but demonic, its teeth too long, the lips peeled back from them like those of a mad dog. This creature seized Geburael in its jaws. Geburael fought back. From what Loki could make out, the initial invasive presence had vanished. It was insane. His serene realm had become a maelstrom of hostile energy.

Loki redoubled his efforts, trying to push all distracting images from his mind. He must find a quiet space in his head, otherwise both he and Geburael were surely dead. Geburael was clearly in no position to open a portal himself. Concentration was almost impossible and although Loki sensed a portal was forming, it was too slow. He uttered a cry of despair, projected his intention with every shred of will he possessed. Then the portal was there, hanging before him: a splash of pulsating light. Loki leapt towards it, grabbing hold of one of Geburael's arms as he did so. Sensations of his surakin's pain shot through his fingers. He could feel the *sedu* pulling against him.

'No!' Geburael cried. 'Go, Loki! Go now!'

'I can't!' Loki yelled back, and his voice seemed to fly away from him and be swallowed by hurricanes of energy. 'I can't leave you!'

'You must!'

At that moment, a shout vibrated through the hectic air, like the voice of a dehar. It stripped the last leaves from the trees and cracked branches that began to crash to the ground. It flattened the grass and caused the waters of the lake to boil. This voice boomed Geburael's name and the entire realm shattered into fragments of whirling colour. At the same time, Zikael manifested in the portal; a tall dark shape with flying hair, beckoning urgently. His summons could not be disobeyed. Loki's body complied with it beyond his will.

Just before Loki was sucked through the portal, Geburael uttered a hoarse cry. There were entities all around him. He was consumed by them.

Loki came to his senses on the floor of Ninzini, gasping painfully. He felt he'd inhaled acid and coughed up liquid, which was like sour water, but perhaps something else. Diablo and Zikael stood over him. Zikael too appeared shaken; his breath was laboured, his silken hair in disarray. For once, Diablo had an expression other than disdainful contempt on his face. He looked distraught.

Loki scrambled into a sitting position; his head swam. He was covered in a strange, oily deposit, as if he'd walked through greasy smoke. 'What happened?' he managed to say. 'Zikael...'

'Our enemies seek to pre-empt us,' Zikael said grimly.

'Geburael...' Loki's voice was a plea.

'He was taken,' Zikael snapped. 'There was nothing I could do to prevent it. I had to take you to safety.'

'But what took him?' Loki asked. 'What *were* those things?'

'You met your brother,' Zikael said. 'The abomination was there in that realm, along with other entities. I have no idea how or why.' It was clear this lack of understanding had unsettled the Hashmal greatly, since it was rare he felt that way.

'My *brother*...' Loki clasped his head, which was aching in a deep, pulsing manner. A brief thought of the Thanax crossed his mind.

'He must have been looking for you,' Zikael said. 'He obviously meant to kill you. Geburael must have followed you, and it's fortunate he did. He sacrificed himself to save you. He called for me.'

'And now that har has taken Geb?'

Zikael shook his head. 'No. A *sedu* came, but also something else. I believe an agent of the Aralisians has taken Geburael, no doubt at the injunction of the *sedim*. Your family is in league with the *sedim*. This is difficult, Loki. The time has come for you to make a choice. Your family is misled. Only you have clear sight now. Only you can save them.'

'He's so much stronger than me,' Loki said. 'You warned me.' He stared at Zikael fiercely. 'If you want my compliance, make me as strong. Help me to vanquish him.'

Zikael held out an arm and Loki took hold it, let the Hashmal pull him to his feet. 'Are you with us now, Loki?'

Loki bared his teeth. 'I am your avatar,' he said.

Behind him, Diablo laughed. Loki shuddered. He heard madness in that sound.

Chapter Twenty-Eight

In the garden of the prison house, Abrimel and Caeru sat on the ground, holding onto the young har they'd pulled from the Otherlanes. Pellaz sprawled on the grass, some distance away, dazed. He had no clear idea what had just happened to them.

A few moments before, in an uncomfortable cauldron of prickly energy, the three of them had projected their minds to try and locate Geburael. There had been nothing, a blank, and then something Pellaz could only describe as a psychic fanfare announced Geburael's whereabouts to them. Pellaz had received the impression that the young har had manifested spontaneously in a realm that was accessible to them. Pellaz could not travel without a *sedu*, and neither could Caeru or Abrimel, but suddenly, against their wills, they were dragged into another realm, in the midst of a bizarre conflict. It had all happened so swiftly, Pellaz could barely remember the details, but they'd pulled Geburael back with them. Or rather, a *sedu* had become involved and facilitated it.

Pellaz turned his head. Behind him stood Peridot, whose entire body was shaking. The Tigron stared at the *sedu* unblinkingly.

How did you know? Pellaz demanded. *How did you know what I was going to do? You spied on me. You followed me.*

You don't trust me, beloved, Peridot told him.

Pellaz uttered an involuntary snarl. *And you don't trust me, since you've clearly been monitoring my movements.*

Peridot shook his mane and took a few steps forward. *You don't understand. Our enemies have set your sons against each other. You were there, with Loki, yet you did not recognise him. You were there, with your lost son, Darquiel, and you did not recognise him.*

Pellaz leapt to his feet. *What? How can that be? I'd have known.*

Peridot closed his dark eyes, his equine features set into the nearest to a sorrowful expression they could get. *But you didn't, beloved. Can't you see what's been done to your progeny? Darquiel and Loki were fighting. If I hadn't intervened, it could have been disastrous. If you wanted Geburael brought to you, you should have asked.*

Pellaz was so incensed, he spoke aloud. 'This is preposterous! As if you'd have done that!'

I could have done.

Pellaz gestured abruptly at the hara behind him. *If you're telling the truth, complete our family. Bring Loki to me. Bring my other son… Darquiel. Do it now!*

Peridot snorted softly. *I can't bring Darquiel to you, and it's too late for me to help you with Loki. Why did you not ask for my help before?*

Pellaz clasped his head for a moment. *Why didn't you offer? You knew he'd been taken. You could have just fetched him home for me.*

It's not that simple. I could have done nothing until you asked me.

Again, Pellaz spoke aloud. 'A hint of that might have been useful, Peridot! I'm sick of these games and their ridiculous rules.'

Peridot stamped a front foot and his head went up. For just a moment, his image flickered, as if he was about to manifest in his true form. *You have no comprehension! What I do for you, I do in secrecy. Our kings have their own agendas. It's not permitted for me to help you in any way, but there's a clause of the ancient contract concerning being asked the right question. There are many truths in the ancient legends. You should have thought of this.*

Pellaz turned away. Caeru was wholly occupied by tending the young har who lay before him, but Abrimel had turned his head to watch his father's exchange with the *sedu*. Pellaz smiled bleakly at his son and turned back to Peridot. *Just exactly why are you trying to help me now?* he asked.

Peridot turned his head to the side and stared at Pellaz for some moments. Then his body shuddered with a deep sigh. *I wonder that myself, often. I've estranged myself from my kin, as have other sedim who've come here. Such things have happened before between the creatures of earth and our kind. I took a great risk interfering today, and could only do so because I'd been directed to observe certain events. My task was to help Darquiel, ultimately, but he does not need my help. Pellaz, Loki is lost to the Hashmallim. He has become expendable to the kings of the sedim.*

A chill passed through Pell's flesh. An image of Loki as a young harling flashed across his mind; his innocence, his untouched beauty. *What must I do to save him? Tell me that, at least.*

I believe his fate lies in the hands of the Kamagrian, Lileem. You can do nothing. His fate lies with Darquiel also.

Pellaz clawed the air with desperate hands. *Why were Darquiel and Loki fighting? Who's influencing Darquiel?*

Your sons have been set against one another. I dreaded this would happen. The Hashmallim have persuaded Loki to support their cause. As you know, they always wanted to dispose of Darquiel. It appears they're using Loki for that purpose. What the two were doing together in that realm, I don't know. It was a temporary realm, perhaps an arena created purposefully for them to do battle in. I managed to separate them, and both escaped that realm before it collapsed. But no doubt there are plans for them to meet again.

'Great Aru!' Pellaz put his hands over his face. *We must stop this. My sons must be taken beyond all influences. If you have any real love for me, Peridot, you'll help me with this.*

Peridot's response felt cautious to Pellaz. *There are limits to what I can do.*

Pellaz was sure that Peridot had made a decision to conceal something. This unknown information hung between them, like invisible poison. *Peridot, you're troubled. If you want me to trust you, tell me why.*

Peridot uttered a groan from deep within his body. *It pains me to tell you this, beloved, but Darquiel could be a danger. He's unprepared to ally himself with any faction, as yet. You know how you made him; he's not the same as any other har. He's come into himself. He's aware and knows who he is. But he's a lone agent, unattached to your family.*

For a moment, Pellaz was swept by a surge of disorientation. He had this son he had never seen, who had grown up and now had opinions of his own. Where had he lived? What was he like? *I want to meet him, Peridot. You must help me. It pains me to say this too, but I beg you!*

Peridot tossed his head. *I can't. All I can tell you is that our king, Lurlei, approached Darquiel and offered to convey him here. Darquiel refused to accept it. He has learned very recently, to some degree, how to negotiate the Otherlanes on his own. So has Loki, because the Hashmallim have given him that skill.*

It occurred to Pellaz then that Cal might be involved, since he was absent from Immanion, with no explanation. This was not unusual, as Cal often liked to escape the city for a few days. He came and went as he pleased. But this time, was there a reason for his absence? Pellaz knew he wouldn't have had this thought without his instincts sensing some truth. Could Cal have found Darquiel and begun to teach him? If Darquiel was a dangerous har, it was likely that would appeal greatly to Cal. He was not beyond keeping secrets from his consorts either. Pellaz resolved to make every effort to contact Cal as soon as he could.

Peridot, Pellaz said, trying hard to keep emotion from his thoughts, *do you know if Cal has found Darquiel?*

The *sedu* answered at once, which reassured Pellaz he was telling the truth. *I can't tell you that. Lurlei has forbidden any of us near Darquiel, in the earthly realm, but for himself.* He paused, then said, *Darquiel is strong-willed, Pell. He might not be what you expect.* The *sedu* turned his head to regard Abrimel, who was observing the conversation speculatively, not least because he would only be able to hear his father's occasional outbursts. *He could be more trouble than that one.*

Pellaz couldn't suppress the shudder those words conjured. He couldn't think too deeply about Darquiel now. One thing at a time. *Will the sedim take action against Loki?* he asked.

If they get the chance, they might. I will not take part in any such action, I assure you.

Pellaz stared the *sedu* in the eye. *Just where* do *you stand, Peridot?*

The *sedu* did not respond. For some moments longer, he regarded Pellaz with his dark intelligent gaze, then ducked his head and disappeared into the Otherlanes.

For some moments, Pellaz remained staring at the space where Peridot had been. He felt bewildered.

'Pell!' Caeru's voice.

Pellaz turned round. It seemed that in the midst of crisis, Caeru and Abrimel had been reconciled, at least temporarily. Geburael was still unconscious, his head in Caeru's lap. His face and hands were badly scratched. It was impossible yet to discern what other damage his body might have taken.

Pellaz pressed his fingers against his eyes. *Cal, where are you?* It was not an idle thought, but projected like a mind call. *Don't do the disappearing in time of need act again, please!*

Pellaz waited for a responding call, however faint, but there was none. He sighed and went to his family. Caeru had placed his hands on Geburael's face, presumably to project healing energy.

Pellaz stood over Abrimel and put a hand on his son's shoulder. 'How is he?'

'Shocked, I think,' Abrimel said. He took Geburael's hands in his own. 'If that *sedu* hadn't shown up…' He shook his head.

'He didn't exactly show up,' Pellaz said. 'I think he took us there. He helped us.'

'It was Peridot, wasn't it?' Caeru said. 'He's different from his brethren, because he cares for you.'

Pellaz exhaled heavily through his nose. 'He's certainly different, yes.'

Caeru smiled tightly at Pellaz. 'This is our high-son, Pell.'

Pellaz nodded. 'Yes.'

'He's beautiful,' Abrimel murmured. 'He's mine.'

Geburael had the Cevarro look, but also hints of the height and facial appearance of Ponclast. Pellaz felt dizzy with the thought that Abrimel, his own son, had created this life with the Varr leader. A harling who was now an adult.

'I think we should take him to the infirmary,' Caeru said. 'He doesn't feel badly hurt to me, but I'd be happier if he was checked properly.'

'I agree,' Pellaz said. He addressed Abrimel. 'Once Geburael has been examined, and if the physicians allow it, I'll bring him back here.'

'You'll let him stay with me?' Abrimel asked, surprised.

'Why not? You *are* his father.'

'Then essentially he will be in confinement too.'

Pellaz took a deep breath through his nose. 'No. I just think he would prefer to be with you.'

Caeru removed his hands from Geburael and Abrimel began to lift him. At this point, Geburael stirred. He did so quite aggressively and pushed his father's hands away. It was clear the har was frightened and disorientated. He uttered a cry, put a hand to his eyes, then lowered it.

'Geburael,' Abrimel said, reaching out towards his son.

Geburael backed away from his father in a crablike scuttle, and then stared at him from a safe distance. 'I know you,' he said. 'I know your face. Who are you? Where am I?'

'Don't be alarmed,' Abrimel said softly. 'You're safe.' He touched his own breast. 'I'm Abrimel, your father. Do you remember what happened?'

Geburael sat up, his hands braced against the ground, as if he feared it would disintegrate beneath him. His skin looked waxy. 'Loki, something… A terrible force. Then a creature had me.' He looked around himself. 'Where's Loki? How did I get here?' The reality of the situation appeared to dawn on him. '*Father?* Is it really you?'

'Yes.' Abrimel gestured towards Pellaz and Caeru. 'And this is your high-father and high-hostling.'

Geburael glanced at Pellaz, looked away, glanced back. 'I'm in Almagabra?' he asked abruptly.

'Yes,' Pellaz said. 'Welcome to Immanion.'

Caeru stood up and bowed to his high-son. 'I wish the circumstances of meeting you could have been different, but we're very glad to have found you.'

Geburael flicked the briefest glance at the Tigrina. 'What do you want with me?' he asked Pellaz.

Pellaz strove to keep his voice pleasant. 'Your hostling has advised me to speak to you concerning Loki. We think you might be aware of his whereabouts. We wanted to find you, to ask you some questions, and also, well…' He held out his arms. 'We *are* your family, Geburael. We should have looked for you long ago.'

Geburael uttered a caustic laugh. 'Yet you didn't. You were looking for Loki, not me. Ironically, you could have taken him just now, but you took me instead. Why? Couldn't you see what was happening?'

Pellaz nodded once. 'I know what happened. Unfortunately, at the time, we were unable to recognise Loki. We didn't realise he was there.'

Geburael sneered. 'He was in great danger. Something attacked him, and you left him there!'

'He escaped,' Pellaz said. 'I have that on good authority.' He folded his arms. 'Were you responsible for Loki's abduction, Geburael?'

Geburael didn't answer. His face took on a mulish expression.

'Where have you been keeping him?' Pellaz persisted.

'Am I a prisoner?' Geburael snapped.

'Not at the moment,' Pellaz said mildly, although his hackles had begun to rise. 'If you co-operate, it will be well regarded.'

'I can't co-operate with you,' Geburael said rudely. 'We're on different sides.'

Pellaz sighed. 'Geburael, at this stage, I don't think any of us truly appreciate what these "sides" consist of. Your hostling thinks the same. Whatever our differences, the only sensible course is for us to work together, otherwise we risk being used.'

'But you're allied with the *sedim*.'

'Really? What makes you think that?'

Geburael narrowed his eyes. 'Aren't you?'

Pellaz walked closer to Geburael, who visibly became nervous rather than simply hostile. 'I have an open mind,' Pellaz said, 'but a very concerned mind. I've a lot to tell you, not least what your hostling has discovered in his place of exile. I want you to hear everything I know, and hope you'll extend me the same courtesy. We shouldn't be enemies. The competing factions aren't interested in allying with me, or Ponclast. Not anymore. It's the next generation they're interested in. I think they want to get to hara who are impressionable and young. But perhaps you already realise this.'

Geburael swallowed, rubbed his face. 'The Hashmallim have befriended Loki,' he said. He paused for a moment, sighed. 'All right, I'll talk to you. The Hashmallim have told him that the freakish son you made is the enemy of all Wraeththu. They want Loki to be their avatar and destroy his own brother.' He pursed his lips. 'Recently, some things have bothered me. I'm not sure if you're the one I should really be confiding in, but I'm concerned too. I worry for Loki, not least because I think all hara are expendable to the Hashmallim.' He stared at Pellaz. 'I never thought I'd want this, but I think Loki should be brought back to the earthly realm as soon as possible. I'll help you with this, but there must be conditions.' He looked at Abrimel. 'Loki in return for my parents. Release them.'

Pellaz cleared his throat. He wasn't quite sure how best to respond to this demand, but Abrimel spoke for him.

'Don't think of me,' he said. 'Think of yourself. There are many conditions the Tigron will fulfil. Don't wreck the potential before you with useless demands. Find Loki for them. Bring him here.'

'But…' Geburael appeared confused.

'I'm your father,' Abrimel said. 'It's what I want. I've made conditions too.'

Geburael shrugged. 'In that case…' He shook his head. 'This situation is unreal.'

'You feel disorientated,' Caeru said gently. 'We think it might be best if we take you to the infirmary to be checked over. That exit from the Otherlanes was rough.'

Geburael raised a hand. 'I'm fine,' he said. 'I haven't got time for that. I want to take action.'

'Perhaps we should go inside,' Abrimel suggested.

Despite objections from Caeru, Pellaz wished to talk to Geburael alone. He took the young har to a sitting room in the house, leaving Caeru to wait with Abrimel in another room. Geburael was surly and very much on his guard, but he wasn't silent. It didn't take Pellaz long to realise that Geburael and Loki lived in the realm from which Ta Ke had been exiled. Geburael was honest about having abducted Loki and taking him there. He seemed to think his actions were justified, although it was clear he was feeling confused about finding himself conversing with a har he'd taken to be a mortal enemy.

Pellaz too was confused. This young har was of his blood, and in many ways it was a good thing to have found him, but there were issues that made this reunion difficult. Pellaz felt he had to address them. 'If you help us, you'll be rewarded, like I said. However, you do have some things to answer for, namely the murder of a har in Freygard.'

'What?' Geburael snapped. 'I killed no har there. I took Loki, and it was right that I did. At the very least, it has made everyhar more aware of what's going on.'

'Maybe you didn't mean to kill him,' Pellaz said patiently, 'but the har who was supposed to go to Loki for his feybraiha is dead. From his injuries, I find it difficult to believe that death was an accident.'

'I didn't do that,' Geburael said. 'You won't believe me, of course.'

'Then who did kill him?' Pellaz enquired. 'It has to be somehar connected with you – Diablo, perhaps?'

Geburael fixed Pellaz with a stare. 'Diablo helped me,' he said. 'It's possible. Does that let me off the hook in your eyes?' His voice was bitter.

'Geburael,' Pellaz said, 'let's focus on the most important things now. Can you bring Loki to Immanion?'

'I want to,' Geburael said, 'although I can't guarantee success. I don't know what happened after that *sedu* seized me.'

Pellaz tapped his cheek with the fingers of one hand. He came to a decision. 'Together, we'd stand more chance of success. Take me to Thanatep.'

'You?' Geburael laughed. 'The Hashmallim would kill you. They know you're an ally of the *sedim*, and whatever you say to the contrary won't convince them.'

'I'm not that easy to kill,' Pellaz said. 'Loki must be brought home.' He knew that the Hegemony would be furious at him putting himself at risk like this, but he'd taken great risks before in his life. He wasn't afraid.

Geburael frowned. 'All right.' He paused. 'I think Loki's in danger. Like you, I want him out of there.'

Pellaz smiled. 'I can tell you're very fond of him and that you're concerned for his welfare. Do you feel strong enough to go to Thanatep now?'

Geburael nodded. 'Yes.' He held up his hands, examined the scratches on them, then shrugged. 'I won't be able to guarantee your safety. If you come with me, you'll have to look out for yourself. Also, it's not easy for me to take hara to Thanatep. Loki was less of a problem because he's young and his abilities when I took him there were not that developed. Thanatep protects itself, and coupled with that, the Aasp don't want anyhar going there. The wards around it are almost impenetrable.'

'All I ask is that you try,' Pellaz said.

'Very well.' Geburael rubbed his nose and reached out to Pellaz. 'Take my hands. Close your eyes. You don't have to do anything.'

Pellaz did as he was asked. He could feel a warm fizz of energy in Geburael's palms, and a slight fracturing of the air around him, which signified the creation of a portal. Then he was yanked into the Otherlanes, and experienced first-hand the far more terrifying method of travel that is accomplished without a *sedu*. Otherworldly winds buffeted his body, hostile entities screamed in at him from all directions. Geburael was far less of a reassuring presence than a *sedu* would be. Pellaz felt his essence would be sucked away, and then they were crashing out of a portal into a realm.

Pellaz shuddered and braced himself for whatever might face him.

But then he found that he was sprawled on the floor in exactly the same place he'd been before; a room of the prison house.

Geburael was on his knees some feet away. He dragged himself upright. 'It's no good,' he said, and his expression was anguished. 'I can't get in. The Aasp must have sealed the realm from me. Loki's training realm has gone too.' His eyes filled with tears. 'I can't reach him. There's nothing I can do.'

Chapter Twenty-Nine

After Darq returned from Helek Sah, he went for a walk alone in the snow-silent forest above Nezreka. He felt as if he stood at the brink of a great battle, when many lives would be lost and the face of the world changed forever. He also knew this was an illusion and the changes, when they happened, would be subtler than that. He knew he should summon Zu, to tell him what had occurred in Helek Sah, as they'd arranged to meet that evening anyway, but for some reason Darq lacked the will to do so. He wanted to be alone with his thoughts. If Zu wanted him, he could come without being summoned.

Darq wandered farther than he'd ever gone before. He could feel the presence of Tava'edzen in the town behind him, connected to him by an invisible cord, which would always guide him home. He had no fear of becoming lost.

He came to a place that reminded him strongly of the forest around Samway. It was almost as if he'd somehow stepped through space and time into a winter of his childhood. Surely, around the corner of this path, he would come across the ruins of the old church and the pool where the moon came sometimes to bathe. Perhaps Amelza would be waiting for him there.

He did find a glade, and it was a place of uncanny power, but it was not of Samway. Somehar, perhaps in his travels east to sanctuary in Jaddayoth, had erected a statue of a dehar in this place. Considering it must have been hastily created, it was a work of beauty. Darq went up to it and saw that words had been etched into its base: 'Here is Panphilien, he of the many aspects, lover of all, dehar of the cycle of Arotohar, the turning wheel of life. Pause, here, traveller and reflect.'

Panphilien held out his arms and gazed towards the horizon. It wasn't as if he was poised to embrace those who came to him, but rather embraced the future, since he faced east, the place where the sun rose and new days began. Darquiel climbed up onto the plinth of the statue and stood with his back to it. He copied its pose, reaching towards tomorrow. For some moments, he closed his eyes, and felt his heart pump blood in time with the heartbeat of the earth. She was close to him; he was living in her breath, walking upon her skin.

Suddenly, Darq's flesh prickled; he was being observed. He thought it must be Zu, or somehar from Nezreka, or even Lurlei, but when he opened his eyes, he saw a stranger standing among the shadows at the edge of the glade. It was a tall har, dressed in a grey travelling cloak, with the hood thrown back. His hair wasn't very long, which was unusual to Darq, but it was as pale as moonlight.

Darq lowered his arms. The har was watching him with a faint expression of amusement. 'Who are you?' Darq demanded.

The har came forward. He was one of the most beautiful creatures that Darq had ever seen, and most of that beauty, he realised in a moment, was beneath the skin. The har radiated an air of great experience and strength, and also of sensuality. He must be Gelaming, Darq thought.

'Don't you know me?' the har asked him. 'Look closer.'

Darq approached this har. He could smell the stranger's personal scent, an intoxicating blend of freshly mown hay and warm animal fur. Darq stared into his eyes, unafraid. Yes, he did know this har, but he had no idea of how or when. Perhaps they had met only in dreams, because Darq was sure they had never encountered one another in reality. 'I know you,' he said, 'but not. Tell me who you are.'

'I am your father,' said the har. He smiled. 'One of them.'

Darq took a step back. He was surprised at how shocked he felt. He could barely draw breath. Tomorrow had just stepped into today. Had he wished for this? 'How did you find me?' he asked.

The har folded his arms. His posture was easy, as if he met lost sons every day. 'Thiede communicated with me. I am Calanthe… Cal. And you are Darquiel, I'm told. You've no idea how glad I am to see you well. The circumstances of losing you were… traumatic.'

'I don't know what to say to you,' Darq said, which was the bare truth. He felt hot.

Cal gestured languidly with one arm. 'Then say nothing. Or at least, let's just talk together generally, as if we were strangers meeting for the first time.' He sat down on the plinth of the statue and gestured for Darq to sit beside him. 'Tell me of Anakhai,' Cal said, 'for this is one place I've not really explored. Tell me of your childhood.'

'I lived in Samway,' Darq said. 'West of here. That is where it began.'

'I know of that place,' Cal said. 'Your father, Pellaz, went there once, although it was a long time ago. He's not spoken to Phade har Olopade since.'

Darq sighed. 'Phade was my guardian. We didn't always get on. I've always been different.' He glanced at Cal. 'I think you made me that way.'

'Then tell me about it,' Cal said.

Darq told his story, all of it that he could remember. Cal listened, his eyes half-hooded. He crossed his legs and clasped the upper knee, in exactly the same way Divozenky had earlier. He stared at the trees while Darquiel talked. On one level, Darq delivered an eloquent narrative, but on another he felt dazed and disorientated. The pieces of his puzzle were all falling into place; so quickly now. This magnificent har beside him was one of the mysteries that had haunted his childhood. Cal had not come as a haughty Tigron, but simply as an ordinary har, who had discovered the whereabouts of a lost harling. He did not hide his feelings; Darq could sense them. Some of Darq's story upset Cal, other parts surprised and delighted him. He did not interrupt or even ask questions. He simply listened, with full attention.

When Darq reached the part about when his identity was revealed to him by Zu, over an hour had passed. He paused now and asked, 'Is it true my brothers will resent me?'

Cal drew in his breath through his nose. Still, he did not look at his son. 'I can't speak for Abrimel. He's a stranger to me. All I can say is that Loki, as I know and love him, would embrace you as a brother - under normal circumstances. Unfortunately, he's no longer in normal circumstances. I believe he's been influenced. He's far from home. Once he used to call to me, but now his cry is silent. The place he's in is selective about who it lets into it. I don't have enough connection with that realm to breach its boundaries - yet.'

'He's been influenced by the Aasp,' Darq said softly. It wasn't a question.

'We'll get Loki back,' Cal said, 'and then I defy any influence to oppose mine.'

'I think,' Darquiel said, 'that I should go to Immanion very soon. Will you take me?'

'Oh yes,' Cal said. 'First, I'm quite interested to meet your new friends, not least the one who was once the leader of the tribe that incepted me.'

'Do you mean Tava'edzen?' Darquiel asked.

Cal nodded. 'I knew him as Manticker. I didn't know him very well, because I was so young, newly incepted. Wraxilan ousted Manticker shortly after that.'

'*You* were Uigenna?' Darquiel couldn't help laughing at the thought.

'Most were,' Cal said. 'Uigenna was the primal tribe. All the oldest Wraeththu you meet will have some connection with them. An embarrassing stage of our development that many seek to deny.'

There was a short, tense silence, and then Darq announced: 'I love

Tava'edzen.'

Cal grinned and wound an arm round Darq's shoulders. 'Now why am I not surprised?' He pulled Darq to him and Darq was happy to curl into Cal's side. He felt great strength in this har.

'Who is this Zu you spoke of?' Cal asked. 'Summon him here. I'd like to meet the creature who hijacked your most intimate moments.'

'He's not bad,' Darq said. 'Don't be angry about that. I haven't told you everything about him. He was incepted from the Krim Sri. He says he's the only one who was. And he *has* helped me.'

'Summon him,' Cal said. 'He can tell me the rest himself.'

'All right.' Darq drew away from his father and got to his feet. 'I have to call to him by swinging a weighted cord.'

Cal raised an eyebrow. 'Different. Well, do carry on.'

Darq took the cord out of his pocket - he always kept it to hand now - and closed his eyes. He swung the cord and the stone at the end of it sang in the cold air. Almost at once, he could feel Zu approaching, and sensed the har was in some way cautious. Perhaps he was aware Darq was not alone. His presence flickered, as if Zu was debating whether or not to manifest. Then Darq heard Cal say, '*You?*' in an icy tone. He opened his eyes.

Zu stood some feet away, clad in his travelling clothes. His arms were folded defensively and he was not at all the commanding, confident creature with whom Darq was familiar.

'I'm sorry, Cal,' Zu said. 'I'm sorry I couldn't tell you about Darquiel.'

Cal stood up, radiating a type of energy Darq felt could blast holes in rock. 'Does Thiede know about all this?'

Zu shook his head. 'No.'

Cal bared his teeth. 'I don't envy you when he becomes aware of it. And that will be approximately as long as it takes me to walk to Nezreka.'

Zu came forward. 'I did what had to be done. You couldn't be with Darq, and neither could Caeru or Pellaz, but I could, because I'm different to you. I'm one of a kind, Cal.'

'Quite,' Cal said.

Zu displayed his palms in a gesture of appeal. 'When Darquiel was conceived, I felt responsible for him. It was me who encouraged Rue to become intimate with you. I've always felt that Darq is partly mine, and I've watched out for him.'

'Rather more than that,' Cal said, apparently unmoved by Zu's words. 'Please remember you're speaking to one of his parents and that he has just related to me the content of his *friendship* with you!'

'It's all right,' Darq said hurriedly. He didn't like to see Zu so cowed. 'Please don't be angry with him.'

Cal turned to Darq. 'This har you know as Zu is one of Thiede's agents, as well as an official of the Hegemony in Immanion. I've always known he's a slippery fish, since he was instrumental in taking me from the earthly realm at the time of your pearl's abduction. Now, it appears he's also been working independently, but then that doesn't really surprise me. His name to us is Velaxis.'

When Darq returned to the Drudehall with Cal and Velaxis, Jezinki swooped down on him in the entrance hall and told him, in an icy tone, he must go to the phylarch's office at once. There, Darq found an impatient group of hara awaiting him: Tava'edzen, Thiede, Ookami and the Weavers. It was clear that Thiede had told the others about Cal's arrival, and also that Cal had gone to speak with Darq alone, since nohar questioned Cal's presence. It was also clear that Tava'edzen and the Weavers had already related their side of what had taken place in Helek Sah. Darq formally introduced his father to everyhar and once this was accomplished, Thiede turned to Velaxis and said, 'What are *you* doing here? Did you travel with Cal? He didn't mention it to me.'

Cal laughed. 'Velaxis has something to tell you, Thiede.'

Velaxis appeared to be very uncomfortable, and because he was still "Zu" to Darq, Darq felt sorry for him. 'Let me explain,' Darq said. 'I don't want you to be angry, Thiede.'

'Angry?' Thiede said archly. 'Why would I be angry?'

Darq cleared his throat. 'You know when we first met and I heard that voice in my head?'

Thiede nodded, his eyes narrow.

'Well…' Darq glanced at Velaxis. 'It was him.'

'What?' Thiede snarled.

'He's been with me ever since… in one way or another. He's been my teacher.'

Ookami, who had remained politely in the background, now couldn't help an outburst: 'Teacher?' he cried. 'He's committed shameful acts.' He pointed at Velaxis. 'Don't think I've forgotten, *Tiahaar!* There's unfinished business between us. You were foolish to show your face here.'

Velaxis looked horrified. Possessing Ookami's body was one thing, but facing the wrath of an indignant Ikutama warrior was another. Darq could tell that Velaxis was afraid, and in Darq's opinion, he had good reason to be. This was all going horribly wrong. 'Tiahaar,' Velaxis said to Ookami, 'I...'

Thiede raised his hands. 'Hush, all of you,' he said.

Ookami lowered his accusing arm. He was furious, but he held his tongue.

Thiede folded his arms. 'Darquiel, be so kind as to finish your story of your... *relationship* with Velaxis.'

Darq did so, keeping the more personal details to himself. All the time, he looked into Velaxis' face, this har he'd come to look upon as a friend. As he spoke, he was aware that Ookami was upset by what he heard, but Darq didn't know what else he could do to defuse the situation, except show Velaxis in as positive a light as possible. Perhaps he was wrong to do that, but he didn't care.

Thiede listened to the whole story in silence, his expression inscrutable. When Darq finished speaking he said, 'Ookami, you will take no action.'

Ookami came forward. 'Tiahaar, my honour has been offended. I demand retribution.'

Thiede remained expressionless. 'Do you want to skewer him with your swords, is that it? Will that make you feel better?'

Ookami stared back at Thiede. 'You don't understand me,' he said. 'He took possession of me against my will. Let him put his will against mine when I am prepared.'

Thiede closed his eyes and uttered a short sigh. 'Ookami, I do understand, but quite frankly, there's no time for this. Velaxis can make compensation to you in some other way, at a later time.'

Ookami inclined his head. 'I respect your desires. However...' He glared at Velaxis. 'I won't forget this matter.'

'I apologise,' Velaxis said stiffly. 'Although I doubt that is enough.'

Ookami said nothing. He retreated to the back of the room.

'Velaxis,' Thiede said, 'we'll speak in private shortly. We have much to discuss.' He shook his head. 'I'm annoyed with myself I never realised how different you were. You *are* adept at disguise, aren't you?'

Velaxis bowed his head. 'I've worked well for you; you know that. I've done nothing against the Hegemony or Wraeththukind. If you wish to punish me, I'll accept your judgment. I just want you to know I acted with Darquiel's welfare at heart.'

Ookami expelled a wordless sound of fury.

Again, Thiede raised a hand to silence him. 'You've played with Darq, Velaxis. I have issues with your methods. And you had more than his welfare at heart. But we'll not speak of this here.'

'Thiede,' Darq said in appeal. 'Please don't be angry. Zu... Velaxis... has been helpful to me.' He turned to Ookami. 'What he did to you was wrong, but I'd not have gone to Helek Sah without him.'

'A lot of what he's done is wrong!' Thiede said. 'I appreciate your feelings on the matter, Darq, but I can't just ignore this... *interference.*' He sighed through his nose. 'I'll deal with it, but at the moment there are more important things to discuss. Tell us everything you experienced with the Krim Sri.'

Grateful for the change of subject, Darquiel addressed the gathering, and related everything that had happened to him in Helek Sah. He didn't include the information Divozenky had given him about Wraeththu's creation, as he'd already decided he wanted to tell Thiede this privately first. At the end of his narrative, Thiede and Cal launched into a discussion about it.

'This must have been Darq's purpose all along,' Cal said. 'It's what Pell sensed when he was so driven to create him.' He shook his head. 'A har who can communicate with the world itself. It's unprecedented.'

'It means that highly evolved souls are waiting to find suitable vessels among us,' Thiede said, his expression thoughtful. 'What we'll need to discuss is whether we should actively seek to repeat what you did, Cal.'

'The Aasp and the Zehk won't like that,' Velaxis interjected. 'I would recommend caution.'

Thiede fixed Velaxis with a bleak stare. 'I think you'd be wise to keep your mouth shut for now, Tiahaar.' He turned back to Cal. 'We've much to discuss, and it should take place in Immanion.'

'You'll return to us, then?' Cal asked. 'Is it safe to do so?'

Thiede nodded. 'Darquiel's existence has changed things for me. I was seen as a threat because I was too curious, but now my threat factor is negligible. Darq is far more potent than I am, or he will be.'

'Many will be glad to see you back,' Cal said. He paused. 'I have to ask - what role do you see for yourself?'

Thiede grinned. 'Fret not, protégé. I see myself as an elder stateshar. I have no wish to take back control of the Hegemony, but I hope I can be of use to it.'

'You'll always be that,' Cal said.

Thiede glanced back at Velaxis and flared his nostrils. 'Anyway, the time has come for me to depart this gathering and speak alone with my faithful servant.'

Velaxis bowed. 'Of course, Tiahaar.' He allowed Thiede to steer him from the room.

Now that Darquiel had delivered his report, and the atmosphere in the room was lighter following Thiede's departure, Tava'edzen sent a message to Jezinki to bring food and ale. Darq felt obliged to approach Ookami, who was still clearly angry. 'I'm sorry,' Darq said, wondering whether this particular spell of words would work; somehow, he doubted it.

Ookami did not speak and would not even look at Darq.

'You've done so much for me,' Darq pressed on. 'I'm grateful. I don't condone what Velaxis did to you, but in his own way he was important to me.'

'I understand,' Ookami said. 'My part in your life was brief. The moment we came here it ended.'

'No,' Darq said. 'That's not right. You mean a lot to me.'

'Some things you just have to accept,' Ookami said. 'We all do. Will you excuse me?'

Without waiting for a reply, Ookami left the room. Darq wasn't quite sure what the har had meant. He turned to face the room and noticed that Cal was studying Tava'edzen intently, in the manner of a cat watching potential prey. Darq wasn't surprised when his father moved swiftly and took Tava'edzen to one side. Darq decided he had to be part of any ensuing conversation; he went quickly to join them.

Cal gave his son a stare, then clearly decided it would be pointless to ask him to move away. 'Well, well, Manticker is still among the living,' Cal said to Tava'edzen. 'You've hardly changed physically. Not that I knew you way back when, really.'

'I remember *you,*' Tava'edzen said. 'Weren't you the one that Wraxilan lost his reason over?'

Cal shrugged. 'Most likely.'

Tava'edzen eyed Cal shrewdly. 'He took it upon himself to destroy me round about the same time.'

'I met him again some time ago,' Cal said hastily, clearly attempting to divert the conversation a little. 'In Maudrah.'

'Oh.' Tava'edzen raised his eyebrows. 'And?'

'In some ways the same, in others greatly changed. He's done well for himself.'

'I heard.'

'But then so have you, if not on such a grand scale.' Cal's tone changed, losing some of its levity. 'I hope you'll consider bringing Nezreka into the Federation of Tribes, Tiahaar. Darquiel has spoken well of you.'

'Thank you for the offer,' Tava'edzen said stonily, 'but it's not appropriate for us. We keep to ourselves out here.'

Cal inclined his head. 'I appreciate that, and we'd not require you to change anything. However, it might be useful for you to be kept apprised of current events. There would be other benefits too. I'm sure you don't need me to spell it all out, at this time.'

Tava'edzen grimaced. 'You want to shepherd us into the fold,' he said, 'but we're quite happy roaming out on the hillside.'

'As you wish, but I hope some kind of relationship can be maintained.'

'You can be sure of that,' Tava'edzen said. He glanced at Darquiel and smiled.

Darquiel sensed that Cal wouldn't let it rest at that, but his father did not mention the subject again that evening. Cal dropped into the role of ambassador and politician, and took care to speak to everyhar who had been part of Darquiel's life.

Very late at night, Darquiel managed to get some more private moments with Cal. Tava'edzen had invited the high-ranking hara of Nezreka to the Drudehall, and now there was a party atmosphere within it. Everyhar had moved to the room where the Natalia rite had been held, and the wine and ale were flowing freely. Cal and Darq went out into the yard beyond Tava'edzen's office and there sat muffled in thick furs on an ice-covered wooden bench, their breath clouding on the air.

'I've become utterly Gelaming,' Cal said, somewhat despairingly. 'It's my instinct now to organise and facilitate. I'm considering offering Ookami a position in Immanion, because he'd no doubt refuse. I admire what he's done for you, though. He's a good har.'

'He is, and I would like to keep him as an advisor.' Darq grimaced. 'He's furious about Velaxis, of course. But once he's cooled down a little, I hope that if I ask him to stay with me, he'd be less likely to refuse than if you asked him.'

Cal laughed. 'Ah, now our blood speaks through you! Have you mentioned anything about this potential position to him?'

Darq shook his head. 'No. A lot has changed over the course of one day, and I haven't had a chance. At the moment, he's angry and disappointed in me. But I will ask him when the time feels right.'

'And Tava'edzen…'

Darq glanced furtively at his father. 'What about him? Do you disapprove of the age difference?'

Cal stuck out his lower lip. 'No, not at all. Why should I? I can see how you feel for one another. I just wonder what you can do to bring him onto the stage, as it were. Manticker was a respected leader. If he hadn't been ousted by Wraxilan, it's possible Ponclast wouldn't have ended up with so much power.'

Darq pulled his fur coat more tightly around his body. 'Manticker might have ended up like Ponclast. Tava is scathing of his early days. He thinks what happened to him was for the best.'

Cal raised an eyebrow. 'Well, Wraxilan turned out fine.'

'What does it matter? The past can't be changed.'

Cal reached out and pushed a stray strand of Darq's hair away from his eyes. 'No, it can't, but the future can. Having met your Tava, I think his voice should be heard.'

'Maybe he'll feel differently when he knows you better.'

Cal twisted his mouth to the side. 'Maybe. Gelaming do tend to throw their weight around. I even feel myself doing it, as I told you.'

Darq sighed. 'I'm more worried about my brother, Loki. I don't want to have to fight him.'

'I'm sure it won't come to that,' Cal said. 'Not if I've got anything to do with it, anyway.'

The following day, Darq began to acquire the instruction he craved, concerning Otherlanes travel. It appeared that Cal had decided to forgive Velaxis, because they agreed to work together with Darq, and Thiede had obviously given his permission. Ookami, pointedly, kept well away. Darq felt slightly guilty that he spent so much time with Cal and Velaxis, thereby side-lining the Ikutama, who had been his protector for so long. At one time, Ookami had virtually been the centre of Darq's life, and he'd believed they'd somehow end up together, at least for a short time, but fate had decreed things turned out differently. Darq thought that perhaps hara swam into focus and faded away all the time throughout life. He hoped a time would come when he could talk to Ookami about it, and explain how he felt, but for now all he could and did care about was his training. Tava'edzen provided a large empty room near the top of the Drudehall, which he said he occasionally used for meetings and ritual. It had a wall of windows that looked out over the town and pale winter sunlight streamed into it.

Although Cal and Velaxis regularly had differences of opinion, Darq could see they liked and respected one another. One day, he intended to get Velaxis' full story. Darq had to admit that Velaxis had taken a lot of liberties with him, but he couldn't find it within himself to be angry about it. It hadn't done him any harm, and in fact had been quite an adventure, even if at the beginning he'd been resentful of Zu's intimate meddlings. He found it difficult now to equate this fairly urbane creature with the mysterious entity that had haunted his journey east. Velaxis was theatrical; he liked playing a mystifying role. But he couldn't keep that up in front of those who knew him well.

Unlike Loki, Darq was confident with the procedure of opening portals and travelling through them. He became proficient at it far more quickly. Once he knew how to do it, he was surprised he hadn't discovered it by accident before. He could travel both physically and astrally, and over the next few days experimented with Otherlanes journeys, both with and without his physical body.

Despite Cal's constant requests, Velaxis was insistent that Loki could not be prized from the grip of the Aasp, or more accurately their agents, the Hashmallim. Darquiel, heady with success, felt he was more than competent enough to try and breach the barriers around Thanatep. Both Velaxis and Cal were adamant he should not attempt it.

'The Aasp failed to kill you once,' Velaxis said. 'Don't be so foolish as to go wandering alone into a realm they control. I doubt they'd fail if they got another opportunity to get rid of you.'

'Why don't they just come here and do it, then?' Darq said. 'I'm not in hiding anymore. I don't think they're as powerful as you say.'

'Darq, you must wait,' Cal said.

Darq blew out his cheeks. 'Why? So they can poison Loki against me even more? Has it occurred to you that he might be the tool they could use to destroy me?'

It obviously *had* occurred to Cal, who appeared pained. 'We'll return to Immanion soon, and talk things over with Pell.'

'Immanion is full of *sedim*,' Darq said. 'I wonder whether I should go there yet. I'm surprised Lurlei hasn't turned up again here, to be honest.' He frowned. 'I accept your counsel, but I'll have to decide myself what I should do next.'

'By Aru,' Cal exclaimed, 'there's a lot of Pell in you! Don't you think so, Vel?'

'Indeed, there is,' Velaxis said, grinning.

'What do you mean?' Darq asked.

'Never mind,' Cal said. 'We should break for the day now. I'm hungry. Don't we have another formal feast to attend this evening?'

Left alone, Darq went to his room and was pleased to find Ookami wasn't there. He had at least an hour of spare time before dinner, and although he didn't really intend to try and visit Thanatep, he thought he could do a bit of sniffing round. He could try to discover where its boundaries were, at least, and he could remain alert for Otherlanes signatures that resembled his own. Part of him yearned to present Loki triumphantly to the older hara, but he wasn't stupid, and knew it would be folly to take senseless risks. Still, nosing around wouldn't hurt.

Darq composed himself cross-legged on the floor beneath the window, and decided he'd project his consciousness into the Otherlanes rather than visit them physically. He presumed this was a safer option. Like Loki, he could control the appearance of the Otherlanes, but had far longer sight than his brother did within them. He could visualise them as an immense shining web, upon which nodules of different coloured lights represented potential exit points to other realms. Cal had already taught Darq how to recognise the signature that represented the physical and psychic makeup of a member of his family. He extended his sight to search for such signs, not really in the hope he'd find anything. Therefore, it was a surprise when he stumbled upon an energy signature that was as familiar to him as his own being. He found it in a small realm, the security for which was not that intense. He did wonder about this. Surely, if Loki was there, he'd have more protection? Still, Darq's excitement at his discovery overrode any caution and he formed a portal to exit the Otherlanes.

Beyond the portal, Darq found a young har who looked so much like Cal it had to be Loki. His essence also felt familiar. But it was clear at once that Loki did not perceive Darq's true form. Darq could see himself through Loki's eyes: a manifestation of aggressive energy. He could tell that Loki's indoctrination, some of which was subtler than he knew, had taken over. His purpose for being, carefully groomed by the Aasp, swung into action.

Darquiel was confronted by a murderously hostile force and he could do nothing but react defensively. In the moments before they made contact, he tried to communicate with Loki, but there were barriers in place he could not breach. Their conflict began to destroy the fabric of the realm, which was not that stable. Then there were strange forces shooting in from all sides, and everything became utterly confused. When the *sedu* appeared, Darquiel fled. He was disorientated and shaken; it was extremely difficult for him to return to his home realm. When eventually he pulled his consciousness back into earthly reality, he lay exhausted and trembling upon his bedroom floor. Then he wept. He had to admit he was not as strong or as clever as he'd thought.

Velaxis found him in that state. He came into the room and said, 'I felt something was distressing you, I had to come. What have you done?'

Darq raised his head. He was incapable of speech.

Velaxis came to kneel beside him and placed a hand on Darq's back. 'Where have you been?' he asked. 'I know you've been somewhere.

What happened?'

Darq could only shake his head. Velaxis sighed through his nose, stood up and went to the bathroom. He returned carrying a glass of water, which Darq accepted gratefully. He drank it all, and wiped his mouth.

'Better?' Velaxis asked.

Darq nodded and put the glass down on the floor. 'I found Loki,' he said.

Velaxis raised his eyebrows. 'What? You'd better explain.'

Darq told him all that had happened. 'I didn't expect to find him. I wasn't prepared.'

'You were warned,' Velaxis said. 'Darq, don't do that again. It's just not safe.'

'Loki hates me,' Darq said. He closed his eyes. 'It's such an unreasoning and mindless hatred.' He stared at Velaxis. 'We *have* to get into Thanatep. Before it's too late.'

'It might already be too late,' Velaxis said softly.

Darq felt emotion welling within him and decided to let it spill out. He wept again. To come face to face with such unjustified loathing as Loki felt for him was shocking. What had he ever done to his brother? It didn't make sense.

Velaxis made a wordless, soothing sound and hauled Darq into his arms. Together, they sat on the floor, while Darq vented his confusion and bewilderment. Velaxis stroked his hair. 'We must go to Immanion,' he said. 'I agree that we must take action. Thiede told me that Pellaz is also trying to get to Loki. He might already have discovered some useful information.'

Darq rested his head on Velaxis' chest, wiped his eyes with the backs of his hands. 'Has Cal told Pellaz about me yet, do you know?'

'I don't think so. Everything's been so hectic. You have to prepare yourself for Pellaz, Darq. He's a mighty force.'

'I like Cal,' Darq said. 'That's a relief.'

'He's not a typical Gelaming,' Velaxis said dryly.

'Neither are you,' Darq said. He hesitated. 'Was your name once really Zu?'

Velaxis laughed softly. 'Bizarrely enough, yes. I supposed you'd picked that up from me.'

'Maybe I did. I think I met family of yours in Helek Sah. A man called Nimron.'

Velaxis rested his chin on the top of Darq's head. 'My father,' he said. 'I knew he was still alive.'

'Why don't you go to him?'

Velaxis sighed, deep in his chest. 'If you want the truth, it's because I can't bear to see what's become of my people. I have to put it behind me. But that doesn't mean I can't fight for them out here in the world.'

'I think you should go,' Darq said. 'I'll go with you, if you want me to. When all this is over.'

Velaxis was quiet for some moments, and then said, 'Darq, do you resent what I did to you?'

Darq pulled away from him. 'No. I was annoyed at first, but you ended up being a kind of lifeline for me. I'm pleased we can be together like hara now, in a normal way. I prefer it. Was Thiede angry with you?'

'Impatient,' Velaxis said. 'He thinks I should have kept him informed, and maybe I should have done.' He smiled wryly. 'The fact is that I wanted to communicate with you alone. I spend so much time paying lip service to other hara's needs and demands. I have to act continually in Immanion, playing whatever roles are required of me or are appropriate. With you, I lived out a kind of fantasy. I enjoyed it. You were my private escape.'

'Despite our strange beginnings, I look on you as a friend,' Darq said. 'That won't change.'

Velaxis inclined his head. 'Thank you.' He frowned. 'Pellaz will be furious with me. We don't exactly get on. It's fortunate that Cal and I do, because otherwise Pellaz would gladly use my behaviour with you as an excuse to get me out of the Hegalion. I'm your hostling's best friend, though. You'll like Rue. He's easy to be with.'

'A lot of hara to meet,' Darq said. 'I'm not looking forward to it. I can't do what you do, Vel; pay lip service. I'm bound to say all sorts of things that I shouldn't.'

'Just be yourself,' Velaxis said. 'Remember, the Aralisians thought they'd lost you. They want you to return.'

'It's not so much my family I'm worried about,' Darq said, 'but everyhar else. They'll think I'm a freak, or too full of myself because of what I can do… or something. Anyway, I'm just not looking forward to it.'

Velaxis kissed the top of his head. 'Don't worry. You have Thiede and Cal behind you, and you have me. It won't be as bad as you think.'

Darq rested his head on Velaxis' chest once more and closed his eyes. He hoped Velaxis wasn't just humouring him. He wished Tava'edzen would be with him, but knew that would never happen. Soon they would spend their last night together, if not for a long time, then perhaps forever.

Chapter Thirty

Early one morning, five days after Cal had come to Nezreka, Darquiel har Aralis left the realm of snow and wolf magic and emerged from the Otherlanes with Thiede, Cal and Velaxis into the far balmier winter season of Almagabra. Darq had spent his last night alone with Tava'edzen. Their parting in the morning had been brief yet poignant. All Tava'edzen had said was, 'Come to me when you can.'

Darq resolved he'd keep away from Nezreka until he felt events had come to a proper conclusion. His reward for whatever tasks lay in the future for him would be to lie once more in Tava'edzen's arms.

At Cal's suggestion, the party arrived at a hilltop outside Immanion, which was a favoured area for Otherlanes portals. A chill wind fretted the dense branches of cypress trees, but there was no snow. In summer, sheep and goats would roam these high slopes, but most were safely in their stables during the winter season. Below, the city glowed white, even though the sky was overcast. The ocean beyond it was the colour of iron.

Darquiel had never seen the sea before. Its immensity stirred him, even from a distance. Its smell swept inland, bringing a taste of salt to his mouth.

'As soon as we get a chance,' Cal murmured, leaning close, 'I'll take you there.'

Darq glanced at him askance. 'I was always told it was rude to pry.'

Cal grinned. 'Your eyes speak as eloquently as your mind.'

'The sea is new to me,' Darq said. 'I want to get close to it.'

Cal nodded and draped an arm around Darq's shoulders. The wind blew Cal's hair over his face in shards of silky spikes. 'It's a bit of a walk into the city, but I thought you'd appreciate the time to gather your thoughts and take a look around.'

Darq reflected that in only a few days he had become completely comfortable with this stranger who'd simply arrived and announced paternity of him. Cal had an easy way with him. Darq had watched him carefully and had noted how Cal could drop the casual demeanour in an instant and become the wily diplomat instead.

Darq looked down upon the domes, tiered roofs and spires of Immanion and thought: *They conceived me there. They did the impossible and now here I am, coming back.*

Cal pointed out the hill in the centre of town, which was like a piece of countryside in the middle of sprawling buildings. 'That's our home,' Cal said. 'That's Phaonica.'

The building on top of the hill looked like something from a dream. It seemed alive to Darq. He shivered.

Thiede came to walk on Darq's other side. 'Be assured that we'll *both* be greeted with surprise,' he said. 'Cal banished me from Immanion once, and the last thing anyhar expects will be for me to walk back into it at his side.'

'Why did he banish you?' Darq asked. At this question, he sensed a certain reserve creep into Cal's aura.

'A long story,' Thiede said. 'You've a lot of history to catch up on, Darq. So much to do! Family, friends and oily-tongued hegemons to meet!'

Darq was consumed by weariness at the thought of that. 'Do they know we're coming?' he asked Cal.

'No,' Cal replied. 'I like surprises.'

'Tell them,' Darq said. '*Please.*'

Velaxis was trailing behind. Now he sent a mind touch message to Darq. *Never mind Cal's games. I've contacted Rue. He knows.*

Thank you. I'll say nothing.

Cal, meanwhile, only laughed. 'It'll be a joy to see their faces!'

Thiede joined in with this laughter. Whatever bad history might exist between them, it was clear why they had become friends.

When they reached the city gates, Thiede pulled up the hood of his travelling cloak. Darq saw no reason to do likewise, since nohar knew who he was. The guards on duty made gestures of respect to Cal and Velaxis, but paid little attention to their companions. Clearly, Thiede had cast a glamour around himself. The gates were dragged open and the party passed through.

'This is the way your father Pellaz came into Immanion,' Thiede said to Darq. 'It was such a long time ago.'

Darq wondered about Tigron Pellaz: what would his other father think of him? What would be his first words? Was he as beautiful as Cal? And there would be Darq's hostling, Caeru, as well. Hara didn't speak much of him. Darq wondered what he would be like too.

The areas Darq passed through on his way to Phaonica were mostly residential. The city seemed enormous and so clean. There were no chickens or animals running about, as there were in Samway. The hour was still early, so few hara were out in the streets. Now that Darq was here, in the city of his creation, he felt disorientated. He had never been in a place where so many hara lived together, and the psychic residue of a multitude of souls pressed upon his being. He realised that, should he let it, that feeling could easily descend into panic.

Then they were at the walls of the palace estate, and the moment Darq had increasingly come to dread was almost upon him. A long curving driveway wound around the hill where Phaonica sprawled at the summit. Lesser buildings, workshops, staff quarters and stables spread downwards behind the palace, but at the front was a magnificent series of tiered gardens. Darq could only catch glimpses of follies, waterfalls and fountains, as there were so many trees. He thought that Amelza and he would have enjoyed playing in such gardens when they'd been children. Would he ever bring her here?

All too soon, Darq was climbing the front steps to the building. The palace reared over him, magnificent and strong. His heart was beating very fast, his breath laboured. He felt extremely light-headed.

Then, from the shadows of the columns at the top of the steps, a willowy figure emerged. It was a pale-haired har, of exquisite, almost otherworldly slenderness, dressed in garments of matte violet silk. He looked at nohar but Darq, and Darq felt an unaccountable and immense tug in his chest. Involuntarily, his eyes filled with tears, so that the figure before him became shimmery and unfocused. He knew he was looking at his hostling.

Cal, or maybe Thiede, said something, but Darq's ears were filled with a high-pitched humming. His hostling came down the steps to him and enfolded him in a warm embrace. 'Welcome home,' Caeru whispered and kissed Darq's cheek.

It was almost like the time before feybraiha, because Darq was overwhelmed by emotion. He couldn't help but weep, even though that was the last thing he wanted to do. When he held onto Caeru, he could feel ghosts of the terrible thing that had happened, the way they'd been ripped apart unnaturally. He also knew that at the moment Caeru had touched him, some deep inner hurt had begun to heal. Darq understood now why he could never have felt close to Phade, and why Olivia had drawn him to her without realising it. He'd missed the contact of the body that had held and nurtured him, and he'd never known it.

Caeru drew away, his hands still clasping Darq's face, thumbs lightly stroking his cheekbones. 'Well, Cal,' he said, without taking his gaze from Darq's. 'Sorry to spoil your surprise. What a good cat you are, bringing home such a delightful gift.'

'He's hardly hanging from my jaws,' Cal said.

Caeru wiped his eyes with one hand. 'No?' He now turned his attention to Thiede. 'Welcome to you, too. We've just about managed to mature without you. Isn't that a wonder?'

Thiede took Caeru in his arms and hugged him rather roughly. 'Amazing,' he said. 'Phaonica still stands.'

'And Pell and I are now always what you wanted us to be.'

Thiede glanced at Darq. 'So it seems. Well, lead us in, fair Tigrina. Why isn't Pell with you?'

'I wanted to meet Darq myself first,' Caeru said. 'If Pell was here, he would have been, well… just Pell.' Caeru held out a hand to Velaxis who came forward to take it. He appeared slightly defensive. 'And you, Vel, have many things to tell me,' Caeru said. 'I always knew you were a horse of the darker variety, but you've exceeded my imaginings. The hints you've given me in mind touch are intriguing. I want to know the rest!'

'I vowed a long time ago to find your son,' Velaxis said. 'I never forget a promise, even if I haven't voiced it aloud.'

Cal took Caeru's arm. 'I think you should take everyhar to your apartments, Rue. Have you told Pell anything?'

Caeru shook his head. 'Not yet.'

'Then I'll go and see him, tell him what to expect.'

'What about the element of surprise?' Thiede asked.

'Outside the city, it sounded like a good idea,' Cal replied. 'But if there is any surprise to be registered, only I should witness it.'

'I think I should come with you,' Thiede said.

Cal raised a hand. 'No. I must do this alone.'

Thiede inclined his head, although he didn't appear too pleased. 'As you wish.'

Cal ran up the rest of the steps and disappeared through the great doors.

'Come with me,' Caeru said, in a bright tone. 'I'll get my staff to prepare you the best breakfast you've ever eaten.'

Pellaz was already up, having been disturbed from sleep by nagging dreams, which had left him exhausted. Geburael had been staying in a bedroom of the Tigron's apartments that was reserved for staff, though never used. Nothing had been stated overtly between Tigron and high-son, but it was accepted that Geburael had moved in, even if only temporarily. Pellaz presumed this was because Phaonica was situated more conveniently than the prison house. Geburael had lost no time in exploring the city of his family. Pellaz knew he couldn't discuss anything personal with Geburael, because if he did, his high-son might take umbrage and bolt. He seemed intent on finding excuses to be affronted. He was like a skittish, high-spirited colt, and needed careful handling. Pellaz was surprised that he was not more impatient with this behaviour, since he wouldn't have tolerated it in Loki.

Geburael spent every day with Abrimel, and Pellaz made no comment. Sometimes he'd come back from the prison house and go directly to his room, where he'd eat his dinner. Then he'd disappear into the city until the early hours of the morning, all without uttering a word to Pellaz. Geburael had quickly discovered he could charge drinks, meals and other purchases to the Phaonica account. Again, Pellaz said nothing. Not yet. Once the dark, poisonous storm that he felt massing on the horizon had passed, Geburael's conduct could be addressed. For now, all Pellaz wanted was his high-son in Immanion. If that meant the har racked up huge bills in the nightclubs of the city, so be it. Pellaz thought it a small price to pay. In some ways, it was gratifying that Geburael was making friends and actually having a social life, since it must be completely new to him. It would be interesting to hear what he thought about it all, but Pellaz knew that any frank discussion with Geburael was unlikely.

Geburael traipsed into the Tigron's dining room just as Pellaz was drinking his second cup of coffee. It was a miserable day. In the sky beyond the long windows, seagulls were tossed like scraps of rag upon the air; too white against the sullen grey.

Geburael yawned and threw himself into a chair next to Pellaz, who sat as always at the head of the table.

'Good night, last night?' Pellaz asked, hoping the question didn't sound too sarcastic.

'Mmm.' Geburael helped himself to a bread roll, which lay in a basket that had come fresh from the palace bakery. He tore this apart and stuffed it into his mouth.

'You're up early,' Pellaz said.

'Something's happening,' Geburael said.

'What do you think that is?'

'I don't know. It doesn't feel bad exactly, but it woke me.'

'Have some coffee.'

Just as Geburael was slopping coffee over the pristine tablecloth, Cal came into the room, still wearing his travelling clothes. Pellaz stood up at once. 'Cal, thank the dehara! Where have you been?'

Cal raised his hands, his gaze fixed on Geburael. 'Busy,' he said. 'Who's this?'

'This is Geburael,' Pellaz answered. 'Abrimel's son.'

Cal came forward quickly. 'And Loki?' he asked. 'You took Loki, didn't you?'

'He's not here,' Geburael said. 'And yes, I did take him.'

Cal glanced at Pellaz. 'Clearly, a lot has happened while I've been away!' He sat down opposite Geburael. 'So, what are you doing here? Where have you been hiding Loki?'

Geburael's voice was surly. 'You should ask *him...*' he jerked his head at Pellaz, '...if you want to know why I'm here. Loki is, I presume, in a realm called Thanatep.'

'Ah, Thanatep!' Cal said. 'Now that's interesting.'

'Abrimel, Rue and I were searching for Loki in the Otherlanes,' Pellaz said. 'Peridot helped us get this one instead. Geburael has been trying to find Loki for us. It's a long story.' Pellaz narrowed his eyes at Cal. 'How do *you* know about Thanatep, anyway?'

'Sit down,' Cal said.

Pellaz did so, his eyes never leaving Cal's face.

'I heard about it from our son, Darquiel,' Cal said. 'I found him, Pell. I found our lost pearl.'

Pell's jaw dropped open. 'What? Where? When?' He screwed up his face. 'Oh, why am I surprised? I suspected something like this. Tell me everything.'

Cal smiled uncertainly. 'You'll hear it all soon. How angry are you with me, on a scale of one to ten?'

Pellaz shook his head. 'Angry? Hardly that. I'm resigned.'

'I have to see him,' Geburael announced.

Cal gave Geburael a contemplative stare. 'Darq's with Rue,' he said to Pellaz. 'We'll go to him soon. I just wanted to tell you first, Pell. I didn't want it to be too much of a shock.'

Pellaz took Cal's hands in his own, shook them. 'Why didn't you contact me?' he asked. 'Why do you just disappear and go off doing things on your own? This is as important to me as to you. What's he like? Where did Thiede hide him?' He realised he probably shouldn't be talking so openly in front of Geburael, but couldn't help himself.

Cal raised Pell's hands to his lips, kissed them. 'Hush. There's another thing you should know.'

'For Aru's sake, what?'

'Thiede is here too. He's come back to us, Pell.'

Pellaz withdrew his hands from Cal's grasp and pressed them against his eyes for the briefest moment, then he was on his feet again. 'Geburael, come with us,' he said.

For once, Geburael did not drag his feet.

When Pellaz laid eyes on Darquiel for the first time, every other har present in the room became mere blurred outlines. Darquiel shone. Pellaz saw in him vestiges of his own lost youth and hints of an inner sadness that was deeper than any petty considerations of mundane life. Pellaz knew that feeling, even if it stole over him only rarely. It was concern for the world and all hara upon it, and misery for the harm that some still did to others, mimicking earlier human ways. Pellaz also knew, from the briefest of inspections, that Darquiel himself was probably as yet unaware of what he felt inside. *I'm looking at our true heir,* Pellaz thought. *We were right to make him, whatever it cost. He's literally our hope for the future.*

Darquiel had stood up from his chair next to Caeru. Pellaz approached him and saw many different feelings and thoughts cross his son's eyes: awe, wariness, excitement, fear, relief. Pellaz took his hands. He saw the flecks of gold in Darquiel's black eyes, and the threads of it in his hair. He was a creature of light and dark, possessing the beauty of all his parents, the best parts of each.

'I can see,' Pellaz said, straining to keep his voice level and light, 'that this moment has indeed been worth waiting for. Darquiel, I don't have the words to express what I feel, but I trust you sense my heart.'

Darquiel closed his eyes briefly. 'May I touch you?'

Pellaz opened his arms. He held Darquiel close, aware keenly how he'd never felt this way for either of his other sons. He was glad then that Loki was not present, and this reminded him who was. He pulled away. Thiede had come to stand beside him.

'So, the rogue returns,' Pellaz said. 'Are you the champion in our hour of need, Thiede?'

Thiede grinned. 'No. I'm an aged relative who wishes to retire into his old apartment here.'

Pellaz laughed. 'You'll *never* be aged, Thiede. Don't ever try to pull that one with us.' He indicated Geburael, who was still standing at the threshold, his expression unreadable. 'This is Geburael, son of Abrimel. Slowly, the Aralisians are coming together again.'

Pellaz sensed Darquiel tense. He sent his son a brief mind touch, gratified at how easy it was to make contact. *Are you afraid of him? Don't be.*

They wish me harm, Darquiel replied instantly. *He works for the Hashmallim. Forgive me, I must tell you that.*

Pellaz sent a stream of soothing energy in his son's direction, and put within it the message that if anyhar tried to harm Darq in Phaonica they would have the Tigron to get past first. *I know his history, but he's here now. Things are changing.*

Can I speak to you alone?

Soon.

'I've ordered breakfast,' Caeru said, into the silence that accompanied this brief unspoken conversation.

'Good idea,' Cal said. 'We can sit around a table and get acquainted, like civilised creatures.'

'I'll summon Raven and Terez,' Pellaz said. He laughed. 'I'm almost tempted to drag Snake and Cobweb over from Galhea although it'll be the middle of the night in Megalithica.'

'Oh, save that treat,' Cal said. 'Don't even summon Terez and Raven. We should keep it a small gathering today. We have a lot of ground to cover and too many voices will make it difficult. Socializing should come later.'

'You're right,' Pellaz said. 'This is unlike me. I feel strangely euphoric!'

'There is one other who should be here,' Thiede said abruptly.

'Who?' Pellaz asked him.

'Isn't it obvious? Abrimel.'

There was a moment's silence, during which Caeru shot Pellaz a sharp glance. 'I don't think he'd want to be here,' Pellaz said.

'Whether he does or not, he should be present,' Thiede argued mildly. 'Let me bring him. Where is he?'

'He's in confinement,' Pellaz said. 'Really, Thiede, I don't think…'

'Be quiet. My autocratic days are over, but allow me this one last demand.'

Pellaz considered for a moment. He wondered what the likelihood was of Geburael and Abrimel slithering off into the Otherlanes, with manic laughter, and a host of evil intentions. Unexpectedly, Geburael came to the Tigron's side. 'I'll vouch for him,' he said. 'He won't try to escape.'

Pellaz fixed Geburael with a stare. 'And you?'

'I wish to speak to Darquiel,' Geburael said. 'Believe me, I'm not going anywhere just yet.'

Everyhar continued their breakfast while Thiede went to fetch Abrimel. Darq's mind was in a spin. He could barely keep his eyes off Pellaz, who was the most beautiful creature he'd ever seen or could imagine. The Tigron's beauty was more than skin deep too. No wonder Darq's parents were legends among Wraeththukind. Velaxis had absented himself before Pellaz arrived, perhaps understandably. Nohar had objected to him leaving. Occasionally, during the conversation, which Pellaz and Cal deliberately kept light, Darq's eyes would be scalded by the intense gaze of Geburael. Darq could see into the har as if a spiritual light shone through him. He was Loki's lover. He was suspicious of Darq and thought the worst of him. He was preparing to reveal Darq for what he believed he was. Darq was not at all happy to be sitting at breakfast with a har whose hostling had wanted to kill him.

But any shadowy emanations from Darq's surakin were kept at a distance by the love of his parents. Caeru was like summer sunlight, an open door into a beautiful landscape. There was no way Darq could be anything but comfortable in Caeru's presence. He might veer strongly towards a soume aspect, but he had a she-cat's instinct to protect his young. If Pellaz and Cal were prepared to protect Darq, then so was Caeru, and when the sheaths came off his claws, he would be an unexpected force to be reckoned with. *I am blessed,* Darq thought, and the only thing that marred this gathering, apart from the hot murky presence of Geburael, was that Tava'edzen wasn't there to share it, nor all those who'd been a part of Darq's childhood and adolescence, including Phade; a realisation that surprised Darq.

Thiede returned after about half an hour, bringing Abrimel with him. He was, of course, much older than Darq, nearer in age to his parents than to his brothers. Life had not been kind to him, Darq could see that. But Abrimel politely inclined his head to Darq when he was introduced and gave him a brief wry smile. *He's not all bad,* Darq thought. *Whatever he's done.*

The meal was over and it was time for serious discussion. Before Darquiel related his own story to the gathering, Pellaz gave everyhar an account of what had occurred in Shaa Lemul. Listening to it, Darquiel became conscious that he was somehow reassured. He wasn't sure why this was so, but perhaps it was because somehar else was confirming some of the extraordinary things Darq had learned from Divozenky. When Pellaz finished speaking, he asked that nohar questioned him until they'd heard what Darquiel had to say.

'Where shall I begin?' Darq asked nervously.

'Tell us everything,' Pellaz said. 'We're in no rush. We want to know about you.'

Darq drew in his breath. 'OK.' He grinned uncertainly at Cal and Thiede. 'You've both heard all this before, but…'

'I have no objection to hearing it all again,' Cal said. 'This time, I want *more* details.'

Darq sent him a quick mind touch. *You won't get that. Not here! You want lurid details? We talk privately.*

Cal responded instantly. *Oh, we will!*

Darq related the main points of his life story again, this time with more temerity. He was conscious of Pellaz's stern view of Velaxis for a start, and there was also the uncomfortable dynamic of the shamed

Abrimel to deal with, not to mention the hot scrutiny of Geburael, who appeared to think that Darquiel might sprout horns and breathe fire at any moment.

Darq took comfort from the fact that his parents had welcomed him freely and with genuine relief to have him back among them. Not once throughout his admittedly short life so far had he ever considered how they might have felt about his abduction. The excision of his pearl was a wound that had never truly healed. The Aralisians had done something special and new to create him, and he was to them a miracle. He knew they did not feel quite the same way about Loki, no matter how much they loved him, and their feelings for Abrimel were difficult to intuit. He had been dragged from prison for this reunion, but surely this would only be acid in his throat; seeing how another son of the family was regarded so favourably. For this reason, Darq found himself addressing Abrimel more than anyhar else. In a subtle way, he was trying to apologise for being preferred. He didn't care what Abrimel thought of him, but was strangely moved to care about what Abrimel thought of himself.

At the end of his story, Darq simply grimaced and displayed his palms, his eyes upon Abrimel's face. He would wait for reactions.

Everyhar began talking at once, but Abrimel regarded Darquiel steadily. When he spoke, his voice was soft, but somehow it managed to silence every other har in the room. 'Geb and I have spoken in great depth about you over the past week,' he said. 'When you made your desperate call into the ethers, you were heard. Geburael heard you, even though at the time he was in Thanatep. He and Loki heard from the Hashmallim that you were a threat – an abomination, to use their words. They said you would become a tyrant. Geburael said to me he'd only know whether this was true once he'd met you. Now, his voice should be heard.'

There was a silence as all eyes turned to Geburael. Darq's mouth went dry. This was Geburael's moment. He wondered how his surakin would use it.

'His life force is different to any other har's,' Geburael said. He'd considered that opening remark carefully, Darq could tell.

'Of course it is,' Pellaz said in an even tone. 'That doesn't make him a danger.'

'What do you see, Geb?' Caeru asked. 'Speak honestly.' He was obviously of the impression that nothing dark could stain the wondrous soul of his son.

'It's my talent,' Geburael said to Darq, by way of explanation. He narrowed his eyes. 'I don't see bad in you, Darquiel. In fact, I see very little other than surface beauty. You hide a lot inside yourself.'

'That's not intentional,' Darq said crisply. 'Do you wish to establish mind touch? I'm quite prepared to allow you in deeper, if that will prove my *innocence*.' He could not keep a sting from his voice.

'I've not been able to read you, Darquiel,' Geburael said, 'as Velaxis hasn't been able to, nor Thiede. Perhaps they blind themselves to this fact, because they have their own plans for you, and emotions are involved, but you're a sealed tomb to them.'

'Thank you, Geburael,' Pellaz said. 'Your assessment was interesting.'

'But true,' Cal said.

Pellaz shot him a dark glance.

Cal shrugged. 'But it is. Believe me, I don't see that as an aberration.' He smiled at Darq. 'I admire it. Because of how he is, he can communicate with entities beyond our understanding or perception. Aren't we all overlooking this most salient fact? This is obviously why you were driven to create him, Pell.'

Pellaz nodded. 'That makes sense. So, what do we do now? How does Darquiel end this conflict around us?'

'There is no conflict,' Darquiel said.

Pellaz raised his eyebrows.

Darq shrugged. 'Well there isn't, not for you. There is for me. I have to combat whatever the Hashmallim have done to Loki. It's not my responsibility to reactivate Thanatep, and we have to hope those involved in the task will be successful. My job is to safeguard the resources of our realm, but first I have the personal issue with Loki to resolve. I bear no ill will towards him. He's my brother. I want to undo what's been done to him.'

'Darquiel,' Thiede said, 'we can't assume Ta Ke and Lileem will automatically succeed. Given our combined strengths, we should attempt to assist them. I think you're focusing too much on Loki. He is only a har. Look at the broader picture. If Thanatep isn't reactivated, the Hashmallim can still do as they please. That might mean you'd always have to be on your guard.'

'Do you think we should speak with the *sedim*?' Pellaz asked Thiede.

Thiede sighed through his nose. 'If we don't, they'll simply have their agents crawling around Phaonica. Pell, you, Darquiel and I should do this.'

Darq had no desire to confer with the *sedim*. Instinctively, he distrusted them.

'There's something else you should consider,' Geburael said.

'Yes?' Pellaz asked him.

'Darquiel says there is no conflict. I disagree. Well, it's not a matter of conflict, but of interests. Before you speak to the *sedim,* in my opinion you should be sure whether you still wish them to harvest this realm.'

'We'd hardly want the alternative,' Pellaz said.

Geburael leaned back lazily in his seat. 'Why? Isn't it obvious that if Darquiel wasn't set against the Aasp, the Hashmallim would not regard him as a threat? Isn't that what you want, your *unusual* son to be safe? You should speak to representatives from both sides. Whatever you think of the Aasp, the fact is that the Zehk would prefer to stifle Wraeththu's advancement. Personal issues aside, are the Zehk really what you want for the world?' He looked again at Darquiel. 'What does the world itself want, for that matter?'

Darq was surprised by the eloquence of Geburael's speech. He wondered if he'd underestimated the har. 'She's left that decision to us,' he said. 'I doubt the Hashmallim are willing to speak to me, in any case. I had to face the murderous wrath they've put in Loki. Once Thanatep is reactivated, both factions will have to abide by the contracts. The Thanadrim passed guardianship of earth to us. I don't think either the Zehk or the Aasp would have that much influence over us afterwards. We might not have the benefit of their superior knowledge to evolve, but we could do it ourselves, naturally. Are you still loyal to the Hashmallim, Geburael?'

'I'm loyal only to myself and those I love,' Geburael answered, smiling icily.

'Then do what's best for them,' Darquiel said shortly. 'And if that puts us on opposing sides, so be it.'

'Stop it,' Cal said. 'We're going round in circles. Let's just concentrate on Loki for now.'

'I know what has to be done,' Darq said, looking Geburael straight in the eye.

'Tell me,' Geburael said.

At that moment, Darq realised he didn't want to speak aloud. What he had to say was for Geburael's ears alone, and now everyhar in the room was quiet, waiting for him to speak. 'I think, maybe, you should return to Thanatep.' And at the same time, he sent an arrow of thought: *There is more we should discuss.*

Geburael regarded him steadily. 'I've tried, Darquiel. The Aasp are now taking more precautions regarding security.'

'That avenue is closed to us,' Pellaz said. 'I think perhaps I should summon Galdra back from Freygard.' He glanced at Cal. 'What do you think?'

'You should try to work with him, yes,' Cal said. 'You should do whatever you can.'

'There's little more we can discuss now,' Thiede said. 'We know that the Hashmallim might well use Loki to move on Darq, and we should be prepared. I still think we should try to give Lileem our assistance, but...' He raised his arms. 'How we do that, I'm not sure yet. I'll have to think about it. What do you think, Bree?'

Abrimel appeared to have been lost in private thought and was clearly surprised Thiede had addressed him. 'Perhaps you should discuss these matters in the Hegalion.'

Thiede rolled his eyes. 'Your personal thoughts, Bree. Come on!'

'I have no idea. All I can say is that I think both the Hashmallim and the *sedim* are untrustworthy.' Abrimel pulled down the corners of his mouth. 'What difference does it make what I think?'

'You've been invited here,' Pellaz said, 'so what you say makes a difference.'

'Thank you, father,' Abrimel said coldly. 'In that case, I stand by whatever my chesnari thinks.'

Pellaz ducked his head from side to side. 'Well, I don't disagree with Ponclast's thoughts.'

Caeru put his hands on the table in a businesslike gesture. 'Big concerns aside, we should let this rest now. I want to show Darquiel around Phaonica, and then take him into the city. Does anyhar have an objection to that?'

'No,' Pellaz said. He smiled at Darquiel. 'This must all be overwhelming for you. Take some time to find your feet. We'll meet again later.'

'I'll return Abrimel to his accommodation,' Thiede said. 'I'd like to spend some time with you, Bree, if you've no objection.'

'Not really,' Abrimel said. 'I'm quite interested in hearing about your life since I last saw you.'

'That's settled, then,' Pellaz said. 'Today, I have to inform our beloved Hegemony of recent developments. Of you all, I have the least enviable task.'

Immanion was an impressive city, but as Darquiel explored it with his hostling, his mind was only half on his environment. He wanted desperately to see Geburael again, and this time alone. Fortunately, he already knew how to behave affably while feeling in turmoil. He did not think that Caeru suspected his attention was anywhere but on the wondrous sights he was being shown.

'Every har in Immanion will throw themselves at your feet,' Caeru said. They were walking through one of the market districts, palace security unobtrusively in tow. Darq noticed he and his hostling were attracting a lot of attention from hara in the street, but because these hara were Gelaming, they were discreet about it.

'Looking at everyhar here, I doubt that,' Darq said. 'They are far too composed to throw themselves anywhere.'

Caeru chuckled. 'Perhaps, but you have to be the most beautiful creature ever born. You'll be fighting off admirers all your life.'

'I already have a chesnari,' Darq said.

Caeru frowned at him. 'Oh? But you're so young.'

Darq shrugged. 'It just happened.'

'Who is it? Why didn't he come here with you?'

Darq paused for several seconds. He already knew that Caeru's feelings for him were the most intense he had ever encountered. It was frightening, because his awareness of it brought a responsibility that he had never thought he would feel.

'Please answer me,' Caeru said. He sounded afraid.

'All right. He was a leader of the Uigenna, and now lives in Anakhai. His name is Tava'edzen, but he used to be Manticker. He doesn't want to leave Anakhai. That's it.'

Caeru stopped walking and tugged on his son's arm. 'Darquiel! No! Now I wish I hadn't asked. Manticker, as in Manticker the Seventy? You can't be serious.'

'I am. He's different now. Cal met him. He's my love, Rue. Hara in Immanion will have to accept that.'

Caeru had gone very pale. 'You didn't mention any of this back in Phaonica.'

'Of course I didn't. I knew what the reaction would be.'

'Do you intend to return to Anakhai to live with him?'

'I don't know.' Darq took hold of Caeru's hands. 'Please don't worry about it. You're not going to lose me again, I promise.'

'I couldn't bear it,' Caeru said. He took a deep breath. 'If you go back to Anakhai, I'd have to come with you.'

They both laughed and continued their walk, but an uncomfortable feeling stole into Darq's heart. Very soon, he would confront Loki and no matter what Cal or anyhar else thought, it would be a fight. He hoped he could keep his promise to his hostling. If he should die, he had no doubt it would kill Caeru too.

Throughout the day, Darq was simply waiting for the evening. He presumed Geburael would be at the meal and that they might get the opportunity to speak in private. Caeru had insisted that Darq take up residence in his apartments, so after their walk Darq was forced to pretend he cared about which rooms he took. Caeru's affection and enthusiasm were endearing, but he was beginning to get on Darq's nerves a little. A great deal of fuss was made over what Darq should wear to dinner; again, a subject in which Darq had little interest. Caeru brought his dresser, his hairdresser and his beautician to Darq's bedroom, all of whom were clearly itching to get their fingers on him.

'Line your eyes with kohl,' Rue advised, standing behind Darq as he sat glaring at himself in his dressing table mirror. 'Perhaps some golden dust upon your eyelids.'

'For Aru's sake, why?' Darq snapped. 'I'm fine as I am.'

'Oh…' Caeru sounded wounded.

Darq felt guilty and relented. 'Sorry, do what you like. Just don't make me look…' He shrugged. 'I just want to look like me.'

Caeru hugged him from behind and kissed him on the side of the head. 'Forgive me, Darq. I just want you to have everything, I suppose. Even Cal, whose idea of dressing up is to run cold water over his head for some minutes, wears kohl. It makes your eyes stand out.'

'What, on stalks?' Darq couldn't help laughing.

Caeru clicked his fingers and a dresser swooped forward, holding out a garment of sumptuous fabric that spilled from his arms. 'How about this outfit in dark green?' Caeru asked. 'It's almost black, but there are gold threads in the material too.'

'Fine.' Darq sighed. 'Will this take much longer?'

Caeru shook his head. 'I'm afraid there's too much of Cal in you. You should want to look good tonight. Members of the Hegemony will be there.'

Darq's fear was that Caeru would make him look ridiculous. He cared a lot that Geburael shouldn't see him that way.

Eventually, after what had felt like a mighty battle over the minutiae of his appearance, Darq accompanied Caeru to the Tigron's apartments. As Caeru had warned, the dining room was full, and hara were no longer discreet about submitting Darq to close inspection. He was introduced to so many, he couldn't remember their names. He met new members of his family, such as Raven and Terez, and was asked dozens of questions he was too tired to answer. His face hurt from smiling.

At one point, before they sat down to eat, Pellaz came up to Darq and drew him aside. 'You're bearing up well,' he said. 'I can see you enjoy this kind of function as much as I do, which is to say not very much. Keep smiling. You can plead exhaustion and leave after we've eaten.'

Darq smiled gratefully. 'Thanks. I won't have to do this sort of thing all the time, will I?'

Pellaz raised an eyebrow. 'Sadly, yes, you will. It's your fate, Darq. You're Aralisian. But you'll learn how to cope with it.'

Darq sighed dismally and thought longingly of Anakhai. 'Is Geburael here yet?'

Pellaz scanned the room. 'No, but that's not unusual. Why?'

Darq experienced a moment of envy that his surakin wasn't forced to attend the gathering. 'I just wondered.'

'He's your own age, of course,' Pellaz said. 'You'll meet others, Darq. You'll soon have a host of friends, and you can be picky about who you let close.'

At that moment, Darq could think of nothing more tedious than having to consort with Gelaming hara his own age. He imagined them to be preening creatures to a har. What would they do all night? Talk about makeup and clothes? His heart slumped. Had he gone through everything in Anakhai just to reach this point? It seemed farcical.

'I don't want to stay in Immanion all the time,' he said and took a deep breath. 'I have a chesnari in Anakhai.'

Pellaz regarded him steadily. 'Cal has spoken to me about that,' he said. 'He's your first love, Darq, this Tava'edzen. A chesna bond takes time to develop. What you feel is something else. I'm not denigrating your feelings, and I think you should live them to the full while you have them. It might be that you and this har will remain together, or you might not. I'll not stand in your way, in either case. I know what it's like when others tell you how you should feel.'

'Thank you,' Darq said. 'I thought you might disapprove.'

Pellaz laughed. 'I'm the last one who should disapprove of controversial choices in matters of the heart, or of how young you might be when they take a hold.' He put a hand on Darq's shoulder. 'Enjoy yourself. I wish you well.'

'Come with me to Anakhai some time,' Darq said. 'I want you to meet Tava.'

Pellaz stroked his son's face. 'I'd like that.' He paused. 'Do you want to go somewhere we can talk alone soon?'

Darq shook his head. 'Not tonight, if you don't mind. I can hardly think straight.'

'Well, when you're ready, just come to me.'

'I will. I want to.' What Darq didn't say was that he wanted to speak to Geburael first.

But Geburael did not put in an appearance that evening at all, which in some ways Darq found puzzling. He knew Geburael was interested in him, if only to prove Darq really was some kind of demon. Hadn't he intuited what Darq wanted to speak to him about? If he hadn't, he wasn't the har Darq had decided he was. But perhaps it was a deliberate ploy on Geburael's part to keep away.

Darq was also aware that he was being watched carefully by Cal and Velaxis. He hoped he was only being paranoid and they hadn't worked out what he planned to do. Eventually, as Pellaz had promised, Darq was able to plead exhaustion and leave the gathering. Unfortunately, Caeru insisted on escorting him back to his rooms.

'Everyhar thinks you're amazing,' Caeru said. They were walking along one of the high galleries that led between the different wings of the palace. The lighting was dim, and the corridor seemed endless.

Darq grunted in response. 'Where was Geburael tonight?' he asked.

'Oh, he goes his own way,' Caeru answered, a little coldly. 'He's in love with Loki, it's obvious. Draw your own conclusions as to his absence.'

'I don't want anyhar to feel pushed out because of me,' Darq said. 'I can't be bothered to deal with senseless enmities.'

'You're our true son,' Caeru said.

'So are the others.'

Caeru sighed. 'Abrimel, yes of course, but… I should tell you about Loki's parentage, Darq. It's complicated.'

Once Darq knew the facts he realised that Loki had even more reason to resent him than he'd imagined. Was having family always this messy for hara? He yearned to return to the winter stillness of Anakhai and the haven of Tava'edzen's arms. But he must deny himself that. He wouldn't return there until everything was resolved; only then he could feel justified in rewarding himself.

When they reached the doors to Caeru's apartments, and the guards on duty had admitted them, Caeru said, 'Do you want to come for a final drink with me before bedtime, Darq?'

Darq screwed up his face. 'Not really, Rue. I'm feeling har-drowned, if you know what I mean. No offence, but I need time alone to unwind. Thanks, anyway.'

Caeru hugged him. 'I quite understand. See you at breakfast, then.'

Alone in his bedroom, Darq sat on the edge of his bed and rubbed his face slowly. His head was aching. *Geburael, come to me!*

He extended his senses and was sure that Geburael had heard the call, because he felt a slight flex in the ethers that suggested attention, but the har didn't respond. This was ridiculous. Darq could also sense other disciplined minds scanning the vicinity. Perhaps that was a customary security measure in Phaonica, but he was wary of transmitting too forceful a mindcall, because then it could be picked up easily. A soft touch caressed his mind. *Darquiel...* It wasn't Geburael. Darq shuddered. He suspected it was a *sedu*.

Geburael, come now, or I'll come and find you. You want Loki safe? I know how to accomplish that.

It wasn't exactly the truth, but at least had the required effect. After only a few moments, the shadows in a corner of the room condensed and shivered, and then Geburael stepped out of them. He was in fact quite dressed up, which suggested to Darq that his surakin had been in two minds about whether to attend the dinner party or not.

'At last!' Darq said. 'Are you avoiding me?'

Geburael shrugged. Like Darq, he was dressed in deepest green, which was an amusing coincidence. His hair hung loose over his breast. 'What do you want with me?'

Darq could see no point in dissembling. 'I want us to go to Thanatep,' he said. 'Together.'

Geburael grimaced, folded his arms. 'I told you, I can't get back there. I tried taking Pellaz with me. It won't work.'

'Yes, it will... with me.'

Geburael sneered. 'The Hashmallim will kill you.'

'Or you will? Isn't that right?' Darq stood up, gestured at himself. 'Come and try it.'

Geburael didn't move. 'You could be everything the Hashmallim say you are.'

'Then come and find out. Come on. What are you waiting for?'

Geburael flared his nostrils. 'Is this what you want? You want us to fight?'

Darq laughed. 'No! I can simply see your mind, Geburael. You can't protect your thoughts from me. The Hashmallim are right to fear me.'

'I won't take you to them,' Geburael said.

Darq could tell the har was on the point of creating a portal to leave the room and projected his will firmly. It was like a hand closing over Geburael's intentions.

'No,' Darq said. 'Don't run. It has to be done. You have to help me get to Thanatep. It is destiny. Maybe Loki will kill me, or maybe I'll kill him. Maybe we'll all die together, or there might even be a happy ending. Who knows? But you must help me end it, Geburael.'

'You're unnatural,' Geburael hissed.

'Maybe so, but I exist.' Darq sighed. 'I don't want us to fight. Listen.

If I can, when this is over, I'll pull those thorns for you. I can take the taint of Gebaddon from you completely.'

Geburael bared his teeth. 'How dare you! You have no right to pry so deep.'

Darq shrugged. 'I know. But don't you want to be like a normal har? It bothers you that Loki might still find your *unusual* trait disturbing. I can help you, but you must help me first.'

Geburael took a step forward, fists clenched at his sides. 'Will you just shut up? Stay out of my mind.'

Darq raised his hands. 'I'm out! Well? What's your answer? Don't you want Loki back to normal too?'

Geburael exhaled slowly. 'All right. I'll help you. But if you try to hurt Loki, I *will* kill you, even if it takes the last breath in my body.'

Darq gestured to his surakin. 'Come. It's up to us. Nohar else can do a thing.'

Geburael placed his hands over Darq's. What Darq sensed in him was not the wistful longings and hot passions like those he'd sensed in Zira and Amelza. Geburael was full of sorrow, because even though he and Loki had become close, Loki still thought that part of Geburael was contaminated. 'Loki is a fool,' Darq said softly. 'Doesn't he realise that his own love for you would remove this taint he despises so much?'

Geburael shook his head. 'Don't speak of it. We have work to do.'

Chapter Thirty-One

Lileem sometimes felt tremors from above, as if Thanatep were flexing muscles that were stiff from long disuse. She spent most of her time exploring Thannaril Below, which was vast. She wandered through towering empty apartment buildings that were like something from a narcotic dream. The people had left so much behind; their clothes, their tools, even their letters. Some homes were jungles, just like the greenhouses. Mechanisms in the buildings had continued to nurture houseplants after the owners had left.

While Lileem roamed the city, Ta Ke remained sitting on the strange black throne in his work area. He appeared to be doing nothing, although Lileem knew his mind was attempting not only to re-establish communication with his tower but to rebuild it. Ta Ke had wept the first time he'd done this. Mutandis was crippled and he felt its pain.

'How will you rebuild it without going to the surface?' Lileem asked.

'The way it was created initially,' Ta Ke replied. 'Through sound.'

'Won't anyone on the surface notice it's rebuilding?'

Ta Ke made an airy gesture. 'I'll do what I can to disguise the process.'

But it all appeared to be taking too long. Lileem was starting to feel impatient. She sensed some kind of deadline approaching.

Then she ran smack into it. It happened as she was walking in one of the farms, between tall trellises that were overgrown with rampant vines hung with swollen purple fruit. Without warning, the ground shook, and she was thrown from her feet. This was far more than the slight tremors she sometimes felt. Leaves and fruit rained down upon her. She had to curl up into a ball to protect her head. Once the tremor subsided, she scrambled to her feet and ran at once to Ta Ke. The Thanad had been disturbed from his meditations and was prowling round his workroom, his eyes feverish.

'What was that?' Lileem demanded. 'Something's happening above us.'

Ta Ke picked up a small vitreous sphere of indefinable purpose, which had fallen from one of the tables. 'A portal opened,' he said. There was a trace of blood at the edge of one of his nostrils. 'It took some effort by whoever was responsible. Basically, they had to punch a hole through some well-constructed defences.'

Lileem scraped back her hair; it was still full of leaf bits. 'Who came? Can you tell?'

Ta Ke wiped his nose with the back of one hand, stared in some astonishment at the blood he found. 'I'm not sure. Not Aasp, or their agents. That's all I could tell.'

'Ta Ke, I want to go up there!'

The Thanad frowned. 'No, you mustn't. That would be the worst folly. You have no idea what's happening up there.'

'Exactly!'

Ta Ke considered for a moment, then shook his head. 'No, no, I can't permit it. I'm so close to a breakthrough. Nothing must threaten that.'

'But what if whatever's up there is a danger to the tower? You have to let me investigate. I'll be careful. Help me make a portal, so I emerge somewhere discreet.'

Ta Ke stared at her for some moments. 'Very well,' he said. 'But there's no need to create a portal. I can show you how to travel up through Mutandis.'

Geburael had neither lied nor exaggerated when he'd spoken of being unable to return to Thanatep. He was quite open about the fact that he considered his Otherlanes travelling ability to be second to none. He intimated to Darq that he thought the Hashmallim believed he'd defected to the *sedim* and now they wanted to keep him out of Thanatep, perhaps for obvious reasons.

'That may be so,' Darq said. 'But I really believe we can get in there if we do it together. It's a gut feeling I have. I have to obey it.'

Even with this focused intention, Darquiel and Geburael still had an immense struggle to break into Thanatep. Darq could perceive the realm beyond the Otherlanes, but whenever he and Geburael tried to create a portal, an invisible solid wall sprang up to obstruct it. It was only by repeatedly bombarding a specific point with intention and energy that eventually the barrier began to weaken. It was exhausting work, not least because hara are vulnerable in the Otherlanes. Parasites are drawn whenever they perceive weakness. They hovered at the edges of Darq's perception, waiting to strike. It was almost impossible to keep up his guard and assault the barrier at the same time.

We need more power, Darq told Geburael. *It's rebuilding itself almost as quickly as we can break it down.*

Geburael's response was an enraged cry in Darq's mind. *I'm tired of this! We can't keep it up. They won't keep us out any longer! Believe it, and throw out every bit of energy you still have.*

They directed a final searing blast of will at the weakest spot and for a moment Darq thought it hadn't worked and they'd have to abandon their plan. Then suddenly, the barrier broke and disgorged them, almost like expelling a nauseating irritant. They were falling from the sky, perhaps from five feet above the ground, into the stark realm of Thanatep.

Darquiel landed heavily on top of Geburael, who expressed a sharp cry of agony. For some moments, neither of them moved and then Darquiel crawled away. He scanned himself for broken bones or other injuries and was relieved to find none. 'Geburael, are you all right?'

Geburael hauled himself into a sitting position. 'Barely.' He was rubbing one wrist.

'Is that broken?'

Geburael shook his head. 'Hurts, but no, just twisted.'

Darq got to his feet. They were perhaps half a mile away from the city of broken towers, which lay at the bottom of a long slope. It was an amazing place, beautiful in its strangeness, but Darq could perceive no sign of life. 'Where will Loki be?' he asked Geburael.

Geburael also stood up. 'In his tower, or in the Otherlanes with Zikael… he could be anywhere.'

'Well, let's go and look for him.'

'What do you intend to do when we find him?'

Darq had no idea, but realised Geburael needed an answer. 'Talk. What else? I'm here with *you*. That must count for something.'

Geburael looked around himself. 'Keep on the lookout for Thanax. They're inhabitants of this realm, and sometimes dangerous. Loki seems to have an empathy with them, but I wouldn't recommend getting too close.'

'What do they look like?'

'I'll tell you about them,' Geburael said. He indicated a path that led slightly to the west. 'We'll follow this trail. I don't think we should enter the city head on. Diablo is there too. I'll leave you in a safe place and go to find Loki.'

As they followed the path that skirted Thannaril, Geburael related to Darq all that he and Loki had learned of the Thanax, details that had been left out of the discussions in Immanion.

'Shouldn't you have told hara about this?' Darq asked. 'I mean, if these creatures are failed inceptions and so on…'

'Darquiel,' Geburael said firmly, 'this is a side issue.'

'Though probably not to the Thanax,' Darq insisted.

'Then *you* sort it out, once you've given us all a happy ending.'

Darq flared his nostrils. 'I'll certainly not forget it.' He paused.

'Lileem and the Thanad must be in Thannaril Below. After the *happy ending*, as you put it, we should try to contact them. You know how to get down there.'

Geburael nodded, frowning slightly. 'I suppose so. You're assuming Loki will be open to what you've got to say. I wouldn't count on that.'

'I don't think he's stupid,' Darq said. 'He'll surely listen to reason, whatever's been done to him. I believe I can reach him. I have to believe it.'

Geburael merely sighed.

Loki sat meditating at the summit of Ninzini. Zikael had given him power, even if it was so alien he could barely understand it. His whole being was focused upon destroying the brother he'd been told was an abomination. He would do this thing, and he would find a way to get Geburael back.

His trance was disturbed by a mind touch from Diablo. Loki opened his eyes and saw that Diablo was also with him physically, only a few feet away.

'It's nearly time,' Diablo said. Ever since Geburael had gone, Diablo had been different with Loki. His behaviour could not be called kindly exactly, but there was a new empathy between the two of them. He didn't even appear so freakish to Loki now.

'How do you know?' Loki asked.

'I received a communication,' Diablo answered. 'The abomination is with your family. They have embraced him.'

'What?' Loki's voice was a rasp.

Diablo sat down opposite Loki, who couldn't help thinking that if circumstances had been very different, Diablo could have been more like Geburael was. He felt a pang of sympathy for this har who'd been born in the poisoned realm of Gebaddon. 'Demons are often very beautiful,' Diablo said. 'The Aralisians admire surface beauty and, in this case, have been seduced by it.'

'What of Geburael?' Loki asked. He could tell that Diablo was thinking of Geburael.

'He's with them too,' Diablo said, 'but he'll bring the demon here for you, Loki. I feel them approaching, like a hot wind, full of stinging sand. You must be ready.'

'I am,' Loki said simply. He stood up.

Diablo also rose to his feet and took hold of Loki's hands. 'You won't be fighting alone,' he said. 'Use my senses. Use my strength. They are yours to draw upon.'

Diablo leaned close and Loki realised the har meant to share breath with him. He had a feeling that Diablo might never have done this before. Somewhere deep inside himself, he was shocked that he was willing to comply with Diablo's wish, but he wrapped his arms around Diablo's cold thin body and pulled him close. What lay in Diablo's breath wasn't cold, though, it was unnatural heat. It poured into Loki's flesh, invading every cell. It was a roar in his head; a hurricane scouring his inner landscape. It filled him with strength so vital and beyond compassion he lost himself to it.

Loki pulled his head away from Diablo's. 'More than this,' he panted. 'Give me more. Is there time?'

Diablo smiled grimly, one hand running purposefully down Loki's back. 'I'm pleasantly surprised by you, Loki har Aralis,' he said. 'Yes, there's time.'

Darq and Geburael had reached the shadow of the outermost tower of Thannaril Above. Darq could feel strange energies wheeling around him, like invisible flying fish with huge diaphanous tails. He felt light-headed. Geburael put a hand on Darq's right arm and pointed to one of the towers with his free hand. 'Go in there. It's empty. Wait for me.'

Darq didn't like the idea of waiting, but could see the sense in Geburael's suggestion. 'All right. Try not to take too long.'

Geburael grunted in response and jogged off between the clustering towers.

Darq examined the edifice before him for some moments and then walked up the worn steps to the entranceway, some fifteen feet above the ground. He felt he was being observed. Thannaril was too silent for his liking, because the silence didn't really indicate emptiness; something other than that. At the threshold to the tower, a dark red lizard-like creature regarded Darq with intelligent eyes. After a moment, it sped off down the steps. Darq went inside.

He could tell at once that a very faint residue of power remained in this place. He walked around the circular room, touching the walls. As he did so, a weak vibration shivered up his arm. He came to a flight of stone steps that led to the next floor. There was something about the uninviting black hole of the room above that called to him. He began to mount the steps, one hand still touching the wall. Something was waiting for him up there; a revelation.

Darq had no sooner set foot on the dusty floorboards at the top of the steps when a powerful force hit him full in the chest. He would have been thrown back down the steps if he hadn't willed himself to fall to the side. He rolled over, on his feet in an instant, his body held in a defensive crouch. Something was in there with him, but it was invisible to him, and neither could he gain any information about it with his inner sight. He calmed his breath, mustered his strength in the way that Ookami had taught him. If another assault came, he'd be ready for it.

Unfortunately, the next blow came from behind and caught him full in the back of the head. Darq was thrown to his knees; red lights pulsed in his eyes. He realised that whoever or whatever was attacking him was darting in and out of the Otherlanes. Warmth ran down his face; his head was bleeding. *Hashmallim!* He thought. But they were playing with him. If they'd wanted to, they could have killed him outright.

He directed healing energy into the wound to stem the flow of blood, and drew his strength in around him like a shield. At the same time, he extended his perception to observe Otherlanes portals forming. He had to move into a kind of quick time to be faster than whatever came for him. He perceived it then, a pale blur flashing past him. There was a further flicker of movement, which he focused his perceptions to identify; a weapon. It looked like a metal bar. He whipped out a hand and grabbed hold of it, swinging all of his weight into the movement. Whoever or whatever held the weapon would be thrown off balance. A body slammed onto the floor beside him, and rolled over several times before it came to rest, stunned.

Darq felt a jolt in his flesh. His assailant was Loki. Darq recognised the pale hair, the face too like Cal's, which was bizarre considering Cal wasn't really his father. But Loki's inner essence had somehow changed. Darq could feel no sense of familiarity. What had the Hashmallim done to him, and what was he doing here, at this precise moment? Darq wondered if Geburael had betrayed him and had simply told Loki where to find him.

Loki was still only for an instant. Before Darq could even say his brother's name, he was faced with another attack. Loki moved unbelievably fast; undoubtedly the results of Hashmallim training. He pushed Darq backwards until they were up against the far wall. Loki's face was a snarling mask. His hands were round Darq's throat, pressing it with an iron grasp. Hostile energy streamed from those hands; the intention to explode arteries and shred the heart. Darq could barely fend him off. He sent an arrow of crippling energy into Loki's eyes and in the brief lessening of Loki's grip managed to free himself. He knew it was impossible to negotiate with this har. Loki didn't utter a word, not even a threat or an insult. He was a single purpose; a killing machine.

Darq ran to the stairs, hurtled down them. He intended to get outside, give himself enough space to clear his head. He had to formulate a strategy to incapacitate Loki. It was impossible to do that in the face of such mindless aggression.

Loki attacked him again before he reached the entrance. Darq sent a loud message: *Stop!* But it was ignored. He realised that part of his defences must be to stop caring whether he hurt Loki or not. He had to survive.

Uttering a hoarse cry of anger, Darq stopped defending himself and fought back. He fought with his fists and his feet, but also his intention. He projected himself into the place where his mind had been throughout his training. He was stronger than Loki; he had to be.

In Phaonica, Cal awoke from sleep and sat up in bed, the covers falling from his body. The room was utterly without light; not even the soft sheen of the lamps from the city below penetrated the murk. He could see nothing, not even Pellaz, who he could tell still slept on beside him, breathing deeply and evenly. Earlier, they had dared to think that everything might turn out all right, that danger would pass, that Darquiel was the shining herald of a new, more enlightened, age.

Pellaz had asked Cal to come to him after the dinner party and, from the mere glance Pell had given him, Cal had been waiting all evening for the party to end. Part of him had been concerned about Darquiel; he had sensed their son had private plans. But mainly he'd wanted to see what lay behind the look in Pell's eyes. He quickly found out. Perhaps for the first time since he'd come to Immanion, Cal had felt that Pellaz had given himself fully, without cares of the past marring their union. It was as if Darquiel's return had healed ancient wounds, and brought soothing awareness.

The sweet oblivion of aruna had lasted for several hours, until both Cal and Pellaz had fallen asleep. But now Cal knew, in the deepest fibres of his body, that everything was not all right, and that passion can be a brightly-painted veil. He could feel it in the unnatural dark; he could feel it in the listening stillness.

'What?' he said aloud.

In the distance, he heard wolves lamenting. His skin prickled. There were no wolves around Immanion.

'What?'

A figure appeared before him, limned in a soft radiance. It hung at the end of the bed, like a vision of an angel. It was Tava'edzen. 'Go to him,' Tava'edzen said. 'You must go at once.'

Cal opened his mouth to speak, ask a question, but then his body flinched sharply, and he found he was waking from a dream. He opened his eyes and the room was dimly lit by a lamp on a table near the door. Cal swallowed. His mouth was dry. He glanced at Pellaz, who was lying on his stomach, covered by the shawl of his hair. Cal carefully got out of bed and reached for his clothes.

Dressed, he padded from the room and went to Pell's office. Tava'edzen must have been referring to Darquiel, and at first Cal was in two minds whether to go directly to his son's room in the Tigrina's apartments or not. But his instincts advised him he should investigate first, while the essence of the dream was still strong and vital. If Tava'edzen was attempting to contact him, he should act upon it without delay. And Cal intended to work alone: he didn't consider waking Pellaz or contacting Velaxis or Thiede. He composed himself on the floor and focused his intention upon Anakhai. The ethers were disturbed; not as badly as when Ponclast had been freed from Gebaddon all those years ago, but certainly not how they usually were. Cal perceived a faint strand of awareness at the end of the shining cord of his will. Should he go to Anakhai through the Otherlanes? Before he could make a decision about this, Tava'edzen made an extraordinary effort to contact him, because the message, when it came, was clear: *Go to Thanatep. Darq is in danger, terrible danger.*

Cal knew he must keep this dialogue to the point. He could find out how Tava'edzen knew this information later. *It's difficult to break into that realm. Is the danger coming from there? Shall I send Darq to you for safety?*

Too late. He's in Thanatep.

Cal was so surprised by this, it nearly severed his contact. The little fool!

The barrier has been breached, Tava'edzen told him. *You'll be able to get through.*

Against his usual instincts, Cal made an offer: *Come with me,* he said urgently. *I can come to Anakhai swiftly and collect you.*

Tava'edzen's connection began to waver, but Cal could feel the har pouring all of his will into maintaining it. He was in awe of the Nezreka's force, but then, of course, he had once been the legendary Manticker. *No.* Tava'edzen told him. *Unable. I'll add my strength to yours. Only you can go.*

Give me guidance.

I'll try. Go now. Hurry.

Cal ended the contact and leapt to his feet. He closed his eyes, opened a portal.

To Darquiel, his conflict with Loki had become utterly surreal. They were fighting as spiritual creatures, no longer exactly in their own bodies. They tumbled and leapt and soared into the heart of Thannaril Above, where the tower of Mutandis shuddered to emanations from Below. Darq and Loki shrieked like maddened angels, tearing at the etheric fabric of each other's beings. Personality was lost. All that existed was the essence of the conflict: one will against another. And in that elemental fight, so the towers suffered. Their fragile, untended stones began to crumble, buffeted by hurricanes of hostile force.

For a few moments, Darq came to his senses, outside of himself. There below, huddled against the wall of a tower, was Geburael, his face set in an expression of horror. Darq could see that the har had not helped initiate this fight.

His senses zoomed out. All around the city, attenuated spectral shapes were converging from the outer lands. They must be Thanax, drawn by the heat of the event. Darq realised a dreadful truth. This was what the Aasp had wanted all along - Darquiel and Loki har Aralis in battle. They were both the products of unusual conceptions, possessed of abilities and awareness few other hara owned. Their conflict would destroy what was left of Thannaril, the heart of Thanatep, and then no creature alive could reactivate the towers.

Even as Darq realised this, he was powerless to stop the inevitable. It could only be a fight to the death. With this realisation, he snapped back into the moment. He was an angel of devastation.

In Thannaril Below, Ta Ke writhed upon his black throne. He was so close to breakthrough, so close. If only he had others to help him, but destiny had decreed he must work alone. A sphere of energy was forming in Mutandis, which was the initial requirement for reactivating the towers. Ta Ke projected every shred of strength he possessed into its creation. Blood streamed from his nostrils and his tightly-closed eyes. His body shook fiercely. Above him, through the strength of his will, and the pure sounds he could direct from the heart of the universe, Mutandis was rebuilding itself, atom by atom. And now this terrible maelstrom had come, tearing apart all the painstaking work Ta Ke had done. He cried out in desolation.

Lileem emerged from Mutandis to find herself in the heart of a storm of hatred. The air was full of the groan and thunder of cracking stone. For some moments, she was disorientated and her first instinct was to flee back to the base of the tower and hide in Thannaril Below. Then she noticed a young har crouched against the outer wall of Mutandis, his hands over his head to protect himself from flying debris. Ducking the bouncing chunks of stone, she went to his side, pulled his hands from his face. 'What's happening?' she yelled. Her words were blown away from her mouth; she wasn't sure he'd heard her.

The har stared at her; his eyes full of hopelessness. 'They fight,' he mouthed.

It was obvious to Lileem that she and this har couldn't remain outside. She took hold of his clothes and dragged him into the relative shelter of the tower. They were both panting like exhausted dogs. 'Who are you?' Lileem demanded.

'Geburael har Teraghast,' said the har. He had a cut on his forehead and now wiped blood from his eyes. 'And you?'

'Lileem... Kamagrian...' She had no idea if he'd know of her or her kind.

But Geburael nodded. 'I know of you. You know my hostling, Ponclast.'

Lileem smiled sardonically. 'Small world... or rather multiplicity of worlds! What a strange way for us to meet.'

Geburael grimaced. 'I know you were in the city below. Have you just come up through the tower?'

'Yes. What the hell's going on?'

'The Aralisians are fighting,' Geburael said. 'Loki and Darquiel, sons of the Tigron.'

Lileem leapt to her feet. 'What? Why? We have to stop them.'

'You can't,' Geburael said. He coughed. 'I think it's meant to be.'

'I don't care!' Lileem cried. 'They're tearing this place apart and that mustn't happen. Ta Ke has nearly finished working on Mutandis. Get up, Geburael! You must help me stop this fight!'

Geburael made a helpless sound. 'You can't stop it; they're like elementals. I couldn't even get near them. Believe me, I want to stop it as much as you do, but it's hopeless.' He moaned, pressed his face against his hands. 'I brought Darquiel here. It's my fault.'

Lileem couldn't be bothered to comfort or argue with him. Neither was she prepared to stand by and do nothing. She ran out into the storm of stone and dust.

In a pool of calm within the madness, Diablo sat in Apanage and shivered. He could feel the fabric of the towers starting to unravel around him. It would soon be over. As he'd lain in Loki's arms, he had perceived Darquiel and Geburael break into Thanatep and, even at the height of aruna, had informed Zikael by mind touch at once. Geburael was a fool. He would need severe chastising later. But at least he had brought the abomination to this realm, albeit for the wrong reasons. As for Loki, he had turned out well. Diablo had been a soume-well of dark strength for him; Loki was now more than ready to take on the abomination and complete something that had been started so long ago. When it was over, Diablo would consume the remains, as should have happened back in the beginning. Ponclast hadn't been strong enough. He'd been weak, ravaged by his exile in Gebaddon. No, it was up to his sons to finish his business for him.

Diablo rocked back and forth, pouring all of his spite and meanness into Loki's conditioned mind. *Tear. Rend asunder. Destroy.* He was the battery of Loki's power and he was inexhaustible. Not even a demon like Darquiel could stand up to it, for he fought alone.

Tears ran down Diablo's face as waves of hot and cold energy streamed through his flesh. He felt he was Darquiel's complete opposite; dark and shrivelled in places where Darquiel expanded like a sun. This demon was an insult to all who had born and suffered in Gebaddon. He was the Gelaming's ultimate sneer at those they had oppressed and disempowered. For a brief moment, Diablo cursed the fact that the Hashmallim had given him awareness. When he'd been ignorant, almost like an animal, there hadn't been so much pain. *You must help me end it now,* Diablo thought. *Let me destroy their shining avatar as they destroyed all our hopes.* He sensed Zikael observing him, but the Hashmal wouldn't manifest now. What was happening was a ritual that only hara could perform. It was Diablo's job to make sure it produced the right results. He cared nothing for the desires of the Hashmallim and the Aasp; he saw them merely as tools to achieve his own ends.

Then Diablo sensed a new presence. At first, he ignored it as inconsequential, until a voice penetrated his mind. *I should have finished you off at Fulminir, you scrap of offal!*

Diablo opened his eyes, while the major part of his being still concentrated on feeding Loki with power. He saw a tall pale shape standing before him, which gradually swam into focus. It was the har who had prevented him from killing Pellaz har Aralis at Fulminir, the har Diablo had occasionally observed throughout the years; he had planned all kinds of satisfying ends for him. Calanthe.

Diablo snarled; a low venomous sound.

'Please,' said Cal in a reasonable tone, displaying his palms. '*Do* take me on, Diablo.'

This was just a minor irritation. Diablo knew he had the power of the Hashmallim at his disposal and through them the mightier power of the Aasp, those shadowy entities he had never encountered. It would take very little concentration or effort to squash this Wraeththu fly. There was no point in attempting to communicate. He leapt up and lunged forward, but Cal did not attack or defend himself. He merely grabbed hold of Diablo's arms and hauled him into the Otherlanes.

Diablo screeched in fury as the hectic vortex enveloped them. He fought with all his strength, but Cal was like vapor, enfolding him totally. They tumbled in and out of the Otherlanes, through multiple realms and lightless voids. Cal was taking Diablo further and further from Thanatep, so that his connection with Loki was broken. Diablo could no longer perceive what was happening in that realm. He gave up trying to attack the essence that held him, and concentrated simply on escaping it, but Cal was too strong, too driven. He was driven by love, not hate, and Diablo found, too late, that his bitterness was no match for it.

After what seemed like many days had passed, but was perhaps only minutes in the strange time-sense of the Otherlanes, Cal dragged Diablo into an uninhabited realm of bare, wind-scoured mountains. It was perhaps a temporary area, much like the one Zikael had created for Loki, that had been formed for a purpose and then abandoned.

Diablo thought he might have a chance to escape now, but Cal, trained by Thiede himself, put restrictions upon the fabric of the realm, so that portals could not be formed until the wards were removed. Cal released Diablo and folded his arms.

Diablo sank to his knees. He needed to restore his strength before he could attempt to vanquish this Gelaming warrior, for that was how he perceived Cal.

'I could leave you here,' Cal said, 'like your hostling was left in Gebaddon. Would that be a wise choice, do you think?'

Diablo did not answer. He was putting every shred of effort into preventing his body from trembling.

'Diablo, anger and hatred are a sour code to live by,' Cal said. 'I know. Can you be redeemed? I could take you to your hostling. You could live with him, if you'd only give up your purpose to destroy us.'

For a few mournful moments, Diablo saw the truth in Cal's words. He saw himself with Ponclast again. His heart hung in the balance. But it was short-lived. He could not live as a Gelaming prisoner, whether it was with Ponclast or not. His head snapped up. 'I'd rather die than submit to your will!' With these words, he leapt for Cal's throat, meaning to tear it open with his teeth.

Cal staggered back with the impact, then flowed with it. Diablo found himself falling forwards as Cal virtually floated back to the ground. He looked into Cal's deep violet eyes, which were serene. 'It's your choice,' Cal said. He flexed his body and became partly etheric. He plunged his right hand into Diablo's chest and closed his fingers around the heart. 'You poor wretch,' Cal said. 'Did you really think you could be stronger than me? I end it now, Diablo. I release you. If you ever return, do so in light.'

For a brief moment before the darkness took him, Diablo cried out like a desperate harling. The horror and loneliness of his existence crashed through him. Ultimately, he gave himself willingly.

At the very moment that Cal stopped Diablo's heart, Darq's mind found a quiet place in the middle of madness, and here he regained his identity. He saw what was happening and the senselessness of it. While his etheric body still battled with Loki, his inner mind came to a quiet realisation: he did not have to win this fight to be victorious. The way to win was simply to end it.

All around Thanatep, immense presences hung in the sky like pulsing vessels of light. They were beyond form; the Aasp and the Zehk. Darq observed them and could only perceive them as greedy, selfish beings. They were spectators, gloatingly watching the destruction of the realm that had been designed to control them. They were without compassion or feeling of any kind. All they craved was the essence of realms and the nourishment it gave them.

A soft feminine voice flowed through Darq's being: *become yourself again*. It was Divozenky.

Darq paused for a moment longer, gazing around his inner self, with a wistful fondness. *I like the har that I am. Thank you, Divozenky.* Then he willed himself back into a corporeal form. He would not be an instrument in the schemes of selfish beings.

The moment Darq made this decision, he was free of Loki's assault in the upper air. He did not fall to the ground, but merely found himself there, kneeling before Mutandis. For some seconds, the realm was utterly still. Darq was entirely surrounded by a ring of Thanax, but was not afraid of them. Although they were strange to look upon, they possessed their own beauty; attenuated forms with smoking eyes and waving hair. They might have come to feed, but they were not hostile to him, as Loki was. They also had a keen interest in what was happening, even if they didn't know why they did. Darq could sense that more and more of them were being attracted to this site. Did they have a purpose or were they only witnesses? Their ghostly hair waved in the soft breezes of Thanatep, their smoking eyes were fixed upon him.

Darq shifted his body and was conscious of the deep wounds to his flesh, but he could feel no pain. His head became filled with a high-pitched sound like the song of a celestial choir. There were *sedim* near too, and Hashmallim with their fearsome *teraphim.* The Aasp and the Zehk hung silent and immense above them all.

Darq heard the sound of footsteps, and looked up to see that Loki had also reassumed his physical form and now stood panting before him. Loki's eyes were wide, their expression manic. For just a short time, there was peace between them. Loki's whole body shook. His clothes were torn, his body rent by deep gouges. He wiped his mouth with the back of one trembling hand, his hair hanging over his eyes. Like Darq, he was covered in blood. Darq saw before him a vision of Cal, but a Cal he had never known, who had murder in his heart.

Loki never took his eyes from Darq's. He pulled a knife from his belt and turned the blade round and around in his hands. So far, he hadn't used it.

Above them, the amorphous entities expressed a wave of irritation. Why had the fight ceased? The towers still stood; the work was not finished.

Darquiel opened his arms. He felt faint from loss of blood but had to hang on to consciousness. 'Do you still want to kill me, brother?'

Loki's posture became stooped. 'You're not my brother. You're a wrongness. I can *see* it.' He uttered a low growl and a few stones tumbled down from Mutandis.

'I won't fight you, Loki,' Darquiel said. 'It's what they want.'

'I don't want to fight you either,' Loki said. 'I just have to do what has to be done. You must be unmade.'

Darq sensed then a feeling of concern from the vast incorporeal entities around them. This was not the way it was supposed to proceed. Emanations of violent emotion pulsed out from them, with the intent to feed Loki and Darq's animosity. Darq would not let it into him. He wished there was another way for this to end, but there wasn't. He knew it in his being. He knew it from Divozenky. And he was not afraid.

'Tell Caeru,' he said, 'that I demanded this from you.'

Loki appeared uncertain for a moment. Darq could tell it was in his mind to drop the knife.

'No,' Darq said. 'If we do this, they lose all power over us. Trust me.'

Loki raised his arm.

From behind him, a voice cried, 'No!'

Darq saw a har he did not know running towards them, Geburael some distance behind.

To Darquiel, they moved in slow motion. He tore open his shirt. 'Do it now,' he said. 'Loki, you must!'

Loki uttered a sobbing cry and lunged forward. He plunged the blade into Darquiel's chest. It went in to the hilt. For a moment, he gazed into Darq's eyes. Then he pulled out the blade and stabbed again. He would have carried on if Geburael and his companion had not thrown themselves upon him and dragged him back.

Darquiel, who even throughout the assault had managed to keep fairly upright, knelt with his arms outflung, his head back, blood pouring down his body into the dust. He felt no pain and no fear. The tower ahead of him began to bloom with red radiance. It was incredibly beautiful. Through his blurring vision, Darq saw it reconstruct, stone by stone. A crimson beacon blazed at its summit: it was his life force.

The Aasp and the Zehk were confused. Darq could sense it. They conferred among themselves, one faction with another, then began to withdraw. He could see them howling back through the layers of reality, furious with disobedient lesser beings, furious with each other. The *sedim* and the *teraphim* fought, as they often did. It would come, as always, to nothing.

They might be more evolved than us, Darq thought, *but in many ways, we're superior to them.*

Divozenky whispered in his mind, his failing heart. *Hush, my love. Lie back in me. I am with you. I always will be.*

Darquiel surrendered himself to the will of Divozenky. She had always known this would happen.

Chapter Thirty-Two

When Cal returned to Thannaril, he had no idea what he'd find, but had entertained the hope that his destruction of Diablo would have had a positive effect. He was not prepared for what he saw.

Lileem was hunched kneeling on the ground, her hair hanging forward. Darquiel lay in front of her, his head in her lap. All Cal saw at first was the redness; so much blood. He felt faint. He thought of Pellaz, another death a long time ago. That death had driven him mad for many years.

Painfully, he scanned the scene. He saw Loki sitting nearby, his legs splayed out. He held a knife in his reddened hands. He looked mindless.

No, Cal thought. *Not this. It's too cruel.*

Geburael was trying to staunch Darquiel's wounds, but it was clear his efforts weren't helping that much. Cal realised his wondrous son was dying. It was like a replay of ancient tragedies. Pellaz. Orien. This mustn't be. Thoughts flashed through his mind; the possibility of taking Darquiel back to Immanion through the Otherlanes, or doing healing here himself. All of it would take too long.

He fell to his knees beside Lileem. 'I tried,' he said. 'I was too late.'

Lileem turned her face to him, her expression full of anguish.

Darquiel made a faint sound. He reached up with a bloody hand. Cal took hold of it, felt the weakness in its sinews. 'No,' Darq murmured. 'You were exactly on time.'

At that moment, Loki began to scream. It was the cry of a har beyond despair.

'He had to do it,' Darq murmured. 'Don't punish him, father.'

'Geburael,' Cal said. 'Go to Loki.'

Geburael lifted his hands from Darq's chest. 'He did ask Loki to do it. I heard him.'

'Go to him,' Cal said. Loki was not his son by blood. It seemed so unfair he'd been chosen to enact Cal's destiny, to become him at his worst. A tower was alive, but the price had been too great. Anything would have been better than this; slavery to the Aasp or the Zehk.

Geburael went to Loki's side and tentatively touched his shoulder, but it appeared Loki didn't realise he was there. Cal knew exactly how Loki felt. The aftermath of this day would be hideous, but for now they were still in the moment. Cal mustered his strengths. He was different to the har he'd once been.

'Lileem,' Cal said. 'Is there anything you can do for Darquiel?'

'He gave himself,' she answered in a dull voice. 'He's still giving himself and will do until… until he's all gone.' Tears ran down her face. 'Loki did what had to be done, and now he knows what he did.'

Cal put his head in his hands. 'We can't lose them. We can't.'

The ring of Thanax, who had been watching silently, now began to draw closer. Their apparent leader stepped forth from the throng. Cal stared at this peculiar creature. *And what is your part?* he wondered.

'We have to get away from here,' Geburael said urgently. 'The Thanax will feed on this. There are too many of them.'

'No,' said the Thanax leader. He bowed to Cal.

'Cal, Lileem, help me make a portal!' Geburael cried.

Cal raised a hand. 'Hush, Geburael.' He addressed the Thanax. 'What do you have to say to me?'

'I am Atoz.' The Thanax bowed again, touching his own forehead. 'I ask that you allow us to feed on this pain.'

'No!' Geburael yelled. From the edge of his vision, Cal saw that Geburael was attempting to haul Loki into Mutandis. 'Cal, do something. Fight them off.'

Cal looked into the eyes of the Thanax. He glanced also at Lileem, who nodded her head once. From what he knew of this parage, Cal was inclined to trust her instincts. 'Do you know my heart?' he asked the Thanax.

Atoz inclined his head. 'Let us feed.'

Cal got to his feet. 'Very well.'

'Bring Loki to me,' Atoz said.

Cal nodded and turned. Geburael screamed another ragged denial, but Cal took Loki from him. There would have been a struggle, but Lileem wrapped her strong arms around Geburael and held him back.

Loki's head lolled upon his neck. His reason had left him. Cal pulled Loki to his feet, looked into his unfocused eyes. 'Whatever your biological parents, I'm the father of your being,' he said. 'Come back to us, Loki. Your work isn't over.'

Cal guided Loki's staggering steps to where Darquiel lay. As torn as he was, so damaged, Darquiel was still beautiful.

'Make Loki kneel,' Atoz said.

Cal pushed Loki down, but still maintained a grip on his shoulders, directing Agmara energy into him, in the hope it might help. Atoz took hold of one of Loki's hands and placed it upon the knife wounds in Darq's chest. Loki shuddered, made an incoherent sound.

The Thanax joined hands in a vast circle. They threw back their heads and began to sing. It was like the cry of wolves, only softer. They drew closer and closer together, their arms extended.

Cal knew that he should back off. He guided Lileem and Geburael away from the circle, until they could no longer see Loki and Darquiel in its centre.

Geburael was weeping. He thought that the Thanax would take the life force of both Darquiel and Loki. Cal couldn't find the will to comfort him. He wasn't sure what the outcome of the Thanax's interference would be, only that he felt it was right. He also felt there was something else he had to do, but his mind was too numb to work it out.

It was Lileem who knew what to do. She turned round to face Mutandis and stared up at it for some seconds. Then, she reached out and took the hands of both Cal and Geburael. 'Come with me,' she said. Her fingers were slippery with Darquiel's blood. Cal felt relief at her words; he trusted her. Together the three of them went into the tower.

Inside, the light was like that of a radiant sunset. The stones of the tower glistened, and the light made the beads of moisture upon them look like fresh blood. Lileem led the way towards the steps that led to the summit. As they began to climb, Cal became aware of other presences drawing close. He saw them as shadowy figures that walked past him on the steps. There were so many of them. The shadows streamed through him, and each time they did, he sensed a small sphere of radiance within each one. These were hara, or rather the spiritual essence of hara.

By the time, Cal and his companions reached the highest room, a throng was waiting there. They had taken on more substance and Cal was able to identify the astral forms of Thiede, Velaxis, Caeru, Pellaz, Galdra, Terez, Raven, Mima, Flick, Ulaume, Tava'edzen, Swift, Snake and Cobweb, and many more: all those who were part of Wraeththu destiny. They had gathered around a tall and beautifully-wrought silver plinth that supported a large globe of crimson radiance in a nest of glittering wires.

'It's beautiful,' Lileem murmured.

'Pellaz is here,' Geburael said, in a slurred voice.

Cal pointed and said softly. 'So are your parents, look.'

And true enough, Abrimel and Ponclast were within the circle. Cal knew that the beings he saw weren't conscious projections from the hara concerned. Rather, he supposed, they had been conjured by Divozenky from her storehouse of memories. They were representations of significant hara, not the hara themselves. *You're near, aren't you,* Cal thought, directing it at the entity that only Darquiel could properly meet. *I hope you're with Darq. I hope you want to keep him alive.*

And the briefest caress touched his mind, like a tiny curled feather floating down from an invisible bird in the high branches of a tree.

'We're part of this circle,' Cal said to his companions. He squeezed Geburael's hand. 'Let's take our place.'

The ring of hara surrounded the pulsing radiance. Cal knew instinctively what they must do, as did everyhar else. They raised their arms in a single sweeping movement and then, with the intention to feed and empower it, plunged their hands into the centre of the light. Bright gold and orange sparks flew out of it. There was a smell of ozone and a high-pitched whine filled Cal's head. An immense alien energy coursed into his being. He was linked with every other being present and their life force augmented Ta Ke's work and the energy Darquiel had sacrificed for it.

Cal saw within the centre of the sphere the symbol of Pyralis, which was the second level of Ulani. It was the symbol of fire and life. This symbol vibrated for a few moments and then, with an immense realm-shattering roar, a ring of red-gold radiance pulsed out from the sphere. It was strong enough to encompass the whole of Thanatep. Cal's perception extended beyond Mutandis. He saw myriad lights appear throughout the realm as the radiance spread outwards. Myriad towers came to life in thousands of cities.

And as the light touched the Thanax, so night became day. The sun rose over Thanatep for the first time in thousands of years.

Darquiel opened his eyes and saw a dark-haired har leaning over him. Was this a new life? Had he just been born again? He blinked and reached up to touch the face that gazed down on him with such tenderness. 'You have given us life, Darquiel har Aralis,' said this har. 'And we have given it to you.'

Darquiel felt tired, but there was no pain in his body. 'Who are you?'

'Atoz. I was Thanax.'

Darquiel struggled to sit up. Loki was kneeling beside him, his hands plunged between his thighs. They stared at one another for a long minute. Then Loki's face crumpled, like that of a small harling. 'I want to go home,' he said. 'Can we go home?'

'Yes,' Darq said. He reached out and gripped one of his brother's wrists. 'I think we can.'

'I was in your mind,' Loki said. He shook his head. 'I *saw*. Darquiel…' He looked anguished.

'Hush,' Darq said. 'Not now. We succeeded. We're alive.' He tried to get to his feet, but he was still weak and it took great effort.

'Let me help you,' Loki said and took hold of Darq's body.

Once Darq was standing, he leaned upon his brother, who continued to support him. They were surrounded by naked Thanax, but these were no longer spectral creatures. They looked more or less like ordinary hara, if rather gaunt. Around them, Thanatep had changed. The sky was a deep blue and within it blazed a huge sun that brought colour to the world. A cloud of gauzy-winged insects swarmed overhead, dancing like butterflies, as if in mad abandon at the new dawn. In the hills, and among the towers, local creatures were chittering, whistling and croaking. A group of red lizards ran past Darq's feet, with spined ruffs erect around their necks.

'We have never seen this,' Atoz said, making an expansive gesture with both arms. 'Maybe that's why we were drawn here, to wait for this event. You and the sunlight have brought us life. Or maybe we were drawn here simply to be of service to you.'

'What did you do to me?' Darq asked. 'I was dying. I thought I was meant to die.'

'You gave your life to Mutandis,' Atoz said. 'We fed on your pain, and took it away. You lay back in the arms of a being who has more than enough life for a simple creature like you. We simply helped her work.'

'Divozenky,' Darq said. 'I wonder…'

'Wonder what?' Loki asked.

'How much she manipulated events.'

Loki frowned. 'Who is she? Kamagrian?'

Darq shook his head. 'We have a lot to talk about,' he said.

Cal, Lileem and Geburael came out of Mutandis. There were no others with them, because those who had taken part in reviving the tower had now evaporated: Divozenky had taken them back into herself. For some minutes, Cal and his family were allowed the joy of reunion and relief. Perhaps Ta Ke knew this was necessary, because he delayed his emergence from Mutandis.

When he finally stepped forth from the entrance, which was around fifteen feet above the ground, he appeared to be as revitalised as his home realm was. His hair and skin glowed with life. He smiled. He stood upon the top step, behind a new balcony rail, and addressed all those gathered below him. 'The Thanadrim are dead,' he said, his voice ringing far, 'yet Thanatep lives. I thank those who have helped me achieve my aims.' He gestured at the hara below him. 'But Thanatep needs new guardians for her towers, and she has helped create them. Thanax, this is your duty! Once we have had time to discuss the future, I ask that you go to the towers that will call to you, be they near or far. You are the new Thanadrim and there is rebuilding to be done!' He threw up his arms and grinned widely. 'Your cities await you, and they have been waiting for a long time.'

The Thanax, mad with the joy of release, cheered and howled. Darquiel laughed with his companions, because the mood of ecstatic renewal was so infectious.

Cal had to shout to make himself heard. 'Let's go home! Lileem, you're coming with us.'

'Try and stop me!' she yelled.

They joined hands to create a portal, but before it formed, the sky shivered above them. Another portal was opening, and before anyhar could even comment upon it, shapes came out of it in a throng. The Thanax scattered in all directions, perhaps panicked by what they perceived as the return on the Aasp or the Zehk.

Darquiel saw that the new arrivals were in fact *sedim*. They came thundering down into Thannaril in their equine form. There must have been a hundred of them. Some of them were bloodied, as if they'd recently taken part in conflict. Darq could only assume the agents of the factions had squabbled and fought over who got to present themselves here first. His heart sank. He was exhausted. He wanted it all to be over.

'Wonderful,' Cal breathed sarcastically.

One of the *sedim* approached them, and Darq sensed that it was Lurlei, not least because he shone with magnificence beyond physical form. At one moment, he appeared as a horse, the next as a tall creature very similar to a har.

'Darquiel, we meet again.' He spoke aloud, even though his mouth did not move. The sound came from deep within him.

'Go away,' Darq said, rather helplessly. He suspected this feeble command would have no effect.

'Have you come to give us a lift home?' Cal said coldly. 'If not, we've no use for you.'

Lurlei, as a horse, bared his teeth and his ears went back. His head snaked out and his jaw snapped meaningfully. 'Silence, har. My business is with Darquiel, not you.'

At this moment, Ta Ke's voice boomed out from Mutandis. '*Sedim*, you have not obtained my permission to come here. Depart at once.'

Lurlei looked up and assumed a harish shape. He would not have looked out of place in the court of Phaonica. His long hair was tied up in a fashionable Gelaming type of style, and his clothes were robes of costly fabric, stitched with jewels. His eyes were the colour of polished citrines. 'Indeed, I will not!' Lurlei shouted. 'Listen to me, Thanad. I have been sent by my masters to ascertain that the old contract still stands.'

Ta Ke gripped the balcony rail. His eyes appeared furious, even though his tone was level. 'You must negotiate with the creatures of earth. I've learned that Divozenky has become tired of your cavalier attitude to her resources. She has created and appointed her own custodians.'

'She is being wayward,' Lurlei said. 'She should know it is in Wraeththu's interests to remain allied to us.'

Ta Ke shrugged. 'Influencing her decisions is not my concern. I merely abide by them.'

'It *is* your concern,' Lurlei insisted. 'Wraeththu are not yet advanced enough to be responsible for this resource.'

At these words, Cal made a wordless sound of disgust. Darq put a hand on his father's arm. He felt that Ta Ke should speak for Wraeththu now. He suspected Lurlei had more respect for the Thanad than he did for "lower species", whatever arrogant tone he chose to use with the guardian of this realm.

'It is Divozenky's decision,' Ta Ke said. 'Her avatar is Darquiel har Aralis. I suggest you stop being rude and address your remarks to him.'

Lurlei wheeled round and faced Darquiel. He did not appear remotely happy.

Darq bowed his head. 'We *will* speak with you, King Lurlei,' he said. 'And we will speak to the Hashmallim also.'

Lurlei returned briefly to the form of a horse and stamped a foot. 'Darquiel, that is not acceptable. You can't use the resource of your realm yet, so you should allow the standing contract to remain. To do otherwise is to interfere in processes above your understanding.'

'If the essence of our home realm is so *delectable* to you,' Darquiel said, 'it's my thought both factions should learn to share it. We might not be so *advanced*, but I like to think that Wraeththu are learning a lot about co-operation and selflessness. Isn't it sometimes the case that a teacher can learn much from their students?'

Lurlei expressed a snort. 'The Zehk will not take kindly to this.'

'I really don't care,' Darq said. 'Leave us be.'

'Leave you be?' Lurlei laughed. 'And that will include removing the resource we've given you, I suppose? The Gelaming will be able to maintain their control over the tribes without the *sedim,* will they?'

Darq thought it might be quite gratifying to hit that smug beautiful face, but he restrained himself. 'Well, if you do that, then the Hashmallim can teach all hara and parazha how to use the Otherlanes themselves,' he said. 'You don't mind that, I suppose?'

'You're really quite amusing,' Lurlei said. 'A small child stamping his dear little foot in the hope he'll get his own way. Do you have any idea what you're dealing with, Darquiel? You can't order us around, or the Hashmallim for that matter.'

'I have no desire to order you around,' Darq said. 'I'd rather just not *have* you around.'

'That is not going to happen,' Lurlei said. 'We'll not let this rest.'

Darq glanced at Cal, who was smiling delightedly. 'How about this, then?' he said to Lurlei. 'We'll summon you when we've had time to discuss matters.'

Lurlei uttered a disgusted whinnying noise, which sounded amusingly equine, even though his physical shape wasn't. 'Divozenky will regret this. She is mad to invest power in such creatures as you.'

'Take that up with her,' Darq said. He turned to his companions. 'And now, we really are going home.' He smiled at Cal. 'Let's go *now* before the Aasp agents turn up.'

Cal laughed. 'An excellent idea.'

Chapter Thirty-Three

While the debris of Thanatep was cleared up and its former glory restored, Darq and his family had other debris to deal with, of the more personal kind. Rather than be given respite after his ordeal, Darq was plunged into political life in Immanion, and at first he had little time to deal with sensitive issues.

The *sedim* were impatient to enter into negotiations with the guardians of earth, but Darq managed to hold them off. They could wait. He wanted to get to know his new life properly first. Despite Lurlei's threat, Wraeththu did not lose *sedim* support entirely. This was because of a division within the ranks of the *sedim*: those who'd worked and lived with Wraeththu for many years were reluctant to storm off and take umbrage. They had, in effect, become part of the world.

Velaxis said to Darquiel that it was simply a replay of history. 'It's like when the rebel Zehk first came here,' he said. 'There's something about this realm that makes you love it, I suppose.'

'At least your people are safe now,' Darq said. 'I imagine the last concerns of the Zehk are the Krim Sri now. They're too busy being affronted by me.'

Darquiel yearned to return to Anakhai, but knew he should spend some weeks in Immanion first. He allowed himself one brief visit to Tava'edzen, just to tell him all that had happened, and to spend a blissful night ignorant of all cares. He learned that Tava'edzen had worked with the Weavers and the Krim Sri to keep track of his movements, in the event that support might be needed. Darq realised that Tava'edzen was responsible for his success. If Cal hadn't been informed of what was happening, and hadn't taken Diablo out of the equation, things might have ended very differently. Pellaz might think that Darq's love for the Nezreka was a youthful crush, but Darq thought otherwise. He felt, in his heart, he'd never really been a child.

Darq also sent a message to Amelza in Shilalama, to say he would like to visit her in the near future, when things had calmed down. He even contacted Phade and promised to visit Samway as well. It was his intention to take Amelza with him. In an effort to tie up as many loose ends as possible, he asked Thiede to track down Ookami and ask him to come to Immanion. Rather to Darq's surprise, the Ikutama did not refuse this request. Thiede found him quite easily, because he was still in Nezreka.

One evening, Darq went out with Ookami for dinner; just the two of them. Darq thought Ookami would be scornful of anything too grand, so opted to take him to a small tavern near the sea front, where ordinary hara went to dine. Here, they ate lobster by candlelight, and drank the spicy white wine that was produced further down the coast. At first, Darq kept the conversation formal, describing events since he and Ookami had last been together. Then he realised he must speak more personally. 'Are you still angry with me?' he asked.

Ookami regarded him inscrutably for some moments. 'No. I did my work and then others came to replace me.'

Darq reached out to touch Ookami's right arm. 'Never that,' he said. 'You gave me so much. I'm sorry I faded away from you.'

Ookami drank some wine. 'I always knew you had a momentous destiny awaiting you. It would be arrogant of me to be angry about anything. Although…' he ducked his head to one side, '…I'd still like to get my hands on that Velaxis. It's a personal matter. I realise I can't do anything about it.'

'Hmm.' Darq paused. 'I have to ask you, Ookami – that Grissecon you were preparing for; did I ruin it for you? You know what I mean.'

Ookami stared at Darq in silence, and Darq feared what he might say. The Ikutama put down his wine glass very carefully. Then he folded his arms and rested them on the table. 'All right,' he said. 'Before I came to Samway, my teacher told me I should prepare for a Grissecon event. I asked him what it would be for, and he said only that I would know when the time came. I'd assumed it would be with you, and that we'd perform some rite as part of your great destiny, but it wasn't that.' He took another drink of wine, while Darq waited tensely for what he'd say next. 'You really should have gone to Tava'edzen on Natalia night, Darq.'

Darq sighed. 'I know. I simply had fantasies.' He shrugged, gestured. 'You know… I didn't want to be part of a public ritual. I wanted it to be just the two of us, something more meaningful.'

'Which is what you got,' Ookami said. 'Eventually. But the rite of the wolf was part of the pattern. You couldn't bring yourself to do it, because of your feelings, and that was your weakness. I couldn't let that mar your future. So, I took your place. For just a few minutes I became you. I was your avatar and that was my Grissecon. Tava'edzen will tell you the *real* details, one day. I saw what was in his mind. He was hardly aware it was me.'

'Thank you,' Darq said. 'You do understand why I couldn't do it, though?'

'Yes. You're young.' Ookami smiled. 'But like I said, you eventually got what you wanted, and I'm glad you did.'

'No hard feelings?'

Ookami shook his head. 'Not at all.'

Darq summoned the waiter, because the meal was nearly finished and he wanted Ookami to sample the local liqueur. After the har had taken their order, Darq braced himself to address another sensitive topic. 'Do you have plans now?' he asked carelessly.

Ookami sniffed the liqueur and sipped it, then regarded the glass. 'Interesting,' he said. 'As to your question: not particularly. I'll return to my teacher. He might have further work for me.'

Darq took a breath. 'Would you work for me?'

Ookami considered this, then asked, 'In what capacity?'

Darq shrugged. 'I'm not really sure yet. I value your counsel, and I expect I should have security staff. If I must have somehar for that, I'd prefer it to be you.'

Ookami nodded, pulled a face. 'I might not be able to give you more than a couple of years, but if you need me for a while, I'm sure that will be acceptable. I'll have to discuss it with my teacher, of course.'

Darq was flooded with relief. He'd expected he'd have to do more persuading. 'Yes, I understand that. As long as you're happy with the idea.'

'It will be an interesting experience.' Ookami turned the glass in his hands. 'I haven't spent any time in Immanion before. It seems an ideal place to indulge the senses. Occasionally, I allow myself that.' He laughed.

Darq grinned and raised his glass. Ookami did also, and they clinked the glasses together. 'To interesting times,' said Darq.

Darq had intended to speak with Thiede alone concerning certain things that Divozenky had told him, but ultimately decided that Lileem should also be included in the conversation, simply because a lot of what he had to say concerned her. They met at Thiede's apartment in Phaonica. Thiede had spent a couple of weeks refurbishing the rooms, so as to make a completely new home. Now, it was an airy abode of simplistic design.

Thiede conducted them into his sitting room, where jewel-coloured tasselled cushions were arranged upon the floor; they were the only ostentatious touch in an otherwise fairly bare yet elegant chamber. The room was at the back of the palace, facing the hills rather than the ocean. The day was overcast, so Thiede had drawn down the window blinds. The room was lit by soft lamplight and sandalwood incense filled the air.

Househara brought out hot spiced wine and thin orange-flavoured biscuits, which they arranged upon a low table as Thiede's guests sat down.

'This is a lovely room,' Lileem said and then laughed. 'How many times have I said *that* over the past few days?'

'You like Immanion?' Thiede asked, handing her a glass of wine held in a silver casing with a handle.

Lileem accepted the cup. 'I do. Very much. But then I like Shilalama too. This room wouldn't be out of place there.'

Thiede smiled. 'Opalexian and I no doubt share a liking for soothing environments.' He gestured at Darq. 'Well, now you're here and you want to talk, so please, let's not waste any more time. We can indulge ourselves in small talk later.'

Darq inclined his head. 'OK.' He turned to Lileem. 'I know how long you've worked in Shaa Lemul and why you kept doing it. You wanted to know about our origins. It's something Thiede also wants to know, and now I can tell you what Divozenky revealed to me about it.'

Lileem's eyes were wide. 'Go on...'

Darq looked at Thiede. 'Wraeththu were created deliberately, as you suspected.'

Thiede nodded, but did not interrupt.

'Opalexian was not the first experiment,' Darq continued, 'but she was the first successful attempt, in that she survived, even if she didn't fulfil all the expectations her creators had had. She *is* unique. You came after her.'

Thiede shifted upon his cushion, rested his chin in one hand. 'So, the most important question: who created us?'

Darq ducked his head. 'I'll explain. The Zehk have always considered humanity to be tainted, because their blood had mingled with the rebel Zehk's. The fact was that humanity's treatment of this world, through the governments and corporations that were controlled by the descendants of the rebels, was affecting Divozenky's essence. The Zehk felt they had to act to preserve this realm from further depredation. Divozenky was somewhat affronted by this, because she's quite capable of taking action herself if things get too bad on her skin, as it were. She felt that humanity, and the Krim Sri too, were simply undergoing a change. It was like puberty; perhaps uncomfortable, but essential. She saw humans as being like teenagers, belligerent and selfish, because that's simply part of growing up.

'But anyway, the Zehk didn't have her perception or patience. They were concerned only about her resources. It was they who subtly influenced a certain scientist to create a new being, what she supposed would be a kind of super human. Falling fertility levels through pollution meant that something had to be done. Certain animals in the wild were already subject to gender alteration. An agent of the Zehk gave this woman the knowledge to create an androgynous being that would be genetically superior to homo sapiens. She and her team unwittingly created the race that would supplant their own kind. She was intoxicated by the knowledge she'd received, but she didn't know everything.'

Thiede nodded. 'It's what I've suspected for a while, almost down to the fine detail.'

Darq drew in his breath, because he wasn't sure how Thiede would feel about what he would say next. 'Your father knew what you were, Thiede. The place where you lived as a child, the facility where your father worked was where the idea for Wraeththu was born.'

Thiede frowned. 'But they took me to doctors and so on. They thought I was a freak.'

'Your mother did,' Darq said. 'She was an unwitting guinea-pig. She thought she simply had fertility treatment, but it was more than that.'

Thiede frowned. 'I see. Of course, this shouldn't matter now…'

Lileem reached out to touch Thiede's arm. 'You're allowed to feel something about this,' she said. 'It must be a shock.'

'I don't know if it's that,' Thiede said. He looked at Darq. 'I ran away, I escaped, so I must have ruined their plans, whoever *they* were.'

Darq shook his head. 'No, Thiede. You might think that you escaped a life you hated, but in reality you were… *released*.'

'Like a virus,' Thiede said. He exhaled slowly. 'I did their work for them. What an astounding revelation.'

There was a silence, which Lileem eventually broke. 'What about Kamagrian?' she asked. 'If Opalexian wasn't the complete success that her creators wanted, then why are there so many of us?'

'That's because Kamagrian is a Wraeththu tribe,' Darq said, 'just like any other.'

Lileem laughed impulsively, then sobered. 'What do you mean?'

Darq gestured at her. 'Well, that's a slight exaggeration. Women can be incepted, by Kamagrian or even hara. I've proved that.'

'But you're different.'

Darq shrugged. 'I know, and the first hara clearly were incapable of incepting females, but things are changing. Not that it's too relevant now, since inceptions have become few. The fact is that an incepted female could turn out to be either har or parage. An incepted male is always har.'

Lileem put her hands to her face. 'I can't believe it. All this time we've been so wrong. How do we tell the difference?'

Darq poured himself more wine. 'Kamagrian lean towards a soume aspect,' he said, 'and certainly have superior psychic abilities to Wraeththu, but essentially they're not that different from hara. A lot of it is down to how individuals see themselves. Kamagrian identify with the soume aspect more, not just physically, but in another more spiritual sense. Divozenky told me that if a har or parage leans more towards one aspect, it shouldn't be seen as wrong, or as being like a human. We'll never be that. We are what we are, and we should be free to express ourselves as we like. There are different spiritual facets to soume and ouana. The terms male and female don't accurately apply to them; we just use them for convenience, because that's what first generation hara understood. It's our job to expand knowledge and experience, to truly embrace our potential.'

Lileem pursed her lips. 'This sounds like paradise to me, but we can't get away from the fact that very strange things happen if a parage takes aruna with a har.'

Darq nodded. 'We'll need to undertake our own experiments,' he said, 'because Divozenky wouldn't tell me everything. She said that she'd give us information about the past, but we should discover the future for ourselves. For that, of course, we'll need Opalexian's co-operation.'

Lileem groaned.

'There is always a downside to every miracle,' Thiede said sardonically. He took a biscuit and bit into it. Darq thought Thiede looked somewhat dazed, which was unusual for him, but perhaps not that surprising, given what he'd heard.

'Kamagrian are not like Opalexian,' Darq said. 'She *is* unique. She's very strong psychically, but as an androgyne, she can't procreate. That was why she was a failure and Thiede wasn't.' He gestured at Thiede. 'Well, I know you haven't actually had harlings yourself, but those you incepted have.' He turned back to Lileem. 'What I'm really glad to tell you is that Kamagrian as a whole are as capable of reproduction as any other har.'

'Are you sure about that?' Lileem asked. 'No parazha have ever had harlings or...' she grinned, '...parazharlings!'

Darq grinned also. 'I don't know about that, but I do know that their views of aruna have been influenced by Opalexian, and she's desired to maintain a certain status quo. Have any of you have actually tried to make pearls?'

Lileem pulled down the corners of her mouth. 'I really can't say. I know *I* haven't thought of it, but that's just me. I'm not exactly the domestic type.'

'Well, when you go to Shilalama, it's something you can discuss with your tribe,' Darq said.

'You can be sure I will!'

Thiede's expression was thoughtful. 'There are political implications in this that it's Wraeththu's job to address,' he said. 'Parazha born to hara shouldn't be cast out or regarded as unnatural.' He looked at Darq. 'This will require education. Hara fear Kamagrian harlings, because they are seen as symbols of reverting to a human state. They'll need to get over that. If a parage is born to a har, it should be her choice whether she leaves her tribe to become Roselane or stays with them. Do you agree, Lileem?'

'In principle,' she said. 'This information is all too new to make such judgments. As you said, it'll require education and discussion. But it presents astounding possibilities, to say the least.'

'Even I can see that it does,' Darq said, 'and I have little knowledge or experience of the situation. As far as I see it, Wraeththu and Kamagrian should work towards making hara understand that parazha aren't freaks but simply a variation.'

Lileem nodded. 'We still can't ignore that a har and a parage can cause striking effects on reality, if they come together physically. As you said, this must be studied, but then I've always thought that. What we need is the freedom and openness to do it. We know more about the Otherlanes now.' She sighed. 'You know, Mima and I always thought we were har. It was others who told us we weren't.' She grimaced. 'Opalexian isn't going to like any of this one little bit, Darq.'

'She'll have to accept it,' Thiede said. 'She can't hide her head in the sand any longer.'

'Well,' Lileem said, 'she was afraid of her parazha taking aruna with hara and then popping out of existence. It wasn't an unreasonable fear, really. To give her the benefit of the doubt, I think she was mainly concerned about our safety.'

'Divozenky spoke to me about you specifically,' Darq said.

Lileem's eyebrows went up. 'Really? What did she say?'

'Just that you are Kamagrian's natural leader.'

Lileem blinked a few times. 'She said that?'

Darq nodded. 'She said that Opalexian should be like Thiede, a spiritual mentor, the highest of hienamas, but leadership should fall to a parage with the proper understanding and capabilities. That's you!

Congratulations.'

Lileem didn't react with embarrassment as Darq expected. 'I know you're right,' she said. 'I *am* the natural archon of Roselane. There were many things I was unhappy with when I lived in Shilalama. I'm not so modest as to pretend I'm not itching to get back there and make changes. But first there's Opalexian to deal with.'

'Oh dear,' Thiede said, smiling, 'does this mean I have to go and talk to her?'

'Perhaps you should,' Lileem said. 'She looks on you as a brother, despite the fact you've always disagreed on things.' She put a hand on Thiede's left arm. 'Will you help me? I'm not sure Opalexian sees herself as being a distanced mentor for her kind. She was always reclusive, but it was clear who held the reins in Roselane.'

'Of course I'll help you,' Thiede said. 'It's about time Opalexian and I overcame our differences. Some fur might fly, but…'

'I think she already knows how things will be,' Darq said. 'Divozenky didn't imply you'd have a problem. You might be surprised when you get back home, Lileem. Opalexian might simply have been waiting for you to return.'

'Hmm, I hope you're right,' Lileem said. 'You didn't see what she was like when I had my little fling with Terez! She's against the idea of parazha and hara being together. Even if she allowed me to lead, she'd still advocate separatism.' She raked her fingers through her hair. 'Well, dealing with her will be part of my job. I can brace myself to confront it. And now I'm armed with information that comes from the greatest source possible; our own world.'

Darquiel felt he was working systematically through a list of jobs that had to be accomplished. He saved the most difficult until last: Loki. They met fairly regularly, which was unavoidable in Phaonica, but did not converse about the one thing they really needed to lay to rest.

Loki wondered if Darq would ever talk about it, and harboured the frightening paranoia that what he'd done would be a monstrous spectre hanging between them for the rest of their lives. He could see how much Pellaz loved Darq, and that was difficult to accept. Loki was no longer the golden harling who'd never had cause to say sorry. He knew, from the moment he'd come back to his senses in Thanatep, that life could never be the same for him again. He felt that hara treated him with wariness now. They were always too jovial around him, as if they were humouring him. Cal was still the same, of course, and often tried to initiate a deep discussion, but Loki couldn't bear the thought of it. He saw the concern in Cal's eyes and hated it. He didn't want pity.

The first thing Loki had had to face on his return to Immanion was a series of tests at the Infirmary to make sure the influence of the Aasp no longer remained in his mind. That was humiliating. He *had* let Zikael influence him. He'd done the very thing he'd vowed he'd never do. He had let his family down. It didn't matter how many times Cal and Caeru reassured him they did not blame him for anything; he blamed himself. Pellaz asked Loki to work for him closely, clearly in an effort to make him feel better, and there were frequent visits to Freygard when he could talk things over with Galdra. But even though Galdra, like Cal, was keen for Loki to open up to him, Loki found it difficult because he felt so ashamed.

Also, Loki could not help but feel he was an insignificant piece of rock in comparison to the blazing sun of harakind that was Darquiel. Maybe his brother was an aberration, as Zikael had insisted, but he was not evil. He was simply a har with greater abilities than most. He could have turned out bad, but he hadn't.

Loki dreamed constantly of the moment he'd plunged the knife into Darq's chest. Darq had asked him to do it, and at the time Loki had partially regained his senses, but another part of him had still been full of hate, and it was this part that had guided the blade. Loki could not forgive himself for that. It was not part of the har he'd wanted to be and he wasn't sure who he was now.

He was surrounded by hara who loved him, and who tried to help him get over the past, but he felt distant from them. He knew this hurt Geburael, who also had grief to deal with, namely his conflicting feelings over the fate of Diablo. Loki knew he should be helping Geburael with that, but hadn't the energy to think about it. They were never intimate. Aruna too had become tainted for Loki. He'd taken aruna with *Diablo*, for Aru's sake. At the time, he'd *wanted* to. Geburael didn't know about this. Nohar did. If Loki's mind even skimmed over that event he felt utter self-loathing.

While struggling with all these issues, Loki was forced to watch as Darq straightened out his life to perfection; getting things in order, finding his place in Immanion, reporting to everyhar what the world wanted. *As if I can compete with that!* Loki thought. Also, he noticed that as the weeks progressed, Geburael spent more time with Darq, presumably because he was better company than Loki now was. Sometimes, Loki felt very jealous of Darq, and then berated himself for that too. Perhaps he should just disappear. Maybe Ponclast and Abrimel needed an assistant in their distant, rarefied realm.

The festival of Rosatide takes place eight weeks after Natalia, and is a time in Immanion for parties and feasting. It is the time when sap begins to rise in the trees and the hold of winter begins to weaken. Caeru had organised a huge event in Phaonica, and had invited the Parasilians from Galhea, who had yet to meet Darquiel. Loki was hardly looking forward to it. He'd be forced to watch, once again, as hara fawned over his brother and listened in awe to his heroic exploits. What could they possibly say to him? 'Oh, you're the one who hated Darq and stabbed him, almost fatally. How lucky that what you did helped him save the world.'

Two days before the event, Loki confronted Caeru in the Tigrina's apartments, and asked if he could be excused from the party; perhaps he could visit Freygard instead. But Caeru was adamant. 'No, Loki. You must be there. Think how it would look otherwise.' He took Loki's face in his hands and kissed him. 'Come on, now. Just relax. We all want you to be there.' He stroked Loki's hair. 'I just wish you'd let us in a little. We love you.'

Loki pulled away. 'All right. I'll *be* there.'

He walked away from Caeru's bewildered concern and went out into the palace gardens. It had been a bright afternoon, but now dusk was approaching. Small white flowers that hara call Eburniel's Tears had begun to sprout in the moist earth beneath the leafless trees. New life. Soon the soft murmur of regrowth would become a glorious shout.

Loki sat down in the rose garden, in a gazebo that was covered in dead climbers. There were no hara around, because the gardeners had already finished work for the day. Loki put his head in his hands and wept. He couldn't imagine how life could improve for him.

Then a soft mind touch caressed his thoughts. *Loki…*

He looked up, wiped his face. Somehar was standing at the entrance to the rose garden, about twenty feet away. He saw that it was Darquiel.

Loki stood up. He meant to go back to the palace by another route. He couldn't face Darq now.

Don't go.

Loki hesitated, then waited while Darq came to him. It was unfair this har was so radiant. In the half-light, his black hair glowed with golden strands. 'The Parasilians are arriving tomorrow,' Darq said. 'You, Geb and I are supposed to be holding a dinner for the second-generation hara. I thought I should come and speak to you about it.'

'Don't worry,' Loki said. 'Our staff will see to it. There's nothing to organise.'

Darq shrugged. 'Well, are there any things I should know?'

Loki grimaced. 'I suppose it might be difficult. Aleeme and Azriel were captured and tortured by Ponclast some years ago. I don't know how they'll react to Geb, but I guess they must already know he'll be here.'

'Hmm, right…'

'Yeah…' There was a silence.

Darq folded his arms and sighed. 'Oh, this is bullshit! You know why I'm here.'

Loki swallowed. 'What do you want to say?'

'Stop beating yourself up, Loki. You were used, brain-washed.'

'I was weak enough to let that happen,' Loki said. 'You wouldn't have been.'

Darq rolled his eyes and laughed. 'What? You think so? Ookami was possessed by Velaxis, and he's one of the most disciplined hara I know. You've no reason to be ashamed, really. Ookami wants to beat six shades of blood out of Vel, and he knows he can't, which really annoys him. But he's forgiven himself. He's just moved beyond it.' Darq paused and suggested carefully: 'Maybe you should talk to him.'

'No,' Loki said. 'I don't want to. Thanks for the concern but…'

'Shut *up*!' Darq said. He took hold of Loki's arms. 'Look, what will it take to stop this?' He shook his brother. 'What? I can't bear it, Loki, and Geb's out of his mind with worry. Stop indulging yourself.'

'Indulging myself?' Loki felt a stirring of anger.

'Well, you are! I bear you no ill will, and neither does anyhar else. The only har who blames you is yourself.'

Loki brushed Darq's hands away roughly. 'You have no idea!' he said. 'How dare you! You know nothing.'

Darq folded his arms again. 'Nohar does, because you don't *say* anything.'

Loki hesitated. He felt words rising within him, like blood from a wound. He realised he wouldn't be able to stop what he'd say next. 'Before I attacked you…' He closed his eyes and spoke quickly. 'I took aruna with Diablo. I let him feed me with his essence, to give me the power to kill you. I became somehar else, somehar foul. I despised Diablo. He repulsed me, yet I did it. I craved it.'

Darq was silent and Loki opened his eyes. 'See! Now you know. Still so forgiving?'

It was fully dark now, yet the delicate cups of Eburniel's Tears still glowed beneath the trees and the moon had begun to rise. Darq sighed. 'Yes, I do see,' he said. 'That must have been…' He shook his head. 'Vile.'

'At the time, it wasn't,' Loki said. 'That's the problem.'

Darq screwed up his face. 'Hmm…' He nodded. 'I understand. I was wrong in what I said about self-indulgence. I'd have trouble with that too.'

'Geb doesn't know,' Loki said.

'You know you have to tell him,' Darq said. 'For you two to be OK again, you have to.'

Loki pushed back his hair from his forehead. 'I'm not sure we can be OK. We weren't exactly OK to start with. Also… well, I'll always be the har who stabbed you in the chest.'

Unexpectedly, Darq laughed. 'Yes, you will. Think about it; it's good that you were. If it had been Geb, hara wouldn't have been so forgiving, I'm sure.'

Loki sighed. 'I suppose so.' He realised then that his heart felt lighter. Perhaps it was simply because he'd squeezed a little poison from it.

'You look better,' Darq said tentatively. 'Has it helped to talk a bit?'

'Yes, yes, it has.'

'Then we should do it more. We're brothers. I want to help, and that isn't patronising, so don't take it that way. It's inconvenient if you're loopy, OK?'

Loki pushed Darq's arm playfully. 'Why does it have to be perfect *you* who makes me feel better? It's not fair. Are you useless at *anything*?'

Darq pulled a face. 'Doing what I'm told?' He linked an arm through one of Loki's. 'Let's go in and find Geb. We could go out for dinner. Then…' He squeezed Loki's arm. 'You can work on just how OK you and Geb can be.'

'It's not going to be that easy,' Loki said.

'I know, but…' Darq smiled. 'We survived. All four of us.'

Loki narrowed his eyes. 'Four of us?'

'You, Geb, Lileem and me. Four second generation hara. In the future, hara will talk about Thanatep, and what we did there, and that we survived.' Darq kissed Loki's cheek. 'That's all that matters.'

Epilogue

Three weeks before Bloomtide, the festival of the Spring Equinox, Pellaz suggested that the Aralisians should go to Freygard together for a brief holiday, as he could see that everyhar needed respite after recent events. The *sedim* who'd remained in Immanion were happy to facilitate travel, as always, but Peridot had vanished from the earthly realm. Pellaz was hurt by this, because they'd been together for so long. If the *sedu* had chosen to remain loyal to his kind, Pellaz could do nothing about it. He'd learn to work with a new *sedu*. Still, it would never be the same.

One of the reasons Pellaz suggested Freygard was because Galdra was always so desperate to see Loki. Galdra had been informed of all events in Thanatep, and was of course pleased that Loki now knew who his father was. At the beginning of the visit, Pellaz met with Galdra alone to discuss Loki's condition.

'He came out of it the worst,' Pellaz said. 'I can't lie to you, Galdra. I'm concerned for him. Geb and Darq are helping him, but it'll take time. I suppose it's understandable.'

'He should stay here for a while,' Galdra said, 'once the rest of you return to Immanion.'

'If he wants to, then yes. I think Geb should stay here with him.'

Galdra grimaced. 'Shouldn't we disapprove of two hara who are so closely related being chesna?'

'I don't think they are that,' Pellaz said. 'But if Geb can help Loki get well, I don't give a damn about their close relationship. And neither should you.' He hesitated. 'I'm here to relax. We all are. I take it we're staying in the house we used here before?'

'If you like it,' Galdra said.

'Good. Raven and Terez can take the younger ones out tonight. I was thinking of having a private party.'

Galdra raised his brows. 'Oh? And who's invited?'

'Rue and Cal will be there,' Pellaz said. 'You will be the only guest.'

'I see.'

'Do you?'

Galdra laughed and took Pellaz in his arms. 'If you're sure.'

'I want it to be this way,' Pellaz said. 'I won't deny how I feel about you anymore, but…'

'I understand,' Galdra said. 'Occasionally, though, I think we should be alone together. You should allow yourself that.'

'Maybe, but I want you to know Cal as I do.'

'Nohar will know him as you do,' Galdra said. 'Is he aware of your plans?'

'I've said nothing, but he'll know. I don't have to tell him.'

'And Rue?'

'Oh, no problem there, trust me!'

Galdra sighed. 'It feels like it was a thousand years ago I first met you. So much has happened. Will we be allowed a happy ending, do you think?'

Pellaz plunged his fingers into Galdra's hair and pulled handfuls of it forward to smell it. 'Mmm,' he murmured, then smiled. 'My friend Flick once said to me that there's no such thing as a happy ending. Life just goes on, and there's always another episode to the story. All we get is peaks and troughs. Let's just enjoy this high shining peak, shall we?'

Cal and Caeru seemed somewhat bemused by the fact they were to take dinner with Galdra that evening, but neither of them argued about it at first. Late in the afternoon, Caeru cornered Pellaz in his bedroom, as he was changing his clothes. The house around them reverberated to the shouts and laughter of other hara preparing to go out for the night. 'I have a strange feeling about this,' Caeru said, his arms folded. 'What is it you want from tonight, Pell?'

Pellaz buttoned his silk velvet shirt, admired himself in the dressing mirror. 'What do you think?'

'I think you'll throw into close proximity a selection of highly combustible and unstable materials,' Caeru answered. 'It's too staged, too convenient. I don't think it'll work.'

Pellaz shrugged. He sat down before the dressing mirror and began to brush out his hair.

Caeru took the brush from his hand and took over the task himself. 'Go carefully,' he said. 'Judge atmospheres. If things go badly, you should have a plan B.'

'If things go badly, you take Galdra off to your scented lair and do what you will with him,' Pellaz said. 'Will that suffice for plan B?'

Caeru laughed, somewhat stiffly. 'I suppose so.'

Galdra arrived after all the other hara had left the house. He brought with him a scent of wood fires, and there were snow crystals melting in his wolf skin coat. Cal had a predatory air about him, which Pellaz watched carefully, but conversation appeared to flow fairly easily.

Househara brought the meal to the dining room, but Pellaz didn't feel much like eating. He drank steadily, observing his companions from the side-lines of the gathering, even though they were all seated closely around a table. Cal told anecdotes, with much gesturing, and Caeru laughed too loudly. Galdra smiled and appeared to be enjoying the stories.

Pellaz found himself remembering the first time he'd met Cal, and how he'd entranced the Cevarro family with his stories then. So much had happened since that time. The beginning of his life almost didn't seem real anymore. Now, after decades of heartbreak, war, anger, bitterness and grief, he had Cal at his side. Surely, he should put Galdra from him. Hadn't he got enough from life? Was he so greedy?

Pellaz realised the others had been watching him when Caeru said, 'Are you with us, Pell?' He stared into Caeru's eyes and saw his consort's concern. Caeru was still unsure about this little party.

'Yes,' Pellaz put down the glass he'd been nursing. The wine within it was now warm. 'I was just mulling over memories, that's all. Very old ones.'

'It is his tendency to brood,' Cal told Galdra in a humorously confidential tone.

Galdra laughed, nodded. 'I know that only too well.'

Pellaz tensed, wondering how Cal would take that remark, but Cal only joined in with the laughter and poured himself and Galdra more wine. 'Lighten up, Pell,' he said. 'We're done with things for the time being. We deserve this holiday. If there's any more to come, let our sons deal with it.'

Galdra raised his glass. 'I'll drink to that.'

'The househara have built a fire in the sitting room,' Caeru said. 'Have you all finished eating? Shall we move there?'

'Yes,' Cal said, getting to his feet and scooping up several untouched wine bottles. 'Let's toast our feet and get mindlessly drunk.'

Cal and Galdra appeared to be more intoxicated than Pellaz and Caeru and had become mildly rowdy. As they threw themselves onto the rugs before the hearth in the sitting room, and Pellaz seated himself on a chair beside them, he thought about how alike they were: they really could be brothers. Galdra was probably younger than Cal's son Tyson, yet he seemed older. Now, they were behaving exactly like brothers, making jokes about members of the Hegemony that weren't really funny, yet for some reason were hilarious to them.

Caeru, sitting opposite Pell, raised his hands and grimaced. He sent a mind touch. *Somehow, I get the feeling we should leave them to it.*

I think you might be right.

Caeru got to his feet and Pellaz did likewise.

Cal stopped laughing and stared up at Pellaz. His hair was falling over his face, so he had to squint. 'Where are you going?'

'Retiring,' Pellaz said. He bowed his head to Galdra. 'Thanks for coming.'

Galdra appeared to sober up quickly. He looked wary. 'It was a pleasure.'

Cal grabbed hold of one of Pell's legs. 'No, you don't,' he said. 'Sit here with us.'

Pellaz staggered as Cal pulled on him. 'Cal…'

'Come here!'

Pellaz turned to Caeru, who raised a hand. 'I'm going,' he said.

'Rue?' Pellaz said. 'Do you have to?'

'Yes. I do. Really.' Caeru waved his hand. 'Good night. Have fun.'

Pellaz stared down at Cal and heard the door to the room close. Cal raised an eyebrow, smiled lazily and leaned back against the chair behind him. What har could resist so beautiful a creature? 'You know what?' Cal said.

'What?' Pellaz dropped down and straddled Cal's lap, conscious of Galdra's cautious scrutiny beside him.

Cal wound a lock of Pell's hair around his hand. 'This is the happy ending. This time, I think it really is.'

Pellaz exhaled through his nose, closed his eyes briefly. 'That would be good.'

Cal pushed Pellaz off him, laid him down between himself and Galdra. 'Imagine your dearest fantasy,' he said, and kissed Pellaz on the mouth. 'It's about to happen.'

In the morning, Pellaz and Galdra were the first downstairs, and sat waiting in the dining room for breakfast. The night had gone better than even Pellaz had expected; he still felt dizzy from it. Images kept replaying upon his mind's eye, and the one that warmed him most was that of when Cal and Galdra had, for some time, forgotten he was with them. Pellaz had realised that Cal actually liked taking aruna with hara with whom he'd been intimate himself. Certain moments between Cal and Galdra had been fairly intense. Pellaz had felt stunned at the time to discover that they felt something for one another. Maybe neither of them knew precisely what it was, but it was feeling, and it wasn't hostile.

Now, in the bright light of morning, Galdra appeared dazed, as if he was shocked at himself. He'd been subjected to the full force of Cal's arunic accomplishments, of course, so reality must be rather hazy for him at the moment. Pellaz thought he should introduce a neutral topic of conversation. 'With all that's been going on,' he said, 'I haven't thought to ask before, but is that weird portal still here in Freygard?'

Galdra nodded. 'Yes. We still don't know where it came from. I thought Geburael or Diablo made it, but I asked Geb and he said he didn't.'

'I know. That's a dangling thread, Galdra. What if it represents another threat?' Pellaz twisted his mouth to the side. 'I think I want to go and look at it today.'

'Shall I come with you?'

'No. I want to go alone. I feel I have to.'

Pellaz walked out to the cliff top, trudging through deep snow. He could feel the portal as a tingle in his flesh, long before he reached it. Within the grove of hawthorns, he saw a pulsing violet glow. What was this thing?

Among the huddling trees, Pellaz sat down on the hard ground. There was little snow in the grove, because the hawthorns clustered so closely together. He extended his senses to examine the portal. His faculties felt highly sensitive, not least because of the previous night's events. But Pellaz knew he must not think of that now. He must penetrate the mystery of this portal. He didn't want anything to spoil the peace that had come to his heart.

Do you never rest, beloved? The voice was familiar in Pell's mind.

He opened his eyes. 'Peridot?'

'Here I am.'

Pellaz turned round and saw a figure silhouetted at the entrance to the grove. It looked like a har, clad in close-fitting garments of animal hide, like a hunter. This figure came towards him. It was a har he'd never seen, a har who looked young, but who had long white hair and whose eyes were golden. 'Do you approve of this form?' the har asked.

'Peridot, is that you?'

'Yes.'

'Why have you changed?'

'Because I can.' Peridot sat down next to Pellaz in front of the portal. 'I can talk to you now.'

'How? Why?'

Peridot hugged his knees. 'I asked Lurlei to grant me - us - this favour and he agreed. I told him how you'd always wanted to speak to me aloud, like hara do.'

'I see,' Pellaz said crisply. 'So, this is a bribe, is it?'

'Lurlei might well see it as that, yes, but I just see it as something we've both wanted for a long time.' Peridot gestured at the portal. 'It still puzzles you, doesn't it?'

'Of course it does. You said it wasn't a danger, but I wonder. It's still here, and it doesn't appear to belong to any faction, enemy or friend that I know of. I worry that something might come out of it.'

'It won't,' Peridot said.

'You're not always right, you know. Can't you help me close this thing down?'

Peridot rested his cheek on his raised knees, and stared at Pellaz unblinkingly. 'I'll close it for you, if you wish.'

'You said you couldn't before. Is this another *favour* of Lurlei's?'

Peridot sighed. 'Pell, I'll close it for you, because it was me who created it.'

'*What*? Why?'

'To bring you to Freygard.'

Pellaz shook his head slowly. 'Maybe you shouldn't go on, Peridot. I'm not sure I want to hear anything else.'

'But you should,' Peridot said. 'I can talk to you now, so take advantage of it. All those years ago, when Galdra first came to you, do you remember why?'

Pellaz snorted. 'I can hardly forget. His chesnari Tyr was slaughtered by unseen assailants. He thought the Gelaming could help him.'

'Mmm,' Peridot murmured. 'I'm going to tell you something now you probably should never reveal to Galdra. Agents of the Zehk were responsible for Tyr's death. It wasn't the *sedim,* though; don't think that.'

Pellaz had gone utterly cold. 'Why?' he asked dully.

'It was always the Zehk's desire for you and Galdra to get together. The *sedim* monitor hara carefully. We're aware of what different essential combinations can produce. You and Galdra were an effective force against the Aasp's attempt to take control of this realm.' Peridot paused. 'You can imagine that the Zehk were not exactly pleased to discover that Loki, the fruit of your union, was being used against them.'

Pellaz rubbed his hands over his face. 'I don't want to know these things.'

'Don't lie to yourself. Of course you do.'

Pellaz gestured abruptly. 'But why tell me now? You give me secrets to keep, and I don't like that. It makes no difference to the way things are and only brings pain.'

Peridot's voice was wistful. 'Between friends, there should be truth.

You won't believe me, I know, but I've wanted to tell you these things, so many times.'

Pellaz grimaced. 'I believed you to be one thing, and you were another. You have used me, Peridot, or whatever your real name is. We can't be friends, because I'll never be able to trust you. You want there to be truth between us now? Then why not before? So many times, you could have helped me or told me the truth. Always, you obeyed your masters. Don't come to me now like this and expect me to be pleased.'

'I carried you to Samway,' Peridot said. 'I carried you to rebirth. I've been with you since the beginning. I've seen you grow as a har and as a Tigron. Over the years, we've both had to take action we've not liked.' He sighed deeply, as if it pained him. 'The birth of Wraeththu is over, Pellaz. The *sedim* were midwives to it, and have stayed with you throughout. Your pain was often mine, beloved. I could not remain impartial.'

Pellaz laughed harshly. 'If we're going to stick with that analogy, isn't the time after the child arrives when the work really starts?'

'The birth of Wraeththu,' Peridot said patiently, 'involved your generation coming to terms with what you are. Now, it is the time of your sons.'

'In my case, sons who have been damaged by your meddling with my *birth*.' Pellaz got to his feet. 'Can you deny that?'

Peridot, still resting his face on his raised knees, stared up at the Tigron. 'I did what I could, when I could.'

Pellaz nodded his head once and walked out of the grove. He was full of anger and frustration and disappointment. He wanted to talk more to Peridot, yet he didn't. A subtle shift in the air made his body go cold, but he didn't look round. The portal had gone, and he supposed Peridot had gone with it.

For some minutes, Pellaz stood on the cliff top, gazing out to the sea. Humanity had lived and died in ignorance over so many things. The world still shook with the echoes of their cries: the voices of countless children screaming. *Did you ever care for them, Divozenky? Your children went bad, perhaps, but you were their mother in the beginning. Did you never weep for their pain?*

Pellaz was not Darquiel. He could not perceive a response, even if there was one.

It was not our birth the sedim *watched over,* he thought, *but our coming of age. It has happened so quickly. Our childhood was too brief. Now we are free to walk away from those who sought to guide us. Parents can be wrong sometimes, as can children. With maturity comes the ability to accept and not condemn the fallibility of those who came before us.*

He smiled to himself. He'd heard no voice in his head, but perhaps Divozenky wasn't as far from him as he'd believed.

Heal Loki, Pellaz said in his mind. *Please.*

That was all. He turned towards Freygard. He must go home now.

Snow had begun to fall again, because spring comes late to the northern lands. Pellaz pulled his wolf skin coat, borrowed from Galdra, more tightly around his body. He felt very young and very old. His feet slipped upon the frozen ground. He thought longingly of the hearthfires of Freygard, the hearthfires of those he loved. If only the town was nearer. These last minutes out in the cold were almost too much to bear. Pellaz missed Peridot, not just as a *sedu*, but as a friend. How could he judge Peridot, when he was far from perfect himself? He wished he hadn't walked out of the hawthorn grove like that. They should have talked some more. Now, it might be too late.

And then, as if Pell's thoughts had invoked it, from amongst the swirling flakes came a large shadowy shape. It seemed made of snow itself. A *sedu* took on form, shaking its heavy mane, stamping one foot against the hard ground. *Do you need a ride, beloved?*

Pellaz sighed, then smiled. He went to the *sedu*, grasped its mane and vaulted onto its back. 'There is still work for us to do,' he said.

I know. I've walked away from my world, Pellaz. This is where I belong now.

'Then let's go home,' Pellaz said.

Peridot lifted his head and made his way along the cliff. He did not go into the Otherlanes, but placed his hooves surely on the path. Once they'd left the narrow trail behind and reached the wider road through the rough heath to the town, he picked up speed. His powerful body surged through the whirling air.

Pellaz laughed aloud, snowflakes stinging his face, blinding his eyes. It was like the time when he'd first met Peridot, when he'd cast off a dull skin to become Tigron. They had travelled through snow in a cold northern country then too.

I've left another skin behind, Pellaz thought.

Ahead of him, the gates of Freygard opened to them.

Glossary of Wraeththu Terms, Places and Key Characters

Aasp	A highly-developed sentient species, who harvest worlds for their essence.
Abrimel	A Gelaming, son of Pellaz and Caeru.
Aghama (AG-am-ar)	Allegedly, the first Wraeththu, worshipped as a god by some.
Almagabra	Country of the Gelaming, across the sea from Megalithica.
Aldebaran, Ashmael	A high-ranking Gelaming, general of the Almagabran forces and a member of the Hegemony in Immanion.
Aleeme	The first son of Flick and Ulaume har Sarestes, friends of Pellaz in Roselane.
Althaia (al-THAY-uh)	The period of changing, usually around three days, during which as human mutates into a har following inception.
Amelza	A human girl of Olopade, friend of Darquiel.
Anakhai	A country corresponding roughly to North Eastern Europe in the Human Era.
Apanage	A tower of Thannaril, where Diablo and Geburael made their home following their escape from the Second Fall of Fulminir.
Archon	The leader of a tribe and its phyles.
Aruhani	A dehar of aruna, life and death.
Aruna	Sexual communion between hara.
Atoz	Leader of the Thanax, befriended by Loki.
Azriel	Son of Swift and Seel har Parasiel.
Bithi	A har of the Nezreka.
Bloomtide	Seasonal festival of the spring equinox.
Calanthe (Cal) har Aralis	One of the Tigrons of Immanion.
Caeru har Aralis (KY-roo)	Tigrina of Immanion, consort of Pellaz and Calanthe har Aralis.
Carvanzya Mountains	Home of the Nezreka tribe in Anakhai.
Cobweb	A har of the Parasiel tribe, hostling of Swift.
Darquiel har Aralis	A son of Pellaz, Calanthe and Caeru.
Darzu har Nemodilkii	A har with whom Darquiel had a brief dalliance in Anakhai.
Dehar	A Wraeththu god, (pl. dehara).
Diablo	A son of Ponclast.
Divozenky	The mind of the earth.
Drudehall	Meeting hall of the Nezreka.
Drudehar	A hienama of the Nezreka.
Eyra Fiumara	A Hegemon in Immanion, overseer of the

	Listeners.
Faceless Ones	Leading order of the Aasp.
Farn har Olopade	One of Phade's guards in Samway.
Ferelithia	Wraeththu settlement in Almagabra, home of the tribe of Ferelith, place of origin of Caeru.
Feybraiha	The coming of age ceremony, when a harling reaches sexual maturity.
Forever	See We Dwell in Forever.
Freygard	The principle town of the Freyhellan tribe.
Freyhella	A tribe in what was in the human era a part of Scandinavia.
Fulminir	The Varr archon's fortress in Megalithica.
Fyala	A Freyhellan, who acted as housekeeper to visiting Gelaming in Freygard.
Follet	The pony Darquiel rides on his journey through Anakhai.
Galdra	A har of the Freyhellans, chesnari to the archon Tyr.
Galhea (GAL-ay-a)	Parsic town in central Megalithica, governed by the archon Swift.
Ganaril har Olopade	A har of the mountains settlements near Samway.
Gebaddon	An otherworldly forest where Thiede confined Ponclast and his surviving followers following the First Fall of Fulminir.
Geburael	Son of Abrimel and Ponclast.
Grissecon (GRISS-uh-con)	Sexual communion between hara to achieve power; sexual magic.
Har	Wraeththu individual (plural: hara).
Harling	Young har until Feybraiha, the coming of age.
Hashmallim	An order of higher beings who are agents of the Aasp.
Hegalion	The governmental building complex in Immanion.
Hegemony	The ruling body of Gelaming in Immanion.
Helek Sah	The hidden underground city of the Krim Sri.
Hienama	A har who is both teacher and priest, who is responsible for hara's caste training and well as officiating for communities in a spiritual capacity.
Hostling	Har who carries a pearl (Wraeththu foetus), who hosts the seed of another.
Househar	A servant.
Hegemony	Governmental body of the Gelaming tribe.
Imbrilim	Gelaming camp headquarters in Megalithica.
Immanion	Capital city of Almagabra.
Inception	The process by which a human is transformed into a har; the transfusion of blood and the attendant ceremonies.
Jaddayoth	A collection of lands in what was once Northern Europe/ Asia.
Jezinki har Nezreka	Drudehar to the Nezreka tribe.
Kaimana	The first tier of the magical caste system,

	consisting of three levels: Ara, Neoma and Brynie.
Kakkahaar	Desert tribe of Southern Megalithica.
Kamagrian	A branch of Wraeththu that favours the feminine aspect of their being.
Keroen har Olopade	One of the Phade's guards in Samway.
Krim Sri	A hybrid species of human and Aasp, who were hidden among humanity throughout its existence.
Lantovar har Gelaming	A har of the Listeners, stationed in Freyhella.
Laukumati	Ruling hara of the Nezreka tribe.
Lileem har Sarestes	A Kamagrian parage, who researches the stone library she found in Shaa Lemul.
Lion of Oomar	An epithet of Uigenna Archon Wraxilan, referring to his original phyle.
Listeners, The	A group, employed by the Hegemony in Immanion, dedicated to psychic communication over long distance.
Loki	A son of Pellaz har Aralis.
Lurlei	A king of the sedim.
Manticker the Seventy	A legendary archon of the Uigenna, who was overthrown by Wraxilan.
Maudrah	A province and tribe of Jaddayoth.
Megalithica	Western continent, where Wraeththu allegedly began. Its leading tribe is the Parasiel, formerly the Varrs.
Mima Cevarro	A sister of Pellaz har Aralis.
Moon har Parasiel	Sori of Pellaz, son of Snake, chesnari to Tyson.
Mutandis	A tower of Thannaril, once belonging to a Thanad named Ta Ke.
Natalia	Seasonal festival of the winter solstice.
Nayati	A building or sacred space given over to spiritual practices.
Nemodilkii	A tribe of Anakhai, and their town where Darquiel and Ookami paused on their journey.
Nezreka	A tribe of Anakhai.
Nimron	Leader of the Krim Sri.
Ninzini	The tower in Thannaril occupied by Loki, during his captivity there.
Olivia	A human woman of Olopade, appointed to care for Darquiel as a harling.
Ookami har Ikutama	A har who became Darquiel's guide and teacher, during his travels in Anakhai.
Opalexian	Leader of the Roselane tribe, a Kamagrian.
Otherlanes	Etheric pathways beyond this reality that can be travelled through the use of a *sedu* (which see).
Ouana (Oo-AR-na)	Masculine principle of hara.
Ouana-Lim	Masculine generative organs of Wraeththu.
Parage	A Kamagrian individual (pl. parazha).
Parasiel (Pa-RA-see-el)	New name given to the Varrs after the fall of Fulminir and conquest of Ponclast.
Parasilians	Hara of the leading family of Parasiel, including Cobweb, Swift and Tyson.

Parsics	Hara of the tribe of Parasiel.
Pearl	Wraeththu embryo, the shell that contains it.
Pelki	Rape.
Pellaz har Aralis	A Tigron of Immanion, figurehead of the Gelaming Hegemony
Peridot	A *sedu* who works with Pellaz.
Phade har Olopade	Archon of the tribe of Olopade.
Phaonica (Fay-ON-icka)	The Tigron's palace in Immanion.
Phylarch	The leader of a tribal phyle.
Phyle	A community within a tribe, with its own land and leaders.
Ponclast	Archon of the Varrs, defeated by the Gelaming.
Pureborn	A second-generation har born of hara rather than incepted from humans.
Raven har Aralis	Chesnari of Terez har Aralis.
Raymer	A human male of Olopade, partner of Olivia.
Reaptide	A seasonal festival associated with the first harvest in summer.
Roselane	A country of Jaddayoth, and also the tribe who inhabit it, who comprise Kamagrian, hara and human.
Ryander har Calvel	Chesnari of Tharmifex.
Samarchis har Gelaming	A har of the Listeners, stationed in Freyhella.
Samway	Principle town of the tribe of Olopade.
Sarestes	The name of a family in Roselane, who are friends to Pellaz, including Flick, Ulaume and Lileem.
Sedu	An otherworldly entity, which appears in earthly reality as a horse, which can be used by hara as a vessel to travel the Otherlanes. Plural: *sedim*. Agents of the Zehk.
Seydir har Freyhella	A Freyhellan appointed to guide Loki har Aralis through feybraiha.
Shaa Lemul	A realm where the Thanadrim kept their vast library, which Lileem discovered by accident.
Sharing of Breath	A kiss of mutual visualisation.
Shayd	One of the Weavers of the Nezreka.
Shilalama	Capital city of Roselane.
Silbeth	A human girl in Olopade, sister of Amelza.
Skripi	A name used by Geburael.
Slinque	One of the Weavers of the Nezreka.
Soume (SOO-mee)	Feminine principle of hara.
Soume-Lam	Feminine generative organ of Wraeththu.
Stelph	One of the Weavers of the Nezreka.
Sulh	The largest tribe of Alba Sulh, which in the Human Era was the United Kingdom.
Swift	Archon of the Parasiel tribe.
Ta Ke	A Thanad, who was exiled to Shaa Lemul.
Taldri	A young har of the Freyhella.
Tava'edzen	Archon of the Nezreka
Teraphim	Otherworldly entities, similar to *sedim*, who serve the Aasp.
Terez har Aralis	A brother of Pellaz har Aralis.

Terzian	Former Autarch of Galhea, Varr, father of Swift.
Tezarae	Crystalline stones used by the Thanadrim to create specific tones that they used in their technology. Singular: tezar.
Thaine	A country bordering Anakhai.
Thanadrim	A race of beings who were the former inhabitants of Thanatep.
Thanatep	A realm accessed by the Otherlanes, where a race named the Thanadrim once regulated the commerce of the essence of worlds.
Thannaril	A city of Thanatep, where Diablo and Geburael went into hiding following the second fall of Fulminir.
Thanax	Creatures inhabiting Thanatep, who are the products of failed inceptions.
Tharmifex har Calvel	A member of the Hegemony in Immanion, its chair-har and chancellor.
Thiede (THEE-dee)	Leader of the Gelaming, he was the first Wraeththu, and the most powerful.
Tiahaar	Respectful form of address (plural: Tiahaara).
Tigrina (Tee-GREE-na)	An Archon of the Gelaming, symbolising the hostling/soume aspect of Wraeththukind.
Tigron (TEE-gron)	An Archon of the Gelaming.
Tiy	Eye Priestess of the Krim Sri.
Tyr	Archon of the Freyhellans.
Tyson har Parasiel	Har of the Parasiel, the son of Cal and Terzian.
Uigenna (EW-i-GEN-a)	Warlike proto-tribe of Megalithica.
Ulani	Second tier of the magical caste system, consisting of three levels: Acantha, Pyralis and Algoma.
Unneah (Oo-NAY-ah)	Wraeththu tribe of Megalithica.
Varrs	Originally the most powerful and organised tribe in Megalithica, eventually defeated by the Gelaming, and thereafter became known as Parasiel.
Vaysh	A Gelaming, the Tigron's aide.
Velaxis Shiraz	An official of the Hegemony in Immanion.
Weavers, The	Three Sulh hara who are magical advisors to Tava'Edzen of the Nezreka.
Wraeththu (RAY-thoo)	The race of androgynes who came to replace humanity on earth as the ruling species.
Wraxilan	Archon of the Uigenna, after defeating Manticker the Seventy in combat.
We Dwell in Forever	Home of the ruling family of Parasiel in Galhea.
Zehk	A highly-developed sentient species, who harvest worlds for their essence.
Zikael	A Hashmal who came to Loki in Thannaril.
Zira har Olopade	A young har appointed as a teacher of Darquiel in Samway.
Zu	The name Darquiel gives to the entity who follows him on his journey through Anakhai.

Books by Storm Constantine

The Wraeththu Chronicles
The Enchantments of Flesh and Spirit
The Bewitchments of Love and Hate
The Fulfilments of Fate and Desire
The Wraeththu Chronicles (omnibus of trilogy)

The Wraeththu Histories
The Wraiths of Will and Pleasure
The Shades of Time and Memory
The Ghosts of Blood and Innocence

The Alba Sulh Sequence
The Hienama
Student of Kyme
The Moonshawl

Blood, the Phoenix and a Rose

The Artemis Cycle
The Monstrous Regiment
Aleph

The Grigori Books
Stalking Tender Prey
Scenting Hallowed Blood
Stealing Sacred Fire

The Magravandias Chronicles:
Sea Dragon Heir
Crown of Silence
The Way of Light

Hermetech
Burying the Shadow
Sign for the Sacred
*Calenture
Thin Air

*Silverheart (with Michael Moorcock)

Short Story Collections:

The Thorn Boy and Other Dreams of Dark Desire
Mythangelus
Mythophidia
Mytholumina
Mythanimus
A Raven Bound with Lilies: Stories of the Wraeththu Mythos
*Splinters of Truth (NewCon Press)

Wraeththu Mythos Collections

(The 'Para' anthologies are co-edited with Wendy Darling, including stories by the editors and other writers)

Paragenesis
Para Imminence
Para Kindred
Para Animalia
Para Spectral

Songs to Earth and Sky: Stories of the Seasons,
by Storm Constantine and Others

Non-Fiction

Sekhem Heka
Grimoire Dehara: Kaimana
Grimoire Dehara: Ulani (with Taylor Ellwood)
Grimoire Dehara: Nahir Nuri (with Taylor Ellwood)
*The Inward Revolution (with Deborah Benstead)
*Egyptian Birth Signs (with Graham Phillips)
*Bast and Sekhmet: Eyes of Ra (with Eloise Coquio)
Whatnots and Curios
SHE: Primal Meetings with the Dark Goddess (with Andrew Collins)

All books listed are available as Immanion Press editions except for those marked with *

Other Wraeththu Novels

By Popular Mythos Writers

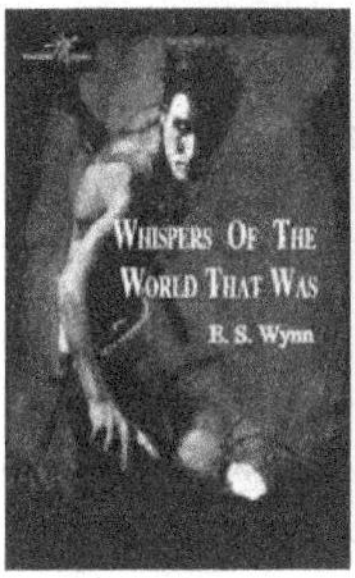

Breeding Discontent by Wendy Darling & Bridgette Parker
Terzah's Sons by Victoria Copus
Song of the Sulh by Maria J. Leel
Whispers of the World That Was by E. S. Wynn
Echoes of Light and Static by E. S. Wynn
Voices of the Silicon Beyond by E. S. Wynn

Further details of Wraeththu Mythos and other fiction can be found on our web site

The Alba Sulh Sequence

Storm Constantine

Set in the land of the Sulh tribe, far from the world-changing politics of Wraeththu leaders and influential tribes, this trilogy explores in vivid and poignant clarity the lives and loves of ordinary hara, their tragedies and triumphs, and the darker side of desire. The narratives are linked but are also separate stories.

In *The Hienama*, the respected and charismatic spiritual teacher Ysobi bewitches the young har Jassenah who comes to him for training in the rural town of Jesith. Blind to Ysobi's faults – or unwilling to admit them – Jassenah eventually has to face his teacher's darker side and attempt to avert the ruin that the unsettling truths he discovers seem destined to invoke.

Student of Kyme tells the tale of the damaged, disruptive young har Gesaril, whose presence in *The Hienama* instigated much of the strife that afflicted the community of Jesith, where he came to train with Ysobi. Banished to the scholarly city of Kyme, to sterner teachers who seek to rehabilitate him, Gesaril is haunted devastatingly by ghosts of his past, which appear to have followed him north.

In *The Moonshawl*, Ysobi, chastened and shaken by the consequences of his actions in Jesith, is estranged from his family. He takes work in the far town of Gwyllion, where the land is drenched with horrific memories of Wraeththu's early history, as well as the blood of those who died. Ysobi unwittingly disturbs echoes of the past, so that secrets long buried begin to emerge from darkness, threatening the whole community. For Ysobi to be capable of averting a hideous tragedy, he must face and fight his own phantoms, the legacy of his past.

These novels are ghost stories, yet not all that manifests are spectres of the dead.

http://www.immanion-press.com

CPSIA information can be obtained
at www.ICGtesting.com
Printed in the USA
LVHW050557080620
657648LV00002B/528

9 781907 737947